THE DEMON BE DAMNED

BEFORE WALKING BETWEEN WORLDS
- BOOK 1 -

The Demon Be Damned

Before Walking Between Worlds
- Book 1 -

J.K. Norry

The Demon Be Damned
Before Walking Between Worlds Book 1
Copyright © 2018 by J.K. Norry
Cover Design and Author Photo by: Dawn Norry/Dear23

Publishers note:
This book is a work of fiction. Names, characters, places and incidents are either the product of the author's imagination or are used fictitiously, and any resemblance to actual persons living or dead, events, or locales is entirely coincidental.

All rights reserved. No part of this book may be reproduced in any form by any electronic or mechanical means including photocopying, recording, or information storage and retrieval without permission in writing from the author.

ISBN 978-1-944916-74-9

First Edition, Published Fall 2019

www.SuddenInsightPublishing.com
Indie publishing for the Indie Author

Dear Reader,

Before you start reading this book, there are a few things you ought to know. Actually, there are a bunch of things you should know. The most important of these things is that this is not the first book in this series.

Let me rephrase that. Although this is the first book in this particular series, it is not the first book in this universe. There are three other books you should definitely read before this one; if you need to know why, I'll be happy to tell you.

The first trilogy in the 'Walking Between Worlds' universe details events that happen long after the story in the pages that follow. In light of this, it might seem to make sense that you would start with the book you have in your hands. However, this is most assuredly not the place to start.

In order to understand why this story needs to be told, you've really got to read those first three books. You'll have all kinds of information at the end, which you're going to need to properly assimilate what happens in these pages; as the author, I can confidently say this book will be much better if you read those three first.

Perhaps you have already read '*Demons & Angels*', '*Rise of the Walker King*' and '*Fall of the Walker King*'. If so, I would like to take this opportunity to extend my gratitude. Those were important books for me to write, and I am glad you are here after sharing those spaces with me. You are completely prepared for what is coming next. I hope you love reading this book as much as I loved writing it.

If not, please find those books and read them first. They are available wherever you purchased this from, and they really are essential reading for anyone about to begin this book.

That being said, I do very much hope you enjoy this story. I'll check in with you again at the end, to let you know what the plan is for the rest of this series; and I'll let you know how you can find my other books, and what you can do to make sure I write more of what you would like to see from me.

Now, I'd like to share a book that I wanted to write for a very long time with you. It's finally done, and I couldn't be more proud to present '*The Demon Be Damned*'.

Thanks for reading!

All the best,
Jay

PROLOGUE

The first thing he knew was everything.

He knew the form his consciousness had taken was the body of a devil, that he was capable of taking many forms, and that each was more powerful and destructive than the other in some way.

He knew the power guilt carried, and that the humans on Earth had only begun to toy with this great power. They were creating demons from that guilt, demons they couldn't see. Demons they couldn't resist.

Demons they couldn't stop.

In the first moment he was, he saw it all. The past stretched forever behind him, the future trailed off into eternity, and he saw every ecstatic and agonizing moment of it before he had taken his first breath.

He knew the one that created him was obligated to ignore him forever. In the same moment he had been made, he had been cast out. For the same reason he had been made, he had been cast out. In seeing it all, he saw there was no reason and no purpose to asking why. A million whys would be answered by a million silences, and he knew before he asked the silence would be too much to bear.

He knew his name was Roche, in that first moment.

In the next moment, he breathed in.

A darkness entered along with the breath, invading every part of him. His ecstatic vision of a moment ago was gathered up in the darkness and swept away with his breath. Everything he had just known was gone, replaced by a bottomless emptiness within him. Now he saw where he was, in a place of light and clouds. Although he had been made here, he did not belong here. He knew it like he had known everything a breath ago, as a certainty that knew no doubt.

Then he saw her.

She was like him, but different in every way. Her soul was pure and clear and empty, and on the rise. Her mind was without thought, without reason and without doubt. Even her name was the same as his, while being exactly the opposite of his.

"Ehcor," he murmured.

She turned, and the light shone forth from her. Lifting a hand to cover his eyes, Roche felt his skin soak up the blinding luminescence. The pain was almost too much to bear, yet his skin seemed to hunger for the light. While the pain soaked in, the hunger rose up to greet it; and as he stared through splayed fingers he saw her clearly within the brilliance.

Twisted in hate, her face moved to form the first words he had ever heard spoken. The words were thrown at him violently.

"You!" she cried. "You don't belong here! You are cast out!"

Roche felt his own voice trying to burst forth. He listened to the whirling thoughts in his head that told him they were the same, that she was a part of him and he a part of her. While he hesitated, she acted.

Two bright hands of light burst forth from the cloud of brilliance enrobing her. She extended them toward him, hands bent at the wrists to show him her palms. A ball of light erupted from between them, and shot toward him. Roche felt his eyes go wide as it hit him, felt his arm thrown back over his head, and felt his body go skittering helplessly across the soft clouded floor.

Somehow he slipped over the side, or through what they had both been standing on, and Roche felt himself falling. Lights and sounds passed him as he fell, but he could find no way to grasp anything. His body began to spin as it descended, and his eyes rolled back in his head as Roche felt his consciousness slipping away from him.

CHAPTER 1

Just because it wasn't home didn't mean he couldn't learn to live here. The only home he had ever known was in a mind that would never think of him again, and he had to live somewhere.

Roche surveyed the landscape, and smiled for the first time.

He had come awake on a low hilltop, with gradual slopes rolling in every direction away from him. The land was nothing more than dirt, but the soil was streaked in blacks and browns and golds in a way that made it seem alive. Off in the distance he could see where the rise began again. Gradual at first, the soil became rock and the rock became a wall. The wall stretched up and out of sight, as did the similar vertical face far behind him.

Surely it met to form a stone ceiling overhead, but Roche couldn't make out its features for all the light shining down on him. Warm and invigorating, the light kissed his skin and put another smile on his face. He let his eyes wander the horizon once more, and spied a dark spot where the ground became wall.

Roche left his vantage point behind, moving forward over the packed dirt. He thrilled at the feel of the wind on his face, his feet against the ground, and the sweet pungent scent that entered his nostrils with every breath. The only other place he remembered had been odorless, the air itself without texture. In this place he could nearly taste the dirt as he strode across it.

Had he not been so caught up in the experience of being alive, Roche surely would have noticed the forms gathering behind him. First two came together, matching his pace; then three more fell into step with them, and moved along with him towards the dark spot in the distant rock face. When the last two caught up, a lone voice called out from the group.

"Ho there," the voice said. "I think you may be lost."

Roche stopped, and turned.

He watched them as they continued to move toward him, spreading out to form a loose circle around him. They looked like he did, sort of; yet there was some distinct difference he couldn't put his finger on.

While he glanced from one to the other, without turning to see them all, Roche heard one speak behind him.

"He looks like an old devil," he said.

Roche whirled toward the new voice, only to hear another comment from one of the devils that was now behind him.

"Old and senile," he said.

This time when Roche turned the last one that had spoken continued talking. He had gotten a glimpse of each of them, of their metal coverings and their array of weapons. Most of them carried a curved sword, with a dagger sheathed and hanging from their belted waists. Two had spears, and one hefted a club with metal spikes sticking out from every angle around the rounded thick end.

The one with the club was still speaking.

"Who else would wander around naked and alone, this deep in Hell?" he asked no one in particular. "Only a new devil or an old one that has lost his mind."

One of the swordsmen nodded.

"Look at the size of him," he said. "And those horns. He must be ancient. He probably lost his mind a long time ago." Roche stood still, letting his eyes flit from one devil to the next as they passed the thread of comments. The next voice came from behind him, and he didn't turn to see who it was.

"He's got nothing," the devil said. "And maybe he hasn't lost his mind. Maybe he likes to battle bandits. We got nothing to gain by finding out."

The armor they wore was finely wrought, contoured to each of their bodies to give their muscled torsos room to flex and move. A single piece of steel bent over each devil's shoulders to cover their backs and chests by simply fitting it over their heads. From the waist down, they were covered in loin cloths that hung between their naked legs. Although they were a ragged band, with hair and beards that looked both unwashed and uncut, the armor lent a uniformity to the group.

That was not the difference between him and them that Roche couldn't figure out. He was bigger than all of them, but a couple were near his size; yet somehow he could feel they were all the same in some way, some way in which he was different.

One of the largest of them was directly facing Roche. He had been doing much of the talking, and he leaned to one side to speak once more.

"Someone is scared," he sneered.

He was looking past Roche when he said it, narrowing his eyes at the devil that had expressed his doubts. After speaking, he let his eyes find each of the others in turn.

Roche sensed movement behind him.

"I'm not scared," the one behind him responded.

The words were followed by an audible gulp, and hesitant footfalls.

Roche felt a different internal response to this movement. Everything inside of him seemed to stand still, while his senses all became immediately and almost painfully heightened. He turned, to see what approached from behind. The turn was not rapid, or panicked; yet he could see that he was moving much faster than the devil as he brought his sword up over his head and stepped forward once more. Roche had time to cock his head curiously to the side, and narrow his eyes, before the curved blade began its arc toward him.

With no hurry to his movements, Roche easily moved aside and grabbed the devil's sword arm by the wrist as it passed harmlessly through the spot he had just been standing. The motion was punctuated by a loud cracking sound, and the devil howled in extended slow motion as he dropped the weapon. It had hardly fallen when Roche let go the devil's wrist and grasped it by the hilt. He swung the blade three times before his opponent could react with anything but a look of shocked surprise.

The first swing was awkward testament to the fact that he had never held a sword or seen one in action. It glanced off the devil's breastplate, driving him further off balance but doing no real harm. Stepping back and swinging again, Roche felt as though the blade had become an extension of his arm. He cut the devil just below the shoulder, and the appendage with the crushed wrist fell cleanly to the packed dirt at his feet. Before blood could flow, Roche swung the blade once more.

Another arm hit the ground with a thump, and Roche drifted back as the dark syrupy spray began to fountain from the devil's stumps. Purple wetness covered the soil, coloring it as it sunk in. It began to puddle immediately, in several small pools. When the devil made to take a step, still howling, he slipped in his own blood and pitched backward.

His head struck rock, and the devil fell silent.

Roche glanced at the others. A few were staring wide-eyed, but the rest were clearly seeing a challenge where those few saw danger. Two of the larger devils rushed forward; one from behind, the other from his right.

Whatever had slowed the world down or sped him up was still with him, and Roche imagined and discarded three possible ways to respond before he chose one and acted. He stepped forward, letting them crash awkwardly into each other, spun to face them and brought their skulls together with a satisfying thunk. One went down, his eyes rolling back in his head; the other dropped to his knees and swung his spiked club at Roche's legs.

He let the blow land, curious what effect it would have. It nearly drove his legs out from under him, and the points of pain that dotted the larger concussive ache almost made him cry out. Roche held his ground, and pried the weapon from the devil's hand and then from his own leg. Bringing it down on it's owner's skull, Roche watched the light go out of the devil's eyes as his body dropped lifelessly the rest of the way to the ground. He had stepped back again, to let the body fall; and he had stepped right between two others when he did.

Two blades were coming at him, and each bit into his torso in the same moment. First he felt the pain, and a fury rising within him; then another shift washed over him, and the scene stood nearly still.

Roche felt a thirst deep inside, a pure killing steak that wanted to turn his body from what he was to what it was. Part of him wanted to let it loose, and watch the cloud of darkness rain stark destruction on the remaining devils. Another part of him feared that transformation, and wondered if he could even make it happen if he wanted to.

The time he spent warring internally over whether to resist the impulse or surrender to it felt like a brief eternity to him. For the others, it was a passing moment; they remained nearly still, moving in exaggerated slow motion while he contemplated the choices he didn't know he had. The fury rising in him passed in that eternal moment, and Roche calmly spun in place. What felt like a measured response to him looked like a whirlwind blur to them, and their weapons were yanked painfully from their taloned hands.

He spun again, and the swords let go the flesh they had bitten to fly in opposite directions and clatter harmlessly outside the broken circle. By the time he stopped twirling the wounds were healed. Roche pushed the two devils away with a casual explosiveness, surprising himself with how far they sailed away from him. He saw the first that had fallen rising again, and saw the arms he had chopped off growing back slowly.

Roche dropped the spiked club and grasped the hilt of the curved sword with both hands. Some instinct within him told him what to do, and the next devil was already rushing at him. Roche let him come, swinging the sword with all his might at his charging adversary. The blade cut past the charge, between the devil's defenses and through his neck. His body took one more step before it fell and began gushing thick purple blood.

A moment later the devil's head rolled to a stop at Roche's feet, eyes vacant and unseeing. While the other wounded regained their feet and their limbs, the headless one stayed down.

They all came at him at once, and Roche found himself wondering if he would die should one take his head from his shoulders. The thought was fleeting, and was left behind as he stepped gingerly around the converging attack. One head after another fell behind him. By the time he returned to the place he had begun the thought, seven crimson corpses dotted the field. An equal number of heads lay lifeless in the dirt, streaks of purple describing the paths they had taken away from their bodies.

Roche felt time begin to settle into its previous slow pace, just as he saw another devil approaching from the distance. At first he saw every feature of the figure as it neared; giant legs pumping as he ran, he seemed to be moving at the same rapid speed Roche was watching in. As his perception slowed, the devil became a dark red blur streaking across the landscape.

Distant and thunderous, a rumbling sound punctuated by regular cracks seemed to be coming near at the same pace as the racing devil. The noise grew louder as the blur came closer, and Roche expected it to cease when the devil halted a dozen paces short of him. Rather than stop, the rhythmic rumbling continued to increase in volume.

The devil didn't seem to hear it at first. He looked at the carnage surrounding Roche, glared hatefully at him, and howled his rage to the sky. The roar was deafening, and Roche could feel his chest trembling with it. While he was being attacked by the smaller devils, Roche had briefly wondered for the first time whether or not he could be killed. Now he stared at a devil nearly twice the size of any of his previous opponents, and considered the possibility that he was about to get a very final answer to his earlier internal question.

When the devil's roar fell silent, he noticed the approaching sound at last. His face went from a mask of rage to a confusing mix of surprise and terror, and he began to lift his eyes to the sky.

In a startling blink, Roche was no longer looking at a devil. A deep scarlet winged serpent stood where the devil had just been, in a trench created by its halted descent. The ground trembled beneath Roche, while dust and rock and liquid devil rose into the air only to fall all around him. He stared at the creature, wondering why time had sped up at such an inopportune moment. All he wanted to do was run his eyes over the scaled torso, to examine the reptilian visage, and take in the wonder of this horrific killing machine.

"You're a dragon," he breathed.

Roche didn't know how he knew the word, or how to register the flood of knowledge that accompanied the statement. He only knew the teeth and claws on the monster made the swords and spears the devils had carried look like so many playthings.

The dragon laughed, and Roche breathed out.

"I am a dragon," she said, inclining her scaled snout.

Her voice was melodious and flinted at the same time, almost musical. Roche let the surprise show on his face for a moment, and she misread his expression.

"You didn't know dragons can talk?" she said.

Roche shook his head.

"Actually, I did know that," he said. "Somehow. But I've never met a dragon before, and I didn't know a dragon's voice could sound so…"

She interjected, impatiently.

"Normal?" she said. "Intelligible? What?"

Roche shrugged.

"I guess…" he paused. "Beautiful."

A slight smile had settled on her lips while they talked, upturning the corners of her mouth. Roche had thought it was meant to be threatening, as it showed him a considerable number of teeth he couldn't see when she spoke. Now he watched the line take a downward turn, and realized how threatening a dragon's face could be. Her eyes narrowed to slits, and flashed with fire.

Then she laughed, the sound rolling over the field and echoing back to them from the distant walls and subterranean ceiling. Roche noticed a cruelty in it he hadn't heard when she spoke, a sinister note that made him wish time would get on with slowing down again.

When she returned her eyes to his, the slight smile was back.

"The queen would see you," she said.

Her voice had gone flat, as though she had deliberately tried to remove the musical tone. Now he could hear the cruelty in it. He shrugged his shoulders, to show her he didn't know what she meant.

"Who?" he said.

The dragon's body seemed to inflate, as she pulled in a deep labored breath. Roche remembered somehow that dragon fire was not to be trifled with, and had a good long moment to wonder if perhaps he was about to learn more details about that inner caution.

She sighed, and turned away.

"The queen of Hell," she said. "She wants to know where you came from, why you arrived here, and why you began your visit with a killing spree. After you talk, maybe she'll let me kill you."

Roche had begun to approach her, mistaking the way she had positioned her body as an invitation to climb on and ride her. At her last words he stopped, and stared.

Pulling back her wings, the dragon leapt into the air in time with the first powerful down-thrust. That newly familiar loud cracking sound accompanied the motion, as did another blast of dust and rock. Roche was pushed away by the explosive takeoff, and staggered backward a few steps while the thunderous sound filled the air again. He heard her call out to him, barely.

"Try to keep up!" she cried.

The carefree lilting tone was back in her voice, and she was already a dwindling dot overhead. Roche took a good long look at the crimson and purple puddle of goo in the trench she had just vacated. He wondered, while he stared, what sort of creature might command a monster like that.

Roche began running.

CHAPTER 2

The number of possibilities drifting by was a little dizzying. Minutes seemed to stretch to hours as they walked endless corridors carved through solid rock, each punctuated at irregular intervals by entrances to adjacent passageways. They turned one way and then another, seeming to double back directionally without ever revisiting the exact same stretch of tunnel. Some passages were dark and empty, and he followed her footsteps down them more by sound than sight; others were illuminated by torches or candles or mysterious light sources he couldn't see, crowded full of devils going from one unknown place to another.

At the entrance to the cave, she had waited for him in her intimidating reptilian form. She had behaved as though he took a great long time to arrive, but he could tell she had put forth real effort to stay ahead. Once he started running, Roche was able to feel time wanting to stretch until it seemed to stand still. He engaged the feeling, somehow, and was able to make the moments tick by nearly as slowly as he had while doing battle. Every time he had looked up, she was above and a bit ahead of him. She hadn't gotten out of sight until right at the end, and he heard her hit the ground harder than she might have wanted to if she didn't been rushing for effect.

As he had approached, she had transformed. One moment she was a monster, watching him over her shoulder as if he had kept her waiting for some time; the next she was a devil, with an outward form to match the voice he had heard earlier. Smaller than him nearly by half, her face was fierce and unlined. Scarlet and orange curls that looked more like dancing flames bounced with the slightest movement of her head, and her eyes seemed to contain actual fire.

Without a word, she had turned and slipped into the cavern. Since then she had walked quickly, keeping far enough ahead of him to make the only conversation possible between them brief echoed exchanges. Roche remained silent, and watched her lead him deeper into Hell. Whenever they approached a tunnel with anyone in it, she would call back to him not to talk to anyone. Then she would press on, silent but for her swift quiet footfalls.

Everything about her was alluring, an intricately layered attraction that was either completely natural or carefully constructed to appear as if it were. The way she walked, her entire body moving like a flickering candle's flame. How she tossed her flowing red hair over her shoulder, and flashed her fiery eyes at him. Her voice, melodic and lilting. Even her smile threatened to overwhelm his senses, and stir a deep hunger within him. She had become clothed when she transformed, in a flowing swath of fabric so dark it shifted from black to deep purple as she passed through lighted and unlighted sections of the endless passages. Hugging her at her breasts and hips, the dress covered the entire length of her legs and trailed behind her along the path.

Only her laughter pierced the illusion of her beauty. Roche heard it again when she saw some of the devils in the crowded areas stop and stare as they passed. Nearly all of them wore coverings of some type, from a simple loin cloth that left little to the imagination to layered robes that showed nothing but brief glimpses of crimson skin. The larger the devil, the more they seemed to wear. Roche was one of the few without clothing of some kind, and the only one of his size. He did his best to ignore the curious gazes, along with her cruel laughter.

He was convinced she was leading him down a deliberately circuitous path. Without intending to, Roche saw a map drawing itself behind his eyes. The tunnels went from a labyrinthine mystery to a familiar network as they walked. By the time she halted before a closed doorway, he was sure he could find his way back to any and all the places they had been. In trying to confuse him, the dragon turned lady had instead given him a clearer idea of how the passages were laid out.

Turning to him as he approached, she pointed to a spot in the worn rock floor and met his eyes. She had to look up to do so, and he got the feeling she didn't much care for raising her gaze to find his. At the same time, she kept herself from staring at his nakedness like the others had. For the first time Roche realized he was an imposing figure, even among the largest devils he had seen. Next to her, he was a small giant.

Knowing she could turn into a creature that dwarfed him in size in an instant, Roche took no pleasure in towering over her or witnessing her reaction to it. He tried to keep his expression respectful, and diminish the effect of him looking down at her.

"Wait here," she said, still pointing.

Roche glanced at the place she indicated. He nodded, and stepped sideways to be exactly where she told him to be. She glared at him a moment longer, then turned and pushed the door open. Disappearing into the space beyond, she closed it behind her to leave him standing naked and alone in the hallway.

Less than a minute passed before the door was pulled open once more. This time Roche was able to see into the room beyond. Spacious yet sparsely furnished, it was wide from wall to wall and spanned overhead in a tall smoothed rock ceiling. Bookshelves dominated most of the wall space; they stretched high beyond his reach and were loaded with volumes bound in everything from stone to steel, from cloth to clay. A few chairs were loosely arranged on the mostly open floor space, and a dark figure rose from one as he watched.

For a moment she was an amorphous fog in shades of black, flowing from the chair to begin drifting languidly toward him. The dark cloud coalesced into a simple but lovely figure, and he shook his head to clear it. Nothing remained of his original vision as she approached, and he took in her dark swirling eyes and black flowing hair as carefully as he took in her midnight robes. Nearly every inch of her was covered by the dancing fabric, which resembled shifting shadows more than any material he had ever seen. Only her hands and her head were clearly visible, and they were lovely in a way that made him think of danger like he never had before.

The dragon lady had slipped behind him, and he felt her hand on his shoulder before he sensed her movement. Suddenly she was pushing on him, trying to drive him to his knees. Roche let himself be surprised at her strength, and grateful for his own. Resisting still, he heard her whisper behind him.

"On your knees," she hissed. "Bow before the queen."

He couldn't take his eyes off the dark vision before him, but Roche continued to stand up straight. Apparently the dragon was stronger than he had thought, in this form; she continued to push harder, and his legs were beginning to tremble with the effort. Before he could step aside, or lash out at her, the approaching figure spoke.

"Lilia," she said. "Release him. That won't be necessary."

The sound of the dragon lady's voice had been pleasantly disorienting, the first time he had heard it. Just as he had nearly grown accustomed to one sound, Roche was spun in a whole new direction by another. The queen's voice was smooth and sublime, musical layers that carried her soft but sure words beyond his ears to shake the core of his being. One part of it was a sweet and caring young girl, another a kind old woman; altogether it was the most moving sound he had ever heard.

His knees would have buckled, had Lilia not stopped pressing on his shoulder in that moment. The dark figure came closer while he found his breath, and stopped a few steps inside the room.

"Won't you come in," she said. "We have much to discuss."

Denying her may not have been impossible, but it seemed such a ridiculous notion he saw no reason to try. Her presence drew him in with warm comfort, her voice beckoning him gently with every softly spoken word. Roche stepped forward, crossing the threshold into the stark space. A scent climbed into his nose as he entered the room; the smell of something that had been burnt, extinguished and burnt again.

It was not at all unpleasant to him.

Lilia was following, until she saw the dark form shake her head slightly. Her face twisted into a momentary mask of anger, only to relax into its placid beauty once more. Without a word, she turned and stepped into the hallway. Another look from the queen, and another paroxysm of fury crossed her face. Again, she relaxed visibly. She pulled the door shut behind her.

Suddenly alone in the room with her, Roche was even more conscious of the dark being studying him. She was so small, and yet it was hard for him to remind himself of that; the power that flowed from her was nearly palpable, pulling him in and pressing him back at the same time. For the first time he became keenly aware of his nakedness, and he shifted awkwardly under her gaze.

Turning, she flowed like a shadow into the room. He watched her, until she turned once more and gestured at the entire space with a slight subtle wave.

"Please sit down," she said, "if you wish."

Finally tearing his eyes from her, Roche tried to let his gaze drift about the room in a way that appeared natural and relaxed. He found the task nearly impossible, felt the irresistible urge to yank his attention from whatever it wandered to back to her.

"In all honesty," he said, "I really don't know what I should be doing. Surely there is some way to interact with you that shows great respect, and countless ways to behave that would imply my disrespect."

He was looking away, then back at her again, as he spoke. When he paused, his eyes found hers for a moment. She smiled.

"Of course," she said. "You are new, and I understand. Please, make yourself at ease. You have nothing to fear from me."

Roche glanced back at the door that had been closed behind him. He felt Lilia's presence still on the other side, found himself wondering if she was listening somehow.

"Your dragon would disagree," he noted. "She is under the impression that if you don't like what I have to say, you will order her to kill me."

The dark lady's laugh did not resemble the dragon's at all. Like tinkling glass, it was full of humor and delight.

"My dragon?" she smiled. "You mean Lilia? She is not my dragon; she is my friend, my confidante. I would not have the relationship with the dragon community that I have were it not for her. Although she is a little standoffish at first, I'm sure you will warm up to each other."

Roche cast another glance over his shoulder, eyeing the door as if he was afraid the dragon would burst in flame first. The dark one laughed again, and drifted to the seat she had been occupying when he first saw her.

"You are like me, I think," she said. "Created on high, only to be cast out. There will be those that say you don't belong here, as they did when I first arrived. Do not let them trouble you. So long as I have a place in Hell, you will have one too."

Now his attention was drawn to her in a whole new way. Something about the way she laughed, the way she spoke, or the way she seemed to blur about the edges as he focused on her.

"The queen of Hell," he said, almost to himself. "You are like me. That means you have an opposite, another much like you that rules in Heaven. That would mean you are…"

Roche drifted off, and watched her raise her eyebrows in anticipation of what he might say next. When he didn't speak, she smiled and finished his thought.

"The dark one?" she said. "The devil?"

Shaking his head, Roche frowned at the thought.

"You are not like the one who made me," he said.

She smiled again.

"The one who made you also made me," she said. "As well as my counterpart. We were separated from that creative force out of necessity, a necessity that also demands we are given great power."

It was Roche's turn to laugh, and be frank.

"Great power?" he said. "I feel as though I know nothing, as though I could do anything if I could only figure out what to do and how to do it. I feel like a very small point in a very large reality, and I feel as though I am only getting smaller."

He looked down at himself.

"I know I appear to be old, and fearsome," he went on. "But only because I have seen others since coming into being. On the outside I seem to be a powerful devil, but within I feel as though all I am is stuffed into a tiny box I cannot open."

He heard his own voice become strained, exasperated.

"I don't even have any clothes," he blurted out.

With a wave of her hand, a change came over him. Roche felt as though giant arms were encircling him in an enormous embrace. The tension drained from his body, his racing thoughts were slowed until his mind was wondrously still, and another more tangible weight settled over him. His sense of delight at the calm within him made it seem only natural that a set of soft flowing robes appeared about his body. They were dark, edged in crimson and deep purple.

"You are not what you clothe yourself in."

Roche heard her within the comforting reality of her presence surrounding him. Her voice was in his mind, and more beautiful than ever. Much as the soft fabric of the robes tickled his skin, her words thrilled him within.

"These coverings are for those like us," she said. "Rulers of the dark realm, and those who reside here. Yet they cover only one form, the form others see when they look at us. Beneath that is the truth only some of us can see, the light that must be ignited to cast the darkness of our shadowy form. In that light you will always find yourself."

He shook his head, and the sublime presence drifted away from him.

"I remember that," Roche said. "But I cannot feel it like I remember feeling it. In that place I was whole, I saw and knew everything."

Suddenly he did need to sit down, and she sensed his need. Once more, she gestured her invitation. Roche settled across from her, and sighed. She looked so small, and so ordinary, sitting before him. He wondered how bright the light must be, to cast such a shadow.

"You will see that place again," she said. "But first you must fall, so you may rise. Things are sure to get worse, I am afraid. Yet then they will shift, and your inner vision will become clearer than ever. By the time you see the light again, you will understand it as only one who has dwelt in darkness can. In the meantime, I am happy to offer counsel and comfort."

Roche stirred in his seat, threw up his hands.

"I don't even know what my purpose is," he cried. "I don't how you might counsel me, or if I would be wise to heed your counsel."

She nodded, understanding.

"Lilia will show you the common areas," she said, "and the place that has been set aside for you. You may come to me as you wish, and make your way as you please. Despite my reputation, I am here to guide the path this reality cuts through existence in much the same way you are. There are not many like us, and I may need your counsel and comfort one day as well. The only beings that need fear me are the ones not comfortable facing reality as it is."

Meeting her gaze again, Roche lifted his eyebrows.

"You seem to have me at a disadvantage," he said. "You know much about me, and I know so little about you."

She smiled, and waved her hand in a gesture that seemed to take in the whole world.

"Then go," she said. "Learn, and live; and know you can ask me anything, when the time comes for us to speak again."

She paused, and he didn't realize he hadn't heard her utter his name until she said it.

"Roche," she said. "You are a special being, with a unique purpose; but only you can define and determine that purpose. Your urges and desires will find context in the world as you make your way in it, and the light within you is there to guide you."

He nodded, wishing he knew just what she meant. Before he stood, Roche let himself soak up the reality of her presence a moment longer.

"Thank you," he said. "I feel you are doing me a great kindness, and I may not be properly appreciating it; yet I do thank you for this meeting, and for your words. You have given me much to think about."

Rising, he found himself feeling awkward again as he looked down at her. She appeared completely at ease, even as she gained her own feet and drifted toward him.

"You know my name," he said. "But you referred to yourself as others do. Surely you have a name, that I may think of when I think of you?"

Her eyes deepened, the shifting shadows going completely black for a moment. For the first time her smile was less than kind, a twisted smirk that reminded him how dangerous she must be.

"I am indeed called many things," she said, "and many are the names I answer to. With you I would share the name of my choosing, the one that fits me best."

Roche nodded, waited.

"Ximena," she said. "When you think of me, you will be thinking of Ximena. And I do so hope you will find yourself thinking of me."

CHAPTER 3

Neither of them wanted to spend another moment together, or be the one to suggest they go their separate ways. Roche knew the dragon was bound by duty, in whatever form it took for her. Although she might not like it, Lilia would make sure he had been shown around to his satisfaction. She wouldn't volunteer any information he didn't ask for, nor would she refuse to answer any question he did ask. All her answers were brief and to the point, evasive enough to always imply that what she left unsaid was much more relevant than what she had shared.

Roche was bound to her by his curiosity. As far as tour guides went, Lilia may have left a lot to be desired; but she was what he had, and he was grateful for the opportunity to learn more about his new home. Even the vast featureless plains of colored soil were fascinating to him, and how they always had to cross a long stretch of emptiness to get from one peopled area to another. Most of Hell was barren and vacant, striking in its pure potentiality. They crossed these areas at high speed, her flying overhead while he ran.

Devils were crammed in tight in the other places they visited. Pathways were cluttered with them, the markets full of shouting and shoving. Roche found it difficult to ask questions in the confusion, and even more difficult to extract any value from her answers. At the first bazaar they visited, they hung back while a crowd of devils surrounded a nearby cart. Roche had asked what they were selling, and Lilia had spoken without turning to him.

"Goods," she had said, without a touch of sarcasm.

He shook his head, and pressed her.

"What are they buying?" he insisted.

Lilia shrugged.

"Whatever is being sold."

Rather than explode, Roche had taken a different track.

"What are they buying it with?" he asked.

Lilia had begun to drift away, as the closest knot of devils moved in their direction. She called back, as he was absorbed into the loud group.

"Value," she said, and moved away even further.

When they were on the move, conversation was even more impossible. Roche put everything he had into trying to keep up, and appear as relaxed as her when they slowed. Only once did he veer from the path her serpentine body described overhead, when he saw an unnatural feature scarring the distant landscape. He headed toward it, out of his natural curiosity, and was almost upon the strange markings when she struck the ground before him so hard he was knocked off balance by the shuddering underfoot. Nearly bouncing off her, Roche noticed she had positioned herself between him and the turned dirt.

That's what it was, too; turned dirt. Three furrows had been dug in the sand and soil, as wide as his muscled arm and as deep as it was long. They stretched as far as he could see in one direction, and nearly as far in the other. From some distance, he could see where the lines turned sharply and headed away in another set of straight lines. Every twenty or thirty feet, he saw that the furrows appeared to stop and start again. The new marks overlapped the old, angling to one side or the other before continuing the nearly straight long lines.

He looked at her, awaiting an explanation.

"They're dragon markings," she said.

Lilia reached out casually with one of her sinewed forearms, dragged long talons through the soil. Three similar furrows appeared between them, smaller than the long lines but identical in every other way. She inclined her giant serpentine snout, to where the lines in the distance turned and headed away at a square angle.

"These mark a dragon's territory," she said. "Never cross into a dragon's lands without an invitation." His eyes traced what he could see of the markings, wondering just how far they went before they turned again to meet up with the furrows coming the other way. While he considered, Lilia expelled steam from her nostrils and shook her head.

"You shouldn't be here," she said. "You know nothing of Hell. Every devil you have seen earned their way here, as will all the demon hunters that come here. Only you will have the experience of coming here by some fluke, and ruling by accident."

She was staring at his robes as if they offended her.

While speaking to Ximena, Roche had wondered if the dragon lady was somehow listening in. He found himself wondering again, curious about what others knew of him that he didn't know about himself. Rather than point out that he was like the queen, in her own words, he pounced upon something else Lilia had said.

"Demon hunters?" he echoed. "What do you mean?"

Lilia sighed, inflating her giant scaled chest and releasing the breath with a labored and impatient sound. Roche got the feeling she wished she hadn't said anything. For a moment he thought she was going to blast off, and leave him standing in a cloud of dust watching her fly away. Instead she wagged her head back and forth, and sighed once more.

"I know who you are," she said. "I have heard the prophecies. You are not truly a devil, no matter how much you may strive to look like one. You exist because the demons do, and it is your responsibility to manage them; but you belong on Earth, not in Hell. Your place is among people, not with those of us who know and understand life in the lower realms. Your territory should go to a dragon, or a devil. One such as you should not have lands in Hell. You should not have lands anywhere. You are an aberration, made to exist outside the normal flow of events while being able to influence them nonetheless."

Still eyeing the furrows in the dirt, Roche replied without looking at the dragon. He remained convinced it would be unwise to point out that the queen was the same as him, so he let his curiosity lead him.

"My territory?" he said. "Why would I have lands? I have no idea what to do with them."

She lifted her head, lowered it again in affirmation.

"At last," she said. "We agree on something."

Raising his gaze from the lines in the dirt, Roche looked around at the barren landscape that surrounded them. A feeling of certainty came over him, and he spoke before he realized what he was going to say.

"This is the place," he said. "These are my lands. I was drawn to these markings because they are encroaching on my territory."

He waited for her to deny his certainty, to laugh at him cruelly and remind him he knew nothing of Hell. Instead the lines around her long snout deepened into a frown, and she rocked back on her rear haunches as if making ready to take to the sky.

"This is a new territory," she said. "When new lands show up in Hell, they are being created to serve the devils that live here in some way that no other area does. Of course, sometimes the land is claimed before that purpose can be fulfilled."

She looked down at him, still angled for takeoff.

"It would seem you have a dilemma," she mused. "I am afraid I cannot meddle in the affairs of one like you. I act as liaison between devils and dragons, and you are technically neither of these. I have shown you the markets, and the tunnels of the royal city. I have shown you to your lands. My duty is discharged."

Although he knew it was coming, Roche had no way to stop her dramatic departure. One moment she was set to launch, the next she was high in the air above him. He stood quiet and still in the cloud of dust kicked up by her wings, waiting for it to settle. By the time his vision had cleared, the whooshing and cracking sounds of her flight had faded to nothing in the distance.

Turning in a slow circle, Roche took a good long look at the streaked soil that stretched for miles in every direction. He could feel a connection to the area, like he had felt nowhere else. Although everything he could see looked much like so many of the other places he had traveled almost without noticing, this place was special.

This place was his.

He completed the scan, looking down once more at the deep furrows in the ground at his feet. Glancing at the smaller lines Lilia had made, Roche tried to imagine just how much larger a dragon would have to be in order to make such markings.

He sighed, approached the furrows and stepped over them.

CHAPTER 4

The last thing Roche wanted to do was go rushing blindly into danger. He proceeded slowly instead, making note of the landscape as it shifted slowly underfoot. At first it was the same as other similar areas, long rolling plains of rock and soil. The flat lands were cast in muted shades of brown and red, the dirt streaked with granular minerals that highlighted the earthen colors with strips of white and gray. Gradually they became more uniform, giving way to long square stretches of sand and silt and clay spread evenly from corner to corner. Eventually he crested a rise, and saw a giant swath of black before him.

He had smelled it before he saw it, the scent of scorched soil dancing on the wind to tease his nostrils from miles away. As soon as he glimpsed the burnt field, he identified it as the source of the smell; but knowing what it was brought him no closer to knowing what it meant. Roche could tell this field had been like the others he crossed, before it was covered in something and set aflame; under the burnt layer was that same mixture of different dirts. The clay was not bound up in loose wet clumps; it had been mixed with the silt and sand to give it a consistent texture underfoot. Whatever had been laid across the area to be burned had left behind nothing but ashes and blackened soil.

The scent of fire burning or flames long since burned out seemed to be present no matter where he went in Hell, and Roche was quickly learning that different fires had different odors to them. In the queen's presence it was unique, the clean lasting smell of a chimney that had borne the smoke of centuries. Here the smell was fresh, wet and earthy. Still not entirely unpleasant, the scent was refreshed with every step he took across the scorched plain; it drifted up to tickle his nostrils and coat his tongue with its burnt flavor.

After a series of such fields, Roche crested another rise and stopped suddenly. Off in the distance he could see activity, dozens of devils moving about over another clearly marked square of land. He felt exposed, standing there watching them; so he backed up a few steps until only his head would be visible should they sense him observing their movements. For some time he watched them, as they laid long browned stalks dangling dried leaves in a uniform layer across the designated area. After awhile they appeared satisfied, and the devils moved to the edge of the field.

A familiar sound filled the air, a powerful whooshing and cracking that began far in the distance and rapidly moved closer. Roche was not surprised to see a black dragon appear on the horizon, but he was slightly startled by its size. It began as a black dot, growing as it came closer. Several times he thought it must be over the distant plain already, judging by how large it was. Each time it kept coming, and kept growing from his perspective. By the time it slowed to hover far above the field, Roche had felt the breath catch in his chest more than once. He reminded himself to breathe, while he watched the enormous creature begin its dive.

The dragon leveled out some twenty or thirty feet from the ground, flames erupting from its giant maw. Fire touched the plant matter the devils had laid down, and it burst into flame in a straight uniform line across the expanse. Another pass, and another line of fire appeared by the dragon's careful design. Only a few more passes were needed to set the entire field aflame. Roche could hear the devils cheering over the distant sound of crackling, and he watched a massive plume of smoke rise from the blaze to fill the sky.

He had no way of knowing how much time had passed since he had first begun watching the devils at work. As transfixed as Roche had been by their mysterious activity, seeing the dragon appear had captured his attention completely. Curiosity had turned to wonder as he watched, and he had taken a few more steps up the hillside without realizing it. Now he stood completely exposed, as visible to the distant devils as they were to him. None of them had turned his way, and he hadn't thought to consider that he had been spotted until he heard careful footfalls behind him.

The sound broke the spell, and Roche whirled just in time to be struck directly in the chest instead of across his wide back. He saw the tight knot of devils behind the one that had attacked, the spiked club that had hit him, and the ground rushing up to greet him as he spun with the impact. The world began to slow down, and by the time he hit the dirt it had nearly stopped. Even so, they were almost upon him. This group was nothing like the other he had battled, acting as one and moving with practiced confidence. Roche had to defend himself while still on his back, taking the legs out from under two of them as they came close with powerful careless swings of both arms.

Each devil wore virtually identical armor, covered in dull gray metal from head to toe. It creaked and clicked as they moved, and Roche wondered how he hadn't heard them coming up behind him until it was nearly too late. In a moment of sudden clarity, he realized the difference between him and the other devils he had seen. Every set of armor had a single hole fashioned into it, where each devil's tail stuck through. The only scaled crimson skin he could see was all those prehensile protrusions, and he found himself wondering at the most inopportune moment why he had been made with no tail.

Converging on him, the devils moved with such speed and sureness that Roche considered the possibility of his own death once more. Even the two he had knocked down kept their mind on the task at hand, and their eyes on the prize; they crawled toward him as others dove at him, and hands gripped his arms while blades came at his chest. Roche yanked the devils holding him across his torso, still lying flat on his back. Their weight settled on him all at once, forcefully expelling the breath from his lungs. In the next rushing moment, a spear punctured both devils through armor and bone to drive itself deep into Roche's heaving chest.

Rather than panic, Roche felt a strange calm settle over him. He remembered the way he had felt before, like his inner self wanted to break free of his own skin to rain destruction on his enemies. The desire rose up within him again, a rage so powerful it pushed him to transform into something other than he was.

The painful point of the spear was pulled from his chest, and bodies were flung aside by a dozen strong grasping hands. Roche was yanked to his feet, as his body began to tremble with the impending inner eruption. One of the devils holding him glanced sideways at him, and called out to the others.

"He's shaking like crazy," he said. "And he's burning up. I can feel the heat through my gauntlets."

Roche was sure it was the last thing the devil would say, the final sound the others would hear. He could feel the power within him bubbling up, ready to boil over. Something told him he might not survive the explosion, and they definitely wouldn't. The knot of devils drew closer around him, the hands gripping his arms grew tighter, and Roche threw his head back to allow whatever was trying to get out to be released.

"Stand down!"

The voice was a thunderous sound, a giant boom that reverberated in the armor and weapons of the devils standing close, and gave Roche pause. Whatever darkness that was rising within him hesitated, as the devils grasping his arms relaxed their hold on him.

"Release him!"

Same voice, same booming volume. Roche pushed away his captors, shook his head to clear it. The rush of whatever waited inside him was not easy to dispel, and he wrangled it as best he could while trying to see past the tight knot of devils to where the voice was coming from. They parted before him, and his vision cleared just as the dragon came into view.

From a distance, the black monster had been large enough to take his breath away. Roche had admired the way it flew, how it banked and turned to scorch every square inch of the field in minutes; he had thought of it as female, likely because the only dragon he had seen was Lilia. Up close, the dragon was alarmingly large. It towered over the entire assemblage without tilting forward, glowering at Roche. The booming voice dispelled any thought of femininity, as it came again.

"You fools!" the dragon said. "You look, and still don't see what is right in front of you."

He was huge, and angry.

"Stand back!" he boomed. "Give him room!"

The devils slunk away, still acting as one. Roche felt his breath coming back to him, as the steely serenity within him gave way to a far less explosive kind of calm. Glancing around at them, he saw the devils shifting awkwardly where they stood. They didn't know what to do, if they couldn't fight. Although he felt similarly awkward, Roche drew himself up to his full height and met eyes with the dragon.

Lowering its head with a long unbroken serpentine smoothness, the dragon closed the gap between them without breaking eye contact. Roche found himself looking past long rows of teeth, trying not to think of the fact that he had just seen more muscles working in the monster's neck than he had in his entire body. Hot and reeking of fire, he could feel the dragon's breath filling what little space there was left between them.

"You wear the garb of royalty," the dragon said.

His voice was not as loud as before, and the monster seemed to be oblivious to the devils standing and watching. Nonetheless, Roche felt his ribcage tremble with the low rolling rumble carrying the monster's words.

"Yet I've never met you," the dragon went on. "Never seen you, never heard of you. And if I'm not mistaken, you have no tail under those royal robes."

A quiet murmur of assent went through the armored bodies surrounding them, and a few helms turned to each other and nodded. These were the things they had looked at without seeing. As much as Roche was keenly aware of both facts, he had no idea what the dragon meant. Rather than ask, he stood silent. He nodded, slightly.

The dragon frowned, showing Roche some of the teeth he hadn't seen before. His reptilian eyes narrowed, and his head snaked closer.

"Well, then," the dragon hissed. "Who are you?"

Resisting the urge to ask questions that would show how little he knew of himself, along with the desire to point out how many better ways the dragon may have chosen to begin introductions, Roche kept his eyes on the monster's while he shrugged.

"My name is Roche," he said, simply.

The dragon pulled back suddenly, at the sound of his name. He swung his head from side to side, finally acknowledging the small crowd of devils around them.

"Are you all finished patrolling?" he snapped. "Or are you awaiting some punishment for doing such a poor job of it earlier? Keep waiting, if you want. I will deal with those of you still here when I am done dealing with this one."

Now they became individuals, abandoning the group mind to back away at various speeds in several different directions. Not even a minute passed before the last of them had slipped away, and Roche stood on the hillside alone with the dragon.

"I have heard the prophecies," the dragon said. "I would think one such as yourself would know not to cross into a dragon's territory. What business do you have on my land?"

The dragon continued to tower over him, his head at eye level with Roche while his body rose to form a mountain of scaled flesh behind him. He held the creature's gaze, trying not to think of the fact that the dragon's eyes were each bigger than his own skull.

"My name is Roche," he said again.

A subtle shaking began in the dragon's neck, rolling along the length of it to begin a more pronounced shaking of his shoulders. Roche could not tell if it was rage or fear causing the dragon to tremble; he held his ground, waiting to find out.

"You said that already," the monster spat. "I know who you are. What are you doing in my territory?"

"There is much I have not learned yet," Roche admitted. "And few things I know for certain. One if them is that this is my land. Another is that an introduction only works if it goes both ways."

Moving so quickly that it startled him, the dragon reared back on his haunches and let a puff of smoke escape his toothy maw. Roche stood silent and unmoving, and kept the surprise inside. Watching the dragon as if it were a bug he might smash under his foot at any moment, he held his ground and let the creature express itself.

"Only a fool would challenge a dragon he does not know," the monster boomed. "You would be wise to follow the example of the others, and leave my sight before I lose my patience."

Roche inclined his head, slightly.

"Perhaps," he said. "I would think that would go both ways, however. Only a fool would challenge a devil he does not know, and I know you don't know me because I don't know you. Is this how land disputes are typically resolved? Do I have to kill you to secure my territory?"

That giant reptilian head began another slow descent, ending inches from Roche's face. He kept still, and tried not to breathe in.

"What makes you think you can kill me?" the dragon hissed.

Roche shrugged.

"What makes you think you can kill me?" he echoed.

For another long breathless moment, the dragon stared at him and breathed on him without a word. Finally it reared back again, and laughed. Roche could feel the sound fluttering his robes, and saw tiny bits of dust dancing all around them.

"The queen resolves all land disputes," the dragon said, after it had stopped laughing.

"You mean Ximena?" Roche asked.

The creature did not look happy that he called her by that name, but he nodded nonetheless. Roche shook his head, and peered up at him.

"I'd rather not bother her about it," he said. "I know nothing of what you are doing, and have no desire to be the steward of vast expanses of unused land. Perhaps we could come to an arrangement, which might benefit both of us. You can teach me what can be done with these areas, and still keep half of the land in question for yourself."

They were both still, regarding each other silently. At last, the dragon nodded its head, and smiled a little. The expression was a bit terrifying, and Roche was fairly certain for a split second that he was about to be bathed in dragon fire.

"I normally don't make deals with devils," the dragon said.

It left the ground behind in one fluid motion, using powerful hind legs to launch high over his head before beginning to flap its massive leathery appendages. Hovering over him for a moment, the monster called out to him between the deafening cracking sound of giant dragon wings overhead.

"Come back tomorrow," he said. "I'll have made up my mind."

Roche watched him fly away, dropping the stern mask he had worn while they talked to let the wonder show on his face. Long after the dragon had turned into a tiny black dot and then disappeared, Roche continued to stare after him. After a while he turned, and began walking back to the markings.

The journey took some time, enough for him to wonder where he would go once he crossed the lines. He considered finding some area that hadn't been claimed, and coming up with some marking of his own. At the furrows he paused, and look down. Roche thought of the dragon's giant claws, and the seemingly endless fangs that showed whenever it talked or frowned.

A shudder passed through his body, and he stepped over the lines.

He hadn't taken six steps when something drifted lazily down from the sky. Nearly as long as one of his feet, the feather was stark white; it floated to the ground before him, and glowed brightly

CHAPTER 5

Hesitating before the closed door, Roche wondered what he might say once he was on the other side. Coming back here had seemed like the obvious choice, but now his curled fist paused before knocking. He likely would have stood there for some time, trying to formulate his thoughts into words that might make sense, had the door not swung inward suddenly.

Immediately he saw her, far across the room seated comfortably. She gestured, darkness swirling amongst darkness, and called out quietly.

"I've been expecting you," she said. "Come in."

The door closed behind him as slowly and soundlessly as it had opened. Roche moved toward her, conscious that the clothes she had given him matched her own in cut and color.

"Ximena," he said. "I hope I am not being a bother."

Although she was sitting down, he couldn't help but try to get a glimpse behind her. She shifted in her seat, and he peered closer.

"What?" Ximena looked down at herself. "Am I on fire?"

Roche shook his head, averted his gaze. He had shifted his attention from the waves of wonder he felt looking at her to check if she had a tail.

"I'm sorry," he said. "I'm just…curious."

She stood up; or rather, she floated into a standing position. The cloud of darkness around her shifted smoothly with the movement, and she spun about in place with that same smoky fluidity. Light seemed to shine from her every pore, and the darkness disappeared to reveal her nude form underneath. Her body was lithe and light, sculpted to modest perfection; her skin was smooth like none of the devils he had seen.

Roche nodded, as the darkness gathered itself about her once more. Somehow seeing the stark naked lines of the form within the shadows made her more mysterious and dangerous to him instead of less. He felt self-conscious for a moment, and held his tongue until he could get it properly untied.

"You do have a tail," he said, as much to himself as to her.

She smiled, kindly.

"You'll grow one," she said. "You are not grounded to this realm yet, although I hear you are making efforts to speed up the process. Your tail will grow as your connection to this place does. Then it will be safe for you to release the other possibilities within you without endangering yourself or others."

Everything she said brought up more questions for him than answers, but her musical voice made him want nothing more than to hear her speak. Roche nodded as if he understood, and remained silent.

"Did you feel at home in Heaven?" she said. "Or was the mortal realm more to your liking?"

Roche shrugged.

"The mortal realm?" he echoed.

Waving the question away with a swirling shadow of darkness, she smiled once more.

"You must have passed it on the way down," she said. "You may want to explore it before you begin any serious ventures here. There is much to learn for souls like us there, and you in particular are tied to the lives of humanity in a very direct way."

Roche spread his hands, helplessly.

"Why does everyone know more about me than I do?" he said.

Another swirl of shadows drifted lazily in the direction of the tall bookshelf along the wall, indicating the bound writings.

"I read those," she said. "When I am shrouded completely in darkness, and falling in my cycle, I make it a habit to remind myself every day with them. When I am on the rise, everything comes clear to me and I don't need them. That's when I write them, actually."

His eyes moved slowly along the shelves, noting how different and how numerous the volumes were.

"You wrote those?" he said. "All of them?"

Ximena shrugged. The movement was totally different than when he did it, flowing sureness instead of halting uncertainty.

"Who else can I trust?" she said. "When I am clear I can see everything, the past and present and future of Hell. When I'm not I rely on those periods of clarity to guide my way."

His gaze was still on the shelf, on the different bindings and markings on their spines. Without thinking, he took a step toward it. He stopped, and turned to her.

"Can I read them?" he asked.

Making no move to stop him, she shrugged again.

"One day," she said. "You don't really have the time right now, but you will one day. It only seems fair, since nearly all the prophecies floating around about you are my doing. There was a time when I gave cryptic hints of the future, to try and guide this realm from the point of view of the bigger picture. It did more harm than good, however; now I tend to keep what I know to myself, and let life live as it will."

His attention drifted to the numerous volumes once more.

"How did you do harm?" he said. "If the future is fixed, and you have recorded it, what harm could come from sharing?"

Ximena gestured to the seat across from the one she had been occupying, as she flowed darkly back into it. Reluctantly, Roche turned from the collection on the wall to settle opposite her.

"No one said the future is fixed," she replied. "Anymore than the present, or the past. Time is on a cycle similar to your soul and mine, never beginning and never ending. We dip our fingers into the stream, but time flows on around and past us. Each book changes, even as events remain the same. They are my way of finding the best path, or of pursuing the illusion of doing so. All things are both fluid and fixed, from the depths of Hell to the heights of Heaven."

One day Roche hoped to be the devil she seemed to think she was talking to, absorbing her every word and making immediate sense of it. For now he could only file away whatever she said in the back of his mind, and save it for looking at later. He let her mention of Heaven remind him of a more direct line of inquiry, and hoped the answers would be more comfortably within his realm of understanding.

"Something happened earlier," he said. "After I explored a territory I felt a very strong connection to. A feather fell at my feet."

Ximena's eyes widened, darkness swirling in their depths.

"Oh?" she said. "What did you do with it?"

He shifted awkwardly, like he had done as he stood over the feather.

"I left it there," he said. "I wasn't sure what to do."

The way she laughed was completely carefree, joyful gaiety given voice in her melodious tones. He heard no mockery in it, or judgement; in fact, the sound was so uplifting he nearly joined in.

"You met Rendibite," she noted, quietly. "You challenged one of the oldest and most dangerous dragons on land he had marked as his own, and yet you hesitate to pick up an angel's feather. You are long on bravery, but short on trust. Surely both will serve you in Hell, and even more so in Heaven."

She continued to smile, as she went on.

"The feather is an invitation," Ximena said, "likely from an angel who wishes to speak with you. You must do more than pick it up to accept the invitation. You need to give that permission expressly, even if it is quietly within yourself."

Thinking of clouded luminescence all around him made Roche remember the pain of Ehcor's fury. He wasn't sure if the blast or her rejection of him had been worse, or if either had done lasting damage he couldn't see.

"It's not from her," Ximena said, softly.

Roche felt the tension drain from his shoulders. He dragged his eyes from the floor to meet hers.

"Also, you don't have to accept it," she added. "It will bring you directly to the one who requests your presence, but you can go to Heaven on your own if you would rather."

His eyes widened. "I can?"

"Of course," Ximena nodded. "You can go there anytime you'd like. It's not like there are gates to keep us out. In fact, you can go anywhere you can think of that you would like to go. Heaven, the middle world, or virtually anywhere in Hell."

Rather than let the wonder of what she was saying overwhelm him, Roche focused on her omission.

"Virtually?" he repeated. "Where in Hell can I not go?"

She laughed again, as if pleased he had caught it.

"I am the devil," she said, lightly. "Allow me my secrets."

As much as he was brimming with endless questions, Roche realized she was pushing him toward experience in her own gentle way. Rather than burden him with too much of her own perspective, she wanted him to have the chance to form his own way of seeing the worlds.

"How do I learn to travel," he said, "and find my way to wherever I would go? I have no desire to be summoned at will by anyone, even an angel. I am curious who wants to see me, and why. But I'm also curious about the mortal realm. Can you teach me to be where I wish to be?"

Something about the way he worded that seemed to amuse her. Ximena let a soft smile alight on her lips, and he felt as though they were sharing some joke he did not get just yet.

"I can do that," she smiled. "I can do more than that."

Her hands didn't disappear, or slip beneath her robes. One moment they were empty in front of her, the next they were holding something out to him. The object was folded and dented, somewhere between deep brown and faded black. He took it from her, without hesitation.

"What is this?" he asked.

She brought her hands together before her again, and their lines blurred into their shadows.

"It will be called a fedora," she said, "when humans get around to creating it. For now, it will appear to be whatever suits the occasion and the company you find yourself in. Others will see it as a halo or headdress, or a set of horns considerably less magnificent than your own. You will need a disguise when you travel, which this will provide. Humans are not so great at distinguishing us from their own, with minimal effort on our part; but angels will not always take kindly to a devil wandering freely in Heaven."

Roche grimaced at the thought.

"Are they all as powerful as her?" he asked.

The one he spoke of did not need to be named; she knew he meant Ehcor, and that it was pain itself to say her name.

"No." Ximena shook her head. "She is like you, only headed in the other direction for now. You would do best to avoid her. But the rest should not give you any trouble unless you let them. If you must, you can kill an angel by stabbing them through the heart as easily as you have killed devils by beheading them."

Roche looked down at his robed body, showed her empty hands.

"With what?" he said. "I have no weapon."

For a moment, she looked surprised.

"Sure you do," she said. "You kept one of the swords you took when you first arrived here. It is in your mind somewhere, waiting to be drawn forth. That was part of the reason Lilia did not wish to leave us alone; she knew you were armed, although you appeared naked before me. But I knew you were unaware of your weapon, and meant me no harm."

It was Roche's turn to laugh, as freely and openly as she had.

"Harm you?" he said. "Is that even possible?"

She remained silent for a long moment, after his laughter faded.

"We must hope we cannot be killed," she said, "and we must even act like it from time to time. Yet that question can only be answered once, and in one way. Such finality is not to my liking, and the question must continue to go unanswered for us to keep asking it."

Rising once more, she drifted closer to him on a shifting fog of shadows. He put the strange covering on his head as she reached out her hands to him, and found that it fit perfectly. The darkness reached for his meaty paws, and somehow her smaller hands enveloped his in shadow. Something cleared up inside him, some clotted thinking breaking loose with a tingle in his skull. Ximena stepped back, and looked up at him.

"I will show you," she said, "how to retrieve the weapon from your thoughts. Then I will show you how you may travel anywhere at will. First, close your eyes. Feel the weight of the sword in your hand, the texture of the hilt against your fingers."

Roche closed his eyes, and imagined.

CHAPTER 6

Roche could not have been more surprised to find actual gates barring his way into Heaven. Ximena had taught him how to travel, and they had appeared in several places together throughout Hell that he had walked or run miles to reach before. She had remained quiet but for her occasional instruction, urging him with the dark unfathomable hopefulness in her eyes instead of using words.

Every moment he spent with her was steeped in ecstatic darkness. Somehow Roche felt free and easy when she was close, more able to be himself than he could even when he was alone. A deep love had begun to form in him, the kind he imagined someone might feel for a saintly mother or an incredibly accomplished older sister. He felt no attraction to her, other than wanting to be around her continually; although he saw the beauty in both her body and soul, and the simple lovely lines of her face, he was simply not drawn to her in that fashion.

Being by her side gave him the feeling of being embraced perfectly and constantly; there was no suffocation in it, or lack of closeness. She held him lovingly by being close by, and he felt more connected to her the more places they went together. The time they spent was long enough for him to completely let his guard down, and he forgot to put it back up before leaving her for the higher realm.

He had taken the strange hat off, as much as he liked the feel of it on his head. It was stored in the same place as the sword he hadn't known he was carrying, somehow somewhere in his mind. The footing was shaky, at the edge of whatever clouded surface he was standing on. Roche moved forward, closer to the breathtaking obstruction. Like the dragon he had seen earlier, the twin barriers grew in size as he approached. Long before he had reached them, Roche saw two forms take shape from the clouds to bookend the gates.

Ximena had been so offhanded in dispelling the notion that his entry to Heaven may be barred, Roche had begun to wonder as he neared the gates if they were perhaps in his imagination. After what he had learned from her, flitting from place to place and storing things in his mind, he wasn't sure he could trust his eyes to tell him what was and wasn't real. The two figures dispelled any such notions, as they came clear.

They were angels, tall and statuesque and covered in armor that seemed to flow and shift like the clouds around them. Each of them held a sword that seemed to be made entirely of light, and stared at him coldly through narrow slits in their helms. When he got close enough that the barriers would have swung into him had they opened fully, the angels moved in on him. One called out, from several paces off.

"These are the gates of Heaven," he cried. "This is no place for you."

Roche raised an eyebrow, fingered the hilt of the sword in his mind. Something about the way he held his ground when the angel called out caused them to slow in their tracks. Still converging on him, but more slowly, the other angel raised his voice as well.

"Begone, devil," he said. "You do not belong here."

His eyes went back and forth between them, curious. Perhaps their sonorous voices and imposing frames were enough to do their jobs for them, usually. Roche had just spent considerable time with the queen of Hell, however; it would take more than a formidable appearance and a couple of deep voices to sway him.

"Why?" he said, simply.

They stopped then, and looked past him to glance at each other.

"Why do I not belong here?" he went on. "Are we not all made of everything, do we not all carry the light within?"

Exchanging another glance, they still didn't move.

"You are a devil," the first spoke again. "You are of Hell, and that is where you belong."

Roche nodded, understanding.

"Then you don't know who I am," he noted.

Now one of them stepped forward, the second that had spoken. His face was hidden behind the clouded metal mask, but his movements showed both his impatience and his uncertainty.

"We know what you are," he said. "That is enough. Begone, I say."

Roche raised his eyebrow again, and spread his hands.

"Or what?" he said, quietly.

The angel took another step, coming close enough to catch Roche in the swing of his sword. He drew the weapon back, as if he intended to do just that.

"Or I'll send you back to Hell myself," he snapped.

Roche shrugged.

"Come on, then," he said. "Give it a try."

The angel was a full head taller than him, and was either heavily muscled or wearing largely empty armor. While he grew more blustery, and annoyed with what surely seemed a mismatch to him, his companion continued to hold back. Perhaps something about Roche's confidence held him, or maybe he just thought a single old devil would be easily dispatched by the other. Either way, he stood his ground and watched as the one closest to Roche set his stance and began his attack. The sword was pure light, a straight steel sun that didn't shine but contained its luminescence in its shape. Instead of glinting like steel, it flashed like lightning as it came at him.

Stepping easily out of the way, Roche watched the blade whoosh past and carry the angel with it. He elbowed the armored frame that dipped low as the weapon sunk into the clouds, and grabbed the angel's wing where it connected to his shoulder. Pulling and then pushing, he smiled slightly as his opponent was thrown off balance and then lost his footing. He let go, and let the angel fall heavily onto his back. Roche looked down at him, noting that even the biggest enemies seemed smaller when they were lying at his feet.

Now the angel's partner moved, coming forward at what struck him as a dreadfully slow pace. Roche was able to step away from the fallen one, and put the first angel between himself and the second attack. They circled each other around the armored form as it struggled to its feet, Roche kicking the one between them as he moved. Clearly the armor was burdensome, both weighing him down and restricting his movement. All Roche had to do was get out of visual range of those two tiny slits in the fallen angel's helmet, and reach out with his foot. Each time the angel went down again, often rolling directly into his partner's path.

Holding his sword while trying to get up was not working for the angel. Roche was barely able to keep from laughing every time he landed headfirst in the clouded surface underfoot, smirking at the circling angel whenever his stumble nearly toppled them both. When the one on all fours set down his sword to focus on getting up once and for all, Roche kicked away the glowing blade. It skittered behind the angel circling him, and suddenly changed the game.

Both angels glanced in the direction the sword had gone, then at each other. Roche kicked the one trying to stand, just as he was moving from a kneeling to a standing position. With a shrug, he began to stride toward the lost blade. The angel that had been circling with him had been hesitant to engage while his partner was down; even when Roche had tried to speed up or slow down to face him, the angel had changed pace with him. Now his choices had dwindled to engaging Roche with a weapon or without one, and still the angel hesitated to rush forward.

Backing away and glancing behind him, the angel tried to move between Roche and where he thought the sword was. Clouds glowed in that direction, but the glow was faint and the angel only had two narrow slits in his helmet to peer out through. Roche spied the weapon immediately, and walked briskly toward the luminous blade.

The angel glanced back at his comrade, who was once again struggling to a kneeling position. With no help on the way, he threw caution to the wind and came at Roche. In the instant before the swinging blade bit into his back, he thought of the curved weapon in his mind and pivoted slightly at the waist. Whatever the sword was made of, it still made a clanging sound when it met his own.

Startled at the sudden appearance of a weapon in his hand, the angel drew back and glanced over his shoulder at his companion. Finally, he had regained his feet and was glancing around looking a little bewildered. Roche stepped forward, drawing his curved sword back over his shoulder. The angel closest to him retreated even further, bringing his attention back to Roche in an attempt to defend himself. Roche drove forward, swinging the curved blade wildly with every step. Some of the blows sparked when they landed, but he was only trying to keep the angel backing up rapidly. When he took one step too many, another clanging reverberated through the quiet open clouded space.

The angels collided, and for a moment Roche thought they were going to go down in a tangled heap together. Instead they both held their ground, leaning against each other for support. Roche's next blow knocked aside the glowing blade, and sliced clean through the angel's armor. A gash appeared in his breastplate, and light shone out through the hole; otherwise, he appeared to be completely undamaged. One more slash, and another gash appeared as the sword was again swept aside. Light burst forth from it like blood, and the angel was driven back into the other with a grunt.

Roche realized suddenly that this would be a long, slow and somewhat macabre affair if he kept at it. Perhaps he would cut the angel's heart out, given enough swings of his curved sword; but more likely the cuts would close up long before he got to it, like the first two were doing right before his eyes. Taking two quick steps away from the pair, watching them balance back to back against each other, he let the sword disappear from his hand to take up space once more in his mind. He turned away from them, and strode towards the glowing mass of clouds.

Their armor made as much noise as he had noticed in the devils wearing similar coverings in Hell. It also slowed them down considerably; although Roche knew they could never catch him if he kicked it into high speed, even if they hadn't been overly burdened by their protective layer. The entire encounter had been more of a pleasant diversion, an opportunity to learn more about Heaven before entering.

A familiar but different sound filled the air, and Roche realized a few short steps from the spot of luminescence that at least one of them had taken flight. Angel wings were not quite as loud or jarring as those of a monstrous dragon, but the noise was enough to make him dash forward and leap toward the glowing bank of fog. The angel struck the lighted clouds at the same time, pounding against Roche with gauntleted fists as they rolled and tussled. Little wisps of mist trailed behind their struggle, drifting away calmly while they pushed and pulled at each other. Roche let a few more blows land before he tired of the sensation, and balled up his fist.

He struck the angel in the abdomen, to the satisfying sound of the wind whooshing from him and the armor denting inward. Another blow and the angel rolled off him, gasping for breath.

Rising to his feet, Roche held the glowing sword before him.

The other angel had taken wing, and was hovering perhaps a dozen feet directly over his head. He had been poised to strike, and looked as though he was going to dive as soon as Roche was clear of his partner. When he saw the sword in Roche's hand, the angel called out.

"Put that down!" he cried. "You're a devil! You cannot wield an angel's sword! Prostos! He has your sacred blade!" Still going through the slow and arduous process of regaining his footing, the angel that had dive-bombed him looked up from his efforts. On one knee, he creaked his helm to the side as far as it would go and glanced up at Roche. He could barely see the sky blue eyes behind the narrow openings, but Roche was able to watch them widen in disbelief.

"Does it burn, devil?" he hissed.

The words were muffled by exertion and plate metal. Roche turned to regard the angel with his full attention, and shook his head.

"No," he said, befuddled. "It actually feels kind of nice in my hand."

Behind the slits, the angel's eyes narrowed suddenly.

"You will pay for this!" he cried. "You will suffer!"

Despite the fury in his voice, the angel still hadn't quite regained his footing. He glanced up at the one overhead, and waved his arm frantically. As he struggled the last bit into a standing position, Roche could hear the flapping overhead suddenly stop.

Whirling, he brought the blade up before him. A flash of feathers and armor struck him hard, and Roche went down under the weight. However soft the clouds looked underfoot, they hurt for real when his head snapped back and struck the drifting mist. For a long moment he lay there dazed, before realizing the form on top of him was not moving.

The hilt of the sword had been driven into his abdomen, and Roche still felt the ache from the blow. He could see how the blade end of it had taken that pressure, driving the sword so deeply into the angel's chest that more of it stuck out behind him than was still in him. Pushing the body off him, Roche stood slowly and dragged the blade from the wound. A loud screeching sound came from the tempered light as it scraped against the plated covering on its way out, and he saw the other angel visibly shake off a whole body tremble that made his own armor cry out in protest.

Roche took a step towards him. The angel leapt backward, although a half dozen paces remained between them. Nearly falling over from his own swift retreat, the angel held up his empty hands and waved them helplessly between them.

"I'm unarmed," he said.

Taking another step forward, Roche felt his brow knit itself together in anger. The angel moved backward again, nearly pitching off balance once more.

"I was unarmed," Roche spat. "You attacked me."

Still backing away, the angel threw up his hands.

"You're a devil!" he exclaimed. "You don't belong here!"

He said the word 'devil' like it disgusted him to pronounce the syllables, much less consider the feelings of such a creature.

Looking at the sword in his hand with a slow deliberate glance, Roche moved his eyes to meet the angel's as he continued his awkward retreat.

"Don't I?" Roche muttered.

He made as if to leap forward, and give the angel similar treatment to what his comrade had received. Rather than face him bravely, the angel unfolded his wings behind him. Roche knew he could move quickly enough to take him before he fled, but he had no more appetite for killing the angel than the fellow seemed to have for dying. As the flapping began he stepped back, and watched the angel's ascent.

Safely in the air above him, the angel looked down at him scornfully.

"You'll answer for this!" he cried. "The gates themselves will not allow you entrance, anyway. You killed for nothing, and all of Heaven will know of your brutality and cruelty!"

Without waiting for a response, the angel turned in the air and flew over the gates. Roche watched him until he had faded into the clouds, and let the new weapon disappear into his thoughts. He approached the gate, marveling at the way it seemed to glow with a life of its own. Once he got within a few feet of it, he looked up and basked in the light.

The gate clicked quietly, and opened enough for him to pass.

CHAPTER 7

He was not surprised to find he couldn't go far in any direction he wanted to. Instead of barriers preventing his movement, drifting cloud banks evaporated before he reached them; Roche found himself standing at the edge looking down, whichever way he went. He wondered if enough time in Heaven would cause him to grow wings, like it would supposedly cause him to sprout a tail in Hell.

The entire environment felt somehow antiseptic to him. In Hell, the scent of fire and smoke intermingled with countless other odors wherever he went. It made the other place seem more alive under his feet, and more real to his senses. Even the clouds here struck him as too pristine, as if someone had scrubbed the gray from them until each puff gleamed pure white. It didn't help that they kept moving away from him, drifting to nothing before he could move to another large floating mass.

He had approached one edge after another, looking for a way to cross from where he was to where he wanted to be. Beyond the floating island, it seemed to only get brighter the further he could see. Every large and small foggy surface seemed connected to each other, save the one he was stranded on. Turning from the thought of leaping at the same time he turned away from the shifting edge, Roche realized he was no longer alone.

An angel stood behind him, waiting for him to be startled at his sudden appearance. Roche grunted instead, and stopped mid-turn.

"Sneaking up on me is not a good idea," he growled.

The angel seemed disappointed at his reaction, and let his shoulders slump a little before he responded.

"You seem to have acquired bad manners already," he said, "after only such a short time in Hell. First you murder an innocent angel, then you stride shamelessly through the gates. Now you accuse me of skulking, as if I were some... some..."

Roche grimaced, and finished his thought.

"Devil?" he said. "Go ahead. You can say it. I'm beginning to learn what those like you think of those like me."

The angel flinched, as if he had been struck. Roche couldn't honestly admit he wasn't considering it, particularly after his dramatic movement.

"Like you?" the angel scoffed. "You are no devil. There is none like you. You are an original demon. I know what you are going through because I know what you are. Your counterpart and I have been working together, as you seem to have been working with the devils. You have no business relating to them, or behaving like them. Your duty is here, and in the mortal realm. You have a higher calling, a responsibility no devil could bear. We need you to cooperate with us just as Ehcor has been."

Narrowing his eyes, Roche let the angel see his teeth in his grimace. The angel shifted, moving slightly away from him.

"You've got a strange way of asking," Roche growled.

For a moment he looked as though he wanted to laugh; another glance at Roche's face stifled the urge as quickly as it had formed.

"I'm not asking," the angel said. "This is your duty, as it is my duty to work with both you and Ehcor to manage the demon problem in the mortal realm."

Roche looked down from the edge of the cloud, saw the world the angel spoke of far below. Beautiful from far off, it looked different than anything he had seen in either Heaven or Hell; yet there were elements of both in it as well. He sighed, and glanced at the angel.

"What about the demon problem in Heaven?" he said.

This time the angel did laugh.

"There are no demons in Heaven," he sputtered. "I mean, other than you, right now. Angels have a level of selfawareness one such as you cannot understand, a clarity of thought and vision that rivals any devil or mortal. This is why I must be the one in charge of your mission, and broker all your dealings with Ehcor."

Roche bristled, suddenly.

"Stop saying that name," he growled.

Pointing out the fact that Roche was staring straight at a sizable demon riding the angel's shoulder seemed a bad idea at the time. He had grown accustomed to seeing them on many of the smaller devils inhabiting Hell, and was just as used to ignoring them as completely as their hosts did. The thought that no one could actually see them had never crossed his mind, until the angel stood there denying the possibility of the twisted little crimson monster on his shoulder.

He looked down again, realizing he could focus in on what was going on in the realm they were watching. Rather than seeing it over a great distance, he seemed to be looking at it through some clear portal that telescoped to wherever he focused. The view kept changing, from a stream of people walking along a dirt road to a neatly ordered assemblage of huts, then on to a carved wooden ship on the high seas.

The angel spoke, shaking him from his reverie.

"What do you see?" he said.

Grunting again, Roche shrugged without looking over.

"What do you see?" he echoed.

The angel smiled broadly enough for him to see it from the corner of his eyes. Roche still didn't turn.

"My family," the angel said. "Or rather, my descendants. Everyone I knew has long since passed on, but I watch over those that came after them. Many of us do, once we come here."

Now Roche looked over at him, only to catch the angel lost in his own distant internal vision.

"What about the people you knew?" he said. "Where are they?"

It was the angel's turn to continue staring off in the distance as he spoke. Roche couldn't help but notice the demon on his shoulder come alive with his words, but he tried to pretend he didn't.

"Some are here," the angel sighed. "Most are not. Other angels have told me they are likely caught in the human cycle, and must purify themselves with further lessons before they can join us here. But I did not believe in that kind of thing when I was alive, and I don't know that I believe in it now. The highest teachings will reveal all, but I am not to that point yet. I must do my work, and earn my wings."

Roche glanced past the demon, raised an eyebrow.

"You already have wings," he said.

The angel waved him off, without turning.

"Just an expression," he said.

Roche joined him in watching the distant world. More travelers, going the other way; the huts, with people emerging from them at first light; the ship, being tossed about on the waves in the pale moonlight.

"You think they went to Hell," he mused, quietly.

From the periphery of his vision, Roche saw him shrug.

"I hope not," he said.

Roche laughed, clapped the angel on his back. Nearly tumbling forward over the edge, the angel spread his wings and lifted off the clouded surface. He turned in flight and crossed his arms. Looking down at Roche, he grimaced.

"It's not all bad," Roche said, "down there. I mean, you might not like it much; but that's likely because you wouldn't last a day there. The most common devil knows more than you about the human soul, and they certainly don't think as highly of you as you seem to of yourself. Every devil knows the soul is in a long cycle, that every human becomes an angel only to become a human who becomes a devil. Or the other way around. You remember your family, but you've forgotten your soul. Devils remember their souls."

Roche pulled the feather from his thoughts, held it between them.

"Is this yours?" he said.

Still hovering, the angel nodded solemnly.

"It is," he said. "Please return it to me."

Roche glanced at it, then at him.

"Why?" he asked.

The angel swooped in closer, and Roche pulled it away.

"It's mine," the angel snapped.

Shaking his head, Roche let the feather disappear once more into his thoughts. He glanced down at the scene below, watched it shift before his eyes. Something about the distant vision was bothering him, but he couldn't put his finger on what it was. The angel did not like being ignored. Flapping his wings steadily, still looking at him over crossed arms, he spoke down to Roche.

"I am in charge of putting together a council," he said. "This council will determine what shall be done about the demons plaguing mortals. You will carry out our wishes, as will…"

He hesitated. Roche finally looked up at him, bared his teeth.

"As will your counterpart," the angel finished, lamely.

Roche pointed, still glaring up at him.

"What is going on down there?" he demanded. "The light keeps changing, the people keep doing the same things over and over."

The angel's eyes followed his finger.

"Time is different here," he said. "Unless you are focusing on someone or something specific, you will see time as though it is racing by from up here. Time changes as you move through this realm. At the highest places, it nearly stands still. That is where…your counterpart is spending much of her time. Her soul rises just as yours falls, and her path becomes more clear as yours grows more muddied. That is why you need us. That is why you have come here, to…what are you doing?"

Roche had grown bored with the angel, and did not feel like spending any more time biting back his responses to the incongruences in what he said. Stepping forward, he saw the angel back up in flight. He took another step, and felt the spongy surface begin to give way beneath his foot. Rather than step back, he continued moving forward. The angel was crying out, waving his hands in front of him while he slowly reversed in flight.

"What are you doing?" he said again. "You can't—"

Roche stepped over the edge, and let the fall take him where it would

CHAPTER 8

This time when he fell, it felt less like falling and more like flying. Roche was immediately disoriented, but no fear came over him. He was wrapped in white clouds that seemed to cushion his descent, thick and cool and completely blinding. Wind rushed in his ears, but it was the wind of the world; no acrid odors pleasantly assaulted his nostrils, and no scrubbed antiseptic invader climbed up his nose. The world smelled freshly flowered, and its faint pleasant odors tickled his senses delightfully.

Rather than seeing the ground rushing up at him, Roche was kept cushioned and sightless by the fog until it set him gently on the surface of the mortal world. As it cleared away he saw trees around him and felt soft damp vegetation beneath him. The crisp green scent of the woods hit him for the first time, and he breathed it in deeply.

The forest was a dark and shaded place, but he could see light seeping between branches and leaves to warm his face. He couldn't figure how long he sat there taking in the new environment, gaining his feet and looking around in a circle of wonder that seemed it may never stop. The distant sound of voices pulled him out of the daze, and away from the damp shadows.

Thinking of the strange covering Ximena had given him for his head, Roche felt the comfortable weight of it settle on his skull. He had seen what those in both Hell and Heaven did when they saw his true form; something told him it would be much worse here. From the shadows he watched a group of men pass by, walking a wide dirt road at a swift and steady pace. Roche recognized them as the travelers he had seen go back and forth across the same wide path from his vantage point in Heaven. They were dressed in simple clothes, most of which looked as though they had seen better days.

The group took some time to pass by, and he heard the voices more clearly as he moved closer. Roche could tell they spoke a different language than they did in the other realms, although he could also clearly understand what they were saying. Their voices were flat compared to the others he had heard, somehow lacking the tone and texture of the faintest whisper in Heaven or Hell. At the same time the sounds had a quality he had not heard before, a liveliness and urgency that drew him in.

As the last of them passed, Roche stepped onto the road. A few glanced his way, but kept walking. Falling into step behind them, he followed without a word. After only a little while moving with the group, he saw another addition join them. He walked from the side of the road, as Roche had done. Several others called out to him, or waved, as he matched their pace. He found his place in the group and began talking with the others, and after awhile more men fell into step with the roving assemblage. One by one or in small groups waiting by the roadside, more members swelled the group the further they traveled.

Most of the conversation was casual, spoken in the tone of familiarity. The men talked to each other about the weather, about their homes and their families, and about the path they walked on. No one spoke of where they were headed, and several men seemed content to walk in silence with the group. Roche took comfort in their quiet, and eventually tuned out the snippets of conversation he had been trying to follow when some of them spoke. The words seemed secondary, unimportant noises that served some purpose without having any real deeper meaning.

After some time walking, Roche saw a distant structure take shape on the horizon. For a while it blocked out the rising sun, casting a long and dark shadow before the brilliance of the morning light. As they got closer, the sun climbed higher in the sky. Roche made sure not to react to the building as its details came clear in the light, since the others were still conversing casually as the giant stone structure came into full view. As wide as it was, the monolith stretched even higher toward the sky. He could see windows cut into the building, from the ground floor to the highest level. The uppermost part of the structure was the only section that had any jagged edges, where stones had been fitted into place only to leave room for more stones to be added.

He couldn't tell how high the building was going to get, only that it was clearly unfinished. More stones needed to fill those holes for the uppermost section to be completed, and there was no way to tell if it would be the final level or if the construction would continue beyond those pieces once they were placed. The structure grew from their perspective, as the group continued its approach; it was evident long before they arrived that it was their destination.

Roche followed them from the dirt path to the paved street that began shortly after the base of the monolith came into view. Suddenly the quiet countryside gave way to a busy cityscape under their roving feet, and the group's scattered conversations were lost in the sounds of civilization. A blacksmith was tattooing a slow steady ringing beat up the way, carts full of stone and tools and children trundled loudly by, and the low din of countless unheard conversations filled the spaces between the louder and more distinctive sounds.

On the path he had encountered only men, but here women and children were just as numerous. They seemed as engaged in business as the men he saw, pushing carts or hawking their wares along the street. A few of the members of the group he was trailing paused along the way, to purchase a handful of cured meat or a stoppered bladder.

Roche took it all in, seeing nearly every sight for the first time and yet knowing immediately what everything was. He even wondered what liquid the bulging containers held, whether it was mead or wine or water; as he thought of these things, he realized he knew what they all were. He could identify them by taste or smell or sight, and knew it without tasting or smelling or seeing them.

Most of the group he had traveled with pressed on without pausing, and Roche continued to move along with them. They came to the giant building together, and began to stream into the open entrance in an orderly line. He watched the monolith swallow them up easily, until the line led him to the doorway. Roche followed the queue through the entrance, only to hesitate on the other side.

He had been underground, and out in the open; Roche had even ridden along clouds high above all of this. Yet he had never been inside something that was still somehow outside. The endless tunnels of Hell had been cut into rock and soil that already existed, and were drowned in darkness without torches or candles to light the way. This building was lighted by holes cut into the walls, windows that could be covered at night to keep out the cold or opened during the day to let the light in. Standing inside and outside at the same time disoriented him momentarily, and he stood there looking at the walls and ceiling with awe and a touch of fear. He imagined all those stones letting loose, and tumbling down on top of each other. On top of him.

Someone nudged him, one of the men he had been walking with. Roche had taken notice of him, as the man had nodded a greeting when he joined the group on the road. Neither of them had said anything, but they had walked side by side for several miles. The man pointed when he had Roche's attention, to a set of stone stairs that ascended out of sight further into the building. He moved toward them, as did some of the others; at the base of the steps he stopped, and motioned again to Roche.

Many of the other men had dispersed along the ground floor, streaming in every direction to disappear around a corner or move to a spot along a nearby wall. The ones he could still see had already set themselves to some task, sweeping the stone floor or sitting down to mix a bucket of mortar. The rest continued on up the stairs. Roche had one last look around, then followed the man who had gestured to the steps. He ascended the first flight, and paused to have another look around.

Another nudge came from behind him, this one not so friendly. Roche turned, ready to nudge back; when he saw the stream of men trying to climb the stairs behind him, he faced forward again. The next several flights passed under his feet without pause, and the sound of footfalls behind him kept him from getting a good look at what was passing by. Many minutes and quite a few floors later, they came to the last of the steps and Roche felt his face bathed in warm stark sunlight.

They were two of the few that continued to the very top, but he could see several others that had arrived before them. Already busy mixing mortar and layering it on the uppermost stones, one of them shouted at them as they came out into the open.

"Are you the last?" he called.

Roche looked behind him, then at the fellow that he had been following. The man nodded, and cried out.

"We're the last!" he said. "The way is clear!"

Half the men on the open floor moved toward them, and Roche moved away from the steps so they could begin their descent. Backing up, he came closer to the edge than he realized; when he turned, he got a good look at how far up they really were. The sight was different than looking down from Heaven. A touch of vertigo accompanied the view, and he couldn't focus in on the people on the ground like he could from the other vantage point. From up here they looked miniature, moving along the streets with short hurried strides and tiny carts.

A hand fell on his shoulder, and Roche tore his eyes from the scene below. The man who had brought him up here was motioning to another section of wall, where the stones hardly came up to his knees. Beyond the short barrier was a long fall, one he sensed would be much more painful than the one that had brought him here. He followed his companion, and watched him bend to his work.

While the others carefully measured the water and sand and powder they were mixing in giant vats at their feet, he lifted one container and then another. Pouring without measuring, he watched each stream with a careful eye. When he was done pouring them in, he lifted a long stick from the floor and began to stir the mixture with it. Roche saw him grimace with the motion, and moved forward to take the tool from his hands. With slight movements from his head, the man indicated how he should proceed; slower to faster, then in circles instead of back and forth. He indicated that Roche should continue stirring, while he added more of the ingredients. Soon they had a full cauldron of sticky brownish muck, and the man looked up at him with a nod of satisfaction.

Roche watched him scoop up some of the mixture with a trowel, and turn to spread it evenly over the nearest low stone. Another similar tool was nearby, and Roche bent to pick it up and imitate his motion. Reaching into the vat of goo, he tried to put as much on the blade as his companion had. Much of it fell off before he had even cleared the side of the container, and most of the rest slid off to drip to the floor before he reached the wall. Roche tried to spread what was left evenly, like he had done; the mixture ended up thick and lumpy in some spots, and thin to completely absent in others.

In the minutes it took him to bend and scrape up the mortar he had dropped, the other man had returned to the mixture three times. He spread it each time with a single smooth motion, evening out the lumps Roche had left across the stone as he applied his own careful strokes. As easy as he made it look, Roche found himself spending several minutes trying to get the same effect. During the time he spent cleaning up the mess he had made and going over what little mortar he added to make it smooth and even, his companion continued his simple routine and covered the rest of the stone they were working on.

His economy of motion was a bit of a wonder to behold. If Roche had simply sat back and watched, the ease with which he applied the mortar would have made him suspect he could perform the task with as little difficulty. Trying to imitate the other man, Roche found the movements he made to be impossible to recreate with his own meaty paws. The man stood back when he was finished, and gave Roche a satisfied nod. Looking down at himself, Roche saw that as much mortar had gotten on him as he had added to the wall. He gestured down at himself, and grimaced.

The man laughed, and shrugged. He pointed to a nearby stack of stones, and moved to get on one end of the closest block. Roche bent at the other end, and helped him lift it until they were both standing straight up with the carved rock between them. The man grimaced again as he stood, and Roche moved his hands more toward the middle of the stone. Taking nearly all the weight of it, he watched his companions eyes widen with a wonder of their own. Pleased with his reaction, Roche reached out even further and took the entire weight of the burden. All the other man had to do was guide it into place, and smooth the mortar as it squeezed out around the cracks.

Moving to the mix again, the man motioned Roche to stand back and watch. He began that slow competent routine once more, never rushing or slowing as he scooped up mortar and smoothed it across the stone they had placed. When it was halfway done, he pointed at his own eyes and then at Roche. He took the trowel to the wall, and ran it over the smooth layer he had already laid down. Tilting it forward, he ran deep creases along the mortar. Angling it the opposite way, he pushed goo all around and let it clump up where the tool passed. Finally he tilted it to one side, and showed Roche how the mortar squeezed unevenly out one edge and left an ugly line in the mortar on the other.

In one fluid motion, he evened out all the clumps and erased the lines. The stone was as it had been a minute earlier, half covered in an even and smooth batch of the mix. He gestured to Roche, to come close and try it himself. Roche shrugged, and stepped to his side.

"You make it look a lot easier than it is," Roche muttered.

He was talking to himself, but the man heard him. He clapped Roche on his wide back and laughed loudly.

"You know the common tongue!" he cried. "I thought you were a mute, or a foreigner. More likely a foreigner, from the looks of your clothes. But you speak! What are you called, friend? I answer to Adeb."

Roche nearly stepped back, flustered by the man's effusive outburst. He let his eyes find the drying mortar Adeb had just laid, and tried on a smile. It felt as foreign as the man's excitement.

"My name is Roche," he said. "It's, uh…it's good to meet you."

Slapping his flat palm against his leg, Adeb grinned and nodded enthusiastically. His eyes gleamed with delight, and his voice rang out with carefree gaiety.

"I was right!" he squealed. "A foreigner, indeed! How far have you traveled, Roche my friend? Have you walked along the oceans, and crossed mighty mountain ranges?"

Roche shrugged.

"No," he said. "None of that. The only places I have really been are Heaven and Hell. I found no oceans, or mountain ranges."

Adeb laughed again.

"Ah, a philosopher," he said, "or a storyteller. No matter; either way your company is even more welcome than before. Now let's get to this mortar, before it dries up too much."

For the remainder of the day they worked, Adeb explaining building to him while pressing Roche to tell him stories of devils and angels. Roche didn't see the harm in any of it, since Adeb seemed to think it was all being made up as he went. When it came time to tell him about Lilia, the man crowed with delight over his description of the winged beast she had been when she met him. Roche went on to describe her transformation, and Adeb interrupted for the first time.

"Was she beautiful?" he breathed.

Roche nodded, solemnly.

"Of course she was," Adeb smiled. "Go on."

Runners came in batches throughout the day, bringing more water or sand or chalky dust. Every time they checked on Adeb first, filling the containers they were working from before any of the others. Initially Roche wondered why, but as the day wore on it became clear. The section they were building was wider than any of the others, and had started out lower than them as well. Halfway through the day they had built their area as high as the others, and soon after their wall was taller than any of them. Roche made note of it, and saw Adeb grow sullen for the first time.

"I would be a supervisor," Adeb said, "if I could make the right friends. I try to help others learn, but those that have not just begun have their own ways. Most of the people I try to help are new. They realize they can do little to nothing all day when they work with me, and that's what they do. That's how I strained my back, trying to lift those stones the way you do. My power is in my mind, and not my body. A big fellow like you can easily threaten me if I expose them, and sit back for the most part. In fact, you're the first that hasn't. These others are trying to act as though they don't see the progress we're making, but everything I have been telling them is taking shape before their eyes. I know you must get back to your travels, and that Hell awaits your return…"

Adeb threw him a friendly wink, and went on.

"But I hope you stay long enough for the overseers to notice," he said. "If I can get them to listen to me, we could do twice the work with half the men."

Roche looked around, saw nothing but workers layering mortar and stone. The runners had just begun to return, the first of them clearing the way as soon as they reached the floor to make room for the others coming up behind them.

"What overseers?" he asked.

Their buckets were being replenished, and Adeb was encouraging the men filling them to give him all they could.

When he was satisfied he turned, and pointed to the stairs. They were empty again.

"If you're going to see one," he said, "it will be while they're restocking us. They don't come up here much, since we all know what we're doing to some degree. They also don't want to give the runners an excuse to pause, and take a moment's rest. So they only come up here right after a fresh batch of supplies."

As if on cue, a head appeared at the open stairwell. Followed by a body draped in chain mail, both the head and body were unmistakably inhuman. Roche looked away immediately, and set about stirring the mix as Adeb added the ingredients. He muttered under his breath, so only his companion would hear.

"You did not tell me there were devils here," he whispered.

Adeb watched the stream of white powder a moment longer, then tilted the bucket upright again. He glanced over his shoulder, and laughed.

"What, you mean Mandine?" he said. "He's not so bad."

Risking another look, Roche saw the devil had made a cursory attempt to mask his identity. He wore a cloak that covered most of his body, including his tail; and a length of fabric was wrapped about his head, concealing his horns. A small monster rode his shoulder, doing nothing to hide its own demonic nature. Naked but for a ragged black loincloth, the demon held on to the devil's ear and swung happily back and forth on his shoulder. Roche was not surprised the devil paid the creature no mind; he had yet to see anyone acknowledge the presence of their demons.

"Now is not the time to quit working," Adeb remarked.

Roche nodded. He turned his attention from the overseer, and back to the rising wall. When the devil came close, Roche could hear him muttering something under his breath. He kept working, putting his whole attention into stirring the mix as Adeb added ingredients. A minute later the overseer had walked the entire floor, and was descending the stairs after the runners. He and Adeb had moved on to adding another layer of mortar to the wall, and that really did require all of Roche's attention. A day of working alongside Adeb had taught him many things, but he still looked liked an awkward giant child fumbling with toys next to the slight and friendly man.

They didn't see the devil again until the day was done, long after the sun had started its slow afternoon descent. He walked to their section of the wall immediately, and looked in the cauldron. It had been empty for a few minutes, and Roche had spent them cleaning out the pot and the smaller containers. Adeb had looked on with satisfaction, until the devil approached. Moving near the wall, as if to showcase it, Adeb stood at attention until the devil was near. With a nod of his head, he motioned Roche to do the same.

Instead Roche kept his head down, pretending to be intent on his work. His heart was pounding fiercely in his chest, and he was wondering if the devil had planned to come for him all day. Perhaps he had waited until the wall had been built up more to come call him out. Whatever disguise the covering Roche wore on his head provided, he wasn't sure he could count on it to fool another devil. The overseer stopped behind him, and spoke.

"You there," he said. "I haven't seen you around here."

Roche shook his head, his back still to the devil.

Adeb piped up, and Roche relaxed a little.

"He just showed up today," Adeb said. "He's a fine worker."

A quiet pause followed, and Roche wondered how the blow would come. He imagined every possibility, except that the devil was staring at the section of wall they had built. Arms crossed, he nodded appraisingly while Roche prepared for the worst.

"You two did well," the devil said. "More than twice what any other team did. Your pay for the day will reflect that."

Roche wondered why the devil was speaking so loudly, until he heard the chorus of moans around them. He kept his back turned while the devil approached Adeb and filled his hands with coins. The only way for him to collect his own earnings was to face the devil, so he heaved in his breath and turned.

CHAPTER 9

Tension knotted his belly, and his heart pounded so loudly he almost didn't hear the devil's question. Roche remained kneeling before the giant pot, looking up at him and awaiting an explosion. After a few moments, he picked the words up awkwardly where they had fallen around him, and put them together in his thoughts.

"What's your name?" the devil had asked.

"Roche," he said, simply.

The devil nodded as he counted out coins, then held out a fistful of them. Roche spread his palm under the overseer's hand, and watched them form a small pile. Nodding, he closed his fingers around the money.

"You're a big one, aren't you?" the devil remarked.

Roche raised an eyebrow, breathed evenly.

"A big what?" he murmured.

The devil burst out laughing, and threw a wink at Adeb.

"Why are the big ones always the dumb ones?" he said.

Turning on his heel, the devil moved among the others distributing coins among them. Adeb put his hand on Roche's shoulder, saying something about not minding what the overseer had said. Roche was just glad his heart was no longer racing, and that his disguise had fooled the devil better than the devil's had fooled him. Leaning forward to continue cleaning the pots, he felt Adeb's hand still on his shoulder.

"We're done for the day," he said. "If you want to do me a service, come back and work with me again. The containers will need to be cleaned again in the morning anyway."

Roche glanced up, and nodded. Rising to his full height, he looked down at Adeb and extended his hand.

"Thank you," he said. "You taught me much today."

Grasping his hand, Adeb grinned.

"Where are you sleeping?" he asked. "You are welcome to stay at my home, and have a hearty meal before resting. Surely you are tired, and hungry. I've never seen a man work so hard."

The feelings had not hit him before. It was as if Adeb's mention of the words threw two heavy blankets over him, and Roche sagged a little. He was tired, and hungry; now that he had identified the sensations, they felt like they wanted to overwhelm him. Stifling a yawn, he squared his shoulders and considered the offer.

Adeb sensed a hesitation in him, and went on.

"The inn will take all your coin," he said. "Especially feeding a belly as big as yours must be. If your appetites don't stop there, you will find yourself in debt by morning. The places on the outskirts are cheaper, but they have their ways of taking all you've got as well. Besides, even you shouldn't walk the road at night by yourself with coin. Best to have good company. Come, rest at my home."

Roche laughed, letting the tense and guarded layer down.

"Very well," he said. "I will gratefully accept your hospitality."

As soon as the coins had been handed out, the others had streamed down the stairwell. He and Adeb took their time getting down the stacked flights, and Roche noticed that only overseers remained on the floors they passed. Nearly all of them were devils, disguised as poorly as the other he had seen. He made sure not to call attention to himself as they passed by, glad his own deception was fooling them. When they reached the street it was nearly empty.

Roche walked with his new friend, carrying the coins he had earned in his balled up fist. The weight of them was somehow meaningful to him, and put a lightness in his step that dispelled his exhaustion. Adeb was jubilant, talking as they walked about how much they had accomplished, how good it was to make a new friend, and how he was sure he was on the path to overseer now.

All the other workers had hurried down the road, and they walked it alone together. Roche was glad, with the way Adeb was talking. At the work site he had been sure of himself, instructing Roche in no uncertain terms on how each task needed to be performed; now he was giving Roche all the credit for their progress, making it sound as though he had performed impossible feats throughout the day. While Adeb downplayed his own efforts, he exaggerated Roche's.

The praise felt good, and Roche was too tired to protest or correct him. As the natural light began to dwindle, Adeb quickened his pace and lowered his voice. His longwinded compliments became punctuated by furtive glances into the shadows along the side of the road, and he began muttering about walking along the road alone with coin every few minutes. He did not seem surprised at all when three men stepped into the path ahead, and called out to them.

"Hand over your coin," one of them said.

The other two nodded, and advanced slowly. Although there was more shadow than light at this point, Roche recognized them. He nudged his companion, spoke quietly to him.

"They're workers," he whispered. "They were there all day, they saw what we did to earn our wages."

Adeb nodded.

"I recognize them," he said. "They saw us get more than they did, and they probably didn't like that. Be cautious, my friend. There are more behind us. Let us give them our coin, and take the road with everyone else tomorrow. We can recover our losses, and no one gets hurt."

His hand fell on Roche's arm, and only then did they both realize he was tensed for action. Roche felt a low growl begin in his throat, and he brushed away the friendly contact.

"I think not," he said. "These fools need to be taught a lesson."

The men behind them were making no attempt to be silent. Roche could hear them well enough to count them, and knew there were not nearly enough.

"Our coin will remain ours," Roche said, clearly and loudly.

The two that were advancing stopped. They drew daggers from their belts, and let the fading sunlight flash across the blades. More noise erupted behind him, the other three taking out weapons of their own and grinding their boots into the dust to make their footfalls sound heavier than they were. Roche thought of bringing his curved sword out of his thoughts and into his hand, then thought better of it. After seeing the way humans were designed, and how much they could do, he realized he did not really need a weapon.

Adeb's hand was lightly touching his arm again, a caution against the action Roche was considering. His other hand was already emptying the pouch he had deposited the coins into, upending it while leaving it attached to the sash tied about his waist. Roche pulled away, gently, and took two giant swift steps forward. The two men that had been coming at them held the daggers up in front of them, both of them glancing back at the same time to look at the bandit that stood behind them. He rolled his eyes, and drew his own dagger; but before he had taken a step, Roche had taken two more.

He heard Adeb call out behind him, his voice quavering.

"Don't kill them," he cried.

Instead of grabbing each of their hands where they wrapped about the hilts of the knives and crossing their arms across each other to bury the blades in each other's throats, Roche batted the weapons away. Rather than crush their heads against each other until he heard two fatal cracks, he backhanded each of them in turn. One went one way, the other went the opposite direction; and they both stayed down. Roche approached the one that was apparently in charge, and grasped him by the throat.

Lifting him off his feet, Roche grimaced at him.

"He just saved your life," he growled.

Although his face was turning red, the man was smiling down at him.

"Let me go," he gasped.

Roche nodded.

"When you stop struggling," he said. "When your eyes roll back in your head and your body goes completely limp. Maybe."

Still smiling, his voice nothing but a hoarse whisper, the bandit nodded past Roche. He turned, continuing to hold the weight of the man's body casually and without any undue effort.

The other three bandits had surrounded Adeb, each of them brandishing a small blade of their own. Roche made no move to release the man, instead tightening his grip until he hear him sputter.

"Have you changed your mind, Adeb?" he asked. "Is it okay if I start to kill them now?"

One of the men with Adeb grabbed him, crossing his free arm across Adeb's chest and holding the knife to his throat.

"We're not kidding!" he called out.

"Neither am I," Roche shot back. "You may kill my friend, although he might be surprised how quickly I can get to you. That's not much reward, considering you will all die shortly thereafter."

The weight in his hand was doing very little moving about now, and Roche glanced up at his purpled face.

"What do you think they should do?" he asked. "Kill my friend, and then die immediately after you? Or back off, and live?"

He had to adjust his grip, before the man's eyes would stop rolling back into his head. A little color came back into his face, and he reached his hand into his tunic. When he brought it out, he was holding a knife of his own. He stabbed weakly at Roche's chest, barely cutting through his robes. Roche looked down at the tiny weapon, felt the pinpoints of pain it was causing, and saw the fabric grow darker around the continuing jabs. Squeezing his neck even tighter than before, he felt the man's motions grow weaker while his eyes widened in disbelief.

The bandit's arm dropped to his side, the knife fell from his hand, and his head lolled to the side lifelessly. Roche tossed him into the road, and advanced on the men holding Adeb.

"I will kill you all," he growled, still moving forward. "I will rip your arms from your bodies and leave you to bleed out on the road. You can watch while I do the same to your companions, but you won't be able to do anything. Because you won't have arms."

The men all glanced at the sides of the path, where the first two he had knocked out still slumbered. While their eyes were averted, he covered the remaining distance between them in the blink of an eye. Moving too quickly for them to see, he extricated Adeb from his awkward situation and pushed him as far away from them as he could without harming him. In a flash, he was between them instead.

He let the world come to him at normal speed, allowing two of the daggers to pierce his abdomen while the third clattered away from the tussle. An inert body followed, landing with a thud nearby. The next time only one blade bit into him, as another unconscious assailant fell to the ground. Roche found himself staring at a lone aggressor, who had just stabbed him twice. He could feel the wounds closing already, and his robes coming together behind them.

Roche looked down at him, and smiled.

"Are you done yet?" he growled.

Looking down at his blade and seeing that it was covered in blood, the man looked back up at Roche and grimaced. He began to tremble, and Roche took the opportunity to smack the weapon from his hand. A loud crack accompanied the sudden movement, and the man howled in agony. He stuffed his hand under his tunic protectively, turned and ran.

Roche busied himself hunting down the knives and wiping the blood carefully from each blade. He had seen the purple color in the dying light, but he was pretty sure they hadn't. Much of what he had done may have seemed impossible, or at least improbable; but strangely colored blood was the kind of proof he did not want walking around.

Next he went to one of the inert bodies, and bent over it. Adeb had watched him silently until now, standing back while Roche wiped the blades clean. He called out as Roche reached for the unconscious man.

"What are you doing?" Adeb cried.

Roche glanced at him.

"Don't worry," he said. "I didn't kill any of them, and I'm not going to now. I'm just going to take their coin."

Adeb skittered across the road, came close and put his hand on Roche's shoulder.

"Please don't," he said.

Standing swiftly, Roche was suddenly towering over him. He let his anger show on his face, in his stance. Adeb smiled up at him, completely unafraid.

"They meant to rob us," Roche said. "They would have killed us."

Adeb snickered.

"Really?" he said. "I get the feeling they had as little chance of doing either as I do of picking you up and tossing you into the woods. You seemed to have the situation well in hand. If I'm not mistaken, you also seemed to even be enjoying yourself a bit there."

The anger he felt was different than what he had felt before. That had been an explosion waiting to happen, building as an outward threat did; this was a boiling rage at an injustice, and he wanted someone other than him to burn it the heat of it. He looked down at the unconscious man again, letting the boil build; then he moved his eyes to Adeb's. Although he felt the fire behind his own gaze, he saw the other man smiling up at him jovially.

"Tell me I'm wrong," Adeb pressed him, still smiling. "Tell me we were in real danger there, that those men stood some chance of robbing or killing you. Then I'll let you take the coin that would feed their wives and children, or maybe their aging parents. I'll encourage it, even. I'll even tell you to go ahead and break their necks while they sleep, if you'll tell me they really had the upper hand for a minute there."

Roche continued to stare down at him, with his chest heaving his anger and his eyes burning with rage. Fearless, Adeb gazed up at him and smiled like Roche was telling him an entertaining story.

Finally, Roche laughed. He kicked the prone body, and got a satisfying sleepy groan for his effort.

"How far is your home?" he said. "I'm hungry."

Adeb nodded, and pressed on down the road.

"Not far now," he said. "Not far at all."

Roche could tell he was still smiling, although Adeb's back was to him until he caught up. By the time he was walking in stride with the man, he was smiling a little as well.

CHAPTER 10

Hell had been consistently hot, warmer in some places than others but still hot. The heat had agreed with him, and was part of what made the lower realm feel like home. In Heaven, the climate was like everything else; neither hot nor cool, it presented nothing worth noticing unless he paid special attention to it. If sterility had a temperature, Heaven had been hovering at that mark every time he had been there.

In this realm, the heat and cold seemed to be fighting a battle neither of them could ever quite win. The full sunlight had beat down on him during the day, combining with his physical exertion to warm him in a way he had never felt. He had soaked it up, tilting his head back to bask in the soft warm glow whenever he had a moment. The slowly descending coolness had been a welcome respite, after the strenuous day and several hours of uninterrupted sunlight. Once the sun disappeared over the horizon, he felt a real chill for the first time.

Entering Adeb's home was like walking into a giant cozy embrace. The smell of fire hit him first, before he saw the dancing flames or heard the comforting crackle. It brought heat along with it, enveloping him pleasantly as soon as he moved through the doorway. Although the space was small and simple, it reminded him somehow of Ximena and her welcoming quarters. The thought of her made him relax while he waited by the entrance, watching Adeb dance across the dirt floor to sweep the woman inside up in his arms.

He held her and kissed her face over and over, as if he didn't want to miss a spot. For a minute she hugged him back, and they exchanged pleasantries that sounded as though they had been uttered a thousand times without ever getting old to either of them.

"Did you have a good day, my love?" he asked, between kisses.

She nodded solemnly, and sunk deeper into his embrace.

"I did," she said, "but for missing you."

Squeezing her lovingly, Adeb kissed her again.

"I thought of you all day," he said. "I love you so."

She smiled, and kissed him back.

"And I you, my sweet husband," she cooed.

Roche didn't feel as though he was being ignored; he felt like he was part of the exchange, and they were warming him with their love as surely as the flames that burned in the hearth. As comforting as the heat and the smell of the fire were, another scent had captured his attention once the door had closed behind him. Although it was completely unfamiliar, the odor delighted him with layers of subtlety that tickled his nostrils and set his stomach to rumbling.

Still encircled in Adeb's arms, his wife nuzzled his neck and spoke softly into his skin.

"I see we have a guest," she noted.

Adeb nodded, and gave her one more kiss. He turned to Roche, keeping one arm about her waist.

"We do," Adeb grinned. "You'll like this one."

She nudged him playfully.

"You make me sound like a poor host," she said.

Adeb let his smile fall, exchanging it for a serious look. The expression still looked joyous on his face somehow, like all the others Roche had seen.

"Oh, no," Adeb asserted. "I choose friends poorly quite often, and you are still kind to them. This time, I chose wisely."

Disengaging from her husband, she crossed the swept dirt floor to close the space between her and Roche. She inclined her head politely, and extended her hand to him.

"I am called Sela," she said. "Welcome to our home."

Roche grasped her hand.

"Thank you," he said. "My name is Roche."

With a smile that held no secrets, Sela glanced back at her husband.

"Ah, a foreigner," she said. "My husband is fascinated with distant lands and their people. Where do you hail from, friend Roche?"

Adeb laughed behind her, acknowledging his curiosity and the frank thrust of her question. When Roche hesitated, he spoke for him.

"You must hear his stories," he chuckled. "The places our new friend has been make the outlandish claims of other travelers seem dull and plain by comparison."

Roche felt his eyes go wide. As Sela turned to her husband once more, he took the moment her gaze was averted to catch Adeb's attention. Shaking his head sternly, Roche frowned at him.

"But we are hungry," Adeb said, derailing his own train of thought. "As I'm sure you are. And it smells like a delicious dinner awaits."

Glancing back and forth between them, Sela seemed to be taking a moment to consider finding out what was being left unsaid. Instead she smiled at them both, and gestured across the modest room. A small table was set with two places, a pair of chairs pushed to the fronts of their backs to make room for traffic in the small space. Roche noticed the places were set adjacent to each other rather than across from each other. Approaching the table first, Adeb rearranged the chairs so they faced one another and were pulled away from the table enough for them to sit down. He motioned as his wife had, indicating that Roche should pick the spot he preferred.

Given the choice of seeing the fire clearly and feeling it warm his back, Roche decided to take the view. He wasn't entirely certain how warm they might like to be, but after Hell the only way he could feel that kind of heat in this home was to step into the flames. The flickering light and waves of warmth comforted him, and he ignored the chill that seemed to cling to him. He suspected it would be with him until he left this realm.

Sela began to open cupboards and containers, removing items and cradling them in one arm. As soon as Adeb sat down he began talking, and it took Roche a full minute before he realized what she was doing.

"Tomorrow," Adeb said, "we will accomplish even more than today, I am sure of it. You learned more of building in a day than I did the first several years I was doing it."

Roche shrugged.

"I had a good teacher," he said. "If I had been helping any other man on their project, the day would have been slow and the knowledge sparse. The methods you showed me were unlike anything they were doing. Where did you acquire such skill?"

For the first time Roche saw him grow uncomfortable. Turning to watch his wife as she walked by, he waved his hand dismissively and stood to follow her to the fire. Adeb knelt near a pile of wood while she filled the pot that was suspended over the flames. Picking up a small hatchet and a piece of wood, he used the tool to chop the round into four even wedges of wood. First the smell of the cleaved round reached Roche's nostrils, then the scent of the fire as the pieces were added to it. The only odor that abated somewhat was the food that was cooking, as Roche realized what Sela had been up to.

"You had dinner ready," he said, "for the two of you. You're adding more food so there is enough for all of us. I am sorry for making you wait, and take more from your cupboards."

Now it was Sela's turn to wave him off. She did so with a smile, and a glance at her husband that seemed to say she did indeed approve of this friend. Nudging her husband as he fiddled with the fire, she nodded at the flames licking the side of the pot.

"Thank you," she said, kissing his cheek. "Did you not tell our guest that you were once a traveller as well?"

Adeb stood, looked down at her and then over at Roche.

"I have not been to the places he has," he said. "His travels are full of adventures that no normal man could have. I was sure he was but an imaginative storyteller, until we walked alone on the road with coin."

Standing beside him, Sela shook her head. She glanced back and forth between them, looking for some evidence of misfortune. Sela appeared to be torn between scolding her husband and fussing over him. Rather than decide, she did both.

"You need to be careful," she said. "You know what kind of trouble you can get into traveling that road alone with coin."

She looked over his tunic and breeches, smoothing them lovingly and inspecting them for damage. When she couldn't find any she held his face between her hands, and smoothed back his hair.

"You need to be careful," she said again. "What happened?"

The whole time Roche was trying to catch Adeb's eye, and shake his head to prevent the man from telling the story. The thought of words describing his violence and his anger from earlier floating around this quiet and peaceful home bothered him somehow, and he kept trying until he was sure Adeb had gotten the message.

"Nothing," Adeb said, clutching her close to him. "That's what I mean. When you walk around in a giant body like his, folks treat you differently. I'm sure some bandits saw us, and thought better of accosting us. Doors have opened for this fellow that don't exist for the ordinary man. Although his strength is a gentle one, people see him and think he must be capable of great violence. They get out of his way, and clear paths for him that others never get to walk down."

Sela stirred the pot carefully, looking at her husband and then at Roche. The expression on her face said she was aware Adeb was being evasive, and that she didn't mind so much. When her eyes fell on Roche she raised one eyebrow, as if asking him whether or not what her husband had said was true. Roche shrugged, and smiled slightly.

"Do you mind your onions a little raw?" she asked him.

Roche shrugged again. He thought it may be a little strange to tell her he knew what an onion was, but that he had never tasted one raw or cooked. It may lead into him admitting he had never tasted any type of food before, which would require him to do more explaining than he wished to do. Already he was regretting telling Adeb stories from his short past. Adeb had glanced at him occasionally since the incident on the road, as if remembering the tales he had told and reconsidering whether or not they may be true.

After setting another place, and carrying a third chair to the table, Sela ladled generous portions into three bowls and joined them. She looked at her husband, who nodded and took her hand.

"We pray here," he said. "We will not be insulted if you do not bow your head and join us."

Roche tried to ignore the smell of the food before him. Part of him wanted to seize the bowl and consume its contents in one giant mouthful. He put his hands on his lap to control them, and lowered his gaze along with his hosts.

"Today I am grateful," Adeb said. "I have a good woman by my side, a roof over my head, a mind that sees things other often don't, a fine meal to eat and a new friend."

A few moments of silence followed, before Sela spoke.

"Today I am grateful," she echoed. "I have a good man, a comfortable home, a talent at making a garden flourish and food enough to serve our welcome guest."

At the mention of the word 'prayer', a flood of knowledge had opened up in Roche's mind. Like all the other things he knew somehow without knowing, he had an image and an idea of what it was. Common things seemed to be common knowledge to him, while the important questions went unanswered in the darkening recesses of his mind. Of all the things he had expected one or both of them to say or not say when the prayer began, their choice of words had not been among them.

They were silent, either lost in their own feelings of gratitude or giving Roche an opportunity to add his thoughts.

"Today I am grateful," Roche said, quietly. "I have a new way of looking at prayer, a skill I didn't have yesterday, and generous new friends."

For a few more moments, they kept their heads bowed. Roche peeked at them once or twice, and lifted his gaze when Adeb and his wife did. As soon as they reached for their food, Roche followed suit. They ate in silence for awhile. Clearly, they were hungry from a long day and a delayed dinner; Roche was fascinated by the flavors bursting in his mouth, and the feeling of his great hunger being slaked.

Adeb broke the silence, swallowing a mouthful of food and turning to smile adoringly at his wife.

"This is delicious," he said. "You make a fine meal, my love."

The explosive variety of sensations in his mouth was bordering on overwhelming. Roche knew he couldn't tell her the truth, that this was the first or the best food he had ever eaten; but once he knew it was not unexpected to compliment her on the delightful mixture of flavors she had blended for their meal, he stopped holding back.

"It really is," Roche said. "You asked me earlier how I liked my onions. Now I have a definitive answer."

Using his small wooden ladle, he indicated the stew.

"This is how I like my onions," he said. "This is how I like everything you put in here. What a wonderful meal."

Sela waved him off, thanked him quietly.

"You are staying with us tonight?" she asked him.

Before Roche could respond, Adeb cut in.

"We have a room for you," he said. "The bedding is soft and plentiful. You would not be imposing by staying. You are welcome."

Nodding her agreement, Sela echoed the sentiment.

"You are welcome," she said.

Roche watched Adeb rise and tend the fire, observing his careful hands as he chopped a round into pieces and set them carefully over the bed of dwindling coals. He blew on it gently, until flames leapt up and the wood began to crackle.

"If you wake up in the night," he said, "would you throw one of the bigger uncut pieces on the fire?"

He indicated a narrow hallway, leading deeper into the home.

"You can sleep in the first room you come to," he said. "Across the hall is the back door. If nature calls, you'll find the answer straight out from there about twenty paces."

Sela had cleared the table while Adeb tended the fire and spoke to him. They finished their tasks at the same time, coming together to lean on each other between Roche and the dancing fire.

"Sleep well, my friend," Adeb said.

Adeb looked down at Sela, and she up at him. She smiled.

"Good night, friend Roche," she said, still smiling at Adeb.

They slipped into the shadowed corridor, and Roche heard a door close out of sight. Silence descended, broken only by the wood popping as it burned. Roche moved closer to the flames, and settled on the floor before the flickering illumination. He sat there until the pieces Adeb had added were charred and blackened, until they went white and then red. When they crumbled under their own weight and heat, he set another piece on top of the small mountain of coals. He poked at it as he had seen Adeb do, and leaned forward to blow a few more flames into existence.

Roche got up, and went to the table. The coins he had earned today were in a pocket within his robes, and he fished them out quietly. Stacking them silently on the table, one by one, he looked down at them and smiled to himself.

He took one last look at the fire, closed his eyes and thought of Hell.

CHAPTER 11

The marks were in the same place as before; but this time Roche didn't have to walk nearly as far before he found himself slogging through ash. Fresh and pungent, the burn seemed to have taken place only minutes before. He could feel the heat still rising up from the dirt as he stepped through it, and found himself wondering if maybe he shouldn't have made a show of appearing on the other side of the dragon's claw marks and approaching on foot.

Roche had no desire to show the dragon any less respect than he ought to, or any more. He was sure leaning too far in either direction would get him into trouble, but it was a line not drawn as clearly as a dragon's borders. Now he was kicking up dust and smoke, and wondering how far he might have to walk before coming upon the creature or its workers. The smell of soot was clinging to him everywhere, and more than once his foot overturned a smoking ember.

Several times he sensed eyes on him, and he was certain someone was following him. Roche didn't blame whoever it was for not approaching; likely they were part of the patrol that had challenged him last time he was here. Monitoring him from a distance was surely more appealing than attempting to contain him up close. So he walked, and ignored the feeling, until he finally found the swath of land being tended.

The dragon wasn't there, but devils were plentiful. Most of them were bent over, working the soil with subtle movements he couldn't make out from a distance. Instead of standing back and watching like he had done previously, Roche marched directly up to the field and viewed their activity from a little ways off. The devils saw him, nearly every one of them glancing up from their work to eye him for a moment before returning their attention to the task at hand. After only a minute or two, Roche picked up the pattern.

Working in groups of two, the devils were carefully placing something into the soil. Each long straight furrow of raised dirt the dragon had carved out had a team making their way from one end of the field to the other along the line. In front of the first, the furrow was just turned dirt. As he moved to the next spot, the leading devil arranged the soil into a small mound with an indent in the top every few feet. When he was done, he would move on to work on the next section. Meanwhile, the devil behind him reached into a sack at his side as he approached the freshly formed mound. He would kneel down, drop a few of whatever he had in the sack into the hole, and gently cover the hole with dirt.

One devil was working alone, forming the mound, reaching into his sack, depositing the items, and covering the dirt each time he knelt. He was only a quarter of the way across the field, where the teams were approaching the halfway mark. Without a word to any of them, Roche walked carefully around the field to where the lines of soil began. He made sure to tread carefully as he stepped between furrows, and followed the line that led to the lone worker. Sidling past the devil while he was bent over, Roche knelt and began forming the next mound ahead of him.

The devil looked up, then glanced around at the others. Everyone was bent to their work, their eyes on what they were doing. Roche raised his gaze to meet the devil's, as he stood up from the fresh mound. They exchanged a shrug, and moved on to the next spot together. The devil dropped something into the hole, covered it up and moved on once more as Roche did. Without looking at each other again or exchanging so much as a single word, they began working in tandem almost immediately.

First Roche moved ahead of the devil, forming two mounds in the time in took him to fill and cover one. Then the devil began to pick up his pace, and soon Roche was forming a mound while the devil stood over him waiting. He glanced up, and saw a grin forming on the devil's face. Nodding, smiling slightly himself, Roche finished the mound and moved on to the next. He worked as fast as he could without making the pile sloppy or uneven, but it took several seconds for him to form the top of the mound into an indented peak.

The devil approached him, smiling again. He knelt at Roche's side and waved his hands away from the what he was doing. Roche moved back from the mound, and watched the devil reform the pile into what it had been moments before. Looking at Roche deliberately, the devil reached out one hand and pointed his finger at the top of the mound. He inserted it into the soil up to his second knuckle, and left it in the dirt while he glanced at Roche again.

Roche nodded, and moved on. This time when the mound was formed, he sunk his finger into the peak and watched a little hole form easily. He was moving on to the next spot in the same moment the devil was, and they gave each other a smile before bending once more to their work. Then they were off, moving more rapidly than any other team and appearing to completely ignore each other.

Time seemed to twist and stretch as they worked. Roche had seen moments tick by with extreme slowness before, but this was different. He was not moving faster than time, as he had felt he was doing when he had been attacked. Still, somehow each moment seemed to open itself up to him, and let him move around easily within it. His whole attention was on the task at hand, even as his awareness expanded to take in the devil working behind him. A connection formed between them as they moved along the furrow, and Roche felt the quiet clarity of the devil's mind as the same sensation stilled his own thoughts.

Nothing mattered, save the simple repetitive motions of forming the mounds and readying them for his companion. Roche felt as though he was in complete control of his inner world, able to start his mind spinning with activity again but unwilling to fall from the balanced center of their shared silence. Even looking over at the devil felt like it would be superfluous and unnecessary, as he felt the quiet calm of his mind and noted his smooth flowing movements from the corner of his eye. He could feel the devil's mind and motions as if they were his own, and knew his companion was equally aware of Roche in the same strange way.

He heard the dragon approaching, a distant sound that filled the air without really coming to his conscious attention. Even when the cracking and whooshing reached a thunderous crescendo as the creature drew closer, his concentration remained unbroken. The dragon appeared overhead, circling quietly in a steady gliding descent, and still he worked in careful and quick tandem with the devil behind him. All around them, devils stopped what they were doing to stand and watch, but Roche and his partner continued moving along their silent shared groove.

The dragon's glide described a slow spiral over the field, widening as it descended to the ground. Landing alongside the field smoothly, beating its wings to lower itself slowly from the sky, the creature took to its feet almost soundlessly. Roche felt the devil he had been working with rise and stand to attention, breaking the flowing connection they had shared. He stood as well, and faced the dragon like the others were doing.

His voice rolled over the field, booming to reach the furthest ear as easily as the nearest.

"Those of you that wish to retire for the day may do so," he said.

None of the devils moved from their spot, although many of them looked around to see what the others were doing. Roche and his partner continued facing forward, standing still and keeping their attention on Rendibite. The dragon went on, his voice resounding like thunder.

"Those of you who seek a bonus," he said, "may finish the row you are working on and collect that bonus after it is complete."

The devils looked around again, and this time Roche joined them. He hadn't noticed when he and his partner had begun catching up to the others, or when they had passed them. Their row was nearly complete, the only one that was any more than three quarters of the way finished. As he watched the other devils begin to stream from the field, Roche bent without turning. He couldn't see the one he had been working with, but he felt as though they started moving again in the same moment. When Roche moved to the next mound, he caught a glimpse of his partner moving to the one he had just vacated.

Smiling slightly, he kept moving. After just a few minutes more, he came to the last place where the dirt had been overturned after being blasted by fire. Roche formed one final mound, straightened and stepped to the edge of the field. Watching the devil move to the mound he had just formed, Roche saw him reach into the sack strapped to his side and kneel beside it. He held his fist over the hole, opened it carefully and covered the hole with soil. Rising in a motion as fluid as all his other movements, he came to stand beside Roche.

All the other devils had gone. Roche saw them trailing into the distance in a loose line, most likely going wherever they went to receive compensation for their work. The dragon had been watching them go as well, until Roche and his partner completed their row and stood side by side at attention. Now he turned from the dwindling figures, and slithered across the sand towards them. From a few feet away, Rendibite rose up on his rear haunches and surveyed the field.

"You came back," he said, eyes still on the work. "And you showed all my workers you are better than them. Well played."

Rendibite swung his head around, fixed him with his serpentine gaze.

"You each earned a bonus," he said. "Perhaps you might tell me what you were hoping for, and we'll see if I had the same in mind."

The devil Roche had been working with dropped to one knee, rested his hands on his leg and bowed his head. After a moment, he looked up at Rendibite and spoke.

"My singular desire," he said, "is to continue to find favor with you. The influence you have had on me and continue to have would be hard to place a value on, save to call it invaluable. I would remain your humble charge and student, as my bonus for this day."

Rendibite nodded, his reptilian lips stretching into a satisfied smile.

"An easy wish to grant," he said, "for you."

The devil stood, and looked at Roche. The dragon did the same, pivoting his giant skull slightly and letting his smile fall.

"And you?" Rendibite murmured.

Roche glanced at the devil, then the dragon.

"He did most of the work," Roche said, indicating the devil at his side. "The furrow we were working was over halfway done when I arrived, and he was working alone nearly as fast as the others were working in teams. He showed me how to help him, and pay attention while moving swiftly. And although the credit for our progress should fall chiefly on his shoulders, I do have one request."

Rendibite exchanged a look with the devil, and the devil shook his head slightly. Raising a scaly eyebrow, the dragon nodded for him to speak.

"That is kind," he said. "But untrue. I had fallen behind the others significantly. When he showed up the tide turned, because he was working as hard as me. I gave him guidance, but he bore his share of the burden from the moment he stepped onto the field."

The dragon nodded.

"Was he using his speed?" he said. "Were you?"

Roche turned to look at the devil. He had not sensed anything out of sorts with him, or any reason to think he was unlike the others in some fundamental way.

"He was not," the devil answered. "I would have been able to tell. Nor was I, as you have requested. I sensed that he was keeping within his normal abilities as deliberately as I was within mine."

Although he hadn't thought of it that way, Roche realized it was the truth. He had done the same when working with Adeb, and fighting off the bandits that had accosted them. Without meaning to, Roche was trying to test the limits he saw others living with. The dragon's voice shook him from his reverie.

"Would you honor his request?" Rendibite asked.

The devil shrugged.

"I would hear it," he said. "If it were reasonable, I would likely grant it. The devil that values work for work's sake always has some value of their own."

Rendibite formed his thin lips into a straight line, neither a threatening smile nor a dissatisfied frown. He bobbed his head up and down slightly, then swung his gaze from the devil to Roche.

"Very well," he said. "I will hear your request."

The dragon was towering over both of them, looking down at Roche with a carefully considered lack of expression. Roche kept his own face slack, his knees and back straight, and looked up and into his eyes.

"You have already started working these lands," Roche said. "Though I have only recently arrived here, this territory distinctly feels like it was made for me. Rather than lay claim to it in its entirety, I would propose an arrangement that benefits us both."

Lifting his giant head and shaking it, Rendibite shot smoke from his nostrils. His face was no longer expressionless when it came close to Roche's, and he could smell a smoldering fire in the dragon's breath.

"A deal?" he sneered. "You want me to strike a deal with a devil?"

Roche shrugged.

"Technically," he said, "I'm not really a devil."

He held the dragon's baleful stare, and went on.

"Or we could bring this before Ximena, as you suggested earlier."

When the dragon's head went back this time, fire erupted from his mouth. The flame shot straight up into the sky, and his front feet came off the ground. Ashes rained down on Roche and the devil beside him, and the ground shook when Rendibite's feet found it again; but Roche did not move or take his eyes from the dragon. He noticed with a strange kind of satisfaction that the devil was similarly unmoved by the dragon's display.

"I did not suggest—"

Rendibite cut off his own exclamation, to shoot another blast of fire at the sky. Lowering his head, he spoke inches from Roche's face in a low and dangerous monotone.

"You negotiate like a devil," he said. "State your case, then."

Roche might have been mistaken, but for a moment there he thought the devil beside him was trying not to laugh. Rather than glance over, and confirm or dispel his suspicion, he held the dragon's gaze.

"You have started working about a third of the lands in question, by my estimation," Roche said. "I propose we split them in half, and you keep what you have already invested time into and then some. I will be satisfied to keep the other half, if you show me how to work it."

Rendibite frowned, and wagged his head slightly back and forth.

"I can't spare the labor," he said. "Or the time. Every day spent on your fields will mean one away from mine."

Spreading his hands, Roche shook his head without taking his eyes off the dragon's. He was certain of it, now; the devil beside him was enjoying this exchange. Although he showed no outward signs, so far as Roche could tell from his peripheral view, he could feel silent waves of mirth rolling of the devil.

"Train me on your fields, then," Roche countered. "I will work them until all of them are prepared, and learn how to start from the beginning and follow the process through to completion."

Rendibite glanced at the devil.

"It sounds to me like he has no idea what we're doing," he said.

Roche shrugged.

"I don't," he said. "That is why I am willing to give up half of what I feel is rightfully mine to learn. I would rather cooperate with you than make an enemy of you."

The dragon looked back and forth between them, as if deciding whether to consult with the devil or give Roche his decision outright. He chose the devil, which made Roche wonder once more what was so special about him other than the way he worked.

"What say you?" he boomed. "You know I can't take the time to teach him. Can you take on this responsibility? Or shall I flame him?"

Shaking his head, the devil gave no sign of his earlier amusement.

"I don't think flaming him would get rid of him," he said. "Although I support your decision, if that is what you desire. In my view, his contribution would lighten my load enough to make up for the time it will take to teach him. We should define what is meant by completion of the fields, since they are in constant rotation. Surely you wouldn't want a devil of his type to be committed to indentured servitude without a specified end to his commitment."

What followed was a confusing display for Roche. The dragon's eyes went wide, and filled with fire. For a moment he was sure the devil was about to turn to ash by his side, and he prepared to get out of the way. Today was not the day he wanted to discover whether or not he was immune to the effects of a dragon's flames, if there ever was such a day.

Then Rendibite's face untwisted, he gave the devil a knowing nod, and his giant scaled form settled slightly. Roche noticed that he had tensed up considerably more than he thought, as had the devil; Roche noticed him relaxing as well, as the tension drained from his own shoulders.

"Of course," Rendibite said. "Once all the fields are planted, you will be free to go your own way without owing me any debt."

Roche shook his head, held up his hand.

"One more thing," he said.

This time the devil actually moved away from him slightly, as though he was sure Roche had tested the dragon's patience beyond its limits. The calm left Rendibite's reptilian face, and he showed Roche nearly all his teeth in a fierce grimace.

"The marks," Roche went on. "Your markers show all the territory to be yours, but they won't be any longer. I would have you remove your lines from my territory, and make a new one where your lands end."

The dragon snarled, and the devil interjected.

"I'll do it," he said. "I'll erase the old lines. If you wish, I'll make new ones as well."

Rendibite lifted a giant scaled forearm over their heads, and waved off his remark.

"Erase the old," he said. "I'll make the new. You cannot dig deep furrows like I can. Remember that, little one."

Lowering his gaze, the devil nodded without looking up.

"Of course," he said. "My apologies."

Suddenly another devil stood before him, and the dragon was gone. It took Roche a moment before he could reconcile that the slight and weathered being standing before him was also the mighty beast he had just faced. The only real links to his other self were the fine dark robes he was swathed in, and the hateful glare that seemed to be permanently affixed to his face.

"Do you have a witness?" he said.

Roche shrugged.

"I do not," he said. "I did not know such a thing was customary at dealings like these. Is it required?"

Rendibite glared at him, frowning.

"I know very few in Hell," Roche went on. "Actually, only two. I would not wish to bother Ximena unless it is absolutely necessary, and Lilia is…"

Roche trailed off, not wanting to say something unkind but having no other assessment to offer.

"Lilia?" Rendibite arched an eyebrow. "The dragon?"

Roche nodded.

The dragon chuckled, with far less effect than when he was in his monstrous form.

"She is the one who told me about these lands," he said. "I wondered why she was helping me, the way that one works."

He eyed Roche with a new respect, deepened his frown and winked playfully at him.

"What did you do to her?" Rendibite asked. "To have her pit you against one of the oldest dragons in Hell?"

Roche shrugged, and answered honestly.

"I exist," he said.

Lifting his eyes to the sky, Rendibite crowed humorlessly to the heavens. Instead the sound reached the rock wall overhead, and echoed back at them.

"That will do it," he said. "I pity you such enemies."

Roche glanced at the devil beside him.

"Can he be my witness?" he said.

Following his gaze, Rendibite nodded.

"He is my ward," he said. "And my witness. But he may serve as yours as well. If he consents."

The devil shrugged, and inclined his head slightly.

"If you both wish it," he said. "I will serve as witness."

Sticking out his hand. Rendibite spoke once more.

"Very well," he said. "You will work my new lands until the sowing is complete, and I will draw a line to cut separate our areas. My ward will teach you to do as we are doing, and will erase the borders I made around your new territory."

Roche extended his hand, took the dragon's firm grip in his.

"This agreement is final," Rendibite continued, "and witnessed on this day by my ward, Laurentis."

CHAPTER 12

In the moment their hands grasped each other, a strange thing happened. The air shimmered around them, and a wave of churning colors went out in every direction away from where they stood. Roche could see the scintillating effect from the corner of his eye, washing over everything he could see to leave it looking a little brighter. Without a word, Rendibite had nodded and stepped back. He took his dragon form, and launched himself into the sky.

Long after the winged serpent's shape had dwindled into the distance, Roche and Laurentis stood silently and watched the horizon where he had disappeared. The mystery around his companion had deepened, and Roche knew there was more about this devil than a great inner stillness. At last he spoke, still staring into the sky.

"You saved me there, didn't you?" Roche asked, quietly.

The devil shrugged, and let a smile tug at the corners of his mouth at last. Turning to him, Laurentis crossed his arms over his chest.

"I may have," he said. "More likely I saved him, though. You must understand the mind of a dragon to know why he was tempted to challenge you or enslave you, and why he heeded my advice."

Roche glanced at him.

"And you do?" he said. "Understand the mind of a dragon, I mean."

A full smile broke out across his face, and Laurentis uncrossed his arms to take three quick steps back from him. Before Roche could think how out of place the smile looked, or how the face bearing it seemed it would crack like stone if he held it a moment longer, the devil was gone. In his place was a black dragon, half the towering bulk of Rendibite but still more than twice the size of Lilia in her monstrous reptilian form.

"I understand the mind of a dragon well," he said.

Laurentis sounded much the same as he had when he was walking on two much smaller legs. His voice didn't boom out, or change in tone or texture; he spoke conversationally, as if he hadn't just transformed into a giant monster that could possibly turn Roche to ashes with a breath.

"Dragons do not have souls," Laurentis continued. "The dragon is a soul given shape. We wear our souls on the outside, when we are in dragon form. That form grows more powerful over time, as souls do; and each of us has a mind that tends toward pushing the limits of that power. When a dragon avoids taking the shape of the devil within, that dragon begins to lose touch with others while getting drunk on its own power. That is why you will likely never see Rendibite in his devil guise unless absolutely necessary."

Lifting one eyebrow, Roche felt a frown touch his face.

"You were in that form all day," he said. "Are you the exception to the rule, the rare dragon that does not seek power?"

A laugh escaped him, and this time Laurentis' voice did boom with the sound. Roche could hear both the bitterness and the honesty in the laughter, and sensed that the dragon would have dialed it back if he had seen it coming. He transformed once more, and took a step toward Roche. Although his face was grave, Roche again felt waves of mirth rolling off the devil as he came close.

"I seek power," Laurentis said, his tone flat and serious. "The only reasons I swore myself to Rendibite's service was to learn and to eventually inherit his holdings. Dragons don't die unless we are killed, but the temptation to put ourselves in situations where that could happen is too great to avoid them completely. In exchange for my efforts to temper his own desire to self-destruct, I became his next in line. Rather than allow their territories and other holdings to be distributed randomly amongst endless devils when they die, old dragons like to move on knowing their estate will continue to grow under the supervision of another dragon. And we all seek power, make no mistake."

Motioning for Roche to walk with him, Laurentis began to move along one side of the field. He pointed to the mounds that had been covered over.

"I had strange dreams," he said, "from the time I first climbed out of my shell. Fleeting visions during the day, and long elaborate sequences at night that faded almost immediately and completely when I would wake. Always there were fields of green, rows of plants that swayed in the wind and captivated my attention."

He stopped, caught Roche's eye.

"You have been to the mortal realm, haven't you?" he asked.

Roche nodded.

"Was it lush and full of plants?" he said.

Roche shrugged.

"Some of it," he said. "Although I didn't see much, there was a pretty wide array of landscapes. They all seemed quite full of life."

After a thoughtful pause, Laurentis looked around as if to see if anyone else was nearby. Roche was pretty certain anyone sneaking up on the two of them would be noticed, since they were facing each other and the land stretched far and mostly flat in every direction.

"Devils remember their lives on Earth," Laurentis said, "when they first arrive in Hell. From what I hear, souls in Heaven get obsessed with watching the mortal realm at first. We can't see the mortal realm from here, though; as a result, devils are more conscious of their soul journey. Unfortunately, that soul journey is always on its way down when a devil first gets here. Ask a soul that has done nothing but rise how things work, and they're bound to say things naturally get better on their own. A rising soul forgets what they were certain of when they were falling, that everything gets worse no matter what you do. But dragons are so far removed from any mortal thinking, we live with no remnants of such a life. The memories of anywhere but Hell or any feeling but falling are completely foreign to a dragon."

They were walking again, and Laurentis was looking at the field as though he had great affection for the tilled dirt. He continued speaking, and Roche listened earnestly.

"Somehow I remember," Laurentis said. "Not any specific memories of a life as a mortal, but things that meant a great deal to me. I knew Rendibite was trying to grow food, since it is so scarce in this realm; but he was having little success. I came to him and offered my services, although I honestly had no idea what to do at first. It wasn't until I had nearly given up, and Rendibite had threatened to flame me more than once, that I fell to the ground in exhaustion one day. Instead of falling asleep, I had some kind of dream. I saw myself sitting with the seeds, willing them to grow and watching them sprout. When I woke I was sitting up, like I had been in the dream."

Slowing to a stop, Laurentis glanced at the field once more before he locked eyes with Roche. He spoke softly, his voice touched with awe.

"I was surrounded by sprouts," Laurentis said. "They looked like they had in my vision, but different than they did in my dreams. I am curious how our fields compare to what you have seen in the mortal realm. They are the largest here, with yields that no one can match."

The devil's gaze was on the field again, his eyes lit with pride.

"Everyone knows," Laurentis said, "if you want to eat the best of what is grown in Hell, you must offer value to Rendibite."

Without looking away from the seeded rows, Laurentis let the proud light leave his eyes as a dark cloud passed over his features. The expression looked like one he was accustomed to wearing, the thought behind it one he had considered many times.

"Falling souls are dangerous," Laurentis said, his voice low. "Beware of them. Watch for the souls that are on the rise, who have seen the darkness and been reborn to rise again; they can lift you up, here in Hell. Most of our work force is built on each soul's ability to see tomorrow as being made better than today, and falling souls have trouble seeing that. But most of all, watch out for dragons."

Their eyes met again, and Laurentis let his voice drop even lower.

"Dragons are souls that have fallen as far as a soul can fall," he said. "Instead of rising, they became dragons. It is our constant fall that kills us eventually, no matter what circumstances seem to create that death. No soul is darker than a dragon, except an older dragon."

Roche tore his eyes from the bottomless black of the devil's gaze, protesting weakly while looking over the ridged rows.

"Why would you tell me this?" he asked. "Why would you even be aware of this like you are, if you were not different than other dragons?"

Laurentis shrugged, his frown easing up slightly.

"Maybe I am," he said. "I have certainly changed, in the time I have been pledged to Rendibite. Before sitting with the crops, I was a torrent of rage inside. Now I have sat with them for countless hours, and the place I inhabit in this form or my other is a peaceful one."

Shaking his head sternly, Laurentis crossed his arms over his chest.

"No," he said, "not peaceful. Focused. The rage is still there, but I use it now. I transform it, and create with it. And one day I will destroy the thing all that rage is focused on, and perhaps the rage itself will become something different."

Roche felt a connection to the devil he hadn't known he could feel. He knew watching him would not be enough, and he had to ask.

"Will you teach me?" he said. "Will you show me how to grow as you do, and how to focus?"

Their eyes met again, and Roche felt the dragon's presence slip somehow into his mind. Rather than resist, he laid himself open inside. All he had seen and felt were there for the slithering intrusion to explore. After only a moment, the presence withdrew.

"You have your own rage," Laurentis said.

Roche nodded.

"It is like a dragon's," Laurentis said, arching an eyebrow.

Roche shrugged.

Laurentis held his gaze, his eyes bottomless black.

"Will you tell me about it?" he said.

Again, Roche shrugged.

"Will you teach me?" he repeated.

Laurentis nodded, a smile touching his face once more.

"You are still a devil," he said, "and I am still a dragon. But we are similar in more ways than it might seem. I will warn you that the place where you point your rage is the place where I find my peace. You may want to find another direction to take it."

Chuckling darkly, Roche let his eyes explore the dirt at their feet.

"Are you telling me I can't be mad at God?" he asked, still chuckling. "Then tell me what you focus your rage on."

Now Laurentis shrugged, and dropped his gaze as well.

"Rendibite," he hissed. "One day I will tear his head from his neck, I will claw his heart from his chest and consume it, and I will burn the bloody pieces of his body. Then I will feed it to the devils that work for him, and see them start to share in what we are doing here. Whether punishment follows or circumstances permit it somehow, I will be his end."

Roche glanced at him, then back at the dirt.

"Is he that bad?" he murmured.

The laugh that came back had no humor to it, only bitterness.

"Not so much to me," Laurentis said. "He depends on me. But to the workers, yes. The old dragon is convinced they won't come back each day if we give them any more than food for the night. Meanwhile his coffers overflow and his work force is greater than any dragon's, and he brushes off any suggestion of paying workers more. He tells me I need to learn to be hard from him, if I am going to survive to be an old dragon. He says I am trying to make him soft, and spend his wealth before I have inherited it. But I have seen the day in my visions, when I am his end. And I can wait, better than he can, until that day comes."

Laurentis was silent for a full minute, turning over the thoughts in his mind while wearing that dark expression he seemed so accustomed to. Turning his head to look at Roche finally, he smiled humorlessly.

"You will keep my secret, won't you?" he said.

Roche returned his smile.

"You will teach me, won't you?" he said, once more.

CHAPTER 13

The space was as he had left it, dark but for the flames while still warm and welcoming. Roche looked closely at the fire. The stick of wood he had added before leaving for another realm had barely burned. Only a few minutes had passed in Adeb's home, as far as he could tell.

Before settling in front of the hearth, he let his eyes wander the common room one last time. Something seemed off, and his gaze kept going back to the table. In the same moment that he realized what it was, a cool and sudden draft gusted its way up the short hallway and wound its way around his legs. A chill went up his spine, from the cold air or from the realization.

The coins were no longer on the table.

Everything else was in its place, exactly as it had been when he had left. Roche had imagined himself sitting before the fire and gazing into the flames, watching his exhaustion pass as it always did and wondering if he should envy devils and humans their sleep. Instead he inspected the room in the most thorough way he could from where he was standing, until a second chill climbed his spine.

Another gust of cool wind brushed at his skin, and he followed the flowing air into the hall. A door stood open, shifting slightly in the breeze to further obscure his view further down the corridor. He could smell fresh night air coming in, but he saw almost nothing past the framed entry. The night was dark, no moon to light the landscape and no stars to cast their dim glow. Roche stepped into the doorway, and through it.

Immediately he was grasped by strong hands and pulled alongside the house. Roche twisted in the man's grasp, ready to attack, when he heard the familiar calm of Adeb's voice.

"Shhh," he said. "We have unwelcome guests."

Roche relaxed, pressing himself against the wall as he felt Adeb doing beside him. Willing his eyes to adjust, he nearly cried out when they did. Every detail of the small yard and nearby forest came into view as if they were standing there in full daylight. Rows of plants in the garden showed him every leaf and flower, glowing with a soft white light. The trees each had their own luminous presence, lending their soft glow to the pooled effect of dazzling brilliance before him.

As breathtaking as the view had become, Roche did not miss the scattered forms of men in the trees and garden. They glowed with their own light, a thin strip of brightness around them followed by a wash of colors that were individual to each of them. He felt exposed suddenly, not realizing the shapes he could make out were still unable to see him.

"Adeb," he whispered, "I can see the—"

The man's reply was fierce, quietly cutting him off.

"Shush!" Adeb hissed. "They'll hear you."

He remained silent, although Roche suspected if they could hear him they could surely hear Adeb as well.

"Stay here," Adeb murmured. "Make sure none of them get inside."

Turning to reply, he saw that Adeb had already slipped away. Even with the way his vision was turned on, Roche had trouble tracking the man's movements once he cleared the scant patch of grass that was his yard. Trees and brush were between him and the lurking shapes, but Roche only caught a slight hint of movement here and there. No twigs crackled underfoot, no branches swung or snapped, and the first sound he heard was accompanied by one of the glowing shapes going down.

Roche had counted five of them, now he could only see four. Rather than scan the forest for signs of Adeb, he switched his gaze from one figure to the next. They were only partially hidden, lurking behind trees that threw light on their faces for Roche to clearly see their expressions. One of them put two fingers in his mouth and blew out, making a strange off-colored sound; the other three answered swiftly, with their own whistle or click.

All four of them reacted to the missing response, but only three of them had time to form expressions showing their dismay. The fourth turned suddenly, threw his arm into the night and then went down. A branch crackled, a thud followed, then silence reigned again.

Cupping his mouth with both hands, the man that had started the last sound off made a different noise. A flapping and whirring sort of warble, the signal set the other two off in the direction of the house. The first finished warbling, and began closing in with them.

One of the men took three steps, and stumbled. The lighted underbrush showed Roche little but a foot pointing up at the sky for a moment, followed by the same foot suddenly pivoting into an unnatural angle. A blur of movement twisted and turned above the fallen form briefly, only to slip between light and shadows and fade just as suddenly from view. The cracking sounds accompanying the commotion could have been leaves or branches or bones, and they ceased along with the movement. Whoever had fallen did not get up.

From the garden and the woods, the two that remained approached cautiously. Clearly they had heard all the sounds Roche had, and they were both moving with less assurance than they had started out with while still closing on his position. From the way their eyes were darting back and forth, he could tell they were unable to see anything but the lighted doorway beside him. They came closer slowly, their feet finding the lawn at the same time from different angles.

Although they were only a stride apart, the men did not see or hear each other as they neared. One turned suddenly in the direction of the other, perhaps hearing his footfall or sensing his presence. He didn't see the form come out of the woods behind him, but Roche was able to watch it all. He stood in the shadows by the door, letting his eyes also adjust to the speed with which Adeb moved.

The slight and unassuming man he had befriended dashed silently onto the grass and came up behind the man as he turned. He tapped his shoulder, and let the unwelcome guest catch a glimpse of him as the man continued pivoting in alarm. The man lashed out, punching at the spot where Adeb's face had been a moment before; now it was gone, and Adeb's gnarled old hands were in its place. His grasped the man's wrist as his fist flew by, and twisted the man's entire arm until it was upside down. A look of panic spread over the man's face, to be replaced a moment later by a look of pain as Adeb shifted his grip and kept twisting.

A loud crack filled the air, and the remaining man stopped in his tracks. He looked around blindly, seeing nothing until his eyes lighted upon the doorway once more. As Adeb stabbed his fist repeatedly into one man's throat, the other took one more step and came within reach of him. Roche was only another step away, and he nearly dashed out to take down the last of them. Instead he waited, and watched, while Adeb let the body he had been pummeling fall lifelessly to the grass.

Adeb caught the last man mid-stride, slipping one forearm around his neck and the other behind his head. Although the other man was taller, he used the height difference to his advantage. Letting all his weight hang on his arms, Adeb lifted his legs to wrap them about the man's torso. His arms were trapped, and turning about in helpless furious circles did nothing to dislodge the choking burden. After less than a minute struggling he went down in slow desperate stages.

First he dropped to his knees, off balance from the weight on his back and out of breath from his choked attempts to shake it loose. Adeb unwound his legs to find his footing and force the man forward; he barely had time to get his hands out and catch himself before being driven face first into the earth. Next his arms gave out on him, and his face did make hard contact with the ground. Adeb knelt over him for several more seconds, his arm still around his throat. The only part of the man's body not lying flat was his head where it bent under Adeb's hold, and he showed no signs of life.

Finally, Adeb stood and glanced over at where Roche was hiding. His eyes seemed to drift past the spot and back to it, while the man's head hit the grass and lay as still as the rest of him.

"You still there?" he whispered.

Roche nodded, then realized the reason Adeb asking was because the man couldn't see him in the dark.

"I'm here," he said.

"Quiet!" Adeb hissed.

"Okay," Roche whispered. "But that was all of them."

Leaning over the man he had just downed, Adeb put one foot on his shoulder and another on the ground near his face. He bent, grasped the man's chin in both hands, and stood up. A raw popping noise came with the movement, and the man's body lay twitching in the grass with his head turned round the wrong way as Adeb stepped back. Next he went to the other body in the grass, and knelt next to him to feel about his neck.

Roche left the shadow of the house to come close and kick the body.

"He's dead," he said. "All of them are."

Glancing up at him, Adeb searched the darkness instead of his face.

"How do you know?" he asked.

Roche waved his hand dismissively, even if Adeb couldn't see it.

"Life has a certain light," he said. "I saw it go out in each of them."

Another uncertain glance came his way, and Adeb rose slowly to stand beside him. He reached out, touched Roche's arm lightly.

"You can see?" he said, under his breath.

Roche laughed, and Adeb shushed him again.

"I can see," Roche whispered. "And I know they're all dead. Why do we have to be quiet?"

Using the light of the doorway to guide him, Adeb moved past him and to the entrance. He leaned inside, grabbed the door by the handle and swung it closed. It let out a loud click when the door met the frame, and Adeb winced at the sound.

"We must not wake the wife," he said, smiling into the darkness.

Once more he moved to the man he had dealt with last. Grabbing him by the arm, Adeb began dragging the lifeless body across the grass. His eyes searched the trees as he came to them, and the burden snagged almost immediately as he tried to pull it into the woods behind him.

Roche stifled another laugh. He stepped to Adeb's side, and took the arm from his grasp. Lifting the corpse and tossing it over his shoulder, he crossed the grass to pick up the other one that lay nearby. With one body over each shoulder he came back to Adeb, and nodded into the thick forest.

"Lead the way," he said. "We'll come back and get the others after we have dumped these two."

Adeb nodded, and moved confidently into what Roche knew was pure darkness for him. His special vision let Roche see every step the man took, but he couldn't tell why every one of those steps was taken with such sureness. Silently, he followed until they were some distance from the house. Adeb began talking over his shoulder then, no longer afraid of waking Sela.

"There's a swamp not far from here," he said, "where the ocean lets in when the tide rises and dumps all manner of mysteries into the muck. Surely something there will be happy to eat our friends."

Glad for the opportunity to speak freely, Roche watched Adeb's back and called out to him.

"Can you not see?" he said. "How are you making your way, if you cannot see like I can?"

Without turning, Adeb let his laughter loose. The sound was full of gaiety, lighthearted and without care; it seemed eerily out of place as they moved through the woods in search of a grave for several bodies. Roche shifted the weight on his shoulders, and let the man's mirth dwindle to match the reality of their situation.

"The more interesting question," Adeb said loudly, still facing forward as he moved, "is how you can see so well."

Roche shook his head, sped up to follow him more closely.

"Not to me," he protested. "I showed you that I am not like other men, and told you true stories of the life I have lived. You pretended to be common, never letting on that you could fight like that or make your way in the dark."

Now Adeb was shaking his head, and Roche let him speak.

"I never said I was common," he said. "Nothing you have seen me do was done like other men around me. Surely it is what drew you to me."

Glad that Adeb was in the lead, and couldn't see his expression even if he turned, Roche scowled at his back in the light of darkness.

"Are you different, then?" he demanded. "Different like me?"

Adeb waved his hand dramatically, knowing Roche could see.

"Different?" he echoed. "Yes. But different like you? No. I have lived a long life as a human, learning everything I could in every land that I visited. I have learned to stay younger longer, but I am still not anywhere near the oldest man. I am human, my friend, with a lot of knowledge about being the best I can at many things. You are something else, with little history but great power. At my best, I was never able to move as quickly as you do. Yet your movements are as clumsy as they are swift, as random and errant as they are strong."

Roche called back as soon as he paused.

"Can you teach me?" he cried. "Will you show me how to fight as you did, how to move as though you are not moving and defeat anything standing in your path?"

Instead of replying, Adeb held up his hand and slowed his steps. Roche came up closer behind him, looking over his head at what they were approaching. Both the water and the plants growing in and around it were alive, but they gave off a different kind of light than the other living things he had seen. This was a strange sickly kind of luminescence, a hazy glow tinged in shades of brown and green.

They stopped together, and stood at the shore.

"Maybe we'll get lucky," Adeb said, "and a hungry water dragon will be lurking nearby."

Roche snapped his head around to first look at the man in the dark, then scan the swamp for movement. When he heard Adeb's laughter he looked at him again, and watched him shake his head.

"They're just alligators," he said. "But many natives call them by other names. One of them is 'water dragons'.

The tension in his shoulders relaxed, and Roche looked for signs of smaller reptilian life. He could see the light through the murky water, a predatory glow within the soft phosphorescence of the swamp. Nodding toward it, he whispered to Adeb.

"I think I see one," he said.

Adeb nodded.

"I hear it," he agreed. "Try to get the bodies close to where it is swimming, like they are coming after it. One by one."

Hefting one corpse, Roche drew back and tossed the dead thing overhand. He could see it somersault lifelessly through the air before striking the thin muck, and he saw Adeb's eyes go wide when he heard the splash. The monster twisted toward it immediately, clamping long powerful jaws down on one arm and then the torso.

Roche let it tussle with the body for a minute, then hurled the next in after it. The alligator turned again, attacking the other corpse in the same second that it hit the water. Roche watched until Adeb had stopped listening and turned to blaze a path back through the forest. It was easier to follow along behind Adeb than find his own way through the trees, even with the light on his side.

"You didn't answer me, back there," Roche reminded him. "Will you teach me how to fight as you do?"

Shaking his head at him again, Adeb muttered something over his shoulder. Roche couldn't make out what he said, and called out loudly asking him to repeat it. Again Adeb spoke quietly, and into his own shoulder; and again, Roche demanded he repeat himself.

"I don't fight," Adeb said, clearly and slowly. "When someone gives me their hand, I take it from them. When someone gives me their foot, I take it from them. I draw lines generously, and allow others to live as freely as I expect them to allow me to live. But when those lines are crossed, I do not redraw them or extend further generosity. Then I wait for them to offer their life to me, and I take that from them."

He stopped, so swiftly Roche nearly ran into him. Turning and looking up at him, Adeb spoke with quiet calm.

"These were the men that tried to rob us," he said. "On the road, I respected their right to try and best us. Near my home, I will never be up for a fair fight. I will sneak and swindle, and do my best to make every strike a death blow. Life must be respected, right up until it no longer deserves to live."

Adeb found his way easily to the other bodies, and it took two trips to dispose of them all. Roche laughed loudly when they were clear of the house once more, and voiced his sudden realization.

"You were never in danger," he said. "Even on the road alone at night, you have nothing to fear."

Shaking his head once more in the dark, Adeb let all the humor drain from his face so Roche could see it.

"We all have something to fear," he said. "Even you. If you haven't found it yet, you should begin looking for it. Better to find it before it finds you."

CHAPTER 14

The stick of wood he had added to the fire was charred on the outside, but still had some burn left to it. Roche sat and stared into the flames while Adeb warmed himself near the hearth and spoke in hushed tones.

"You must forget what happened here tonight," he said. "We go to work as usual and behave as though nothing did happen. If the sixth man from the road is there, he was surely excluded from the plan tonight for a reason. We treat him as if we have never seen him outside of work, either way. I am past the age of sleeping with one eye open, or picking up and leaving on a moment's notice. I like my home, my wife, my hearth."

As if to demonstrate his words, Adeb inched closer to the fire. The light cast dancing shadows across his face, and Roche ignored the man's demons as they encouraged him to dwell on his greatest fear.

"Once I was only myself, young and strong," Adeb went on. "Now I must care for my wife, and our home. Without these things I have added on to me I am nothing. We must keep this to ourselves. You must keep this to yourself."

Adeb trained his eyes on Roche, until he turned and met his gaze.

"I will be happy to do as you ask," Roche said.

The way Adeb's shoulder's relaxed at the words made Roche hesitate to add more, but he knew he had to.

"If you will do as I ask," he said.

A scowl spread across Adeb's face, made to look almost demonic in the shadows cast by the flickering flames. His shoulders bunched once more, and he shook his head sternly.

"My life of violence is behind me," he said. "I work for my living now, and I would rather die slowly by toil than quickly at the tip of a sword."

Roche let his eyes find the fire again.

"Not if they know what I know," he said. "How you handled those men, they'll be fascinated to hear the tale. Challengers will rise up to see if it's true, and they'll come from far and wide when they realize it is."

No matter how dark or intense the man's glare felt on him, Roche kept his gaze on the flames until Adeb broke and looked away.

"You want me to teach you to kill," Adeb muttered.

Roche shook his head.

"No," he said. "I want you to teach me to fight. I want you to show me how to not kill when it is best, and to cause as little pain as I must when death is the only answer. You already taught me there is a line, you must teach me to draw my own lines."

Adeb sighed.

"You are so strong," he said. "You are so fast. My teachings would be lost on you. I have no illusions of being able to best you, and I have never met a man or woman that could."

Turning to face him, Roche put a hand lightly on Adeb's shoulder.

"Not everyone I face will be human," he said. "Surely there are devils stronger than me, and angels that are faster. If I could face them with the knowledge you bring to a contest among humans, I could prevail."

Adeb's face was twisted with his inner battle.

"You want me to help you defeat angels," he breathed. "What consequence would I face for that in my afterlife? Truly you are the devil, offering two options that are both unfeasible."

Shaking his head, Roche watched the war waging behind Adeb's eyes.

"I am not the devil," he said. "I am a young and inexperienced friend in need of your wisdom and guidance."

Roche thought on that for a second, and went on.

"Also," he said, "I would like to learn how to garden, if Sela would be willing to teach me. There is a dragon in Hell that has told me—"

"Shush," Adeb muttered. "Enough with your eager need to absorb everything without learning it. The things you want to know take years to understand, a lifetime to master. You can't just decide you want to know everything and force all life everywhere to give up its secrets overnight."

Just as Adeb heaved in a breath to go on, a quiet voice came from the other side of the room. They turned to it, together.

"That sounds like someone I used to know," Sela said, "many years ago, back when I married him."

She was leaning on the entrance to the hallway, wrapped loosely in bundled robes that covered from her shoulders to where they puddled on the floor around her. Adeb's eyes went back and forth between them. Opening his mouth, as if to explain, he shut it again without a word. Sela smiled.

"It's late," she said. "You two need to get some sleep if you're going to work as hard tomorrow as you did today."

Roche could see the flush creeping up the back of Adeb's neck, and he smiled down at both of them.

"Sorry," Roche said. "We got to talking, and wanted to come to an agreement before we rested."

Turning where he stood, Adeb made sure his expression was entirely obscured from his wife's view before he scowled at Roche. When he pivoted to face her again, a mild smile lighted his face along with the fire.

"Go back to bed, dear," he said. "I'll be along shortly."

Sela sighed, and shifted in place.

"Just give him what he wants," she said. "I'll teach him, too. He has already saved our lives, and our home. He even left his wages behind, when he disappeared to wherever he went without using any doors. You say you need help choosing friends, my husband. Choose this one. Help him, and let him help you."

Adeb turned to exchange a glance with Roche, a look that said he both suspected she knew everything and that he was afraid to ask if she did; then his face fell into a kind of happy defeat, and he shrugged.

"Very well," he said.

Extending his hand, Adeb grimaced once more as it was engulfed by Roche's meaty paw. Sela looked on with approval, and turned to disappear up the hall in her nightclothes. Her voice floated into the room one last time, while their hands were still clasped.

"You'll find the sixth man in the privy," she called out softly.

They exchanged another glance, Roche trying not to laugh at both her offhanded proclamation and Adeb's bewildered expression.

"I'll take care of that," Roche said, smiling only slightly.

Adeb followed his wife up the hall without a word, glancing back with that grimace still on his face but saying nothing. As soon as Roche heard the door click shut behind them, he slipped into the yard and approached the modest outhouse. The only smell that hit him when he opened the door was fresh death, and he wrestled the corpse from its seated and slumped over position to toss it over his shoulder as he had the others.

Apparently the man had been using the small structure to hide, not for its intended use. Roche was glad for that; he didn't mind disposing of the body, but it would have been a little disturbing to have to pull his pants back up first. Without Adeb to slow him down, and with his vision turned on the way he had learned to do, Roche made short work of the task and returned quickly to sit before the warm hearth.

Roche poked at the fire, as he had seen Adeb do. The log he had added crumbled to fat chunks of burning red coal, and settled on the bed of ash and coal below. Selecting another log, Roche placed it carefully and slowly into the heaping pile of glowing heat. His hand thrilled at the closeness of the fire, and he left his fingers wrapped around the wood as the flames began to curl around the thick log and lick at his skin.

Withdrawing his hand slowly, Roche sat back and watched the fire burn for awhile. He had planned on doing this all night, before; now he heard so many thoughts screaming for attention in his head that he didn't feel like listening to any of them. Rather than lie back and wish he could sleep like everyone else, Roche was glad for the strange exemption. The thought made him think of who else might find themselves awake no matter the hour or the realm, and that thought made his mind come to a quiet halt.

He looked at the log, considered how little time had passed when he left before, and then wondered if maybe he hadn't chosen a strange place to find quiet in his own storm. Nonetheless, Roche let the smell of brimstone fill his nose; he allowed thoughts of Ximena to flood his mind, and closed his eyes to picture another world.

CHAPTER 15

Without thinking it through, Roche had imagined himself materializing in Ximena's chambers. He was surprised when he was deposited into the hallway outside her door instead, until he gave it some thought. Surely the queen of Hell had other things to do than sit around waiting for him to burst in on her with a mind full of questions. By the time a devil approached him in the high tunnel, Roche was prepared for what was coming.

"The demon Roche, I presume," the devil said.

He stopped a few feet from Roche, and looked him up and down. Rather than reply, Roche returned the gesture. The devil was different than the workers he had seen in the field. Thin and tall, he had hands that looked soft to the touch and eyes that glowed with intelligence. His clothes were simple but fine, clean leather breeches and a thin tunic. A light cloak was thrown over his shoulders, hiding his angular frame and preventing any sudden or strenuous movement without entanglement.

"The devil's secretary, I suppose," Roche fired back casually.

The devil laughed, and nodded.

"One of them," he said. "Although there are many realms under her supervision, there is only one queen. She does a fine job of keeping her appointments, but you'd be surprised how many devils think they can just pop in on her and receive an immediate audience."

Looking him up and down once more, the secretary shrugged.

"Or," he amended, "maybe you wouldn't be surprised. Here you are, after all. Please follow me, if you would like to wait."

The devil turned and walked away, not looking over his shoulder to see if Roche followed. With one last glance at the door he wished wasn't standing in his way, he sighed and trailed the slight devil up the wide stone corridor. Flames guttered in torches along the walls at regular intervals, but they didn't account for how bright it was in the tunnel. Some unidentified light source cast a warm and steady glow over everything, and nearly no shadows stretched along the lengthy hall.

When they came to a door, stone set in stone, the devil reached out and pushed it open. Roche could see the comfortable room beyond, overstuffed chairs in gleaming silver and plush purple; he hesitated before going inside.

"Do you know how long it will be?" he asked.

The secretary shrugged.

"Usually she knows when everyone is coming," he said. "Her appointment book gets filled well in advance, by her; often when I receive a request for an audience I find she has already scheduled it. I'm honestly a little surprised she didn't know you were coming."

Roche nodded.

"She's a busy lady," he said. "Maybe it just slipped her mind."

Exploding in a sudden burst of laugher, the devil actually slapped his leg while he shook his head. He pivoted in place, his cloak spreading for a moment with a flourish; then he walked away, muttering about the devil letting something slip her mind. He was still chuckling under his breath as Roche stepped into the room, and closed the door behind him.

The furniture was as comfortable as it had appeared to be, and Roche settled into a chair with a heavy sigh. His inner experience of slowly sinking into greater darkness while being constantly refreshed and renewed was still going to take some more getting used to; even with no need to sleep, he still felt some desire to rest his whirling mind. He closed his eyes for a moment, and breathed in the faint smell of brimstone.

A slight sound came from the direction of the door. His eyes flashed open and he turned, to see the stone slab swinging into the room.

"Well, that was quick," he said, rising. "I guess she knew I was coming after all."

The door opened the rest of the way, enough for him to see who was on the other side.

"Oh," Roche said, trying not to sound disappointed. "Hello, Lilia."

She looked much more happy to see him than he felt to see her. Rather than answer, she swept into the room and swung the door shut behind her in one fluid motion. Roche caught himself thinking it was meant to be a grand entrance, and that he was supposed to be impressed or intimidated. Although he could not deny the beauty of her shape or the allure of her movements, he felt increasingly guarded instead of breathless.

The thin fabric Lilia was wearing was more of a nightgown than a dress. Although it covered nearly her entire body, the dark garment also hugged close to every inch of her curved form. Thin and silky, it shone bright black in the light to inked darkness in the shadows. Like a second skin, the material flexed over her rolling hips while she crossed the room and stretched even tighter over her breasts as she heaved in a breath. The way the shifting silkiness clung to her seemed as calculated as the way she walked, and Roche was glad to see the hidden math rather than feeling its intended sum.

He had stood in front of his chair when the door had opened; Roche realized he appeared to be considering her in a way he had not meant to, and sat down. Choosing a seat across from him that was twin to the one he occupied, Lilia lowered herself to the cushion and crossed one leg over the other. A moment's glimpse of her skin showed in the movement, the soft smooth curve of her calf as it met her ankle; the moment passed and it was gone. Roche found himself thinking of Adeb, and how he had asked if she was beautiful. She was beautiful, but the thoughts animating that beauty put Roche on edge more than it drew him in. Noticing the extra effort she was putting forth made him increasingly nervous.

Even her posture was different than before. Lilia's shoulders were thrown back, her breasts pushed forward dramatically. The dress covered her arms and shoulders thoroughly, allowing her delicate hands to escape the fabric at the wrists. Only the neckline was revealing, plunging past her cleavage to leave a wide swath of bare skin nearly to her belly. The line between her breasts was darker than the shadows of her dress, and she pushed the whole ensemble slightly forward when she saw him noticing. When she spoke, her voice had changed as well.

"I'm so sorry, Roche," she murmured. "You are not to see the queen today. I have come in her stead. Hopefully you are not disappointed."

The tone of her voice did not suit her. Lilia was clearly trying to sound kind, even sweet; somehow it was grating on his ears. Roche felt a falseness behind the kindness, and could think of nothing to say other than pointing it out.

"I wish to speak with the queen," he said. "I am not sure you have the answers I seek, and I honestly don't know if I would trust you to tell me the truth even if you did. It's clear you don't care for me, and I am alright with that. But what is this? I've never seen you this way."

A wounded look crossed her face when he said he couldn't trust her, and Roche might have believed he had hurt her if not for the fire that also flashed in her eyes. The flames suddenly turned to smolder, and her lips went from a frown to pursed sensuality. She straightened more fully in her seat, pulled in her belly and pushed her chest forward.

"Maybe I have been unfair," Lilia purred. "Perhaps I judged you on what you are instead of who you are. Please, allow me to mend the rift between us. We might do well to get along better."

She leaned back, unfolded her legs and crossed the other over the one. Another alluring glimpse of stretching shadow and stark skin accompanied the motion, and Roche tried to keep his eyes on hers. Once she had settled in her seat again, and given him another endless view into the canyon of her cleavage, he starting shaking his head.

"I just can't believe you," he said. "Your words are sweet, and your form is most pleasing to the eye; but I get the sense that you are offering both in order to get something. Without knowing what that might be, I can only feel the insincerity of your behavior."

This time she wasn't fazed by his rebuff. Lilia tossed her fiery curls over her shoulder, stood up and stepped toward him. Leaning over, she looked down at him with a sideways smile on her lips.

"Are you saying you don't like me?" she whispered.

Her scent filled his nostrils, smoky and dangerous and intensely feminine. Lilia held his gaze while he considered the question, and let her hair fall back over her shoulder. A fresh wave of her pleasantly cloying odor washed over him, giving him another moment's pause.

"I'm saying I don't think you really like me," Roche shrugged.

His shrug made her scent dance around his shoulders, swirl around his head and envelope him in her.

"If you liked me, truly," he went on, "I can see no reason why I would not like you as well."

The words were as honest as they could be, and Roche felt his tension mounting as she leaned closer into him.

"Of course I like you," she cooed, softly. "Why else would I be here?"

Roche shook his head, trying to shake off her essence and the illusion of her seduction all at once.

"I don't know," he said, flatly. "I wish I did."

Finally, she straightened and stepped back. Her movements were functional, no longer dripping with sensuality. Lilia looked down at him, shrugged and spread her hands.

"Well, I give up," she said.

Her voice was her own again, full and throaty and flinted. The tension that had drawn his shoulders tight relaxed a little at the change, and he leaned forward in his chair as she took her seat once more.

"I had no idea what you were up to," Lilia said, "when I heard you were meeting with Rendibite. I must admit I expected a mighty battle, and wouldn't have been too torn up about getting you or him out of my hair. Now I hear you're planning to help him, and work together. I find myself intrigued by your actions, and curious as to your intentions."

Sitting perfectly erect, Lilia had dropped all efforts to draw him in like she was doffing a heavy cloak. Her body was still as curved as ever, her face just as beautiful; but the way she held herself and spoke seemed much more natural and sincere. The fire in her eyes burned with the hatred he had become accustomed to.

"I am the appointed liaison between devil and dragon," Lilia went on. "I supposed we might work together, rather than at odds. Yet you rebuff me as though I am not even worthy of your consideration."

Roche sputtered senselessly for a few syllables, shaking his head. Finally he managed to piece together actual words, under her fiery gaze.

"You were acting like you wanted me," he said. "But you don't want me. You quite clearly despise me. You've essentially said so."

With a wave of her slender hand, Lilia made as if to brush aside the past like it was so much smoke. Her lascivious facade returned suddenly, and she pursed thick lips at him while sliding slightly forward in her seat.

"Maybe I do want you," she breathed. "Maybe acting like I despised you was a way to cover up the way I really felt. Or maybe some of us want what we despise."

Lilia's eyes sparkled with fire, watching him shake his head again.

"I don't think so," Roche muttered.

A shrill laugh escaped her lips, and Lilia relaxed back into her chair.

"Or maybe I just wanted to try you," she hissed. "Now even that has passed. You should know I can dissolve any agreement between you and a dragon, that I can bar you from having any dealings with them."

Roche sighed, and leaned forward a little. He tried to smile.

"Lilia," he said, "why don't you just tell me what you want."

Somehow the simple request enraged her. Lilia leapt to her feet, twisted her face into a mask of fury, and glowered down at him.

"If only it could be so easy," she snapped. "Fine. Tell me why you claimed those lands. Tell me why you dealt with Rendibite. Tell me what you plan to do with your territory."

Roche gazed up at her a little helplessly.

"Honestly," he said, "I don't know. I'm kind of running on instinct here, Lil. I'd be happy to share my experiences so far with you, though there really isn't much to tell. If some kind of friendship really is—"

Her shriek cut him off.

"Don't get all chummy with me!" she shouted. "I knew you would be evasive, and play games with me. You need to be wary when in Hell, demon. You made yourself an enemy of the wrong dragon."

Stupefied slightly by her outburst, Roche watched her yell and then watched her storm out of the room. He was afraid she might transform right in front of him for a moment, making the expansive room considerably less spacious; but one look in her eyes told him there was no danger of that. Even in her rage, intelligence sparkled in the fire of her gaze.

He sat there a few quiet moments after the door slammed shut, thinking on what he might do. With the way his thoughts were whirling, the last thing he really wanted to do was visit with Ximena right now. Although he could see the humor in the secretary's surprise at seeing him if he were to leave now the traditional route, Roche really couldn't bring himself to laugh over the situation just yet.

Abandoning the comfort of the plush cushion without such a scene was simple, at least. Roche merely closed his eyes, and thought of the comfort of a warm fire during a chilly moonless night.

CHAPTER 16

Very few of his spinning thoughts could not be burned away by resting his gaze on the fire. Roche watched it flicker and dance through the coldest hours of the night, feeling its warmth and settling into its calm. By the time he heard someone stir in the back of the house, his mind was swaying happily with the rhythm of the flames. He looked up from where he was seated as Sela came into the room. Wrapped in robes, she was smiling sleepily down at him.

"Good morning, friend Roche," she murmured. "Did you not sleep?"

Roche returned her smile, let his eyes drift back to the fire. The last thing he felt like doing was getting his mind started whirling again. Trying to explain answers to questions he couldn't stop asking himself or answer for himself seemed far too much effort this early in the morning.

"I am well rested," he said, instead.

She remained near him, soaking up the warmth of the fire or watching him with curiosity; maybe both. Keeping his eyes on the flickering flames, Roche remembered the body he had carried to the swamp after they had retired for the night.

"The man you killed," he said. "He had no wounds, there was no blood in the privy or on his clothes. How did you do it?"

From the corner of his eye he saw Sela shake her head.

"I killed no one," she said. "He gave me his life."

"So she took it," Adeb finished, from the hallway.

They both turned to look his way. Roche smiled slightly while Sela left the warmth of the fire to meet Adeb as he came the rest of the way into the room. Wrapping her arms about her husband's waist, Sela rested her head on his shoulder and closed her eyes.

"Good morning, my darling husband," she murmured.

Encircling her shoulders in his embrace, Adeb set his chin lightly on top of her head and smiled over Sela at Roche.

"Good morning, my lovely wife," he said, continuing to smile.

With his eyes on Roche, Adeb kept talking to her.

"Did our guest get some good sleep?" he asked.

Still holding him, Sela shrugged and spoke into his shoulder.

"He is well rested," she said.

Adeb nodded, mussing her hair slightly with the motion. Closing his eyes, he breathed her in and melted a little more into her arms. They stood together like that for a long quiet minute, each of them leaning so deeply they would fall forward if not for the other leaning just as completely into the embrace. Something passed back and forth between them, a calm quiet energy that seemed both routine and special.

Watching them closely, Roche had no sense of intruding on their intimacy or the peculiar exchange. He could see whatever it was they were passing between them, when he looked at them the right way. Like a white mist with no vapor, a bank of softly glowing light clung to their shared shape as he had seen fog hover about the earth. The glow brightened around Sela at first, only to move the brightness across the unified mist to hover around Adeb. Whatever he was doing made the shape and the light grow, and he passed the brighter and bigger energy slowly back to her.

The couple continued like this while Roche watched, and he saw the glow stretch to envelope him and the hearth as it passed back and forth between them and brightened with each exchange. When it washed over him, Roche felt a shift. His body relaxed in places he hadn't been aware it was tensed, his mind stopped dancing like the fire to go pleasantly and completely still, and his eyes went from seeing their shapes to witnessing the play of their energy.

Once he became part of it, Roche could sense the boundaries of the energy. First he felt the room and everything in it, as though he was connected to the fire and the hearth and the table as intimately as he was suddenly connected to the two people bringing it all together. Even as he marveled at that, Roche felt the energy shift again. No longer passing it back and forth between them, Sela and her husband had begun to work as one mind. Roche could both feel it in his own silent thoughts and see it in the glowing mist as it continued to grow in both size and illumination.

The light and the awareness ballooned suddenly, going beyond the walls of their home to encompass the surrounding area. Now Roche could feel the woods, the road and the nearby swamp. He got the sense that he could know any part of it as completely as he knew himself by putting his awareness on it; at the same time, Roche felt being part of it all was the aspect of that awareness he needed most. Letting the stillness settle more deeply in his mind, Roche felt the energy explode outward once more.

So much of what he knew was latent knowledge, waiting for a thought to throw open the door to all the information Roche knew as though he had always known it. Concepts and languages were one thing, but witnessing a concrete reality he had not known existed for never thinking of it was quite another. The awareness he was part of knew what a continent was; and without words, suddenly Roche did too. He saw and felt the reality they were in with new eyes, and his being inhabited the space it took up in the realm like never before.

When in Hell, he was in Hell; the delightful stench of everything burning surrounded him as surely as the floor curved to form a ceiling above him. Doorways led to other parts of Hell, more tunnels or vast expanses that were forever enclosed by rock and dirt high overhead or close enough to reach up and drag your fingers along it. Heaven was the same, in its own way. The clouds formed both flooring and roofing, enclosing the realm with only glimpses of sky or Earth now and then. He had never thought to reach his imaginings beyond another layer of clouded luminescence, and another beyond that.

From his new perspective, Roche saw that visiting this realm did not put him in a reality in the same way going to Hell and Heaven did. He was on the Earth, not in it; and as his awareness expanded once again, he saw the planetwhirling in a vast expanse of nothingness. The momentary thought that he should be feeling some shock or fear right now came into his awareness, only to be burned away in an instant by the brightening that followed the expansion. This was not one giant mostly empty space he was occupying somehow; it was awareness, stretched out into eternity to show it had no limits.

As quickly and completely as the inner vision had expanded, it began to draw back. The sensation of being in a bubble of love intensified with the contraction, until it condensed into a cloud of ecstasy. Roche thought again of Heaven, and wondered if the couple was somehow bringing some piece of it down to Earth with them doing whatever they were doing. Like all his other thoughts, it was pleasantly blasted away by the light that seemed to be concentrating in him. Even after they had brought their shared awareness into the room once more, Adeb and Sela leaned into each other and embraced a moment longer.

They disengaged as naturally as if they had only hugged for a second, Adeb taking the place she had been by the fire while Sela moved into the kitchen. She began setting places at the table as she had the night before, and Roche stood silently next to Adeb and gazed into the flames. He wanted to say something, to ask what they had done and if they would show him how to do it himself; he also wanted to exclaim, and jump up and down with a wide childish grin on his face. Roche felt either action would somehow crack the shell of the presence he still felt all around him, so he stood silently and stared into the dancing light until his mind began to creep into his awareness once more.

"Can I help?" he said.

Roche moved from the warmth of the hearth and into the kitchen with three small steps. The counter was covered with fresh vegetables, whites and greens surrounded by every shade of red from deep brown to a dark purple. Rubbing his hands together, he looked over her shoulder to see what she was doing. Sela had set a block of wood on the counter, and a loaf of bread on top of that. She was drawing back a long straight knife as he peeked around her, and turned slightly to show him better.

The blade sunk into the loaf as she leaned slightly forward, gliding gently and evenly the rest of the way through while she withdrew. Sela's motion was unbroken, swift and sure and unhesitating. Looking at it from where he was, the loaf appeared untouched; a thin line showed him where the blade had entered, but the slice remained still and the loaf whole. Sela reversed the blade in her hand, held out the wood handle to him.

"Cut up the whole loaf," she said. "Pieces about that thick."

Roche approached the board, set the blade on the loaf and sawed at it. The slice Sela had cut tipped sideways, and fell off the board; the piece he was cutting was much wider about the middle than it was at the top, and had narrowed to nearly nothing by the time the blade bit into the board. Falling away from the loaf in three pieces and a shower of crumbs, the part of the loaf he had tried to slice buried the perfectly cut piece it had tipped over. A few of the crumbs danced across the counter to drop at his feet, and Roche stepped back surprised.

At the hearth, Adeb had turned in place to either warm his backside or watch what they were up to. He exchanged a glance with Sela that spoke of volumes Roche couldn't read, and turned his back once more.

"Try again," Sela said, nodding at the bread.

Roche came at the loaf with the knife, moving one toward the other with exaggerated slowness.

"Set it down gently," Sela said. "You need the knife to do this, just as the knife needs you to get it done. The partnership you have with the tool is as important as the tool you use. This knife is very sharp, and can teach you something about very sharp blades. Whether you are swinging an axe at a head or stabbing a sword through a breastplate or sawing a slice off a loaf, a good tool will be as important to getting the job done as your will to do it."

Adeb was listening at the fire, his back to them. He tossed his thought over his shoulder.

"Aye," he agreed. "A bad tool can be your worst enemy, a good tool your greatest ally."

Nodding, Sela went on with a smile.

"The knife has its duty," she said. "You have your desire. Allow it to do its duty, by letting it know your desire. Gently. See it as you would do it, and then do it as you saw it."

Working on the wall together the day before, Adeb had said the same sort of thing a number of times. Roche had been so bent on his work that he hadn't really seen the big picture until it had come together. Now the phrase found his ears, and Roche saw himself slicing the bread as Sela had. Without any sort of conscious effort, he watched the blade slide forward and back in one easy and unbroken motion.

Roche stood back, moved his eyes from her to the loaf. Other than the piece he had knocked over and the chunks he had cleaved off with his clumsy first attempt, the bread looked untouched. He had to press at it with his finger to see the thin line appear where he had made his second cut, and a grin broke out across his face.

No one noticed. Sela had moved to the table to season a heavy pan, and she took it to the fire without turning to him. Stepping aside when she approached, Adeb kept his back to Roche and continued to warm himself by the hearth. Roche looked down at the bread, back over at them, and then nodded when he realized they were deliberately ignoring him. Getting it right was not something to celebrate, it was something to repeat. He turned back to the loaf and gripped the knife deliberately.

Just as he was cutting into the loaf, Sela spoke behind him.

"Are you finished with that yet?" she said. "There is a lot more to chop up, and you two need to get off to work."

Roche pivoted, after cutting another crooked piece and nearly slicing his finger in the process. Both of them were watching him, and only barely suppressing their laughter. He received their shared unspoken message: their job was to teach him, to push him, and to test his limits in every way. Rather than be upset at her insistence, he bowed slightly at the waist and smiled.

"Not yet," he said. "Sorry, I will go faster."

After he had turned, and cut another perfect slice, he said one more thing under his breath.

"Thank you," Roche murmured, smiling.

CHAPTER 17

Everything was going so well until the overseer showed up.

The road was just as it had been the last time he had walked along it; and at the same time, it was different. Several of the men nodded at Roche, recalling him from the day before. He didn't recognize the faces, but they probably weren't so much remembering his face either. Towering over the tallest of them was the least of it; wearing clothes that disguised his true nature but still made him look like a foreigner surely didn't help matters any.

Sela had stopped each of them at the door. First she tried to give back the coin Roche had left on the table; he refused, asking her to please take it as some payment for what they were teaching him. Adeb began to mumble about how coin and learning were much different currencies, and how one could be spent but once while the other could be traded again and again in various markets. Silencing him with a smile and a kiss, Sela had sent them on their way.

After they moved their supplies to a new section of the wall, runners brought materials and filled their separate containers. Adeb talked him through mixing the mortar, first showing Roche how to get the desired mix and then encouraging him to switch off and measure out the rest of the batch. When Roche reminded him of the pains he had complained of yesterday, Adeb waved away his concern and grabbed the stirring paddle from him. Muttering about how being old was not the same as being useless, he segued smoothly into instructing Roche on the way to pour each ingredient and in which order he needed to add them.

At some point Roche realized that Adeb was settling into a familiar role as a teacher. The man had clearly guided others on their paths in some way or another throughout his life, and more of him was revealed through his teaching than had been through their initial friendship. Instead of presenting himself as a master, Adeb complained about his own flaws and the difficulties of the world in between lessons on how objective reality has nothing to do with one's feelings.

The morning went smoothly, the wall rising before them in swift rows of smoothed stone. Roche was paying such close attention to Adeb and his lessons within lessons he didn't even notice the absence of the overseer. The supply runners made multiple trips with no devil's head popping up between, and Roche didn't consider the fact that he was missing until Mandine finally showed up. Rather than climb the stairs after they were clear of traffic, the devil pushed himself up the steps between two runners. He even shoved one aside as he made it to the landing, causing water to slosh over the edges of the man's bucket.

Adeb noticed first, and inclined his head slightly in the direction of the devil. They were bent to the task of mixing, down on their knees next to each other to gain leverage over the heavy paddle and containers. Roche had his back to the stairway, and turned to glance over his shoulder. The devil was heading right for them, not noticing any of the workers he passed as he stalked across the stone floor. When he had closed the gap between them, he stood over them and glowered down at Roche and Adeb.

"Hello, Mandine," Adeb said, lowering his gaze.

Roche was glad he had thrown the name out, as it had slipped his falling mind; and he thought maybe Adeb was deliberately setting another example for him. He considered greeting the devil with a humble tone and downcast eyes as well; instead he knelt there looking up at the overseer, meeting his gaze and matching his intensity. For the first time Mandine seemed to notice the other workers around them. He leaned in toward them, and whispered fiercely at them.

"We are short six workers today," he hissed. "Would you two know anything about that?"

From the corner of his eye Roche saw Adeb begin to shake his head while keeping his gaze on the devil's feet. Roche looked around slowly, and answered loudly enough for everyone on the rooftop to hear.

"What workers are missing?" he said. "Why would we know anything about what happened to them?"

The others knew better than to stop work and turn to listen. The only indication that they had heard was how deliberately every man seemed to be focused on the task at hand. Usually they let their gaze wander as wildly as their attention did, as Adeb had put it; now they were keeping their eyes on their work and moving with the slow steady sureness of men whose minds were on something else.

Mandine noticed as surely as Roche did, and raised his voice to reach every ear on the floor.

"Start your meal break early," he called out. "Clear this level, so I may have words with these two."

His tone did not leave time for finding a good stopping point or cleaning up. Roche knew the workers were leaving a mess for themselves to sort out after the break, with mortar being left to harden in their pots and in uneven clumps along the stone. Mandine stood over Roche and Adeb while the space cleared out, and let his voluminous cloak and wrapped headdress make him appear bigger and more intimidating than he was. He raised his voice as the last worker cleared the stairs, and Roche chose the same moment to rise to his full height.

"You two have some questions to answer," Mandine said.

His voice began as an authoritative boom, ending in a hoarse whisper as Roche stood to tower over him.

"Let's say we do," Roche said. "First we should get clear on why you are the one doing the asking in the first place. If we have some reason to account for other workers going missing, and you know of it, surely you have some part in them going missing as well."

Roche could feel Adeb's glare on him, and the hand tugging at his sleeve. He didn't care, and heeded neither warning. Keeping his cool and at the same time clearly getting angry, Mandine let the fire burn in his eyes while he carefully unwrapped a coiled length of leather from his belt. The motion was made as if it was meant to frighten Roche, and the devil eyed him as though expecting him to cower in fear. Instead Roche watched, as if he was mildly interested and completely unafraid.

The next movement was a well practiced one. Mandine flicked his wrist abruptly, and Roche saw the coiled length straighten behind the devil for a moment and then leap forward. He let it strike him, allowed the searing pain to stoke the fire of his own rage, and stood silent and unmoving.

"I'll ask the questions," Mandine sneered at him. "Start giving me answers, or I'll keep it up."

Adeb was still tugging at his sleeve, but with considerably less insistence. Either he knew Roche was past the point of no return, or even Adeb was beginning to feel the overseer had crossed an unacceptable line.

Holding the devil's gaze, Roche showed him his teeth.

"I didn't ask you to stop," he said. "Isn't that how this is supposed to work? You whip me until I beg you to stop, then make me tell you what you think I know?"

Mandine stared at him in disbelief.

"Isn't that the way?" Roche pressed him. "I'm afraid you'll have to work much harder than that. I'm far from begging."

The devil tried to exchange an exasperated glance with Adeb, but his eyes continued to endlessly search the floor.

He took one more look at Roche, and then allowed a wicked grimace to smear across his face.

"Very well," he said. "Perhaps this one will answer me."

Leaning back to drag the whip behind him, Mandine caught the look in Roche's eyes just before seeing his movement. For a moment it looked as though he wanted to stop the weapon's forward momentum, but it was a moment too late. The long braided leather snaked out towards Adeb, and Roche reached to his side casually in the same instant. Winding around his forearm, the whip seared another moment of white hot pain into his consciousness. Roche grabbed the coil as it tried to unravel, and gave a swift sure tug.

Mandine tilted forward, nearly colliding with him. Roche picked the devil up by his neck with one hand and held him aloft. Casually, he began walking toward the edge where the wall was barely built. He spoke as he walked, ignoring the flailing devil's attempts to dislodge his powerful grip.

"You sent those men after us," Roche said. "That much is clear. What isn't clear is why. The two of us got more done than the lot of them, and I would think you would be hoping to see us repeat our performance the next day and the day after that. So you must be working some kind of angle that is more important to you than the swift and proper construction of this building."

The whole time he was talking Roche was walking, carrying Mandine high as the devil's feet kicked ineffectually far above the floor. By this point they were nearly at the edge, and the devil's efforts redoubled as he saw the threat of a long fall approaching. Roche continued to speak, but he let his voice drop low enough so only Mandine could hear.

"Or maybe," Roche murmured, "it's what you are. Maybe devils don't know how to resist any temptation to take advantage that comes along."

Mandine stopped struggling when he heard the word 'devils'. He looked at Roche with eyes shot with red and filled with surprise.

"You are a devil," he hissed. "Yet your disguise fools even me. You are not one of us that came here to live among humans. Who are you, wretch? Will Hell never let us be? Must the realm's slithering tendrils reach us even here, and drag us down into the darkness?"

Roche was holding him out over the side of the building now, feeling the spinning vertigo even with his feet on the ground.

"Go ahead, drop me!" Mandine cried. "Let me fall and fall and fall, let my soul find a bottom lower than any in this bright place."

For a long moment Roche considered doing just that. The devil was clearly not making the world a better place by being in it, but Roche was hardly able to assert that he was either.

"How about instead," Roche said, "I keep your secret, and you keep mine. How about you make Adeb over there an overseer, and give him the whole floor to supervise. He'll teach the others to build better, and this structure will be completed more quickly and skillfully. Also, you can stay off the roof that way. I know how you hate the thought of this fall."

Shaking him for good measure, Roche was glad to see terror widen the devil's eyes. The screaming fright in his own chest was almost too much to bear, standing so close to the edge and considering such a swift descent. He was certain it would not be fatal, at least for him; but that didn't make contemplating the rapid drop any less uncomfortable. Roche had hoped his own primal fear would be indication of what the other devil would feel, and he had guessed right. Watching the devil nod almost mindlessly just to get out of the situation was all the satisfaction he needed. Pivoting, he set Mandine down on the rooftop.

"Also," Roche added, almost as an afterthought, "we killed those men. And we'll kill any more you send after us. Then I'll kill you, in a way that shows you how much I regret not doing it today. So keep your word, and don't waste any more lives trying to end ours."

Rubbing at his throat, the devil nodded. He seemed to be having trouble finding his voice, so Roche let the movement of his head be enough. Pointing to the stairs, Roche gave him a little shove in that direction. Mandine stutter-stepped away, as Roche called out one last parting shot to the devil.

"Now get off our roof," he said. "Adeb will take it from here."

CHAPTER 18

Somehow he knew this swath of land to be his own, although Roche couldn't identify how he knew it. The soil felt like toasted sand under his feet, the air reeked pleasantly of something burning and something long since burnt, and smoke choked the air just enough to give it a delightful texture as he inhaled. Most of the Hell he had seen was nothing but long stretches of similar acreage, but here he felt different.

Not only did he know it was his territory as soon as he set foot on it, Roche also sensed for certain he was not alone. Someone else was on his land, occupying space that belonged to him. Roche tramped in the direction of the sensation, cresting a rise as he walked. The moment he recognized who awaited him, Roche's shoulders dropped the knotted tension he had been carrying. His face nearly broke out into a grin as he descended into the slight valley.

"Laurentis!" he cried. "What are you doing here?"

The dragon was in his devil's form, sitting on the ground with his legs crossed over each other and his hands resting lightly on his lap. Facing Roche, his eyes were closed until he heard his name. Laurentis was a picture of peacefulness, maintaining the pose a moment longer as he met eyes with Roche. Holding his gaze, the devil rose to his feet in one fluid motion.

A familiar wave of energy washed over Roche, nearly stopping him in his tracks. The last few steps between him and Laurentis felt as though he was walking on clouds instead of soil, and he let his steps bounce a little for the feeling. Instead of embracing the devil, like he was tempted to, Roche bent at the waist and gave him a polite nod.

"Did we have an appointment?" Roche said.

Laurentis shrugged.

"In a manner of speaking," he said. "Although nothing has been arranged, some time has passed since you came to an agreement with my master. I thought it would be best if we got started as soon as you returned, so I came here to find a good area to begin."

Pivoting at the waist, Laurentis took a long moment to survey the stark barrenness of their surroundings.

"This seemed a good spot," he added.

Roche imitated his motion, turning in place to have a good long look at the immediate landscape. He tried to see how it was different than any other part of the territory he felt belonged to him. Except for the devil before him, and the feeling of lightness that accompanied him, Roche could not determine how this plot of land might be unique among all the rest. Rather than ask the devil outright, he put the question to the back of his mind and hoped the reason would reveal itself in its own way.

"How did you know when I would come back?" he asked, instead.

Indicating the place he had been sitting, Laurentis frowned slightly. The expression was more of a suppressed smile, and Roche could see the mirth dancing at the corners of the severe line his lips were forming.

"For the longest time," Laurentis said, "I kept the visions I had while dwelling in the quiet to myself. The legends of Hell tell of many with such sight, but no one seems to think anyone has the ability to see the future anymore. After closely guarding my secret for some time, I finally tried to share some of the things I was seeing with others."

He sighed, and cast his eyes back to where he had been sitting once more. The smile no longer tugged at his mouth; instead the frown deepened, and he sighed again as he turned back to Roche.

"Even Rendibite," he went on, "does not believe me. He thinks I have some other way of learning things, or that my dragon death wish keeps pushing me out on a ledge to force me to fall or fly. While that may have been true in the beginning, every path I have followed since then has revealed itself to me first in the silence. I tried to teach him to go to that place, but the old dragon won't listen or learn. He is sure any path with such power would have revealed itself to him at some point in his many years, and he thinks I am trying to get him to waste his time by sitting and doing nothing."

Laurentis laughed, but there was no humor in the sound. His mouth remained downturned, as the bitter noise escaped his lips.

"Funny that I kept the secret so long," he sighed. "Now I realize I could fly through Hell shouting that I can see the future, and all the devils below would just think I was mad. I don't have to keep any secret, the secret keeps itself through their collective disbelief."

Shaking his head, Roche breathed in deeply. He felt buoyant, and light enough to wonder if his feet were truly touching the ground.

"I believe you," he said, quietly. "How else are you here, right now? Why would you continue to spend so much time doing something that netted you no results? And how did you get the crops to grow when no one else could, if not by doing what you say you did?"

This time when Laurentis laughed, the sound was light and genuine. He looked at Roche like he was either the wisest person he knew or the biggest sucker he had ever met.

"You don't know dragons," Laurentis said. "We are all about putting on a show for others, and hiding our true intentions behind that facade. It only makes sense that I would steal onto the fields at night to do my actual work, then sit in silence during the day to pretend it was having some effect. While I sleep soundly, those that doubt me wait in the shadows for me to creep out and reveal my true secret in the dark. I do my real work right under their noses, and they cannot see it."

He leaned in close to Roche, searching his eyes.

"But you see it," Laurentis said. "Why is that?"

Roche held his gaze, letting the devil peer into his soul.

"I don't see it," he replied. "I feel it. When we worked together in the field, and when we spoke before, I could sense a strange kind of peaceful urgency coming off you. And now more than ever, I feel as though I'm standing on a bright and uplifting cloud of your making. I don't know that I deserve credit for seeing what others don't; from where I stand the sensation is nearly overwhelming."

Breaking the intense eye contact, Laurentis motioned once more to where he had been sitting. He began to move in that direction, and Roche trailed him slowly. When he spoke over his shoulder, Roche could see the frown was creasing his face once more.

"Have you figured out why I chose this place?" he said.

They stood over the spot he had occupied earlier, both of them looking down at the soil. Roche nodded slowly, understanding before he could put it into words. Then he looked up, and spoke.

"This is the lowest point," he said, suddenly.

Laurentis nodded, showing he was pleased by frowning with greater intensity. He collapsed into an elegant cascade of folding limbs to sit as he had been before, and waved his hand at the ground in front of him.

Following his lead, Roche bent himself awkwardly into some semblance of the posture Laurentis was sitting in. It felt unnatural and uncomfortable, but he tried to emulate the serene face he had seen the devil wearing when he had first come upon him.

"The lower you go," Laurentis murmured, "the slower time passes. Although time is relative to the individual, it is also relative to the realm the individual is inhabiting. Several days have passed since we last spoke, although I suspect the experience was different for you."

Roche was taken aback, shifting from slight discomfort to actual pain as he moved his body to express the feeling. Leaning back into a more balanced posture and mindset, he gave Laurentis a frown of his own.

"I have only seen two sunsets," Roche said. "I have been among the mortals, learning from them and becoming more familiar with their world and their ways. There is a woman I know who grows beautiful gardens, lush plants that made me wish you could be there to see them."

Although he still wasn't smiling, Laurentis had relaxed his features into a neutral and open expression while Roche spoke. Only his eyes showed some hint of his emotion, black as night but shining brightly.

"Did you bring any seeds?" Laurentis said.

Roche shook his head, and let himself feel the fool. Of course he should have gotten some seeds, and brought them back with him. Sela had made everything an analogy to the growing process, when they spoke in the gardens. The lessons had been multi-layered and circuitous, but they had all started with some version of the same thing.

"It all begins with a seed," Sela had said, so many times.

Roche said it now, before answering the devil.

"It all begins with a seed," he said. "And I brought no seeds."

The fact didn't seem to bother Laurentis as much as it disturbed Roche. He was unable to resist the inner downward pull that seemed to be taking more out of him than he could put back in, but he refused to give in to it. Laurentis waved off the concern casually, while Roche doggedly continued to shake his head.

"No matter," Laurentis said. "I have already planted some around us, for you to practice on. I just wanted to see them, really. From what I understand, they will not grow here. Only the seeds we have been planting can be cultivated in Hell, as far as I know. They are not determinate, like seeds in the human realm. There, you plant a seed and it becomes whatever its parent plant was. Here, you plant a seed and it reflects the inner landscape of whoever is cultivating it."

Getting comfortable was still posing quite a challenge for Roche, until he began to pay closer attention to the way the devil was sitting. He made a few minor adjustments, waited for the pain to come and then to go, and picked up the thread where it had been dropped with a less divided focus.

"Where do your seeds come from?" he said.

The devil's eyes narrowed, and he stared off into distant memory.

"I don't know," he admitted. "I only know that they are plentiful when a plant grows well, and we treat the seed harvest just as seriously as we treat the fruit harvest."

More curious than before, Roche leaned forward once again. Twinges of pain poked at him until he settled back, and straightened his posture.

"Do you have some?" he asked. "Can I see them?"

Laurentis tilted to one side, reaching into a satchel tied at his hip. Taking his hand from the bag and reaching out, he held his palm up for Roche to see. Three tiny objects stood out against his crimson skin, oblong and burnt brown. Each of them had a twisting spiral line that made the rounded shape almost serrated, and all three together only took up a fraction of his hand. They were about the size of the devil's smallest fingernail, rolling around on his palm while Roche peered at them.

"That's it?" Roche asked, trying not to sound disappointed.

The hand withdrew, the seeds disappeared once more into the satchel, and Laurentis nodded solemnly.

"That's it," he said. "In the beginning. But what comes later is so magnificent, in some cases, we are able to harvest thousands more from the product of a single seed. On top of that, we have food to eat in Hell for the first time in its long history. Devils no longer scramble in the dirt looking for nutrients, and souls move faster along their path when their vehicle is nourished."

Roche looked at him, disbelieving.

"Devils used to eat dirt?" he asked.

Laurentis nodded again, his expression growing even more grave.

"Some still do," he said. "That is part of why I am glad you want to grow food on your land, and why I am happy to help. We dragons have a chokehold on the agriculture here, and some of us use it to the distinct disadvantage of others. If we can grow so much sustenance that it is no longer so difficult to come by, we could change the entire relationship between the devils and the dragons."

Lifting an eyebrow at him, Roche pressed Laurentis further.

"But why?" he said. "Why would you want to shift the balance of power away from your own kind?"

Laurentis turned, and spit in the sand. The spot sizzled and popped for a moment, then cooked itself dry.

"My own kind," Laurentis echoed. "When your greatest strength is also your greatest shame, the war within can never end."

He glanced at Roche, and threw him a slow wink.

"But you know that better than anyone," Laurentis went on. "What you don't know is that war is coming, and there will be dragons on both sides. We will fight, and whoever is left standing will take the entire race into the next age. Whoever falls will perish, in the fighting or at the hand of the resulting regime."

Roche let his eyes go as wide as they wanted to.

"You have seen this?" he said. "You know what will happen?"

The devil shrugged, noncommittal.

"Anyone who looks can see it coming," he said. "My visions are more personal, bits and pieces of my life to come. Sometimes I can't figure out what I am being led toward, but often I can. I know enough to see which side I will stand on when the time comes, and that you will be there by my side. That is enough to make me wish to help you, and teach you."

Something about what he had said did not sit right with Roche. He shifted in his spot, as if it were his body that was having difficulty settling.

"What do you mean," he said, "what you are being led toward? Who is leading you, or what? And how can you know to trust it?"

As if it was his only answer, Laurentis closed his eyes and sat there. Roche waited for a long moment, until he felt the waves of peace rolling off the devil to wash over him. He closed his eyes as well, and let his thoughts scurry from his attention like so many roaches in sudden light. After a few minutes Laurentis began speaking, his voice low and slow. He told Roche to put his attention on the seeds planted about them, to see them pushing their way up through the soil to sprout leafy brown shoots.

Roche concentrated, and let the devil's words guide him.

CHAPTER 19

They stood facing each other, looking down at the scorched soil at their feet. Roche wore a disgruntled frown, but Laurentis was peering down with curiosity and a little wonder. Something had pushed its way up from one of the places where Laurentis had mounded up the dirt and dropped a seed. Neither of them could identify it, and it was wilting swiftly before their eyes.

At first Laurentis had told him to picture an abundance of small brown shoots like the ones they were growing in the other fields. Roche had to speak up, and remind the devil that he had not actually visited the fields where anything was growing just yet. The only experience he had with plants was in the mortal realm, and there was no sitting and imagining in all Sela had told him so far. Laurentis appeared a little concerned for a moment, and wondered aloud if they should go visit the sprouting crops first.

Then he relented, and told Roche to imagine his favorite food that grew on the vine. Roche thought of one fruit immediately, a smooth rounded delicacy that Sela grew in her garden. When he rubbed his fingers over the skin, it felt rough and hard; but when he bit into the yellowed meat it gave way easily, and flooded his mouth with flavor.

Thinking of the plant was easy, as Laurentis coaxed him with a gently murmuring voice to see it in his mind's eye. He pictured the stalk, the green offshoots that dangled fat spiky leaves, the light flowers and the fruits that sprang from them. They had kept at it for quite awhile, before Laurentis told him to open his eyes and have a look around. Roche spoke before he had a chance to survey the scene.

"Nothing happened," he said, opening his eyes. "I'm sure nothing happened, although it felt like we were at it for quite awhile."

Roche turned in his spot, surveying their surroundings. He could see the spots where Laurentis had churned the soil, pushed up mounds and planted seeds. None of them showed any sign of disturbance from below, as much as he hoped one of them might.

Waving his hand dismissively, Laurentis scoffed.

"That was only a few minutes," he said. "Besides, I was starting you off with a big job. Let's try something else. Rather than see the plant in maturity, with fruits hanging from the vine, I want you to see the shoot as it pushes its way up out of the ground. Just one shoot, okay?"

"Sure." Roche shrugged. "Just one shoot."

He looked around, pointed at a nearby mound.

"That one," he said.

Nodding, Laurentis closed his eyes and began speaking in that same low commanding voice. The sound lulled Roche's mind into a silent still place, and the words quietly coached him through creating the picture in his mind. Something about trying to conjure up the simple single image was much harder than filling his head with green leafy fullness. He relaxed as fully as he could, and let the devil guide him.

Finally, after what seemed another brief eternity, his thoughts drifted away. No images or words touched the pristine stillness that was his mind, and Laurentis seemed to be speaking to him from the other end of a very long and very dark tunnel. A few minutes of that nothingness, and suddenly the shoot he had been trying to see with his inner eye was there before him. Short and stout and healthy, it was as though it had been there the whole time. He hadn't been creating something that had yet to exist; he had been looking for it, and allowing it to come to him.

He could hear something different in the devil's voice when he spoke again, a quiet delight of triumph behind his words.

"Good," Laurentis said. "Open your eyes."

Right away he glanced over at the mound he had indicated, and saw the shoot pushing its way up from the soil. Even as he caught that first glimpse of it, the green start began to lose its bright color. In the time it took Roche and Laurentis to stand up and walk over to it, the tiny beginning of a plant had gone brown in streaks. The stalk was striped in dull shades of both colors, the twin leaves curling at their edges as the expanding stripes became mottled swaths of wilt.

"It would seem," Laurentis said, "that you would have to keep your attention on that type of plant all the time. Clearly, it would be impractical to do so. You were acting as water and sunlight, and growing a plant I have never seen the likes of."

Roche watched the leaves fall from the stalk, first one and then the other. They drifted to the ground silently, the main shoot leaning over moments later to lay between them.

"You sound happy," Roche said. "Yet at the same time, you say it is impossible to grow anything like that here. Why is that?"

Shaking his head, Laurentis put one foot forward between them. He covered the wilted leaves and stem with the sole of his boot, and ground them into the soil. When he pulled his foot away there was nothing left but some dried bits of brown mixed with the scuffed sand.

"Don't tell anyone of this," Laurentis said. "Just because it would be impractical to grow that kind of thing right now does not mean it will be impossible to do so later. You show great promise, and I'm sure you'll be sprouting entire fields in no time. Then, we'll try other things."

Roche nodded, letting the devil's words cheer him. All evidence of what he had done was gone, but the memory remained. He let a smile pull at the corners of his lips while he gazed for another moment at the spot where the start had sprouted. When Laurentis spoke it shook him from his reverie.

"Let's go to the fields, then," he said. "I'll show you what we're growing, and let you taste what we are eating. You can tell me how it compares to human food."

Nodding again, Roche tore his eyes from the ground and began to follow Laurentis in the direction he was walking. The devil glanced back over his shoulder, and a smile touched his eyes.

"You might want to step back," he said.

Roche stopped, moved back a few paces. One moment the devil was standing there, his back to Roche; the next a dragon occupied the same space, and then some. He craned his serpentine head around, and narrowed his enormous eyes.

"When I was guiding you," he said, his voice the same, "what were you thinking of when you made the plant grow?"

After thinking about it for a few seconds, Roche shrugged.

"I thought I was thinking of nothing," he said. "But now I realize that isn't quite right. Beyond the realm of mortals is a great vast emptiness, sprinkled with stars and endless nothingness. It's like some kind of womb for all this, or something. I had a vision of it thanks to some humans I spent time with, and it really affected me. It made me start to look at things…differently."

The dragon stared at him for a little while, one eyebrow raised higher than the other. Finally he moved his front haunches in a shrug of his own, and unfurled his wings slowly.

"I hear you can run very fast," Laurentis said. "Follow me."

CHAPTER 20

In the first few moments he had existed, Roche could remember his mind racing through the light within him. He had known everything and nothing at the same time, which was a confusing state in its own way; but the light had burst brilliantly through both the ignorance and the knowledge. Now he had memories of his own, and much of that latent information had been connected to people and events through his experiences; yet those recollections and bonds seemed to be pushing out the light, and the darkness taking its place was now eating away at the memories he had gathered.

Somehow he continued moving, flitting from one realm to the other with some end in mind that had either escaped his attention or had never existed in the first place. Roche wanted to think he was moving forward, but his inner compass was swinging so wildly it could only be described as constantly spinning. There had been a bright and blazing fire within him, in the beginning; all that remained were the smoldering embers of a forgotten flame, snuffed out by the gathering darkness within him.

More often than not, Roche started to find himself in the grips of his own forgetfulness. His life began to blur past the narrow band of attention he had remaining to pause and plop him fully into the present from time to time. Instead of being a clear and illuminated moment, each occasion it was a sharp slap of reality across the grasping state of his mind. Every instance found him trying to piece together what had come before and what needed to come next while reeling in the sudden piercing awareness.

Standing on the rooftop for the fifth or the hundredth time, Roche felt that sharp sting of the moment catching up to him. Perhaps the worst part was that he could not even address the sensation with familiarity; every time he slipped into his own life this way, it was both coming home and going somewhere completely foreign to him. His mind tossed memories at him with no continuity, and it was up to Roche to sort everything and bring it together until it slipped away once more.

He saw Adeb nearby, pointing at a fresh section of wall and talking in low tones. Two men stood idle and listened intently, nodding every few moments in agreement with the words Roche couldn't make out. At any time he could turn up his hearing, and he had some recollection of having done so like he could with his eyes; but the lesson was surely one he had learned and forgotten already. He saw no use in forming the memory again, only to have it slip from his mind once more. Instead he took the opportunity to get his bearings as best he could, and put his scant memories into some sort of sensical timeline.

By the time Adeb glanced over at him, Roche had recalled both harsh and gentle moments with the man. Most of them were harsh, the way Adeb felt hard lessons needed to be taught. He would chide Roche for being too slow at a task, then mock him for using his supernatural speed to increase his performance. Even when Roche did something quickly and perfectly, with the laser focus demanded of him, no congratulations came in any form. Roche knew he was doing well when Adeb said nothing, and ignored him.

The other memories that filled in between them were of moments like these, times when Roche slammed into his own body while continuing to be aware that he would slip away again at any moment. Adeb had taken to being gentle with him in those instances, treating Roche as though he might break if prodded. He could remember Adeb teaching him to sort his memories, and appear as though he was pausing thoughtfully rather than reeling mentally.

So when he did look over, Roche gave Adeb a brief and solemn nod. It was an indication of what was happening, and that he was all right with it. Adeb said a few more words to the men and moved to join him.

"Good to have you back," Adeb muttered.

He stood next to Roche, watching the rooftop progress and speaking in low tones no one else could hear.

"You're still getting better," Adeb said. "You are learning faster."

A laugh escaped Roche, sounding bitter and humorless.

"Am I remembering?" he said.

Adeb shrugged.

"You do forget a lot," he mused. "But you pick it up again when you do, whatever it is. You asked me to keep teaching you as long as you kept learning, and you are definitely still learning. Sela says you seem to be in pain when you are present, and completely functional when you slip away. She hopes the pain is not something you feel there too."

Shaking his head, Roche felt a grimace tug at the corners of his mouth. Images of her flooded his mind, always gentle and kind but indomitably firm at the same time. Sela's mannerisms didn't change the way her husband's did when Roche found himself clawing his way through every razor sharp moment; she encouraged him to connect with his own growing process instead. Likening his plummeting soul to falling rain, Sela would tell him the seeds of his growth had been planted deep. The fall had to be long and hard to nourish such a crop.

And one time, she had broke off during a lesson to notice that Roche had ceased spinning and was standing painfully still. She had looked deep into his eyes then, and murmured words he had churned over in his thoughts a hundred forgotten times since.

"You never had a mother," she said.

She didn't say that was sad, or unfortunate; but the look in her eyes in that moment spoke volumes Roche felt he might never unravel. Opening one arm and gesturing him to her with the other, Sela had taken him into her embrace as Roche leaned down. He felt the warmth of her envelope him, and the feeling of comfort overwhelmed him for the first time. Roche had sunk into it, then carried it with him into all the racing past time and clawing through the moments that followed.

A nudge from Adeb shook Roche from his reverie. He wondered how many times he could remember the memory of something, and whether he would miss such a moment should it ever slip away completely. The wondering was followed by another, whether precious moments had already been lost or forgotten; then another, wondering how many times he had spun his mind down this spiral. Even while he screeched his awareness to the rooftop again, all these wonderings plagued him.

Adeb was looking over his shoulder, and Roche followed his gaze. A swath of fabric had been wound around his head to conceal the horns, but that did not make discerning who was coming up the stairs difficult for him. The devil was not the one he had dangled over the side of the building, but he was dressed enough like the other to let Roche know he was an overseer. Spying the two of them standing together, the devil topped the stairwell and moved immediately in their direction. He nodded respectfully at Adeb as he stopped before them, and looked at Roche while he spoke.

"I would like to have words with you," the devil said.

Roche grunted.

"Have them, then," he said.

The devil shifted his eyes to Adeb, and back to him.

"In private," he suggested.

Roche stole a quick sideways glance at Adeb, not sure if this was a conversation he knew about and expected or whether this was a surprise to him as well. With a complete lack of motion or change of expression, Adeb let him know this was not an anticipated visit.

Shrugging, Roche looked more openly in Adeb's direction.

"I'll be fine," he said. "We'll stay right here."

The devil looked frustrated for a moment, and it twisted his features. As Adeb wandered off he surveyed their surroundings, and his face relaxed into a slight frown.

"You don't come here like we do," he whispered. "Have you been sent here to find us, or bring us back? You must say you haven't found us, if you were sent here to find us."

Standing there and appearing to be completely in command of the moment had been part of his lessons, along with remaining quiet in the face of a chatty opponent.

"We're not just here," the devil continued. "More have gone to the sea, and the countryside. I could take you to them, if you will let me and a few others remain."

On the outside he was stone. Underneath, Roche could almost hear his fingernails digging into the dark walls of his constant fall. Resisting was all he could do, as letting go meant slipping away into blurred timelessness once more. He had to count on the devil's perception of his stoic features to convey something other than what he felt.

The devil looked up at him, clearly uncomfortable with Roche's silence. Glancing around furtively, his voice went up an octave without getting any louder.

"At least tell me who sent you," the devil said. "Was it her? Everyone thinks it was her. Tell me it wasn't her. Anyone else, but not Ximena."

The name broke loose another gush of memories in Roche, and he lost his carefully maintained composure in the flood.

"Ximena!" he gasped. "I need to see her."

Wringing his hands, the devil shook his head.

"Oh, no," he said. "You mustn't tell her we are here."

Roche lowered his gaze, allowing the full screeching presence of his current internal state to pass into the devil's eyes. Taken aback, the devil stopped wringing his hands and seemed to hang from the visual contact.

"She is Ximena," Roche said. "She knows all."

The devil shook off the dark connection, raised an eyebrow.

"She knows all," he sneered, "except what she doesn't."

Motioning toward Adeb, Roche held the devil's gaze.

"Treat him well," he said, "I will not tell anyone about you."

The devil laughed.

"And what about when he is gone?" he asked. "How long does kindness to a mortal buy us, when we are trying to escape centuries in Hell? Join us instead, and live like a king amongst mortals rather than being enslaved by a devil or a dragon."

Several times during their conversation, Adeb had glanced over to check on him. Roche felt the man's presence as if he was standing right there somehow, whispering to him that all would be well and to just relax.

"Treat him well," he said, "and show me how you get here. When I talk to her, I will not speak of you or your location specifically. But you must show me how you come through, and where the others are."

The devil nodded enthusiastically, and Roche felt the tenuous hold he had maintained on the moment slipping away from him. He signaled to Adeb with the most subtle desperation he could muster, and waved the devil in the direction of the stairs. As the darkness descended on him and the moment turned back into a blur of shifting sand, Roche wondered if he would remember to track down what he had demanded of the devil. The thought didn't matter as much as the next, that he needed to try to meet with Ximena once more. He held onto an image of her as his last grasping thought unwound itself, and wondered if it was a clear recollection or just another memory of a memory.

CHAPTER 21

Keeping track of where the conversation was going turned out to be a much less simple task than keeping his unintentional appointment had been. Roche showed up just outside her door again, with dim memories of the receptionist and Lilia and thinking he should have come back here a hundred times. As soon as he could see the door clearly, it opened before him; Roche stepped from that strange world between worlds and into her chambers.

"It has been some time," Ximena said.

Rising from her chair in greeting, she met his gaze across the room. Roche diverted his eyes and approached slowly, using the time between the door and the sitting area to collect himself in her presence. Either his memories of her had faded more than he had supposed, or Ximena was exuding power like never before. He felt weak and exposed in his diminished state, sure she could see him more deeply than he could see himself. Every step was taken with caution, and with absolute certainty it was somehow a grave misstep.

She waited to sit until he did, while Roche tried not to feel as though invisible waves were coming off her and knocking him back every few moments. Girding himself, he leaned into the feeling as he sat, and let it wash over him before he spoke. Little by little his mind came back to him, and he wondered again why he had not returned earlier.

"I tried to come see you," he said, meeting her eyes at last.

His mind was a sponge that had been squeezed dry and left in the sun; her gaze was a flowing stream of fresh clear water. At first he was surrounded in her bright darkness; then he began to soak it up, and feel himself again. He noticed that she looked a little annoyed to find out the news, and rushed in to explain.

"Your receptionist put me in a waiting room," he said. "Lilia came in and talked to me for awhile, and I left after that. I guess I could have waited, but for some reason I didn't. I think maybe she said you would be awhile, and maybe I didn't want to talk to her any more."

Recalling the encounter was easier in her presence than it would have been otherwise; his mind was focused and present, but the memory remained dim and amorphous. The sharp awareness of his mind was like a spotlight; but it speared into dense fog, and he watched the memory as if it had happened to someone else a very long time ago. He could see Lilia, although he couldn't picture her clearly in his mind any more; but he could also see himself, squirming under his scarlet skin as meaningless sounds that used to be words floated between the two of them.

Ximena watched him after he spoke, and the way she looked at him put Roche at ease so much that he slunk back into his chair. Even if she could see into his soul while his own vision of it remained obscured, only kindness and understanding were present in her gaze. Somehow, as she seemed to pour dark light into him, Ximena still had a touch of annoyance in her expression. Leaning back into her own seat, she brought her slender fingers together and spoke in low tones over the delicate steeple.

"My receptionist should have told me," she said. "Lilia should have told me as well."

As he soaked up the power of her presence, Roche saw more snippets of memory from his meeting with Lilia. He shifted in his seat uncomfortably, as meaningless sounds shifted to words in his mind. Suddenly the power Ximena was putting off had him averting his eyes again, as Roche wondered if she was seeing the same memories he was.

"I thought you knew everything," he muttered.

Ximena laughed, and the sound put him immediately at ease once more. She spoke quietly to him then, and every word helped Roche remember what he already knew; by the time she was done he had met her eyes once more.

"You of all beings should know I do not," she said. "I come and go just as you do; and it would only serve me to act as your friend while you are falling. Yet even in our best moments beings like us are prevented from literally knowing everything. We can only focus on so many things at any given time, and too much happens in all the realms for that focus to not be diminished even at the height of our soul cycle. And when we plumb our own depths, what we know can feel so vague and disconnected that we seem to know nothing at all. The best we can do is remember that this is only what seems to be, and that we still have abundant powers to draw on wherever we are in our cycle."

She smiled when their eyes met, and lowered her hands to her lap.

"I am not reading your mind," she said, "when I ask if maybe Lilia expressed an interest in you that made you uncomfortable, and makes you anxious to talk about it with anyone."

Startled at her supposition, he immediately suspected her of what she had said she was not doing. Of all the humans and devils and angels he had met, none made him feel the way Ximena did. More than once he had considered the thought that she was sort of the mother to all the realms; but her kind and open eyes seemed more like those of a sister he knew he could trust. Although he had never had either mother or sister, he felt as though she related to him more like a sibling.

At the same time, he had heard humans and devils alike speak of her, calling her by one name or another; and they always seemed to do so with more than a bit of fear. Beyond that, he could easily imagine her doing nearly anything to get what she wanted; Roche had to consider that the understanding he saw in her eyes was an indicator of her own dark confusion, and he knew what it meant to know he would do anything to turn the descending tide.

"How could you guess that?" he said. "If you didn't read my mind, how do you know that's what happened? Maybe you saw my discomfort, but how else would you know the reason behind it?"

She stared at him for a moment, appearing dumbfounded; then Ximena burst out laughing, and swept her hand between them to take in his body from head to toe.

"Have you not seen you?" she said, still smiling. "You stand tall and strong like an angel, yet you are covered in the skin of a devil. Those of us that come from where we do are a unique blend of the energy that drives everything. We tend to be very appealing in form, and you are no exception. If you don't wish to become accustomed to fending off advances from interested parties of all kinds, you may consider altering your outward appearance."

Looking down at himself, Roche tried to see what she did. Memories of feeling stronger and animating his body more completely assaulted him, and he slumped further into his seat. If others viewed him as appealing in any way, they were falling for an illusion; Roche was sure his inner spiral was evident to anyone able to see beyond the flimsy facade.

Ximena frowned slightly, and leaned forward. Not many could boast that they had received a compliment of any kind from her, and for a moment Roche thought maybe she was awaiting his gratitude in some form. Even as he mustered up the gumption to deliver a hollow word of thanks, he realized she was not dissatisfied with his response for the reasons he may have considered. Her eyes shone with compassion, not irritation; she had been hoping to lift him up, and her disappointment was only in understanding how he felt.

"At least your tail is growing in nicely," she noted, quietly.

She might just as well have hit him with a powerful electric shock. Sitting up straight, Roche only barely resisted the urge to jump to his feet. Instead he shifted from side to side, feeling for it as he moved. As soon as he sensed it pressing against his leg, he remembered being vaguely aware of it before; he had sat down and accommodated his own tail as he sat, without giving it any thought at all.

"How did you know?" he whispered.

An expression of pure innocence came over her face, so genuine it had to be both true and completely put on at the same time.

"Haven't you heard?" she said. "I know everything."

He chuckled, letting her hear the unease in the sound. Waving her hand in a familiar dismissive gesture, she shrugged.

"You seem more grounded," Ximena said. "You are becoming accustomed to the idea of being alive, and continuing on as you are. Although I would say you are more grounded to the mortal realm than here, you are definitely weaving nicely into the fabric of the reality that spans all the realms."

It took all he had not to sputter in his response.

"Weaving nicely into…" Roche echoed, then trailed off. "Surely you of all people see me as I am. Nothing feels like it sticks when it happens, and I don't see how I can avoid repeating my mistakes if I can't even remember making them. Time seems to pass most quickly wherever I happen to not be, and I feel as though my purpose is constantly out of reach as precious moments slip through my hands."

While Roche was ranting, Ximena was nodding. When he finished she inclined her head one last time, and smiled. She looked as pleased as if he had told her he had everything in hand, and the plan was proceeding exactly as expected.

"Welcome to life," she murmured, still smiling. "It gets worse."

He could feel his eyebrows knit together, as his heart fell.

"It also gets better," she added, her expression of kind amusement not faltering. "That probably won't help you now, but remind me later that I told you it would happen. I do so delight in hearing how I sometimes do seem to know everything."

The smile he gave her was forced, his best attempt at returning her kindness and showing his gratitude.

"I can see that," he said. "I feel better sometimes, usually when I am in the mortal realm or…or with you. Everything becomes clearer then, and I remember this is a cycle I must endure if I am to recover the rest of what I am. But I can only see that, as if from the outside of myself; all I feel is more of me falling away, even in those moments."

Roche looked around for something to pound his fist on, saw nothing, and slumped back in his chair again. Now he could feel his tail, and couldn't seem to get comfortable around the annoying protrusion.

"Everywhere I go," he went on, "I see nothing but devils and angels and people completely comfortable in their own skin, never wondering why it should belong to them or how it could; yet my mind seems to want to be anywhere but in my body, and whenever it finds its way there I can see why. I feel like my awareness is over here…"

Indicating the empty space to his left, Roche continued.

"…while my body is over there…"

He waved his hand in the other direction, still speaking.

"…and seldom," he said, "do the two collide. Even the devils that live among mortals don't question their ability or right to belong. Instead—"

The look she was giving him evaporated his river of words midstream. Ximena had cocked her head slightly at the mention of devils among mortals, and he had forgotten the promise he had made right up until he had nearly broken it. Instead of pressing him, she let her eyes cloud over as she gazed at him unseeing. After a moment, her mind stopped turning and her attention came back to him.

"Of course," she said. "That would explain a great deal. Would you take me to them? Things must be set right, and I could use your help. I have nothing to offer you but my favor—"

"Please," he said, cutting her off. "I have surely done far more wrong than right so far in my life, but I made a devil a promise. Although nothing would be so valuable to me as your favor, I feel horribly torn. Spending time with you is the thing I most want to do, for my own reasons; but I am afraid going against my own word may leave me feeling more hollow than I already do, and unable to enjoy the reward of your presence."

Ximena seemed touched by his layered confession, and his honesty. The intensity in her eyes softened. Roche had enough time to feel relief that she understood and regret that he could not help her before a mischievous grin spread across her face.

"Promises are easy," she said. "Tell me exactly what you said, and we'll find a way to make sure you don't break it."

CHAPTER 22

More than once, Roche found himself wondering whether spending time with Ximena was the best or the worst thing he could do. He found it strange to consider that it might be a vague mixture of the two, but considering it meant justifying being near her for longer. Of all the beings he had interacted with in all the realms, only she did not seem to want to use him or teach him. Even her suggestion that they visit the mortal world together was put forth lightly. She seemed to be using the trip as a pretense to spend more time with him.

After Roche had told her the circumstances and the arrangement he had made with the devil on the rooftop, she had smiled at him warmly.

"You can keep your word, to the letter," she said. "We have many options, some of which lead to us walking between worlds together immediately."

Her smile widened, and for the first time Roche saw a hint of childish enthusiasm in her eyes. Like every other thing Ximena did, the expression made him find her even more endearing. Roche nodded, wanting her to tell him what possibilities she saw.

"We can go back together," she said, eyes sparkling, "and use this devil the way he offered himself up. That way you aren't telling me about him, you're taking me to him. So long as he proves useful, we can leave him and his companions be."

Letting out a heavy sigh, Ximena gave up her chair and stood to begin pacing. She shook her head at her own idea, and explained why it was not the best option while repeating slow measured steps along the plush carpeting. Roche could see a spot slightly worn into the soft walking surface, described exactly by her turns and strides.

"Those devils would not like that," she said. "At some point they would realize we are going to come for them eventually, and your friend will be used as a bargaining chip. You might go back on your own, and find out what he knows; but even then they might intuit the inevitable, and we're right back to throwing your pet mortal right in the middle of it."

Roche shook his head.

"He's not—" he began.

"I know," Ximena cut him off, continued pacing. "You don't see it that way, but they will. Humans are seen as playthings by devils, not people. That's why we need to make sure all the devils that have escaped Hell are returned as soon as possible. Their presence in the mortal realm is causing ripples here, and likely having even more effect there. However, it seems we will have to prolong the process if we are to spare your mortal friend. The only way we can ensure his safety is to travel immediately to where they are, and take them out first. Any other option gives them the opportunity to use the leverage they have against you."

The same set of problems whirled through his mind. Now that Ximena knew about the devils living among the mortals, she was going to do something about it with or without him. As soon as the group using Adeb to guarantee their safety heard of others like them being banned from the realm, they would keep him close to them and a knife close to him. Roche wasn't sure if his own thoughts were coming clearer because he was near her or if her ideas were somehow supplanting his own, but he knew he had to admit it was surely one or the other. Considering both possibilities, he still liked the option that meant spending more time with her.

"Okay," he nodded. "I'll show you where they are. And I'll help you find the others. I do have some questions, if that's alright."

She stopped in her tracks, and captured his eyes with her own. The innocent eagerness remained, but it burned in the crackling fire of her mind as it baked her plans to perfection. Roche was both glad she was a friend and curious if she was just giving him what he needed to get what she wanted. Stories of her ways abounded even among mortals, and they were always the kind of tales where no one but her knew what was going on until it was too late.

After she poured her presence into his for several seconds, Ximena averted her gaze slightly. Still facing him, she looked to the door. Roche followed the motion, and her eyes.

The slab of stone moved silently, opening to admit a figure shrouded in darkness into the room. When it was inside, the door swung shut without sound once more. The figure seemed to float towards them, shifting shadows inside a loose humanoid form; as it got closer, it took shape slowly with every step. Feet formed, delicate and dark; then a body, small and shapely and unmistakably feminine. By the time she was between them, Roche had guessed what her face would look like.

He tried to suppress the level of awe he was feeling, as he stared at them and wondered which one he should address. Ximena's double was not only exactly like her in every way; the waves of power he felt washing off the one was equally present in the other. The only apparent difference was the cloak the one he had been speaking to had been wearing. Lined in purple and made of darkness, it swam about her constantly in a way that made her look like she might at any moment evaporate into the voluminous shadows it cast.

Taking off the cloak, she handed it to her doppleganger. Roche watched her form come into full view, layered in what appeared to be another swath of darkness. Only her wrists and hands showed at the sleeves, and the neckline followed her own closely; the rest of her body was bathed in black, only taking shape when a light shone behind her. Black boots hugged her calves and ankles, covering her small feet in another layer of shifting shadow.

As the cloak settled about the other's shoulders, Roche realized Ximena was dressed to travel. She glanced at the mirror image of herself and then back at him, her eyes aglow with imminent adventure.

"You said you had questions?" she murmured, smiling. "There is nothing I would keep from you, and so much I want you to know. Ask me your questions anytime, and I will try to help fill in the blanks your experience has caused. Go on, ask me anything."

Roche looked between them, the curiosities he had been entertaining a minute ago blown away and replaced by a whole new set of wonderings.

"Is she you?" he said. "Are you her?"

Settling his eyes on just one of them seemed a challenge he could not overcome right now, so Roche kept glancing back and forth between them. The same expression lighted identical features on both of them, and it was the one closest to him that answered his question. She sounded exactly the same as Ximena, and the effect was a little dizzying.

"We are the same," she said. "I have to divide my attention from time to time in a very literal way, since I cannot ever truly leave Hell. The problem we must solve together is likely due to my own curiosity in the mortal realm, and my difficulty in staying away. Humans engage their souls in different ways than devils or angels, and I find their ingenuity fascinating. My travels have taught me many ways to make our realm a better place, but it may have opened up doorways that did not get properly closed."

Roche couldn't keep his eyes on her, even if she was the one doing the talking. Time and again his gaze drifted to the other Ximena, and basked in the glow of her smile while the other spoke.

"Can I do that?" he asked.

The question was one he posed mostly out of curiosity. Roche could not imagine dividing his attention between two minds right now, any more than he could manage to feel as though he was completely focused within one.

While the Ximena that had donned the cloak settled in the chair the other had vacated, the one he had spent the last several minutes alone with answered him as best she could.

"Maybe," she shrugged. "We each have unique abilities that arise when the need for them does, and perhaps one day you will need to inhabit two forms at the same time. This serves me by keeping some watch over Hell, or dealing with two levels of the realm at the same time. With the way time passes in some parts of every world, the last thing I can afford to do is vacate my office for a virtual eternity. But this will probably not be a need for you. More likely you will develop some power I don't have instead, to deal with your unique purpose as it becomes clearer to you."

She sighed, and looked at him entreatingly.

"I would ask that you keep my secret," she said. "Those that would take my place and my powers could easily use such knowledge against me, and seek to take advantage while my attention is divided. The only real way to keep a bunch of dragons from moving in is to make sure they fear me, and they would have little to fear if they should discover when I was divided. Should they learn when I am falling as well, combining their knowledge to overcome me when I must do both would be their best chance at my undoing."

It was strange how she could ask a promise; and he somehow felt as though she was doing him a favor if he made it.

"I will keep any secret you wish," he said, "although I must admit that the more I learn of you, the more of a mystery you become."

Roche paused, and remembered his question from earlier.

"When we were talking before," he said, "you told me we need to take them out. What do you mean by that? Are we going to go find the devils I stumbled across and send them back here through some kind of doorway? Like the ones you mentioned earlier? Did you mean take them out of the mortal realm? How are we to deal with them?"

The excitement in her gaze began to glow with mischief, as he had seen her eyes do before. While one version of her sat her chair and wore her cloak, the other smiled innocently as a giant axe with twin blades appeared suddenly in her grasp.

"We have to kill them," Ximena said.

She stated it in a tone that said it should have been obvious from the beginning, her voice completely without guilt as she contemplated taking multiple lives. When she saw how his face had fallen, Ximena stepped closer and smiled down at him where he sat.

"They won't actually die," she said. "Not like humans. They will disappear from the mortal realm, and reappear wherever they belong in Hell. We will go through the motions of killing them, but it is really just the easiest way to return them without opening even more unwanted doorways."

Maybe it was the easiest way. The gleam in her eyes suggested it might be otherwise, but it was hard for him to tell. Perhaps everything she did needed to be done, but the queen of Hell looked forward to certain aspects of her job in particular. If killing had to be done, he may as well recall his own excited reaction to battle in the past. Roche remembered the weapon he had stowed away in his mind for future use, and brandished it just as she asked her next question.

"You do know how to kill a devil, don't you?" Ximena said, then let her eyes go wide to reflect the glowing light of the angel's sword.

Roche nodded, pleased at her reaction. When a sudden opening appeared in the shape of a doorway to her right, he did not hesitate to follow her through the portal.

CHAPTER 23

He didn't think to wonder how she had known where they were going until it was all over. The world was dark when Roche came out the other side of the doorway she had opened, and he turned up his vision almost without thinking about it. As their surroundings went from shrouded darkness to stark detailed landscape, he wondered if her eyes were adjusting in a similar manner.

Recognizing the area immediately, Roche checked the woods around them before scanning the swamp for predators. Both were calm and quiet, and no living thing was nearby save the insects and vegetation. He spoke in full voice, to let her know they were alone if she didn't already.

"It's quite a walk from here," he said. "Also, I don't know where they might be at this hour. We're actually closer to my friend's house than we are to the structure the devils are having built. He lives in these woods, just off the road into town."

Ximena cocked her head to one side.

"Do you want to check in on him?" she said.

Roche shook his head.

"I think it's best not to get him involved in this," he said.

Stepping back, Ximena looked him up and down.

"Well," she said, "if you're going to walk around looking so much like an angel, maybe you should get accustomed to using your wings."

Two shadows rose behind her, smoky darkness that took shape as he watched. Each wing was bigger than Ximena, stretching out to brush aside branches on nearby trees as she flexed them to their full length. A cross between a dragon's wings and an angel's, they were beautiful and terrifying all at once. The sight of them awakened a part of his mind Roche had not been aware of, and his back began to tingle in a pleasantly painful way.

One moment he was standing there marveling at the dark beauty of her wings, and the next he had sprouted his own. Roche shifted his body to accommodate the sudden weight as his robes parted to let them spread, and glanced back over his shoulder. His eyes went wide with wonder.

"I have wings," he whispered.

Ximena giggled and began moving her own wings slowly. Her voice was swept toward him when she spoke, along with the pleasant tickling odor of brimstone.

"We all do," she said. "Devils and angels, and those of us that are something in between. Most devils do not use them, since the fear of falling is so common and intense among them; but most angels make up for that by flying nearly everywhere, as if touching their feet to the ground is beneath them."

Pumping her wings harder, Ximena began to rise. She hovered just a few inches above the earth, still looking up at him as she raised her voice over the flapping sounds.

"I try to spend time doing both," she said, "to remind myself that I am both angel and devil, and neither at the same time."

The sound grew louder as her wings moved faster. Now she was above him and looking down, while Roche felt his own wings stretch and flex behind him.

"Besides," she said, "flying gives us a perspective we can't get on the ground. We'll need that, to help us find what we're after."

Her wings blurred, the sound of flapping grew louder still, and her body was lifted up and over the treetops. The noise that had just assaulted his ears seemed dim and distant suddenly, and Roche began pumping his own wings as hard as he could. Leaves twisted on their branches in the draft, the force of his own movements swayed him from side to side, and Roche felt his feet begin to lift off the ground.

At first he headed right for a tree, and had to push off from its trunk as he adjusted the way his body was tilted. Branches crackled and snapped off as he extricated himself from the foliage, and he pumped his wings hard to get up and over the forest. Several minutes passed as he learned a hundred minor ways to shift in flight or change his speed with little effort. Ximena hovered above the treetops, watching him until he was confident enough to drift close to her.

The thunderous chorus of their wings beating in time echoed back at them from the woods below. Ximena gave him a moment to look around before she spoke, and he was glad she did. Everything looked completely different from up here. He had stood on the highest floor of the building he had worked on without quite being affected like this. From up there, his eyes could track the side of the structure as it dwindled from full size and close up to miniature and far off; it only made sense that the people walking the streets would look so small, and that a little vertigo would twist at his belly.

From up here, everything was distant and removed except Ximena. Nothing attached him to the ground, and if he stopped flapping his wings at any time he would fall quickly to the earth. Without turning at all, Roche could feel a twisting unease that made him long for the simple fear of falling. He had to grit his teeth to keep the terror from taking over his features, and he focused unseeing on a bright glow in the distance.

Finally the feeling passed, and he realized as it did that he was looking in the direction of the building he had been thinking of. That glow was the lights of homes and torches hung along lanes for late travelers. Ximena seemed to know when he had recovered himself, and she pointed in the direction his gaze had gone.

"Do you see what we are looking for?" she said.

Roche furrowed his brow, shook his head.

"I don't," he said. "I see the lights from the city, but I don't know where the devils might be."

Tilting her body slightly forward, Ximena began to fly in the direction of the glow. Roche did the same, keeping as close to her side as he could without getting their wings tangled. Still pointing, Ximena seemed to want him to see something specific.

"Don't look for light," she said, "or details of the city others can't see in the dark. Think of what a group of devils here might do at night, when the sun goes down in this realm."

Flying was exhilarating, but as he grew more accustomed to the feeling Roche was beginning to notice the little things he had brushed off before. The night air was clear and crisp, but also full of bugs. He was glad Ximena was not going too fast; the more they picked up speed, the more insects hit him as they flew in the other direction. Down on the ground, he had felt the usual chill of full night; up here it was colder, and Roche gave an involuntary shiver before he answered.

"Fire," he muttered. "A big fire, putting out lots of heat. That's where they'll be, laying around a giant stove or fireplace and soaking up the heat while they sleep."

He didn't know he could look for hot spots in the distant landscape until he tried to. Suddenly the torches along the streets were bright pinpoints, and people walking along them flickered like candle flames. A quick scan of the city showed him what Ximena must have been looking at all along, and he glanced over at her when he saw it.

"That's the structure they're building," he said. "They must have built a giant stove underground or something. The first couple levels are glowing with it."

Tilting forward a little more, Ximena picked up speed and called back over her shoulder as he lagged behind.

"They probably have a lookout," she cried. "We need to move in fast, and make sure none of them have a chance to escape."

Pumping his wings furiously, Roche moved up beside her and then past her. He picked up speed as the building drew closer, and saw that there indeed was a devil standing watch on the open rooftop. Dressed in full plate armor, he was facing the direction they were approaching from. The devil had his hands on his hips, and was peering into the darkness directly at Roche.

Without his ability to see in the dark and from such distance, the devil could not make him out. All he could see was layered shadows, and stars sparkling far off. He was looking at the noise Roche was making, gazing into space like he was trying to identify the sound. When his eyes finally widened in recognition, he turned and bolted for the stairs.

Roche had not noticed Ximena changing course, he was so intent on beating his wings as fast as he could. She had sped up, and ascended at the same time. While he was racing to beat the devil to the stairs, she was poised to strike directly over the rooftop. She stopped flapping her wings, and fell silently for several hundred feet into the path of the fleeing devil. Roche had nearly caught him when he saw her descending, and he slowed immediately so they would not all come together at once.

The devil looked back over his shoulder as he ran, and saw Roche behind him. His eyes widened, and he started to reach for the sword swinging at his side; then the falling shadow hit him, and he was gone in an explosion of concrete and dust. Roche settled his feet on the roof and waved away the cloud, kicking aside debris as he moved closer to the place she had hit.

Once he could see clearly again, he realized one of the pieces of debris he had kicked aside had been the devil's head. Blood oozed out of where his neck had been, and no trace of his body remained but some purple stains on the misshapen hunks of rock that were scattered in a loose circle around the point of impact. He stepped closer, and looked at the damaged floor.

A sizable hole had opened up where Ximena had struck, and he peered into the jagged aperture to see if she was on the level below looking up at him. Roche had to lean forward to see down into the opening, and he felt another twist of vertigo as he saw a similar hole in the floor below him. He bent at the waist, and inched forward to get a better look. The misshapen circles of destruction went on as far as he could see, impact after impact pushing her through the hardened stone in a series of violent explosions.

He stood over the gaping orifice, and stared down at the others for a long considered moment. Taking a deep breath, Roche leaned forward further and fell into the hole.

CHAPTER 24

Roche imagined himself descending smoothly through the series of violently created portals, to land gracefully on the underground level. Instead he pitched forward too far as he fell, and his forehead struck the jagged edge of the first hole. The impact sent him twirling backward, and he careened into the next floor headfirst. His body whacked into the edge of the following opening, momentum carrying his legs and feet into the yawning orifice. They dragged the rest of him after, and Roche bounced back and forth between the lip of the hole on the following floor.

When he tried to tuck his wings behind him, they caught on the exposed concrete and busted rocks free while twisting his fall uncomfortably sideways. One level after another passed him in a confusing shower of dust and gravel. Some came and went swiftly and with almost no contact, while others bounced him back and forth repeatedly before letting him by. Every part of him hit something along the way, but most of the strikes bludgeoned him about the head. Everything in his world was spinning and striking and falling for what seemed an eternity.

Even after he had struck the final floor, Roche could feel his head spinning for several seconds after his body had stopped falling. He reached out for purchase with tentative hands, sifting through dust and the pile of rock that had descended along with him. Everything was upside down, and blurry. Roche shook his head and blinked his eyes.

Turning over, he let the chunks of stone and sand shift onto the floor as his surrounding suddenly started to make sense. The stairs were over there, the only exit from an underground floor; the fire was on the other side of the room, and the devils were not clustered around it for heat at this point.

Ximena stood at the base of the stairs, and the devils were huddled together to get as far from her as possible. Roche had known they were in charge of the project, or at least the workforce; yet he had supposed there were only a handful of them altogether. His head was still ringing a bit too loudly for him to count them up, but he was surprised to note there were somewhere between thirty and forty devils occupying the space.

After another moment, Roche realized they were all looking at him.

His grand entry was not quite over, as falling dust and bits of concrete continued to drift down from the chain of disturbances he had caused on his way to the bottom floor. Even as he gained his feet and brushed clouds of it off his shoulders, more gravel and sand settled in its place.

Turning to his left, Roche turned his back on the devils to give Ximena his full attention. She looked both bigger and smaller than before, a tiny dark figure in a mass of darker shadows. The air around her churned with energy, inky blackness spiraling in a cloud of boiling darkness several feet in every direction. Above her, it loomed like a wave that threatened to break and wash the room away into nothingness; below her, the floor seemed to have turned to layers of shadows instead of sheets of stone.

Within the cloud, light crackled. Somehow it was the darkest part of the mass, electric bolts of utter black flashing in intricate networks only to disappear and be replaced by another sudden flash. Roche could see the afterimage of each flash for a few seconds, and when he blinked the darkness behind his eyes was layered in white lightning. He felt fear as he gazed at her, and supposed it was the natural reaction to seeing her power take visible form.

"My queen," a voice mewled behind him, "please, you must understand. We did not come here out of disrespect, or to cause any offense to you. We just wanted a better life."

Apparently the collective attention had shifted from him, and the pile of dust and rocks around him. Roche was glad. He turned to see which of them had spoken, and if his mind could wrap itself about their numbers. The first thing he noticed was that they all looked terrified, hunkered together as they were against the far wall. Even with the way the power was pouring off her, Ximena should not have caused that much fear in them. They were all just going back where they came from, after all.

"This is not your world."

Her voice caused him to turn again. The conversational tone she spoke with him was gone, replaced by a stern and unforgiving hardness. Whatever power was erupting constantly around her was in her words as well, and they crackled with intensity as Ximena went on.

"Life is meant to be a certain way for you," she said, "just as life is meant to be a certain way for souls in this realm. You have cast aside the way of life itself, for your comfort. Either you are aware that this is an affront to me, or you do not know who I am."

Roche could tell which devil had spoken now, when he pivoted to watch the group react. Every body that had huddled in one group now huddled in two, as they moved away quietly and quickly to leave one trembling devil standing alone. The devil didn't realize it was on its own until he glanced over his shoulder. With a sigh, he shook his head and dropped to his knees.

"Please," he said. "I know I must go back, but have mercy. Let me remember this place, and the life I lived here."

After doing a visible double take, Roche put his attention on Ximena once more. He was sure she would dial her fury back at least a little bit, and assure the devil he was in no danger of losing any part of himself. Instead he saw her eyes flash with anger, and each word she spoke was like a blow to his falling soul.

"You will forget this place," she swore, "but that is not all. You will also forget the time you spent in Hell before. You will be treated as a soul just arrived from the human realm, with all your memories evaporated along the way; except I will make certain you are placed even below new souls. This is the price of what you have done, living in a realm that you do not belong in. Whoever you were as a devil has been undone by what you were in this realm."

The devil was nodding the whole time she spoke, which Roche didn't realize until he moved to face that direction once more. His own jaw had unhinged without him realizing it, and he looked back and forth between them with his mouth slightly hanging open.

"Of course," the devil muttered, still on his knees. "I understand your feelings. A bargain, then. I will help save your henchman's pet, if you let me live here awhile longer. Maybe I could even help you find—"

The words were cut off in the same moment his head was. A sudden flash of black lightning exploded in the dark cloud around Ximena, and one tendril of electricity arced out to touch the base of his neck. He looked startled for a moment, when his voice failed him; then his eyes rolled back in their sockets, and his head rolled off his shoulders. The devil hit the floor in two pieces, one right after the other.

As the cloud boiled over, and black lightning began to darken the far corners of the room, Roche thought about what the devil had said. He'd had a chance to count them accurately before they began to fall, and Roche watched all thirty-six of them meet their gruesome end through a dim fog of mental molasses.

The first wave was random, an electric hand reaching long dark fingers out to touch a half a dozen devils as they huddled together. Their heads simply slid off their shoulders, and both clusters of trembling bodies were shortly covered in purple blood as it spouted from multiple falling fountains. A few desperate souls tried to rush her, and they were the next wave.

Roche realized somewhere between the following flash of lightning and the resulting fall of bodies that the devil had been talking about him when he referred to Ximena's henchman. Although he wasn't doing any of the actual work she apparently thought needed to be done, he had technically come along to join her in the violence. As eager as he'd been to draw his sword before, now Roche could only watch as another six heads left another six bodies and think of what the devil had said next.

A deep rumbling sound cut through the screams he hadn't realized he was hearing, and the crackling energy of Ximena's waves of destruction. Roche saw a couple devils look up at the ceiling, only to watch them lose their heads in the next moment. He saw that the tendrils of power were not just reaching the devils that were falling; they were bouncing off the walls and ceiling as well. In the same moment that Roche realized the devil had been referring to his friend's well-being, the floor above them began to crumble.

He could see wide cracks opening in the walls. Small pieces of gravel and stone began to rain down on them, followed by large hunks of stone. Roche glanced at Ximena, but could not get her attention. The darkness had swallowed her, growing around her until she was a bright face in a vortex of billowing black. Her eyes were drunk with the destruction, gazing past Roche and the falling debris as she struck again and again. He called out to her, nonetheless.

"Ximena!" he cried. "I have to find Adeb! I need to save my fr—"

A chunk of stone struck him on the head. Roche fell to his knees, startled. As he struggled to regain his footing, another larger stone broke loose above him and drove him to the floor once more. The steady falling stream of dust and debris buried him quickly, and the last thing Roche saw before the entire building came down on top of him were the last six devils in the clutches of Ximena's lightning fingers. They hovered above the floor for a long sickening moment, twitching in dark electric clouds as gravel and stone rained down on them from above; then their heads slid from their shoulders all at once, and their bodies tumbled to the floor.

Black lightning flashed one last time, and everything went dark.

CHAPTER 25

All of his parts were present, but they were not at all in the proper order. Roche could feel his face, flattened to the floor and surrounded by hard rock in every direction. The weight of the entire collapsed structure felt like it was bearing down on him; it might as well have been, for all the movement he was able to coax from his burdened body.

His arms were there, pinned to his side. The thick muscles in them could not even flex without painfully taking up more of their allotted space. Using them to sweep aside the crushed rock that held them in place was not just a difficult challenge for his powerful limbs; it was completely impossible. His legs may have been stronger, and more layered in sinew; but they were trapped as well, unable to do anything more than send his brain constant signals that they were in pain.

Giant broken stones had brought him down, and kept him there. Smaller rocks and gravel had filtered in around the giant stones, filling in the spaces between the weight holding him down. Finally sand and dust had found its way around the smaller rocks, stealing the very air from the cracks and crevasses around them. His breath had whooshed out of him with the first boulders that drove Roche to the floor, and the rest had fallen so quickly he had been unable to heave anything but dust into his lungs.

His torso was pressed into the floor on one side. Usually his abdomen was contoured with its strength, but now his chest and stomach formed a painfully straight line along the flat surface. On the other side, his back was pushed into unnatural shape marked by agonizing stabbing sensations Roche could only assume were sharp rocks that had pierced his skin. He couldn't move to verify that it was actually stabbing him deeply in several places; yet warm wetness surrounded each source of that particular pain, and he figured it was likely his own purple blood.

Even his thoughts were pushed painfully aside each time he tried to form them. Roche knew the right sequence of ideas had to parade through his mind to bring him out of this world and into another; that sequence would not come together for him, any more than his body could heal while jagged bits of stone were still lodged in the violent openings they had cut into him.

He was able to wonder if a rock had crushed his brain. If the part of his mind that made him all the things he knew himself to be was smashed flat under countless tons of rubble, Roche knew he might find himself stuck in this position for a good long time. Suddenly the frustration of dealing with his own dwindling presence of mind while moving about freely in whatever world he chose did not seem so bad. His mind could remind him how good he'd had it up until just a few minutes ago, but it would not pull together in a way that gave him full access to that diminished version of himself.

After awhile, he wondered if his powers had been slipping away along with his mental state. Trying to think back on the last time he had walked between worlds on his own made him think of Ximena's ability to bring him through, and thinking of that doorway made him think of the devil herself at considered length. She hadn't needed him to show her where the other devils had been, or to bring her from one realm to another; and clearly, Ximena hadn't required his help to deal with the transgressors.

In fact, the only thing that had come out of him tagging along had been the predicament he now found himself in. Roche had to wonder if all her friendly mannerisms had been an elaborate show, to lure him into a situation that would either kill him or nullify his ability to do anything for the foreseeable future. Whether she had orchestrated the events or not, the reality was the same: Roche was stuck, and every thought in his head was steeped in pain just like every muscle in his body was smashed in on itself and ravaged by jagged stone in every size imaginable.

He tried to remember the times he had climbed the stairs, to calculate exactly how much crumbled concrete was actually weighing him down. The process was the same as taking his body elsewhere: Roche could imagine the steps, but he kept getting stuck in a loop that showed the same images over and over behind his eyes. His own feet hitting the floor, climbing a flight of steps, with no end to the flight and no passing levels to count; then a bright burst of sunlight as he spewed onto the rooftop, followed by his own feet hitting the floor as he climbed another endless single staircase.

Tracking time was like counting steps, and Roche had no idea how long he lay there paralyzed before Adeb came to mind. Suddenly he was struggling like never before, but all the actual movement happened in his imagination. None of his limbs shifted in the slightest, and the only reason he knew they were still there was because every cell in his body was bursting with the pain of the constant crushing. Roche knew he may be his friend's only hope, even as he swiftly ran out of hope for himself. The stark nature of his helplessness brought him nearly to tears, but gravel and dust left no room for the droplets to leak out.

When he finally gave up, a strange kind of calm came over Roche. Just as Adeb had been squeezed from his mind for the longest time, he had not thought of Laurentis or the dragon's lessons since the rocks had trapped him in a state of complete immobility. Roche remembered how his own bodily awareness had seemed to shift when he turned his attention inward, and he longed for that disconnected feeling as dull aches and searing pain tried to tear his thoughts apart once more. He didn't need to close his eyes, since everything was already darkness; and he couldn't take a full cleansing breath, as the air had left his lungs long ago and not returned. Still he made the effort to clear his mind, and empty himself of thoughts altogether.

Somewhere in the middle of all that agony, Roche dove deeply into the darkness within him. He had been tense in a way he hadn't realized until he tried to relax, as if his entire body was still braced for the tumbling tons of stone and hardened crumblings of mortar. Pulling his thinking back helped him see that tension, and he released it only to feel more rock and sand settle in the space it made. Rather than rail against the new weight in his mind, Roche sank further into his own darkness just as the burden pressed deeper into his body.

Another brief eternity stretched out in front of him. The darkness went on forever, and Roche was reminded of the visions of vast endless nothingness that surrounded the mortal world he had seen when Adeb and Sela had wrapped him in their shared energy. He seemed to be traveling and floating in stillness at the same time, and long uncounted moments passed while he drifted in his own inner space.

Had he thought about it, Roche would have had to estimate that at least hours had passed since he had been trapped in the collapsing remains of the monolith. Even if he had discovered that days had gone by, he would not have been surprised. Time seemed to stand still as he drifted in his darkness, and Roche felt as though he was surrounded by everything and nothing simultaneously. It was not until he saw a pinpoint of light in the distance that the concept of minutes ticking by occurred to him.

The thought was as disconnected from his awareness as his physical form had become. A minuscule part of his mind made note of it casually as another tiny piece of him continued to feel the pain that imprisoned his brain as surely as the crumbled building had entombed his body. Roche was suddenly focused on the twinkling spot of brightness within him, and all thoughts of agony and timekeeping were swiftly washed away in the excited obsession. He tried to move toward the light, only to feel himself drifting away from it instead.

As the twinkling faded to a dull distant sparkle, Roche made note of where the light had been. Sure enough, the spot faded into darkness as he reached for it with everything he had, and he seemed to be once more turning slowly and helplessly in the middle of an endless nothing. He kept his mind on the spot, even as he spun about, trying to track the area despite the complete lack of surroundings to orient him. The harder he tried, the more uncertain he became; Roche finally had to admit that he was trying to hold onto the memory of a memory, one which he had long since forgotten.

His mind began to slip once more into the relaxed state it had been in moments or hours ago, before Roche had known there was something in the nothingness other than him. As tempting as it was to fall back into the shapeless pattern, something inside him began to twist in another direction entirely. Where seeds of peace had so recently been sown, he began to scatter all the pieces of rage within him in their place. The vast void around him started to bleed colors, and shifting shades of deep red and dark purple appeared around him in swirling shapes.

In his mind, Roche went back to the beginning. Instead of clear images from his past, he saw everything he had felt exploding in muted colors all around him. He relived his first moments, his own creator turning from him, and his sister soul blasting him painfully from her presence. The moments he had spent with Ximena were not happy memories, now; they were recalled with the knowledge that she had caused him to be here, and every kind word and gentle smile was another swirling vortex of betrayal in his inner dark night.

Roche even fumed at Laurentis in his mind, for daring to try to lead him to a place of peace rather than encourage him to erupt in chaos. Every careful lesson the dragon had imparted was as painful to recall as the cutting edge of Lilia's voice, and her undisguised hatred of him. In the darkness he saw them all conspiring behind his back, planning to poke him and prod him into complete uselessness and then to push him over the brink into utter helplessness.

All around him, Roche could see his rage taking swirling shape. The distant point of light had long since been lost in the ruddy vortexes surrounding him, and in his memory. His entire focus was on seeing the underlying theme in his life up to this point, and realizing he had been driven to a place where giving up was the only choice he had left. Not only had everyone he met betrayed him, life itself had dealt the most vicious blow of all simply by weaving him into its tapestry. His highway had been paved for him, and he had been driven to darkness by the hidden hand steering his wheel.

He didn't realize he was burning up until a bubble of flaming liquid popped beside him. The stone around his body was melting in the fire he was stoking within himself, and Roche felt the boiling wetness burn away rock and gravel and sand to deepen the molten puddle he was floating in. Roche felt a familiar ache rising up within him. Where it had caused him fear in the past, it now stoked his fury. In the same way the rising up had clawed at the edges of his identity, he eagerly and angrily scratched away the last vestiges of what he had been to make way for it. As much as he had fought to keep the feeling down before, Roche cast aside the reins he had held so painfully fast to.

The molten pool he was floating in began to churn around him. Waves of it lapped over his body, growing impossibly hotter as it washed away to be replaced by another wave. Roche could smell the stench of his own flesh as it began to burn; he clung to the hurting in every nerve ending like each point of agony was a long lost love, and steeped in his own suffering as his limbs dissolved.

From far off, the eruption looked natural. The ground shook with it, flaming bits of debris rose to collectively block the sun, and a rumbling boom filled the air for nearly a full minute. By the time the rumbling had ceased, liquid fire began to rain down from the sky. The day went from high noon to full night as fat plumes of smoke and drifting clouds of ash were carried in every direction on the wind.

At the source, the sudden concussive burst was a surprise to Roche. He thought he was disappearing, tearing himself apart with his few pointless powers that remained. First the liquid fire was consuming him, then it was rushing away from him and into the sky. Roche looked out not from his old eyes, but from an awareness that took in the whole of his surroundings in a flash of fire and fury. He rose from the earth like the flaming masses of what had been a great structure, half smoke and half fire that formed a towering blistering likeness of him.

Mortal eyes would have seen only smoke and fire, had they been fool enough to watch the blazing sky and lucky enough to dodge the falling flames; but only an angel's eyes were watching, and they saw the rumbling giant cut swaths of fiery destruction through the woods as it walked. Before that beam of rage had a chance to focus on him, the angel closed the door to the sight and walked into the middle of the small room that was still somehow large enough to hold a kitchen and dining table and hearth. He plucked a single feather from one of his wings and held it between his palms for a moment. Closing his eyes, he muttered a few words under his breath.

Before he placed the feather carefully on the table, the angel turned and spoke to the luminous being beside him.

"Just to focus my thoughts," he said, to explain the muttering.

He set the feather down, and went to the door again. As much as he might be disturbed by being in her presence, he wasn't sure they would both survive the next few moments if they stayed where they were. Giant flaming balls were raining down from the sky, and little ones as well; nearly everything seemed to be on fire, and the flames were the only source of light outside although it was midday. He turned to her, closing the door behind him.

"Ehcor," he said. "I think we better be going."

CHAPTER 26

Power was all he knew. His veins did not course with the energy; they had exploded with it. The strength he had known before was a thin slice of what he knew he could do now, a falling drop of rain next to a rushing tsunami. With a brief glance, Roche could sweep the countryside and see it all. If what he saw didn't please him, it caught fire as his attention moved to something else.

Very little of what he saw pleased him, and soon the landscape was painted in shades of flame in every direction. As far as his eyes could see, things that should not have burned sputtered smoke and melted; everything that could burn did, and the stands of trees surrounding the town became a forest of fire.

At some point he looked down, although looking down was not what it had ever been before. The dirt under his feet melted and flowed away in thick smoking waves of lava. Somewhere in all of it he saw the robes Ximena had given him, floating unharmed on the river of flowing fire. He willed it to burn, then to smolder, then to smoke just a little. The lava around the robes bubbled and spat out acrid plumes of smoke, but the fabric remained unharmed as it rode the next flowing wave away from him.

Roche turned his attention to the surrounding area once more, pleased to see that every structure in the town was a house of flame. As he moved away from the spot the building he had helped build had been, he had to climb slightly for several giant lumbering steps. Looking back at it, he saw a crater where the structure had once stood. Every stone had burned, the mortar had melted, and nothing remained but ashes and flames.

The power was not just intoxicating; it was consuming him. Roche had tossed aside the reins on his own rage only to find it had as much of a personality as he did. The power wanted to consume, to destroy, and to rule; it wanted to see the world on its knees before it, and Roche on his knees right there beside the world. Tight and focused, the desires of his rage were clear like his own had never been. Part of him wanted to step away entirely, and give complete control to the burning monster; the more time that passed, the more that part of him grew like the surrounding inferno.

He remembered Adeb, at some point during his fiery rampage; the thought was like a candle flickering in a world of leaping flames, and it moved to the back of his mind as surely as Roche had been moved to the back of the burning beast's. His own eyes would have been hard pressed to see through the clouds of smoke filling the air; but the monster could see far and wide by only thinking of it, and Roche watched behind his eyes as he surveyed the world.

One giant land mass had cracked under some other surely supernatural pressure, and began to float away in several pieces to put ocean between the lands. The fiery creature looked over them all in a glance, and saw where devils had come together. It looked to the sea, and saw the vast endless blue to the horizon and beyond; then it turned its attention to all the devils that had gathered and all the structures they had built, and it razed both bodies and buildings to smoking fire with a thought.

Roche knew it would be easy to give in to the monster. Like everything else, he could burn away to nothing; the flames would consume his identity, and the beast could roam the planet or extinguish itself in the sea; he did not care, so long as the burden of his falling soul was lifted from him. If his rage was so powerful that only it could kill him, maybe it was time to let it do the job.

The candle flickered in his mind once more, and Roche saw the last grasping tendrils of thought remaining to him drift to Adeb. He remembered the man, and his lessons; then he thought of his home, and realized the fires would reach it soon if they hadn't already. His mind went from the home to Sela, and instantly Roche became a small fire burning within the larger one.

Suddenly he had control of the lumbering body he had morphed into, and Roche was able to see past the flames and smoke to glimpse Adeb's house with the creature's far-reaching sight. He couldn't see inside, but he could see that it still stood. Swinging the giant flaming legs of the beast, he moved in that direction. His thoughts were far from clear, and he didn't realize he would burn the home and the woods around it just by getting close. By the time he stood over it and considered the possibility, the roof had caught fire in several places.

A hole soon opened up in the flames. Roche leaned over, and peered into the main room with the monster's eyes. He saw the hearth, the table where they had eaten so many meals together, and the simple stove Sela had used to create one delicious wonder after another. From the corner of his eye he saw the garden, consumed by weeds of fire; and the orchard beyond, flickering trees of flame. Fruits dropped from the trees as he watched, dripping fire from their shriveled blackened remains.

Looking closer, he saw blood on the walls. Streaks of it painted every surface, and pools of it gathered in several spots on the floor. Between two of the largest puddles of sticky red, a pristine white feather stood out in stark contrast to its burning and bloody surroundings. It sat on the floor, waiting to be found.

Roche reached through the hole, widening it with the monster's fiery forearm and setting the parts that had not been on fire alight. By the time he pulled his arm from the structure, it was a stand of smoldering cinders ready to collapse in on itself. Roche raised the feather to the sky before him, and willed the thing to burn.

Flames leapt up around his giant hands, liquid fire spewed in every direction from his outstretched palms; but the feather remained undamaged between his fiery fingers. Finally he gathered what little of his mind remained to him, and willed himself to follow the feather's trail.

In every direction around him, the flames leapt from one thing to another and set the world to burning. Even within him, the fire burned; and Roche let the rage continue to consume him as he set himself to accept the angel's invitation. His fire would rage in Heaven, as it had on Earth; and the first realm to betray him would burn as surely as the second one had.

The spinning upward vortex threatened to extinguish the flames that had become his arms and his legs, and Roche burned hotter as he stoked his mounting fury. Heaven would not tell him whether or not he could burn, and angels would learn to think twice before summoning an angry demon once this day was done.

He held onto the fire, and stood smoking on a high cloud in the next moment. Roche towered over the only other figure he could see, a winged angel with matching white robes bent over a desk made of mist and light. The angel turned at the sound of Roche blazing over him, and tried to leap from his clouded seat. Somewhere between sitting and standing his legs got tangled up in his robe, and the angel sprawled helpless at Roche's flaming feet.

"You can't..." he sputtered, wide eyes looking up at the burning beast Roche had become. "You shouldn't be able to..."

Although he was clearly terrified, the angel made no move to right himself. Instead he leaned away from Roche, and looked past him.

"Do something," he pleaded. "He'll destroy me."

Roche was leaning down, with full intention to do just that. The feather had burst into flame in his hand the moment he had arrived in this realm; he supposed the angel would do the same, once he got his fingers wrapped around his simpering little frame; then he would see how clouds looked when they were set on fire.

"Roche."

The voice came from behind him, small and quiet and as familiar to Roche as his own. He stopped leaning toward the angel, and straightened slowly. Although it had only been a single word, the sound had struck a chord in him that was resounding through his entire being. As he turned, he expected Ehcor to be facing him ready for battle. He was sure she could take some towering form equal to the one he inhabited, and he would not have been surprised to find a giant angel with a sword of light squaring off with him.

Instead, she was the size of any other angel. Her beauty was luminous, otherworldly in a way no angel could be; but she was in her original form, standing there completely small and utterly open to him. Her arms were outstretched, as if she felt she could embrace the full fiery effect of his burning fury.

Roche turned from her, and advanced on the fallen angel.

CHAPTER 27

Even with his back to her, even caught up in the fiery monster his rage had brought forth, Roche could not deny the effect she had on him. Echor spoke his name again, quietly. He slowed his approach, flaming embers dripping from his arms as they reached out toward the angel. Her next words hit him like love bombs, and Roche felt silent explosions of emotion within him cause him to straighten and turn once more.

"My brother," Ehcor said. "I am so sorry. Since the moment I lashed out at you, I have regretted it. We have lost so much time, so many moments we should have spent together. This is all my fault, my other, my brother. Your anger should be directed at me, not at humans or other angels."

Roche faced her, still towering over her. Looking up at him, Ehcor continued to hold her arms outstretched. She surely couldn't see that his reaction to her had started a battle within him. So long as Roche was willing to wreak havoc wherever they went, the burning beast had been fine with letting him be at the helm; now that Roche wanted to feel things like forgiveness, or at least love, the monster was ready to take charge.

His eyes met hers through the fire, and suddenly Roche knew: she did understand what he was fighting. A smile alighted her lips that said she would not be refused, and Ehcor threw her arms open wider. She took a step towards him, and Roche could see the blaze that was his body lighting her face.

"In that first moment," she sang out, "I knew nothing but the realm I saw around me. Seeing you frightened me, and I did not understand who you were until it was too late. I am not asking you to forgive me, brother; but I would do anything for the chance to make it right. I would give anything for the opportunity to…to know you."

From the outside Roche may have looked like a flaming giant standing in place and rocking back and forth, a fire elemental taking a break from the heat of its own destruction to soak up the cool sterile air in Heaven. Within, Roche was struggling with all his might to keep the monster from destroying him. The thing he had wished for such a short time ago was now the one thing he was bent on preventing, and the burning beast was not giving up without a fight.

Within the flames, they battled. Roche met the creature's fire with anger, and it answered with rage; he attacked it with fury, and it countered with a maniacal hatred. Pain crept into the tattered remnants of Roche's mind, and began to tear the fragments to shreds.

"I watched you from above."

Ehcor's words cut through the pain, brought pieces of him together that had been torn apart and soaked them in the healing balm of her musical voice. She could see what he was going through, and suddenly she was there with him in the midst of his agonized fragmentation. The presence he felt beside him spoke her words as her lips did, and Roche heard them clearly even as she delivered them softly and quietly.

"I saw you with humans," she went on. "I saw you learn from them, and love them. I was glad for you, and envious at the same time. I wanted to be the one you were coming to care for, I wanted to be learning with you as it should have been. My lessons in this realm have been many, but every one of them has been incomplete without you."

Somewhere in all of it, her words and the searing pain without end, Roche thought of the space he had inhabited while trapped under rubble and the star he had seen twinkling in the distance. He had supposed letting down his guard would mean losing who he was forever, but suddenly he got the sense that his fighting was only feeding the fiery monster. Roche let down the walls he had put up around his mind, focused on the sound of Ehcor's voice and began to release every little tension he had summoned up to ward off the pain of battling the beast.

At first it was timeless torture, slow searing hurt turned white hot agony as waves of the creature's presence washed over and through him. When Roche did not tense up to resist, the pain burned deep furrows into his mind and threatened to once more begin tearing him apart. Roche let the feeling come, and go; then he opened his mind up further, and let the fire inside. He welcomed it, flinging his mental arms wide as Ehcor had done with her own limbs. This was his rage, and either it was going to consume him or he was going to hold it so close to him it became part of him again.

"My brother," Ehcor repeated, "we should have learned these worlds together, and because of me we did not. Please, let us have the time with each other we both deserve. Do not destroy me before I have the chance to show you how I really feel about you, how I cherish the thought of knowing you."

She was his star in the distance, rushed up close to shine her brightness directly on his soul. Roche felt the monster he had become break as she fell silent, and in the next moment his awareness became cluttered with a thousand thoughts the beast had burned from his mind. Rather than feeling himself emerge from the dying fire, Roche could feel all that hate and rage condensing once more to the size and shape he had carried it around in before.

From up high, Ehcor looked like a child's toy, an animated doll with wings and outstretched arms. As the flames guttered into crimson skin, Roche came down to nearly eye level with his sister soul. He took a step toward her, smoke still drifting from his naked torso, and collapsed onto the clouded floor at her feet.

Roche considered the possibility that it was a trap, and she had said the words to stop his mindless rampage; he almost didn't care, and he laid his head down on the soft yielding surface to await the leagues of angels set to descend upon him and finish the job she had started. No angels came, except her; Ehcor knelt beside him, then sat with her legs crossed and lifted his head into her lap.

"Relax," she murmured. "There is nothing to fear here. You belong in this place, as much as any angel."

Turning his head, still feeling the softness of her robes cradling its weight, Roche cast his eyes up at her and sighed.

"What you said..." he began, eyebrows arched hopefully.

Ehcor held his gaze, her eyes level and open and beautiful.

"You meant all that?" he whispered.

Her nod detonated another series of love bombs within him, and Roche felt the delightful explosions filling the furrows etched into his mind by the agony that had finally passed. Like fresh cool water, the soothing feeling washed over him and through him. Roche sighed, involuntarily, as she reached her hand to his forehead and began to stroke his skin with the softest touch he had ever known. The calm and loving presence she exuded was not just all around him; somehow his sister was inside him, and every touch of her fingers on his skin fed his soul. Roche felt his eyes fill with tears, as he closed them and rested the weight of his head completely in her lap.

The monster he had become was forgotten, along with every pain that had prodded him into a blazing rage. Only peace existed for Roche in that sublime moment, and he had lost the awareness of where he was and what had brought him here. Just as he had felt the temptation to let the blazing beast burn him away along with everything else, he now felt the desire to let go of everything but the love all around and within him. That had felt like a sure path to losing himself forever, while this felt like the only way to find himself once and for all.

Although he occupied the same clouded surface, Roche had let any thoughts of the angel he had been advancing on slip away along with his awareness of everything else. When he heard the angel's voice calling out across the luminous mist, at first the sound didn't even register. Only Ehcor's response found its way into his ears, into his soul; through that response he understood the angel's words, and his fear.

"Ehcor," he cried to her, his voice strained. "You need to get away from him. He is dangerous, even to you."

Speaking to Roche, her voice had been a healing balm poured over his boiling rage; her words to the angel had an even more profound effect, bursting through the dams in his heart to fill the deepest pools of Roche's inner emptiness. His mind was not just clear; it was silent, as the brilliance of her love chased away the darkness within him.

"This is my brother," Ehcor said, soft but scolding. "I lashed out at him, and sent him away to walk between worlds alone with only that memory of me. If he wishes to destroy me, he should have that opportunity; if my other does not think I should exist any more, I have no desire to go on. But if he wants to come to know me as I want to know him, he should have that chance as well. We both should. We are the same."

She traced her fingers lightly between his horns.

"Leave us," she went on, "if you are afraid. I do not fear him, even if he is one of the few things in all the realms that can hurt me. That means I am one of the few things that can hurt him, and I have already done too much of that. I will stay with my brother, so long as he wishes."

Roche didn't lift his head to see if the angel left them alone together. Nothing else existed for him in the next few eternal moments, but his head on her lap and her touch on his skin. He relaxed into both, and let himself float forever in the bubble of her love.

CHAPTER 28

Roche could not measure the time he spent with his head in her lap and the soft touch of her hand on his rough scaled skin. In some ways those moments would last forever, and he knew as much while he was living them. Her presence overlapped his in more ways than one, and they felt each other's deepest feelings and longest thoughts in that shared space.

She had risen as he had fallen, and he could see every bitterness and disappointment within him matched by love and forgiveness within her. Constantly falling had dug deep trenches in his inner landscape, and he let them be filled with the rush of love Ehcor was pouring into him. The pulsing glow of her radiant presence became almost too much, as her rising tide swamped the banks of his rivers of turmoil. He shared the whole of his life with her, until he felt his own identity begin to slip away on the muddied shores of his own mind; she seemed to be doing the same, opening up to show him the way she had lived without him.

Nearly all her life had been spent learning. Roche could see the lessons in her memories: he watched her paying close attention to every detail of what sounded to him like a bunch of ideas that had gone stale somewhere between being written down and being passed to her. The attention she gave the lessons was of greater interest to him than what she had learned; one of the first things he had realized was that each being has their own perspective, some of which is true and much of which may not be for someone else. His sister soul had been robbed of that vital teaching by having only one teacher.

The angel had not left them. Looking into Ehcor's thoughts, Roche realized he was not going to. Every moment he saw in her memory, the angel was there; every lesson she remembered had been recited in his tone, in his cadence. So many of the thoughts in her head were his, and his voice sounded in her mind as often as her own.

Roche knew the angel, although he had not recognized him before. He was the one whose feather had invited him back to Heaven, and had greeted him on the other side of the gates. The angel's name had not been important then, and he hadn't asked; now he saw it in her thoughts, and lifted his head to address the angel by it.

"Trethis," Roche said. "You have done more harm than good here."

He wanted to lay his head on her lap again, and lose himself in her soft glow; but Roche saw the angel begin advancing on them, his fists clenched at his side.

"You were supposed to be here," Trethis spat. "I tried to make sure you were near her in the beginning, like you were supposed to be; you were the one who balked, and decided to live amongst them instead."

Trethis said the word 'them' like it tasted bitter on his tongue, and accompanied it with a wave of his hand indicating everything under them. Roche considered asking if the angel meant humans or devils; then he reconsidered, and realized it was likely both.

"I needed experience," Roche said.

Rising from the clouded floor, Roche looked down at Ehcor before he went on. Her eyes were the color of the sky, and her radiance made her delicate features swim in and out of focus for him. For a moment he thought he saw a touch of sadness at the corner of her eyes, and a slight frown on her lips; but it was hard to tell, and he quickly looked away. When he had reached his full height, Roche took a step forward to deliberately tower over Trethis.

"Each realm is endlessly varied," Roche continued, "in its own way. She needed to learn that, the only way she could. All your dusty books and ancient lessons can't do that, no matter how much time or attention she gives them."

The angel snorted, and shook his head.

"This is Heaven," he said. "Our books do not get dusty."

They faced off, devil and angel staring hateful daggers at each other while Ehcor glowed quietly behind them. Roche was clenching his fists, as he had seen the angel do; the muscles in his naked body flexed with the motion, drawing sinewed cords of tension across his chest and abdomen.

"You have kept her here," Roche snarled. "You have treated her as a prisoner, instead of the unique and powerful being she is. You cannot teach her the things she needs to live in order to learn, and keeping her here only prevents her from being who she is meant to be."

Although he was clearly cowed by Roche's dominating physical presence, the angel did not back down. Instead of clenching his fists at his side, he folded his arms until his hands disappeared into the sleeves of his robe. He glanced past Roche at Ehcor, as if to remind her of when he had predicted this; then he frowned fiercely and returned his attention to Roche.

"You will learn," Trethis said. "There are rules here, and everyone must follow them. Who or what you are does not make you special, in this realm. It is what you do that elevates you here, and earns you the respect of other great souls. Your time here with us begins now, and that is the first lesson I have for you. Put aside your own arrogant viewpoint, and let a wiser mind take the helm of your soul."

Roche matched his frown, and let the angel feel the fire that burned in his eyes while they stared each other down.

"Do you mean yours?" he said. "You want me to replace my thoughts with your own, and keep me imprisoned here like you have her?"

Keeping his gaze locked on Roche's, Trethis shook his head.

"She is not a prisoner," he said.

Roche took another step toward him, clearly breaching the angel's comfort zone although he did not back away.

"Then let her go," Roche murmured. "Let her leave this place with me, and explore the other lessons this life has to offer."

They had been so focused on each other, neither of them had noticed Ehcor rising from the floor and moving

forward to stand behind Roche. She spoke suddenly, and they both turned to the sound.

"Trethis," she said. "Let us have some time together, alone. Allow me to explain what has happened, and how we can find our purpose here."

The angel shook his head.

"Absolutely not," he said. "He needs to learn how we do things here, and not expect to be coddled. Besides, he is clearly a danger to both you and himself. In light of recent events, the last thing I can allow is for you to be alone with the greatest threat to your existence that we know of. I have been authorized to keep him here using any means necessary, but leaving you alone with him is neither necessary nor an option."

Ehcor sighed, and hung her head. Looking back and forth between them, Roche felt his anger grow along with his curiosity.

"What are you talking about?" Roche demanded. "Are you saying I am your prisoner, and that you plan to keep me here by force?"

He almost laughed; but there was no humor in the way the angel shrugged, as if he was considering doing just that.

"Why?" Roche heard his own voice ask, almost in a whisper.

Turning away from him, Trethis strode to the edge of the cloud they stood on. Wispy walls turned to windows, and he indicated the world below with a wave of his hand.

"Do you not realize what you have done?" Trethis said. "Are you not aware of the destruction you have wrought, or the consequences of unleashing your rage on the mortal world?"

Ehcor moved quickly between them, placing her body between Roche and his view of the scene below. Spreading her wings, she opened her arms to him as she had done before.

"Please, brother," she said. "Come to me. Place your head on my shoulder, and let me tell you what you will see before you see it. Allow me to put the sight into perspective, before it floods your heart with grief."

The way she put it, Roche could not help but feel the allure of losing himself in her lighted aura again. Surely they could exist in that state forever somehow, as that tiny piece within him was so determined to do. The thought that pulled him from the pleasant reverie was how beautiful the world of humans had always been to him, and how each of their bright souls seemed to burn all the more brightly for how quickly they were snuffed out. He saw Adeb's face in his mind, and Sela's.

Roche pulled his eyes from hers, walked around Ehcor and moved to stand beside Trethis. As he passed her, he glanced her way; this time he could definitely see the sadness in her eyes.

CHAPTER 29

At first it was hard to see anything but smoke. Thick dark clouds of it hung in the air between them and the earth below, layer on layer of black rolling heat. As Roche focused his attention downward, the smell of it wafted into his nostrils somehow.

He breathed deeply, and thought of Hell.

Whatever made his vision work at night was able to spear through the smoke as well, and Roche looked despite not really wanting to. The smoke was enough to give him a hint of what he would see; gazing through it would only drive the point home. Nonetheless, he looked.

As far as his eyes could see, everything was burning or burnt. He scoured every square mile of the giant broken land mass with his broad vision. From this vantage point, it was easy; he saw the whole world, or at least all the places people could live. What he didn't see were those people, or any evidence they had ever existed. If he hadn't been looking the way he was, everything would have been dark as well; the smoke from fires long since burnt still filled the sky everywhere, and fresh acrid waves of it were rising to join them as he watched. He couldn't tell if it was day or night there, even from up here.

Roche tore his eyes from the charred remains of the realm below, turning his attention to Trethis. The angel stood there with his arms crossed inside his sleeves, ignoring Roche and continuing to eye the wretched landscape. Disappointment was etched clearly in his features, and the forlorn lines of his face.

"Did I do that?" Roche whispered. "All of that?"

The only answer he got from Trethis was that sad expression, and a slight shaking of his head. Roche didn't think he was saying no, with the gesture; he sensed it was just another way for the angel to express his judgment of the scene below. His vacant stare was still pointed in that direction; and he didn't pay Roche any mind at all until Ehcor stepped forward.

"Tell him," she said. "Tell him everything, or let me. Keeping him in the dark will not benefit anyone any longer."

Trethis scoffed, audibly; he untangled his arms from their folded position to gesture slowly at the world below once more. His eyes remained downcast while he moved, and responded.

"They have to live in the dark," he said, "for hundreds of years. Perhaps he deserves to share their fate, for at least a little longer."

Moving closer to both of them, Ehcor couldn't help but cast bright spears of light into the thick smoke beyond their clouded footing. In the places where it struck, the dense clouds seemed to dissipate. Roche couldn't tell if it was drifting to another bank of noxiousness, or evaporating to nothingness; and he was having trouble keeping his thoughts in some proper order. Every time she came too close, she seeped into him; as much as it felt like she was driving away the darkness within him like so much smoke, he seeped into her as well.

And when she spoke, he nearly lost himself completely.

"Are we here to judge him?" she said. "Is it our place to mete out punishment, or are we supposed to be helping him? Have your plans changed since you made them? Have they changed since last we spoke of them? Have you?"

Ehcor was watching him with the same crestfallen expression the angel was gazing down with. When he turned to her, Trethis saw it and sighed. He shook his head a few times, and nodded slowly.

"You are more of an angel than I am," he murmured.

His response seemed to frustrate her, and they held each other's gaze for nearly a full minute. Some unspoken communication flowed between them, and both angels appeared to be thinking their own thoughts while being aware of what was on the other's mind. Ehcor broke the eye contact at last, and turned to Roche. She opened her mouth to speak.

"I will tell him," Trethis said, cutting her off.

Another silent exchange followed, as the angels debated each other using only their expressions. Ehcor peered at him with insistence, couched in the kindness always present in her face. His look was one of practiced patience, a kind but unyielding set of his features; it was the expression of someone who is accustomed to getting what they want, and is tired of always having to wait for it.

After several moments of this, Ehcor sighed and nodded. Bowing her head, she stepped back and settled her eyes on the clouds at her feet. Trethis inclined his head in return, still looking slightly annoyed that he'd had to overcome the hurdle of her thoughts in the first place. Turning his attention from her completely, he faced Roche and sighed.

"You began what you see below," Trethis said. "You brought a fire to the world of humans that is not easy to extinguish in that realm, and spread the flames quickly across the land you walked."

He sighed again, and stole a glance at Ehcor. She felt the attention, and raised her sky eyes; the insistence was there again, and she waited for him to nod some silent agreement before lowering them once more.

"Most of what you see," Trethis went on, "is not the direct result of that fire. Other events followed, natural events that cannot be directly attributed to you. Although many of us are of the opinion that you began a chain reaction, which would make you responsible for all of it, I am obligated to inform you we cannot prove that is the case."

The angel harrumphed, and hid his hands in his sleeves.

"Regardless," he said, "I have been charged with keeping you here, and given the authority to use force to do so if I must. At this point it doesn't matter who is at fault for the wreckage that is the human realm; we must take great care in preserving what remains. If another incident like that happened, it could wipe them out completely."

Roche had been lost in his thoughts for several minutes, watching the way the two angels interacted while trying not to let the light from Ehcor chase away his identity completely. Part of him wanted to feel her, always; but the rest of him needed to see what he had done, and plumb the depths of his subsequent remorse. He had been imagining the world below was dead, as it appeared to be from where he stood; when he heard the angel say otherwise, Roche felt his mind desperately latch onto the idea.

"They're not all gone?" he murmured hopefully. "I saw no survivors. Did my eyes deceive me? Are there humans left down there?"

The questions hung in the sterile air between them, while the angel made a show of slumping his shoulders and casting his eyes below once more. He looked like he was about to speak, when another thought struck Roche suddenly.

"What of my friends?" Roche demanded. "What of Adeb, and Sela?"

The angel appeared to be gearing up for another round of heavenly drama, and Roche was prepared to endure it; but Ehcor broke suddenly, and sputtered audibly.

"Just tell him!" she cried.

That earned her a fresh look of disapproval from Trethis, but Ehcor was not paying him any mind. Her attention was on Roche, and he felt her light pouring into his soul as her words flowed into his ears.

"Your friends are dead," she said, not unkindly. "But you did not kill them. Trethis and I went to their home, to intercept you there and try to have words with you in a setting that was comfortable and familiar to you. When the fires began, they somehow knew it was because of you. They asked us to help them get away, so they could find some place to live out the rest of their lives in peace."

Stepping between them, Trethis clarified in his own way.

"Away from you," he interjected. "They wanted to go somewhere they could be away from you, and all the consequences of having you in their lives. That's why we brought you here, to this level of the celestial realm. Time passes more quickly here, and they were able to live out their natural years as moments passed for you."

Roche shook his head.

"I was there," he said. "I saw blood on the walls."

With a smirk and a nod, Trethis answered.

"Everything was burning," he said. "Wildlife had thrown caution to the wind in its need to escape the flames, and your friend was easily able to catch and kill something. He splattered the blood of a boar on the walls, to make you think they were dead. That's how badly they wanted to get away from you."

Now he could see it, as Roche looked down at the lower realm: the smoke was shifting too quickly, fires burned with unnatural speed and guttered out just as suddenly. It was no wonder he hadn't seen any people; they had surely found shelter, or gone underground. Any foray onto the scarred surface of the natural world would be brief, and would not even register as a flicker as he watched at high speed.

A hundred questions raced through his mind, leaving tracks in the darkness within him; it had gone a shade darker at the news of his friends, and was seeping in to his every thought to spiral them downward. Ehcor's words barely reached him, and seemed to have no effect at first. Outwardly he stood, staring at the dense smoke below and letting what she had to say next sink in.

"They lived a hard life," she said, softly. "But it was a good one. Trethis watched them, and so did I. Your friends were clever enough to build a good life, even given the conditions they had to build it in. At first they found others and helped them; in fact, they may have been instrumental in making another rise in humanity possible. But after a few years, they went off to live alone together. They fell even more deeply in love, and were able to have a closeness they could not have experienced in their old life."

Part of what he saw, through the smoke below and the darkness under that, were the places where the land ended and the sea began. Roche watched the ocean lapping at one shore, then another; he realized the vast expanse of water he had seen in the past was escaping his vision in this place. Before, he had been able to look at the seas; both in Heaven and in his giant fiery form, he had made note of them. Now they were beyond his vision somehow.

Roche met her light eyes with his dark gaze, and nodded once in thanks. She bowed her head, and stepped back. At first Roche thought it was a habitual movement, she was so accustomed to giving ground to the other angel; then he realized she knew what he needed to do, and was allowing it.

Thinking of the dark wetness beyond the dense smoke he could see below, Roche stepped closer to the edge of the cloud.

"What are you doing?" Trethis demanded.

He angled himself between Roche and the opening in the clouded wall, barring him from going further. Roche was tempted to lift him bodily, as he had so many others; but his swift and violent reactions from the past continued to burn, both below and in his thoughts. Instead he sighed, and turned his attention to Ehcor.

In the same moment, Trethis turned to her as well.

"You must stop him," the angel told her. "You heard what I said, what they said. We are to keep him here, against his will if we must; and I can use any means available to me to do so."

Her face was without expression, tilted slightly forward to keep her gaze on the clouds. Although all eyes were on her, Ehcor's were on the fluffed flooring. Trethis shifted uncomfortably, as if he was suddenly aware of how close he was to Roche and how much smaller he was than the devil.

"Please," he hissed. "You must stop him."

When she finally raised her eyes, they alighted on the wall around the opening to the world below. Ehcor raised her arms, and rays of brilliant light erupted from her chest. The rest of the wall dissolved, as she spoke to the angel without looking at him.

"I am not your weapon to wield," she said. "And I am not my brother's enemy. I will certainly not be his jailer."

They met eyes one last time, Roche watching her with wonder while she gazed at him lovingly. When the light became too much for him, and Roche feared he may end up imprisoned by his own desire to be by her side, he looked away and down at the other angel.

Trethis frowned fiercely, alternating his glare between them.

One short step took Roche around him, and two more forward brought him to the edge of the cloud. Resisting the urge to glance back once more, Roche thought of the vast salted sea.

He leaned forward, and fell.

CHAPTER 30

This time when he fell, Roche had plenty of opportunity to think as minutes ticked by. He thought back over the sights he had beheld from the elevated eyes of the burning beast, and how he had seen them in Heaven once but not again. Reassuring himself that the furthest reaches of the sea had been beyond even the monster's vision led him to think of why he may not have been able to see it from above. He felt the warmth of his own assurances melt away in the smoky night air.

Although he could remember seeing activity on the surface of the waters in the past, Roche could not be sure there were still vessels floating out there. He was sure his intention would land him near one, if one existed to land near; but otherwise all he was picturing was the vast endless expanse that had escaped his fiery eyes and his view from Heaven.

He fell for long enough to begin to wonder if he had made a wise choice, and to question that choice at rather a cool and uncomfortable length of time. Shudders racked his body as Roche fell through smoke and chill, until he could feel the air warming as it whizzed by him. At first he thought of it as balmy evening air, until he remembered the smoke and the fact that he could not tell if it was day or night. Despite the speed at which he fell, Roche began to feel the warm air begin to get downright hot as he fell through it faster and faster.

By the time he hit the water he was really moving. Roche saw the impact of his body on the surface create a giant sudden opening in the otherwise calm sea. For a moment the water surrounded him like a bubble, encasing him in cold wetness without actually dousing him; then he burst through the encasement, and shot dozens of feet into the ocean. Salty water and streaming bubbles were his whole world, and the sea seemed to be sinking into his skin as Roche swiftly plumbed its depths.

The momentum of his fall wore off, only to leave Roche stranded directionless under tons of ocean. He swam, if you could call it that, for the first time ever. Flailing his limbs at first, he calmed down after a minute and began to work his arms and legs in tandem in some way that seemed to move him in a definite direction. After another minute he let some air from his lungs, and felt the bubbles rise past his face through the dark water.

Following the bubbles, Roche kicked and swept his arms through the sea until he broke the surface. Right away he heard shouting, and the clamor of boots on wood above him. Roche blinked away the salt stinging his eyes, and looked up while treading water.

At first all he saw was a giant shadow looming over him, punctuated by dozens of smaller ones peering down at him. Roche turned up his vision, and it all came clear: the boat was bigger than any house he had seen, but shaped to cut through the waves. Only twenty or thirty faces were looking over the edge at him, but that was all the room allowed by the nearest railing; Roche knew as many as a hundred humans could fit on the floating structure with ease.

He tuned into the shouting, and met eyes with some of the peering faces; the language was unfamiliar and completely understandable at the same time, and he listened as waves lapped at his face. Some of the voices were calling out, asking what had caused the explosion of water; they came from beyond the railing, on the deck Roche imagined to be full of curious onlookers who couldn't see. Others complained of themselves or something they were doing getting drenched, but most of the unseen voices were asking what had happened.

When the faces he could see turned away from him and shouted back, they said a man had fallen in the water. Laughter came in answer, and questions about how big a man had fallen overboard. A couple names were sprinkled in, apparently suggesting some of the larger members of the crew. Every guess was answered with a chuckle, and in the negative; until one voice rose above all the others.

"Well, who is it then?"

Something about the way his words carried and seemed to sound on a different frequency than the others caught Roche's attention. He watched men drifting apart at the railing, and saw another appear where the space opened up. A full head taller than any of the others, he leaned over the railing and met eyes with Roche.

Roche didn't think the cold water was what had caused him to shiver; that cold reptilian stare could not be mistaken for human, but the rest of him could. By all accounts, the man looking down at him was just that, a man; but Roche could see the devil in his eyes, and hear it in his voice.

"You're not one of mine," he called down, casually.

Shaking his head, Roche treaded water.

"I'm not," Roche said.

The devil made a big show of looking around, scanning the sea slowly as if he were looking for something he knew wasn't there.

"I don't see any other boats," the devil noted. "What did you do, fall from the sky?"

Roche paddled, and nodded.

"Something like that," he said.

Squinting his eyes, the devil was looking right at him; still, Roche could tell he couldn't see. Since leaving this realm the last time, he had worn no disguise; in fact, he had worn nothing at all. Just as he had confronted the angel in Heaven naked, he was swimming naked in the sea. Yet the devil was clearly more surprised by where he came from than what he was, and that made no sense.

In his mind's eye, Roche saw himself clawing his way up the wooden hull and leaping onto the deck, or exploding from the water with wings spread to drench them in seawater as he descended on them. He tried to put his desire to act so immediately and violently aside, and show the devil with his eyes that he would resort to such measures if it came down to it.

Still, Roche could tell he couldn't see.

Letting the rage rise within him just a little bit, Roche felt his eyes begin to burn with fire. He swished his tail in the water behind him, and lifted his arms above the waves so the devil could see his scaled skin.

Even with all that, the devil stared dully for several seconds as Roche began to reverse his efforts and calm himself. It wasn't until Roche felt the fire in his eyes begin to die that the situation seemed to register with him, and the devil motioned to someone behind him.

"Toss a rope in," he called out. "Pull him up."

CHAPTER 31

Voices reached his ears before his feet found the deck. Roche heard the first of them as soon as he cleared the water, complaining that he obviously had no purse and no possessions; how could he, if he wasn't even wearing clothes? The speaker thought it was good reason to throw him back in, as did a few others nearby.

More voices floated down to him, pointing out that there was not enough food aboard even for them; the last thing they needed was a giant man with an enormous appetite fighting them for scraps. He was nearly to the railing when he heard swords being drawn and the conversation moving to more macabre suggestions. At first he thought they must be joking, talking about eating him or throwing him back; later he would realize they were the only real options they had.

Roche nearly leapt the last few feet, launching himself over the railing to land amongst them and dash any ideas of overwhelming him aside. Again he remembered the consequences of acting quickly, and let the rope drag him up until he could grab the ledge. Slowly and with great care, he pulled himself up and over it to lower himself to the deck. His feet were quiet but for a dull squishing sound, and he deliberately folded his frame slightly to appear smaller.

It didn't help.

"You see?!" one man cried, exasperated. "No purse, no coin, not even any clothes! We should throw him back in!"

The devil was nearby, and stood taller than Roche in his hunched posture; he shifted uncomfortably, and looked back and forth between the rumble of agreement and his wet naked new passenger. Roche kept his eyes averted from the others, but he did flash a quick glance at the devil; he seemed to be dazed, trying to remember why he had pulled Roche aboard and why he shouldn't throw him back in now.

"Are you the captain of this vessel?" Roche asked.

His voice was quiet and slow, just like his limbs and head when he shifted. The others were drawing in closer to Roche, encouraged by his slumped spine and molasses movements. His bulging muscles should have kept them at a safe distance, and his height should have cowed them no matter how much he stood in a way that disguised it; but they moved steadily closer, and Roche had to speak in even lower tones to make sure his words reached only the captain's ears.

"Take me to your quarters," he said. "Away from them."

Lifting his head to meet the devil's eyes, Roche tried to impress the damage he could do upon him with the intensity of his stare. The devil stared back at him, uncomprehending. He narrowed his eyes, and shook his head.

"This is my crew," the devil called out. "They can hear whatever you have to say."

Roche shook his head, lowering it to the muted sounds of cheering.

"I could kill you all," Roche muttered.

He didn't care if the devil heard him, and part of him wanted them all to come at him at once. Holding back the rage, moving slowly and mumbling almost silently, he went on.

"They're all so close," he said. "Before you finish this breath I could kill them all, and your next breath would be nothing but smoke as your little boat burned. And that breath would be your last, if I wished it."

Leaning in close, the devil nearly shouted in his ear.

"What's that?" he said. "Speak up, we can't hear you."

Roche gritted his teeth, took a deep breath. He kept his eyes on the deck, until he had finished speaking.

"We need to talk," he said. "Some tales should not be told in the light of day, and you need to decide if your crew is up to hearing this one."

When he did look up, Roche let the fire burn in his eyes once more. The devil peered at him for a long confused moment, then began to nod ever so slightly. Roche could see the remembrance dawning in his gaze at last, and he was afraid another outburst from any of them might throw him back into dazed forgetfulness.

As if his thought had created the reality, one man started laughing and clapped the captain on the back abruptly.

"What light of day?" he cackled. "None of us have seen the light of day in our lifetimes. Our parents may have told us of their parents telling them of it, but they never took it seriously. Day is dark, night is darker. That's the way it is, and always has been."

A dozen heads bobbed in agreement, voices murmuring assent. Roche held the devil's gaze the whole time, reminding him what they both were.

"Come," the devil grunted. "We will talk, and then I will tell my crew what they need to know."

Waving his hands, the devil raised his voice.

"Go on," he called out. "Get back to work. Pull up the nets, see if we are eating fish tonight."

He pointed at two men standing nearby, and motioned for them to follow him along with Roche. At first he thought to protest; looking at them more closely, Roche realized they were devils as well. Their costumes did not do much to disguise them, if that's what they were; even with cloth wrapped about their heads, their skin was scaled crimson; their loose trousers may have kept their tails from view, but they were clearly moving around under there. The only thing stranger than their crew mates not noticing what they were was Roche not realizing it until now.

Together, they flanked him all the way to the other end of the vessel. The captain's cabin was the only enclosed structure on deck, taking up the frontmost section of the ship. From the outside, it was wide enough to suggest it might go on for some ways; once the devil opened the door, Roche could see that even the most stately quarters on the boat were oddly shaped and a bit cramped at best.

The devils behind him shoved him the last few feet, through the doorway and into the tight space. Roche kept his movements slow, and let his feet stumble awkwardly across the threshold. Again, he felt a cluster of bodies around him; they were too close, too sure he couldn't move any more quickly than he was. The last one in closed the door behind them, and only Roche seemed aware of how tightly they were packed into the small room.

"So," the captain pronounced, looking down at him. "What are you doing here, and what is it you have come to tell us?"

Roche glanced up at him, then at each of the others in turn.

"We are the same," he said, low and slow. "And our kind is not safe in this realm. We must help each other. I seek refuge, and a place to hide. You must be doing the same thing, staying away from the places she might find you. I can help you, both in avoiding discovery and staying one step ahead of her."

The devils exchanged confused glances, and the captain shook his head after the round of looks. It was clear they thought Roche was crazy from the sea, or loneliness; they seemed to have forgotten what he was, and what they were.

"Who?" the captain asked. "One step ahead of who?"

After a few tense moments, Roche breathed her name quietly.

"Ximena," he said.

Roche expected gasps of fear, furtive glances at the darkest corners, and demands that he not speak the name again. Instead the devils exchanged another round of looks, and one of them began to laugh. After a moment the others joined in, and the captain had trouble forming words between chuckles.

"Her?" he said. "Why would she come here? The devil hasn't visited the realm of man in ages, and she certainly has no interest in us. She's got enough to do in Hell, with all the overcrowding and infighting."

The captain was still laughing, and he finished his thought before losing himself in the collective mirth of the others.

"If she even exists," he said.

They all laughed together again, harder and longer than before. Roche began to feel impatient, and straightened his bent frame. As he drew in a deep breath and looked down at the tallest of them, he made sure the imposing nature of his stance was not lost on any of them.

"Very well," he said, his voice rumbling. "You will teach me to captain this boat, to sail the vessel and lead the people."

Six eyes gazed up at him, their laughter silenced by his booming pronouncement. They stared together in disbelief for a long moment, silent and by all accounts completely serious; then all at once, they burst into fresh laughter.

Roche sighed, and moved quickly for the first time since coming aboard. Barely reaching out, he took advantage of the small space and shoved in every direction at once. They each hit walls in the same moment, and he hit each of them again before the moment had passed. None of their feet were moving when they struck the wooden floor, save for a few lifeless twitches. Tearing their heads from their shoulders was a gruesome chore, but his speed did not fail him as he attacked. None of them had any chance to react, before their vacant eyes rolled back in their heads as those heads hit the floor.

Blood was everywhere, covering his naked torso and every wall around him. Roche watched as the purple wetness began to fade, and acted before the bodies could follow. He gathered the pieces in his arms, threw open the door and stepped out on deck. Moving swiftly to the railing, he tossed the remnants of the bloodied corpses overboard. He made sure plenty of the crew members saw, and that no one could tell how many bodies could be pieced together from what he chucked into the water.

After one more trip, walking past men frozen on the deck by his swift steps or his dripping load, Roche had tossed all of what remained into the ocean. He stood at the doorway to the captain's quarters for all of them to see, stretching out his giant frame and bloodied muscled torso; then he turned, ducked his head under the frame and slammed the door shut behind him.

199

The Demon Be Damned   *J.K. Norry*

ocean. He stood at the doorway to the captain's quarters for all of them to see, stretching out his giant frame and bloodied muscled torso; then he turned, ducked his head under the frame and slammed the door shut behind him.

CHAPTER 32

No one knocked on the door while Roche settled into the cabin. As far as he could tell, no one even came near. He could sense the individual minds on the vessel, whirling with wonderings about him; but the voices speaking those thoughts were hushed, and far off. Even below deck, everyone kept their words to a whisper. The only real choice any of them had was to wait and see, or leap over the side of the boat. Roche could feel them making that decision from one end of the floating structure to the other, and he let them wait.

More than their curiosity, he could feel their pain. Every soul on board was wracked with fear, every body withered from hunger. He could feel the day turning to night in the windowless cabin, and was sure they sensed the sky shifting to a darker shade. Although they gathered in their own bunk area under the main deck, none of them closed their eyes to seek the solace of sleep. They reclined on hard makeshift bedding and tossed their own noisy thoughts about in their heads, or sat on the edge whispering those thoughts to one another.

Roche explored the contents of the cabin at his leisure, stacking everything that was of no use to him in a pile to be burned or tossed over the side. At first the clothes he found went into the pile; then he looked down at himself, and realized he should probably cover his own nakedness. Garments of any kind would be hard to find here in the middle of the ocean, and the captain had been closer to his size than anyone else on board. It wasn't until he decided to piece together an outfit that Roche realized he had been holding his breath for some time.

Inhaling, he understood why immediately. The cabin was small, and it stunk of unwashed devil gone sour. The stench was a mixture of sour grape sweat and blood that had putrified before drying, with a strong undertone of sulfur; and the most noxious odors were coming from the pile of clothes. Roche wasn't sure if the garments had ever been washed; if they had, it had not been recently.

The bedding was nearly as bad as the clothes. Blankets and furs were stacked high in one corner of the cramped space, and the pile put off its own unique sweaty sleepy smell. Roche hung all of it along the walls, spreading the garments out across the floor until every square inch of the cabin was covered in the offending fabrics. Pulling his tail to one side, he sat in the middle of the floor cross-legged and began to breathe deeply.

At first it was almost too much. Concentrating on his breathing was difficult when every deep inhale brought a fresh wave of noxious odors with it, but he pressed on. Soon his body began to heat up, and he let the boiling rage within him simmer on his scaled skin. Roche thought of his time in Heaven, his first extended encounter with Ehcor, and the pain it had caused him to leave her.

And he breathed.

Thinking of her was its own meditation. Rather than clear his mind of all words and images, he flooded his thoughts with her. Roche could see her face clearly behind his eyes; even when he imagined her, the light leapt from within her to brighten her features. Her voice filled his head, a sweet musical lilt that repeated the most simple things she had said over and over until the words found his heart. She had called him brother, and said she loved him; as few moments as it had taken her to say the words, the sentiments could not be unspoken. Roche had always had his rage; now, he had something else.

He knew the rage had been tangled up in her from the beginning. The fire had grown in him when she had cast him from Heaven, but that hadn't been where it started. Roche knew where he came from, and why he had been made, in the sacred seconds before she had entered his awareness. The rage had started with knowing he was created as a solution to an impossible problem, and that the one who made him had turned away from him immediately and forever after bringing him into being.

The fire had been stoked by Ehcor's violent and sudden reaction to him, and his subsequent fall; but now that part of the rage was gone, and he could see the moments before more clearly for having let it go. While he continued to fill his mind with images of his sweet other, Roche looked back on those first few moments with new eyes. A combination had been struck within his consciousness, with her loving words and gentle touch; the lock had clicked open soundlessly, and a doorway had opened inside him that he had not realized was sealed.

Rage was a part of him, to be sure; he had been driven by it from that first fall, and had nearly extinguished his own identity in the heat of it. Yet now he could see to the other side of that anger. He could see where it came from, and why the raging fire of fury had been sparked in him.

He had been created by love, in a place of love. The secret inner workings of all the realms had filled his mind and surrounded his body when he was brought into being, to show him they were all aspects of the same world. Roche had begun his journey knowing everything there was to know without having any frame of reference for understanding it. The most important knowledge had been a feeling, and he had lost that feeling almost immediately.

Everything came from love. Either it was pure and playful, and took wondrous beautiful shape with the simple ease of a child stacking building blocks; or it was twisted and lost, and led to endless conflict. Roche was familiar with the fighting, within himself and out there in all the worlds; the love had been lost to him, until now. The sudden shock of falling had separated him from that awareness, so long ago; now he had to look back over all of it, and see everything that had come before from this new perspective.

While he breathed and reintegrated his own memories, Roche was peripherally aware of his body. The rage was still there, and he let it burn until the small space he occupied began to heat up. Any fear of the beast within him was gone, his desire to disassociate from it washed away in the clear pure waters of truth. The burning beast was not a monster living within him, determined to break its bonds and ravage the world again; it was a part of him, the aspect of him that had seen everything except the force behind it all.

As Ehcor's voice had done, the love within him tempered the rage until he stopped seeing it as a beast at all. Roche let the rage burn, and the love flow along with it, until he could feel his own skin wanting to burst into cool flame. The cabin heated up along with him, at first turning the pungent odors of the dead captain into swampy stenches. He ignored the powerful smells, and kept his inner fire just under the scaled surface of his own skin. Eventually the room began to smell like heat, and little else.

Roche breathed in the clean hotness, and reviewed the life he had lived through his new eyes. Soon he found himself floating in familiar space, looking down on the Earth and out at the stars. The point of light was there in the distance, waiting for him. Somehow he had known it would be there without expecting it, and now he knew how to reach it. He let the love flow, setting aside the rage to allow it to fill his consciousness. The light was not something he could push toward, or propel himself to; all he had to do was fling that new doorway inside him open, and gravitate naturally to it.

In the next moment, nothing existed but light. Luminous shades of white brightness surrounded him, and penetrated him. Roche felt his body sigh, far away; he was home, and some part of him knew exactly what that meant.All the other parts were surprised at the sound of a voice in the blinding brilliance; but that small part of him expected to hear her voice, and delighted in the sound while the rest of him contracted in surprise.

"My brother," Ehcor said. "You have found your way home."

The pleasant shock of hearing her was too much for all those parts of him that hadn't been expecting it. Roche was slammed back into his body, suddenly and painlessly. He could smell the dark subtle scent of scorched fabric, and opened his eyes to see that all the garments had been burnt black by his heated breathing session.

Rising to his feet, Roche leaned over to cobble an outfit together from the selection of fabrics. Some of them were crispy, and let loose flakes of darkened dryness when he handled them; others were stiff and dry, but bent at his touch. Wearing the trousers and jerkin he selected for awhile would do them some good, and the sea air would surely loosen them even more. Roche let his feet and arms go uncovered, and did not bother buttoning the jacket.

He stepped out on deck, and had a good long look around. Four men were visible to him in the darkness, two on each side of the vessel. They clung to the railing, looking over the side at inky black sea. Whispers had passed between them at random intervals before Roche had opened the door and exited the cabin. Now they all four stood silent, gazing out at nothing with the intensity of someone avoiding looking at something else. None of them stole even a glance at Roche, or each other; but everyone on deck knew what was on their minds.

Casually, Roche strode to stand between two of them. They tensed when he came near, while trying to keep still and not react visibly. He looked out over the side as they did, and spoke as if he had known them for some time.

"Have you seen anything?" he asked.

Both of them continued looking out at the darkness, silent for a long moment. They each seemed to be expecting the other to answer, and finally one of them did.

"A whale," he said. "Earlier, far off."

Now that the silence had been broken, the other wanted to have his say as well.

"It broke water once," he said. "We could barely see it, from that distance. I thought I saw it again, a few minutes later. It was even further away, though; and I couldn't be sure."

The first one spoke again, nodding as he kept his eyes on the sea.

"Nothing to raise a cry over," he said. "No reason to wake anybody up, as if any of us could get any sleep."

He seemed to realize who he was talking to, and turned to Roche while still holding onto the railing. The man's eyes were wide with fear, but tired around the edges. He had the look of someone who had lived in fear so long the feeling had lost its sharp bite. As if to demonstrate, he gazed at Roche for a long moment with drooping lids, then sighed and went back to staring at the ocean.

Inside, Roche was reeling a bit. He had expected them to laugh at him, and tell him there was no way they could have seen anything in the long dark hours of the night. Instead they had told him what they had witnessed, with no reason to lie about it. Somehow they were able to use their eyes as he did, and see when there was no light to see by. He had to think on it for a full minute, before he realized they had always been that way. They weren't turning their vision up, like he was; they were looking through their natural eyes. Their parents and their parents and their parents had likely adjusted to the darkness over time, and now these people could see clearly in the dark.

Their vision was not like his, though; that explained why the captain and his cohorts had been able to show their skin, as he showed his; colors and textures were not an important part of the way their eyes worked now, so they must not perceive them at all. He let the man beside him relax again, while collecting his thoughts, and spoke once more.

"What are you looking for?" Roche asked.

Both men turned to him, the same tired terror in their eyes. They answered at the same time, and Roche realized they may as well have said the same thing.

"Food," one said.

"Hope," said the other.

They turned back to the ocean as one, and Roche felt a chill creep up his spine. It was all a bit too much for him, the state of the world and their lives. He retreated to the cabin, to clean up the charred contents and renew himself once more before the sun came up to slightly brighten the dark world.

CHAPTER 33

First he found the stillness, and felt his awareness expanding as he steeped in it. Roche could hear the inner voices of all the people on the vessel with him, coming together in a symphony of pain. Either none of their thoughts were clear enough to come through in words, or the cacophony of so many minds together drowned out the individual. None of that mattered right now, anyway; he would come to know them from their words and deeds, while letting their thoughts be their own.

Once his awareness ballooned beyond the boat, the voices faded. Stillness reigned in his mind once more, and soon he found himself floating in spacious nothingness. Roche had time in that place to detect the presence behind the void. Without allowing his mind to think on it, he felt the silent consciousness in every cell of his being. Everything seemed to exist here, somehow present as energy without taking solid shape. He sensed it more than he saw it, and still he kept his mind from thinking on it.

The light appeared next, far off in the distance. Roche found it even more difficult to keep his mind clear here, and to move towards his goal without reaching for it. Now that he knew what awaited him within the brilliance, it was harder than ever for him to simply let it come to him. Several minutes passed in peaceful frustration, until he remembered the doorway within him. It appeared to him as soon as Roche recalled its existence, and opened slowly to bathe him in light.

And at last, he heard her voice.

The sound did not come to him from far off. It was not diffused by the distance between them, or lost in the vast silence. In the spacious emptiness he had discovered during his own quiet moments, nothing could reach him including the thoughts in his mind. Somehow a bubble of stillness formed around him in that place, and he welcomed the respite from the endless voices within him.

Here, it was different. Roche felt as though he had pressed against the edges of that soundless bubble, and slipped through to the other side without popping it. His mind was with him here, but it was not crowded with ceaseless wonderings too persistent to let go and too complicated to grasp. Here he felt more completely present, more keenly aware of his own consciousness but with no body to attach it to. He saw Ehcor as light within light, and heard her voice as clearly as his own scant thoughts.

"You came back," she said, simply.

He felt like he was nodding, even if his head was far away right now; he also sensed she could see the nod, in whatever form it took for her. Still he responded, and watched the glow that was her brighten at his words.

"Of course I did," he said. "I did not know what this place was, or how to get here. Now that I have found it, how could I stay away?"

Something about what he said was not quite right. Part of him had known what this place was, and how to get here; just because that aspect of his inner world had been hidden from his awareness did not mean it had not existed. Roche struggled with a way to say that, to correct the twisted and incomplete feeling the words hung from; then he felt something pass between them, and knew the words would be superfluous. They had a connection in this place, which made his meaning clear as he thought about it. The incomplete feeling untwisted, and he sensed her understanding as easily as she had deciphered the unspoken message.

"We are meant to work together," she said.

Even as Roche nodded again without actually inclining his head, he wondered briefly if she was trying to coax him back into her own realm. As soon as the questioning tension began to form within him, the link between them quelled the feeling and filled in the blanks between her words. She was not speaking her desire; she was simply telling the truth. Her motivations were as clear as her voice, in this place; and Roche knew immediately she was not here to assert any kind of power over him. Ehcor did not want to control anything; she only wanted to walk the straight clear path of purpose.

"I cannot come to you," Roche said. "Even if I could rise to Heaven on my own, which I'm not sure I could do at this point, I could never submit to the rules I would have to live by there. The thing I want most in all the worlds might be there, but the nature of the realm is too much for me to bear. I feel as though I'm losing more of myself with every moment I spend there, like my identity is being slowly burned away by cool bright light."

She probably didn't need to know his thoughts to realize what he meant by the thing he wanted most. The only part of Heaven that was also a part of him was her, and she was clearly touched by him saying he wanted her more than anything in any world. Since they had shared everything, she also knew his memories were slipping away no matter where he was; she knew his identity had nearly evaporated in the violent heat of the burning beast, and that he moved from one part of his life to the next with little or no awareness of where he was going or how he had gotten there once he arrived.

Heaven was different for him, however; even if he couldn't throw a net of words around the experience to explain it satisfactorily to himself, Roche knew that much. In the lower realms, he felt as though parts of him were being locked away inside; he couldn't reach them now, but they would always be there to be mined later. Up there, bits of him seemed to float away invisibly; and they felt as though they were lost to him forever. Without speaking it, he communicated all this to her; and without a word, she understood.

"But you can come to me, brother," she said. "You did come to me. You are here, with me. Maybe you can't come to Heaven, and I can't go to the human realm; but we can both come here."

She got brighter within the light, somehow. When she had glowed more intensely in Heaven, the luminous burst had diffused her features; here it made them come clearer. Roche could sense the excitement in her, and was awash in her emotional upswing as her thoughts flooded his head. He could barely make out her words when she spoke, which was fine; he barely needed to.

"I can learn for us both," she gushed. "The things Trethis teaches me are meant for you as well. I can learn them, and come here to share them with you. I can help you learn more about what we are here to do, and you can help me see when…"

Trailing off, Ehcor stopped glowing quite so brightly for a moment. Roche could sense her confusion, her hesitation, and her decision to share with him like she never had with anyone. All of those feelings passed between them in that moment, and Roche felt a wave of love wash over him as she went on.

"Trethis doesn't tell me everything," she said.

Ehcor's voice was not the calm melody he had grown accustomed to hearing. Clipped and thin, her words shot from her like chips of ice. For the first time, he felt her light begin to put off heat; and Roche found himself basking in the warm glow while she continued.

"He treats me like a child," she seethed, "only reminding me I am among the most powerful and gifted angels when he is pointing out how I need to be humble. All that he sees, I can see; and more. So many of his lessons are simple, obvious things I already know. Yet he speaks them as if he doesn't quite believe them, and will never understand them. Someone else wrote everything he says to me, yet none of them ever come near. He gives me messages, words they supposedly said in response to reports he apparently gave. I have no way of knowing if the messages are accurate, or if he muddled something important along the way; and I have no way of knowing what he reports to them, or who they even are."

Nearly a minute passed before he realized she had run out of words. Her thoughts still whirled noisily in his head, which would have been bothersome in this place had they been his. They were Ehcor's, though; and he delighted in sharing that part of her even as he lamented the angst she was transmitting. He continued to soak up the heat of her anger while she picked up the thread once more.

"My brother," she said. "I can teach you about our powers, and our purpose. You can fill in the blanks left in my life by my isolation, and I can help you learn about yourself in a more gentle fashion than you have been."

Immediately Roche thought of the burning beast, the fires that had burned all around him and the smoke still hanging in the air. He felt their connection begin to slip away, and he saw a dash of darkness flash in the brilliance before him.

"That is not what I meant at all," Ehcor's called to him.

Her voice rang out, cementing him back into the strange space completely. When she spoke again, her words were the sweet song he was used to hearing.

"Perhaps that should be your first lesson," she said. "It would be appropriate, since it was mine. Even as one of the most powerful forces in all the realms, you cannot make the world in your own image. All you can do is shape the realms as they cry out to be shaped, and play the part you have to play as conscientiously as you can. The more unconscious you are, the more you will be a pawn to the unseen forces at play about us all. In the darkest of times, we cannot hope to shine a light without casting even darker shadows. Sometimes the soul of the world rises, and sometimes it falls; all we can do is rise or fall with it, and add our ray to the light or our shadow to the darkness."

The lesson was an overarching one, and a little too impractical for his taste; but Roche saw the thoughts behind her recitation, and shook his head sadly at her hope.

"I cannot accept that," he said. "Not completely. I would have the burden of my destruction lifted from my conscience, just as you would. I know you see that it weighs me down heavily, but I do not think you see the value in carrying that burden."

He could feel how open she was to him, how eager she was to hear something of value from anyone other than Trethis. Roche tried to speak gently, and consider how quickly she might grasp his meaning through their connection.

"Maybe the world was on the verge of this," he said, "and would have suffered a similar fate even if I hadn't come along. Perhaps the world falls and rises, and we are all rising and falling within our own parameters inside that great pattern. That doesn't change the fact that my experiences are mine, though; and it doesn't relieve me of responsibility for what I have done. I must live with that, and let those feelings of regret shape what I do with my powers in the days to come."

He almost said it, that he needed to stay here while the world was dark; Roche let the words go unspoken, and knew she understood. Still, he felt better for the lesson; and she seemed to feel better for hearing his thoughts on it. Roche laughed as he felt her probing him lovingly, soaking into his heart and sponging up his soul just by being nearby. Her desire to know him all at once was pleasantly invasive, but he could only take it for a little while. Of course, she sensed his discomfort as soon as he felt it. Ehcor drew back the instant she picked up on it, and began to fade into the distance.

"I know how you found me now," he called out, as the light began to drift away. "I know how you discovered this place. You have rage in you, just like I do; anger that the world that made you would make a world where you had to be made. I thought you were all love, all light and hope. But you're not. You have the rage, too."

Her laughter echoed back to him, far away but clear.

"Of course," she sang. "You should have known I would have anger, just as I knew you had love in you. We are more alike than different, and it is my hope that we will come together often from now on. I miss you when you are not nearby, brother; and every time I am not with you I am only waiting for the next time I am."

The light still floated in the distance, but her voice and her presence were gone suddenly. Roche drifted in spacious emptiness for moments uncounted, and thought of the time they had spent and the words they had spoken. When the sun finally began to brighten the dim sky, he was ready to step on deck and call out to the first person he saw.

CHAPTER 34

Shrouded in robes and darkness, the figure froze at the sound of his voice. When Roche called out again, the last thing he expected was for the figure to straighten and head away from him; the action surprised him, and threw him across the space between them with sudden anger. Roche jerked at the reins of his rage, but not before he had seized the retreating shadow by the arm. The sound that escaped the cowl surprised him, and he stepped back.

He kept his hand on her arm, but eased up his grip while turning her bodily towards him. If it hadn't been for that involuntary exclamation, he would have assumed she was a man. Bent and gaunt like all the others, the size or shape of her frame did nothing to suggest otherwise. As she glanced furtively up and down the deck to see if anyone was watching, Roche concluded she must be attempting to disguise her sex. He spoke quickly and quietly, to put her at ease.

"No one heard you," he said. "Except me. Whatever reason you have for passing as a man has nothing to do with me, but I won't reveal your secret to the others."

Every time he looked into the eyes of one of the people on board, Roche felt a chill climb his spine. Their gazes were invariably dull and distant, and spoke of souls that had been bent beyond breaking many times. Part of him wanted to know their stories, and hear what they had seen and had passed down to them; another part of him wanted to burn the vessel where it floated, and put an end to all this misery at last.

Her eyes were no different, floating in sockets hollowed by hunger above lips that looked like they had never smiled. Even her sigh was more an exhalation than a sound of relief. When she spoke, she clearly was masking her identity; if he hadn't known, Roche would have been sure she was a man.

"Thank you," she said, gruff and low. "But how am I to believe you? You are a man, after all."

Lifting her defeated gaze from the deck, she caught his eyes briefly. Everything about her was mortal, but he still thought he saw a flash of light. Some fire existed within her somewhere; maybe it didn't burn as brightly as it might have otherwise, but it was there. Roche considered the likelihood of this same thing happening before, and how she might have handled it.

Dull and rusted, the blade did not flash in the light of the morning sun. Even if it had been shiny and new, there were no bright rays to reflect from its surface. Everything here was dark and colorless, including the knife she tried to stick into his belly.

Both of her hands grasped the handle, pushing the blade at him. Roche wrapped one beefy hand around hers, engulfing them, and held the weapon several inches from his skin. Their eyes met once more, as they stood facing each other. He could feel her pushing the blade at him with all her withered might, even as he paused her attack in place.

"I am not like other men," Roche murmured, holding her gaze. "You have nothing to fear from me."

She struggled against him uselessly, still pressing the blade where he had halted its progress. Her feet were planted firmly on the deck, her entire body leaning into the attack. Speaking through clenched teeth, she kept pushing as she responded.

"All men say they are not like other men," she hissed.

Roche did not want to crush her hands under his, or peel her fingers forcefully from the knife; he also didn't want others to see their struggle, and investigate the cause of it. His mind searched for a way to disengage from her without revealing her secret or his.

From the rear of the boat, a sudden shout cut through the dark morning stillness. Another followed, a different voice raised in similar urgency. In the next moment a chorus of cries went up, and Roche felt her thrust slacken under his grip. He stepped back and let her go all at the same time, spreading his hands and anticipating another attack. The woman looked up at him for a moment, glanced briefly in the direction of the voices, and began to move away from him.

Roche let her go, watching her until she had slipped into the shadows and fled his attention entirely. Moving toward the voices, he traversed the length of the vessel in less than a minute. He came to stand between several shouting figures, leaning against the railing and pointing, in the same moment the boat began to turn.

"What is it?" he asked aloud, of no one in particular.

One man spoke without looking at him, responding while keeping his eyes on the water.

"A boat," he said, pointing. "See?"

Following the man's outstretched finger, Roche spied the tiny vessel. It looked like a tree that had been felled and hollowed out by hand; and although the tree had been enormous, the carved trunk struggled to hold all the people within it. More than a dozen men and women crowded in the space, wearing nearly nothing to show bronzed skin over taut muscles. Half of them held paddles, as crudely fashioned as the craft; the other half sat in sedate postures, keeping out of the way of the oars as they lifted from the water over and over to cut repeatedly into the waves.

"They're rowing away from us," Roche noted.

The man that had spoken to him nodded, still not turning to see who stood behind him. He apparently mistook Roche's meaning, and answered a question that hadn't been asked.

"Don't worry," he said. "We'll catch them."

Roche watched the tiny boat, saw the gap between them begin to close as the vessel they were on picked up speed. He could see the faces of the people looking their way, and he couldn't help but think of how much more animated they were than the faces of those around him. Like the muscles that worked the oars, their eyes were clear and alert. He could feel them watching him back, and he could sense the shared consciousness behind those bright eyes.

At first, he had supposed a vessel like this one would offer help to a smaller one; especially when the other boat was so crowded. He could see the fear in those distant eyes, however; and at the same time, he could sense the eagerness in the minds around him. Roche felt as though he didn't want to know, but he had to ask.

"Why do we want to catch them?" he murmured.

The man who had been speaking to him stiffened where he stood, clinging more firmly to the railing. His head pivoted slowly, and his eyes finally fell on Roche. They were dull and distant, like all the others.

"Want?" he said. "We don't want to."

He dropped his gaze to the deck, then turned to stare out over the ocean once more. Roche had to strain to hear what he said after that, and wonder why it shot another cold chill up his spine. The feeling was beginning to become a familiar one, even if he liked it less each time it swept over him. The clawing cold persisted as the man went on.

"We don't want anything," he said. "This is not a life of want. This is a life of need. We do not want to catch them; we need to."

They watched in silence together after that, as the watery gap between the vessels closed. Roche thought of pressing the man further, or peeking into his thoughts; instead he waited quietly until they were nearly upon the little boat, and moved along the deck. Forcing his way through the small crowd gathered at the prow of his vessel, Roche got there just in time to see the first rope fly. A loop was tied about the end, and it wobbled lazily in the air before it struck.

Wherever it had been aimed, the rope missed; it splashed into the water alongside the tiny craft, only to be pulled back immediately through the waves. A half dozen more snaked out in the next moment, and Roche watched several bronze figures get yanked overboard as they stretched taut. He was crying out, yelling at them to stop; but everyone else was shouting at the same time. The men pulling on the ropes exclaimed loudly with each tug, and everyone around them raised their voices in a cacophony of support; the people on the hand-hewn craft and in the water were shouting as well, and their collective cry echoed off the ocean to drown out his own.

Roche may have been bigger than any of them, and stronger than all of them; but somehow he was overwhelmed by the frenzy of bodies on deck. More flooded forward as the first captives were pulled in, and he was buffeted about by the frantic rolling wave. He had to choose between using his strength and speed to control the situation, or losing his footing.

As he went down, all he could see were legs scissoring frantically past him and the first of the captives being dragged onto the deck. Roche wiggled away from the crowd, watching the rope that had been used to lasso the prisoner being wound tightly about his arms and torso to hold him and secure him to the railing. More bodies were being pulled in, as more passengers crowded the deck. Roche finally got clear of them, and regained his feet to helplessly watch the chaos unfold.

CHAPTER 35

Several of the captives looked terrified, as if they knew what awaited them and feared it more than anything; Roche looked on, curious, wondering what thought would twist their features with such stark fear. Each of them were slim and sinewy, including the old men and women; even the young had hard faces with features accustomed to stoicism.

Their captors treated them with surprising gentleness as they were bound to the deck. A few of the prisoners tried to speak, or cry out; they were gagged immediately, but not painfully. Those that attempted to break free or fight were wrestled into submission without blows, and the whole affair went down with a complete lack of undue violence. Roche watched, wondering about the mixed messages as they were sent. Once the clamor had died down, he approached the clothed crowd gathered about the railing.

By the time he shouldered a few of them aside, two more were untying one of the prisoners from the railing. Ropes were still wound about his body, keeping his arms trapped along the length of his bare torso; but his legs were free, and the men standing over him were lifting him gingerly to his feet. Roche noticed again how careful they were being in handling the prisoner, pressing on while he wondered. He came close just as they began to lead him away.

"Where are you taking him?" Roche asked.

The men kept walking, either not hearing or not caring that he had spoken. A few quick steps and he was in their path, blocking them from leading the nearly naked captive any further.

"Where are you taking him?" he repeated.

One of the men sighed, and looked at the other; the other shrugged, and tried to walk around Roche. He moved closer, as if daring the man to walk into him. Both men stopped, and their eyes found the deck at the same time.

Roche felt the prickle of being watched climb his spine, and glanced back. The other passengers were staring at him, or glaring with forlorn expressions on otherwise slack faces. Meanwhile, the prisoners were paying even closer attention to his interaction with the trio. Some of their eyes were shining brightly, and hope lifted their features. He had to do something, and all of them knew it. Either he needed to force an answer from them, wrestle their captive away, or step aside.

With a sigh, Roche stepped aside. They might be able to resist talking to him, but they couldn't stop him from following wherever they were going. Neither of the men holding the prisoner seemed to mind, and they moved sluggishly along the deck to slip past him. Roche trailed them, and soon they came to one of the few doors on deck other than the one to his cabin. The frame was the most imposing piece of the otherwise triangular structure, with a rickety roof over it that angled sharply downward. Even before they opened the door, it was clear it led to stairs that would take them below deck.

One of the men released his hold on the captive, moving to open the door while keeping a wary eye on Roche. He felt the urge to explode, and point out that the two of them couldn't stop him from seizing the prisoner any more than one could alone; but he held his tongue, and checked the angry rise. The man opened the door, and the odor wafting up the darkened stairs hit Roche like a blow.

Something about the way Hell smelled had always pleased his senses. The antiseptic atmosphere in Heaven had a scent to it, but it was characterized more by the uniform lack of odor more than by any truly clean smell. On the other hand, Hell filled his nostrils with pleasant layers of burnt sweetness. The smell varied in its own way from place to place, but it always hinted at fire it its many forms. As much as the odorless air in Heaven put him on guard, the smoky scents of Hell relaxed him in a way Roche had never felt anywhere else.

The human realm was as varied in its odors as it was in its people. Some smells here had made his head tingle as if he was about to spin into some kind of helpless euphoria, although they had all been before the fire. Sela's garden had been full of flowers and fruits that each exploded in his nose like he was tasting them, and they had transported him to blissful reverie for a moment each time he breathed them in. On the other hand, few odors were as painfully offensive to his senses as some of the smells humans put off naturally. Unwashed flesh and unburied eliminations had quickly become his least favorite scents, when he had smelled them.

This was different, in ways he couldn't have imagined. Layers of stench came at Roche, and seemed to wash over him in waves. He stopped breathing immediately, only to feel the smell settle into the back of his mouth as a flavor. The taste was one he hadn't experienced before, but he immediately knew what it was. Excrement was in there, to be sure; but in this case it was the least offensive of the gritty and slimy textures on his tongue.

Diseased and rotting flesh had their own unique odors, and now Roche knew what each of them smelled like. Pungent and sticky, the sickly blend clung to the inside of his mouth and nose as he tried to shake it off. The men had been on board longer than him, and knew to expect the disgusting assault; as far as he could tell, they didn't even notice it. Roche did his best to emulate their casual postures, even as his insides turned over and over uncomfortably.

In comparison to them, the bronzed captive became an unruly mess. He turned his head away from the stench, screwed up his face and spat on the deck. The only thing that kept him from moving swiftly in any direction but towards the opening was the man holding him, and the other as he released the door to seize the prisoner once more. Together they pulled him through the frame and into the darkened staircase.

Roche followed, wondering how they could breathe in the dense fog of rot and waste that got thicker the further they went. He saw the prisoner try to turn, and flee back to the deck; when the men held him firm, his knees buckled and he drooped between them. Roche thought he was resisting, by going limp; then he looked closer, and realized the man had lost consciousness.

Even then, Roche could not determine where the man's panic had come from. It wasn't until they came to another doorway, unlocked it and opened it that the reality of the situation hit him like it had already struck the captive. The stench was stronger here, despite his efforts at not breathing; as soon as he looked into the space, he realized why.

Rows of benches lined one wall, perhaps a dozen in all. Each seat was occupied by two or three people, humans that looked more like the prisoner than any of his captors. They sat idle, every hand in each row gripping a long wooden pole but not moving. None of them turned to see why the door had opened, or who was on the other side; and as Roche looked closer, he wondered why anyone had bothered locking the door in the first place.

Every one of them was tied to their seat somehow, wrapped in chains or thick lengths of rope that wound about each bench and the people sitting on it. Men and women were both represented, as were children; they seemed to be grouped by size, so they would pull on their poles with approximately the same force as the others. Roche realized they were the motive force behind the vessel, rowing their captors from one empty corner of the world to the other while rotting in their seats.

All of them were missing one leg, and many were missing both. The wounds had healed in some cases, but many of the amputated limbs were open sores that oozed odor and pus. In the places where rusted chain or frayed rope met flesh, gashes had opened up and been left unattended; they expelled their own scent into the air, slowly dripping thick colorless liquid streaked with blood.

It all came together for him in one sickening moment, the rancid smells and the terror some of the prisoners had shown at being captured. They had known what he hadn't been able to imagine, to the point where they assumed it was why they were being taken. Although they had been right, Roche had not been able to picture such horror in his mind. Now the reality of the situation sank in for him all at once, and he turned to the men holding the limp body between them.

"You're eating them?" he cried.

The question was more of a statement. When they lowered their eyes together in a familiar gesture, Roche understood why that expression was so common among his shipmates. Their only choice was painful starvation or perpetual shame, as far as they knew; and the only ones that had survived had chosen the shame.

One of the men spoke without lifting his gaze. His words sent another frozen shock down Roche's spine, and the listless voice that delivered them chilled him to the bone.

"It's them or us," he muttered. "What would you have us do, eat each other?"

Roche could not trust himself to be near the man for another moment; at the same time, he clearly could not leave the prisoner with them. Reaching out, furious and frightened, he gripped the ropes where they were wound about the man's naked torso. Although he yanked at the man more violently than they had handled him, he seemed to be relieved when he opened his eyes to see Roche holding him. Together they retraced their steps, until they stood on deck under the clear smoky sky and filled their lungs with pleasantly acrid air.

CHAPTER 36

Up on deck, the air seemed clear by comparison. Roche was all but dragging the wiry nearly naked man behind him, and didn't stop moving until they came within sight of the others. The remaining prisoners were still tied to the railing, and every eye on deck was turned his way.

"This is no way to treat others," Roche called out to them.

He was calm, compared to how he had felt below beck. Still his words were clipped with anger, and loud; Roche was certain they all heard him. Some looked away, others exchanged glances with those beside them. The woman he had discovered earlier was among them, watching him with cautious eyes.

Roche was still holding the captive by his upper arm, and the man made no attempt to break free. Instead he started talking, addressing the other prisoners where they were tied. His language was completely different than any Roche had heard, more a series of sounds than a collection of words. Nonetheless, he understood the meaning as immediately and clearly as he had every other language he had heard spoken. Roche ignored both the sounds and their meaning, and warily eyed his shipmates.

One gaunt figure stepped forward, and met his glare.

"What are we to do?" he said. "Die of starvation? Eat each other? They are like animals, the way they live and the noises they make. That's not language, or anything like it. It's like a bird singing, or a bear growling. They don't have souls, like us."

The bronzed man in Roche's grasp fell silent around the same time as the fellow arguing in favor of eating him. He glanced between the captives and his captor, and gestured excitedly to Roche.

"I think he is trying to help us," the man said, quite clearly. "The others like us, they are beyond hope; but we may not be. The big one seems to be trying to talk the others out of eating us."

Roche kept his eyes on the bedraggled cannibal as he spoke to the bronzed man in his native tongue. Every strange sound struck his shipmate like a blow, and he flinched visibly with every click and pop under Roche's icy stare.

"I am trying to help you," Roche said. "These people think you are without souls, and should be eaten like animals."

Their laughter was sudden and unexpected, considering their circumstances. Several of the prisoners sprinkled the deck with the sound, and the man Roche was holding rushed to explain.

"We are native to the land," he said.

He paused, as if that explained everything. When Roche lifted an eyebrow at him, letting him know it didn't, the man went on.

"They made a choice," he said, "to separate themselves from nature. They used their hands to shape the world to their whim, and used their minds to subvert the very rules of creation. In turning their backs collectively on the natural life, they brought about a civilization that could not help but destroy itself."

Although the prisoners were tied, it did not prevent their heads from nodding as the bronzed man spoke. Every face was grave on deck, and every eye was on their exchange. When the man spit on the wooden flooring at their feet, Roche was glad only half the people present could understand what he said next.

"They are the ones without souls," he said. "We refer to them as the dead that walk, or the dead who do not know they are dead. The way they lived made many things possible that had not been possible before, but they pulled up their roots as they reached for the skies. What you see here are the last gasps of a dying life form, the final mindless twitches of a body whose collective soul has long since departed."

Roche looked from the prisoners to his shipmates, and let the differences between the two groups really sink in. The people he had found on this vessel had grey skin, sunken eyes and hollowed cheeks. All of them were slim, but they held themselves as if the weight of their own bodies was too much to bear. Any place he could see their flesh, it either hung loose from brittle bones or sagged in ashen puddles. Their skin and muscle tone seemed to reflect their collective state of mind, and most of them kept their dull weary eyes fixed to the deck.

The others were also slim, but strong. Roche could see the corded sinew working under their bronzed skin as they shifted within their bonds, and their eyes shone so brightly he thought of Ehcor when he locked gazes with any one of them. Every aspect of the way they moved crackled with energy, and life; even the way the man in his grasp spoke seemed to have another dimension to it, like everything else these people did. Roche could only compare them to beings he had met in other realms, even if their only supernatural power was their intense humanity.

"You must know they are lost."

Even as Roche held him firm, the nearly naked man shook him from his reverie by speaking once more. They turned to each other slowly, and locked eyes while the native went on.

"Only momentum," he said, "carries these people from one day to the next. They have grown so accustomed to relying on those that came before them, they have no idea how to start again at the beginning. Although they came from people like us, they can no longer rely on each other in the present. With all the progress of their people burned or decayed, the only thing they know to do is scavenge the past or eat the future. It is a shame to see, but you cannot prevent their eventual demise. You may be a powerful devil, but even that is beyond you."

Roche jerked his arm, involuntarily. The man skittered across the deck towards him, but did not cry out or resist. He scanned the deck, to see half the faces unsurprised and the other half uncomprehending.

"You know what I am?" Roche demanded.

The man shrugged, as much as he could without giving the impression he was trying to break free.

"Of course," he said. "We all do. Only the minds that were twisted yesterday have eyes that can not see the truth of today. Those with demons may forever confuse you with something else; but we are made alive through our connection to the land. Their souls gain a kind of power through individuality, but ours stay together and remain connected to the planet. In this way, we do not ebb and flow with the rhythms of the world. We remember the natural way, while one civilization after another rises only to fall."

Looking over the crew and passengers that had come with the boat, Roche suddenly saw the motley assemblage in a darker light. He had tried to ignore their demons, as he had learned to do; but those hateful mutterings would have told him all he needed to know, had he only tuned into them. Roche felt trapped between two worlds, unable to keep one alive without feeding it the other.

"How have you survived?" he asked the native. "Why are your people strong and healthy, with the world the way it is?"

He shrugged his naked shoulders once more, and gestured to the sea with his free hand.

"The ocean is full of life," he said. "When the plants shriveled and turned brown, and the hunting became scarce, we knew what to do. Our people have fished nearly as far back as our collective memory reaches, and we all knew the largest catches come from the ocean. We have drifted with schools of fishes, netting the small and spearing or hooking the large, ever since the land became unlivable."

Something still didn't seem right; after a moment staring at the man, Roche realized what it was.

"You live in the sun," he said.

The man flinched, and several of the prisoners exchanged glances. Roche kept staring at him until he looked up, and nodded.

"Your skin has soaked it up," Roche continued. "You have eaten more than just fish in your lifetime, and soaked that up as well. Food may be plentiful on the water, but you can't drink the ocean. You have a place where you go, and the sun shines there. Fruit trees grow, and fresh water flows. Tell me where it is."

Shaking his head, the native smiled sadly and looked away.

"I will not," he said, quietly. "And neither will any of them. That is where the next rise must come from, and the only devil allowed to walk its soil is already in residence."

Roche arched an eyebrow, and shook him a little.

"What rise?" he demanded.

His captive glanced to the others, as if looking for permission to speak on the matter. When none of them voiced any objection, he responded.

"The next rise of humanity," he said. "We are always here to seed the next wave that rises up to claim its greatness, and we stand forever ready to hand the world over to the civilization that ascends to those heights with grace. We also let the old die, so the new can live. Even you cannot stop us from allowing that."

With a sigh, Roche let him go at last. He turned to the gathering of the dead that did not know they were dead, and spoke to them in a calm and steady voice.

"Did you keep their vessel?" he asked, of no one in particular.

A cowled head nodded, and sunken eyes came up from the deck to meet his as one of them stepped forward.

"We did," he said. "There was a little food and water in it, but not much to speak of. The rest is still in there, and the little craft is lashed to the side of ours; but it isn't much use to anyone."

Roche went to the nearest captive, and began to untie the lashings holding him. Some of his shipmates stirred, but none of them raised their voices or their fists to challenge him. As he moved to the next set of knots, he called out to the entire assemblage.

"They are going to help us," he said. "We will send them out with their boat and their gear, and they will bring us back food. A few of us will go with them, and a few of them will stay here. They will teach us to live off the sea, and we will live in peace with them until we can get along without them. Does everyone understand?"

By this time he had untied two prisoners, after releasing the one he had been holding. They were beginning to line up behind him, and present a united front full of lean powerful muscles and bright shining eyes. No one put forth any argument, until Roche repeated what he had said to the natives in their own tongue.

"This will not work," one of the bronzed women said, shaking her head as she rubbed at her unbound wrists. "Nothing you can do will save them. Even if we feed them, or teach them to feed themselves, they will thwart their own survival instincts. Their souls are asleep, and their time has passed."

Roche growled, deep in his throat.

"Would you rather I let them eat you?" he said.

The woman smiled, gazing at him as if she could transmit her calm to him through simple eye contact. She shrugged, and gestured to the dark endless waves surrounding them.

"We will do as you ask," she said, "until we must do otherwise. But do not mistake our assistance for fear, or weakness. My people do not shrink from pain, or run from dying; for our lives do not end with the death of our bodies, and we know it. Just as our souls are tied to each other, our memories are linked to the natural world. We know the way of things, much as the devil herself."

She held his eyes with hers, still smiling softly.

"One day," she said, "you will see there is a time to act in the world, and there is a time to let things be the way they are."

Roche moved on to the next bundle of ropes holding a captive bound to the railing, and turned his back to her. He let himself feel glad for the promise of cooperation, and pushed the rest of her words from his mind.

CHAPTER 37

Roche stood at the railing, staring at the hazy line where the ocean met the sky. He tried to keep his eyes fixed on the spot where they had disappeared over the horizon, but he couldn't be sure he was watching the same stretch of sea after all the time that had passed. The tiny vessel had shot off into the distance sometime in the early evening, paddled by eight men from his boat and eight of the natives. Since then, the sky had grown slightly darker and then a little bit brighter once more.

Still, they were not back.

More of them had stayed behind than had gone, something Roche reminded himself of many times over as the hours dragged on. Even if they killed the men he had sent with them to make their escape, they would be leaving most of their people behind. Something told him they wouldn't do that; but knowing it in his bones didn't stop Roche from considering the possibility, or imagining it in great detail. He was sure someone would voice the same concern, and he waited with every argument he was repeating to himself poised on his forked tongue; but no one spoke while he waited, at least not to him.

No one went anywhere, either. Although the night was long and uneventful, all of the people that had been on deck when the vessel left stayed there. The natives had no quarters to retreat to, and may have been afraid that exploring the ship would lead to violence; but even the people with bunks below braved the night air to watch Roche endlessly scan the horizon. It felt like they were all holding their collective breath, waiting to see what would happen; Roche held his right along with them, hoping for the best while vividly imagining the worst.

A dozen times, he was sure he saw them. A light appeared in the distance, or a shadow took the shape of the craft for a moment. Every time he leaned forward, and squinted his eyes to see better; and every time it was a trick of the light, or his own imagination showing him something that simply wasn't there. He thought of retreating to his cabin more than once, only to realize everyone on board needed him where he was. As much as his heart ached to meet Ehcor in that place that was no place, Roche knew he needed to stand his ground and count on the bronzed fishermen to keep their word.

In those chill hours when the sky was darkest, he found himself wondering if maybe he had imagined talking with the angel who called him brother. Perhaps he was pretending a relationship that was only happening in his mind, and she had given him little thought since he fell from Heaven again. The possibility seemed more likely than any other until the sky brightened once more, and he looked at those memories under the wan glow of the smoky sun.

He couldn't have imagined her the way she was, or made up the things she was teaching him about their shared purpose. The last thing a mirage would offer is to instruct the person imagining in a bunch of things they don't know; if he had dreamed her up, she would have been more focused on filling him with light than teaching him her lessons.

She did that too, of course; but Roche knew she relied on him to ground her to life in other realms just as much as he relied on her to connect him to the place he needed to feel but did not dare visit. Ehcor was Heaven, for him; and because of her, Roche needed Heaven.

Thinking of her for the thousandth time since the little boat had slipped over the horizon, Roche didn't notice the shadow on the water until it had taken clear shape. By then he could count the heads floating towards him, and sigh in relief that all of them were accounted for. Soon after, he could see that many of the faces on those heads were smiling. Roche let out a deep breath he hadn't realized he was holding, and turned his back to the ocean.

"They're back," he called out.

He searched their faces: the bronzed countenances of the people that had been lashed to the railing hours ago, and the ashen features of his shipmates. Joy brightened the eyes of the natives, but they already had life shining in their eyes. It was the others he wished to see light up, and rejoice in the good news.

"They're back," he repeated, louder. "And they have food."

Many of them had been lounging, leaning against each other while they sprawled languidly on deck. The natives jumped to their feet, and crowded about the railing; the others stood slowly, as if it pained them to do so, and moved with molasses steps to gaze out at the sea.

Everyone helped haul in the load, fish that were still flopping and dripping as they were pulled out of the water. A long net had been tied to the end of the tiny craft, and they had gathered catches from smaller nets in the larger one as it trailed behind them. The food was fresh, and plentiful;

and people were biting into the slippery flesh before anyone even made any move to stoke the fire.

A broad stone pot was hauled into the center of the open deck, and a few flames were fanned into existence from the burning embers buried inside. Suddenly everyone was moving, and those that knew where wood that could be burned might be went looking for it. Nearly everyone else took part in cleaning and gutting the fish, and by the time the fire was roaring dozens of sticks with dead pieces of sea meat were competing to get close.

Roche stood back and watched, letting himself be satisfied for a moment. The people were not coming back to life, but they were smiling and acting civil to each other and the former prisoners. With roasted flesh in their bellies, he hoped they might start looking at the others as people instead of food; but he kept an eye on the proceedings until he could be certain.

While he watched, the woman he had discovered earlier approached him cautiously. She sidled up alongside him, so slowly he didn't realize she was there until she spoke.

"You have not eaten," she noted, quietly.

Glancing down at her, Roche shrugged. He could not hide the satisfaction showing on his face, and he didn't want to.

"There's plenty," he said. "Let them eat their fill first."

She looked to the fire, and the ring of people around it. They were eating, but they were also interacting. Those that shared a language exchanged words, but even those that didn't were exchanging gestures or friendly expressions. One ashen man handed a stick of roasted fish to a native as she watched, and she turned to Roche again as the other man thanked him with a nod and bit into it.

"It's true, what you said earlier," she noted.

Roche noticed she wasn't going to great lengths to make her voice sound gruff and deep, as she had before. No one else was close enough to hear, and he sensed that her decision to drop the disguise in his presence had some deeper meaning to it. He kept his eyes straight ahead, and tried to act like he wasn't paying close attention to her words.

"You aren't like other men," she said. "You put your own desires aside, and take satisfaction in helping others. Where other men see only darkness, you look for the light. I know you fell from the sky, and I am beginning to think I know where you came from. You are an angel, descended from Heaven to come and save us."

Turning his head slowly, Roche looked down at her. He met her eyes with his, wanting her to see the fire in them and the darkness that lurked behind it. He hoped a single cold look would chill her to the bones, and send her scampering away to lurk in the shadows of her disguise once more. Instead she held his gaze, her eyes widening with wonder as he held his tongue and his protestations.

"You are here to save me," she whispered.

Even with a spark of hope lighting her eyes, Roche could see the twisted remains of her soul casting long dark shadows within her. He knew what had been done to her could not be undone, and he wondered if maybe she was dead and just didn't know it yet. He shook his head, as she spoke again. The simple motion was meant to dispel all her illusions, and make her see him for what he was; or at least see what he wasn't. She ignored the dismissal, and gestured at the nearby flames.

"You should eat," she said. "Of all the people enjoying the taste of real food in their mouths tonight, no one deserves it more than you. Wait here, and I will get you something."

Roche watched her slip away, looking back to see if he was still there as she approached the fire. As soon as she was engrossed in conversation with someone holding several skewers of cooked fish, using the low gruff tones she was accustomed to, he turned and made for his cabin.

The word she had spoken had thrown him into a swirling tornado of thoughts and emotions, pulling him out of his satisfaction over hungry mouths being fed and sending his mind to think of the angel he knew best. She might agree with the woman, that he was an angel of sorts himself; but Roche was not comfortable being cast in such a bright light, or being placed upon any sort of pedestal.

He was sure everyone would eat their fill, then slumber the rest of the night and perhaps the following day away. Each of them had either waited sleepless on deck, or taken to the sea to forage through the night. In the morning he would check on them, and start a regular foray of fishers to keep them all fed in the days to come.

Right now, he needed his own refreshing escape from the floating crew and all the problems that would arise once their hunger had abated.

CHAPTER 38

When he found her waiting for him, Roche felt an immense burden lifted from his shoulders. It took some time to get to that sacred silent place, since he had to fight his mind from lingering out on deck. Most of the minds outside his cabin had grown silent, and succumbed to exhaustion. The rest were surely not far behind them. From this side of the door, he tried to put all his imaginings about what might be happening on the other side of the door behind him. They would sleep, while he searched the darkness for the light of his other.

He had to believe that, at least for a while; it was the only way to reach that place, which was the only way he could be with her. Roche ignored their sleepy thoughts, and turned down the volume on his own; and suddenly, there he was in that nowhere place with her.

"My brother," Ehcor said. "You have come."

Trying to hide the fears he had entertained would be pointless, and Roche didn't want to anyhow. His counterpart should know how he felt about seeing her, and how he had despaired over the possibility that their meetings were only in his mind.

"I felt the same," she said, as he thought about it.

The angel didn't laugh, but she may as well have: the light brightened around her luminous form, and waves of mirth flowed from her to wash over him. She was laughing at herself, not him; but when he joined in, Roche had to admit he felt a little abashed to have thought that way as well. They shared the humor silently, in the sublime connection they had that required no words.

Ehcor went on, giving beautiful but unnecessary voice to the thoughts she was already sharing with him.

"I also drew the same conclusion as you," she said. "You show me things I could not have imagined myself, and tell me things I would not expect you to say. As much as I feel whole in your presence like nowhere else, I also feel there is a great unbridged gap between us. So much of what you are is a mystery to me, and so much of what you have done is nothing but strange stories set in even stranger worlds. If I wasn't seeing it through your eyes, and your memories, I would be sure nothing like the land of the living could exist as it does."

Without a head to nod, Roche made the gesture somehow anyway. Even he found some of the things he had experienced hard to believe, and part of him wanted to forget his most recent memories rather than share them with her. Roche felt an intense desire to protect her from the ugliness of all the worlds, for some reason; at the same time, he had to see his own memories through her eyes to really feel he had lived them. He saw her light waver, and darken, while he thought over the events of the last few days. When he was done she brightened once more, and set the face she didn't have in this place into a determined smile.

"The natives on your boat," she said, without saying a word. "They are connected to the mortal realm as we are connected to the worlds above and below. Just as we can listen to the endless hum of Heaven or the constant crackle of Hell, they are tuned into the eternal song of the Earth. They see it as a symphony, and every event as an essential sound in that symphony. I admit I have watched you from up here, and felt great pride in knowing you were a part of me as you tried to help them all at once."

Roche knew he would watch her, if he could; the possibility that she was as interested in his life as he was in hers was a bit of a pleasant shock, to him. The next shock was not so pleasant, as he looked into her bright mind. He could see a scene divided, one part of her looking at him while another part of her gazed down at the world his body still occupied.

The first thing he felt was surprise. Roche had supposed everyone had gone to sleep on the ship, after eating their fill; but through her eyes he saw a cluster of people gathered below deck, clearly awake and alert. All of them had bronzed skin, pulled tight over lean muscle that tensed as they spoke to each other in hushed urgent tones. One of the women raised her voice above the whispers, to remind the others what she thought they should already know.

"They are beyond hope," she said.

Although they had each descended willingly belowdeck, very few of the natives looked like they were comfortable being where they were. They shifted in place, looking from each other to the woman that had spoken. She stood between them and a locked door, and one of them grudgingly came forward and began working on the lock when she gestured at him and then the door.

Immediately Roche realized where they were. The natives had clustered outside the room full of benches, oars and prisoners. While the one at the door wrestled with the mechanism, the woman went on.

"We were brought here to deliver mercy," she said. "Otherwise the fish would have forged a different trail for us to follow, the currents would have routed us right around this ship and its cursed crew. The sea is vast, but it brought us directly to our brothers and sisters of the land."

The door swung open, and the small crowd of natives shrunk away from the smell that burst forth. Covering their mouths and noses, they peeked inside one by one. Whatever had weakened their collective resolve was gone by the time they were done looking, and they moved into the room without hesitation when the woman spoke once more.

"Show them mercy," she said, "and deliver it swiftly."

Roche was torn in two by the vision. In this place he saw things differently, and the quiet calm of Ehcor's presence had shown him a fresh new perspective on each memory he had shared with her. Everything was clearly a part of a larger plan, when he was here with her. He knew the spell would be broken if he left this place, and darkness would descend within him once more. Roche needed his time with her, to carry him through all those moments he would have to endure without her.

At the same time, he could not stand to watch the horror that was happening through her eyes. Part of him wanted to stay here with her, insist she tune out the world his body was in, and get on with spending precious timeless moments sharing their experiences in peace. The rest of him knew she would be watching either way, and that he had to leave her to both escape the vision and prevent it.

Of course, Ehcor saw his struggle. Through their connection Roche looked at the vision, and at his own swirling mind; he realized it was not her he was trying to protect. He wanted to keep such savage scenes from her for his own sake, so he could continue to imagine her glowing brightly for all eternity; he wanted to gather all the darkness of all the realms into himself, and keep it from ever touching her.

"My brother," she said, softly, "all shadows are cast by the light. Darkness does not exist to overwhelm the light, or to snuff out its brightness. Without the darkness there would be nothing but endless featureless light, the white glow of love with no thought or experience. None of what you love would have ever been, and there would be no need for the worlds you walk between or any of the lives you have touched. You cannot keep me from the darkness, unless you would remove me forever from the light."

This place seemed to be the one she spoke of, an unending and untainted landscape that glowed with love in every direction as far as he could see. Aside from her, and him, nothing existed here but the light. Roche had assumed it was her presence that created the effect, but he could see now that this place had existed before they had discovered it and then found each other here.

The realization made him want to stay even more. Here he could be near her, and watch the worlds through Ehcor's eyes instead of his own. In this place that was no place, he could see the love in every tragedy; while the light constantly filled him and lifted him up, Roche could let the realms happen on their own without the confusion or rage that came with getting involved. They could be together, always; and the realms of angels and humans and devils could go on without them.

Roche expected her to see his thoughts, and be disappointed in his desire to disengage completely from the world outside their shared presence. In the back of his mind he knew he couldn't stay here much longer, but his mind was way back there on the boat. The part of him thinking about leaving it behind was here, with her; the quiet calm of their togetherness in this place was big enough to push those distant thoughts away forever.

To his surprise, Ehcor felt the same way. She did not want to return to her endless lessons or her angelic teacher; in her heart she was agreeing that they should remain here together, and let the worlds go on without them. Just as he was counting on her to shake them from their shared reverie and be the resounding voice of reason, she was relying on him to do the same. She knew he could not turn his back to the lower realms forever, and she waited for him to break their sublime connection.

It was not his love for those worlds that made him turn from her, or the need to see anything set right; from here, everything looked right already. The natives on his boat had echoed the same sentiments Ehcor had when she shared her lessons with him; although they had said it in their own way, they seemed to be permanently ensconced in the knowledge that the world had its own path and its own direction. With them, it would find the way to where it was going; and without them, it would get to the same place. The particular path it took was not nearly as important as the destination it led to, and there was nothing anyone could do to stop that eventuality.

She expected him to act. Despite his desire to be with her, Ehcor was counting on him to break away and return to the body he had left behind in his cabin. She knew he could not abide simply letting the worlds be as they would, even if he saw the futility in acting. Because she knew that about him, Roche knew it about himself. The only thought more devastating than leaving her presence was seeing her disappointment in him if he did not go. Putting aside his elevated viewpoint and his own regret at their time together being cut short, Roche spoke to her gently within the waves of luminescence.

"My sister," he murmured, "I must go."

Even in a world that was nothing but light, Roche could see the landscape brighten visibly around him as he pulled away. The scene they had glimpsed together had faded while they interacted, and he had no way to know what to expect upon his return without looking through her eyes again and directing her attention downward. Roche was sure merging with her once more would make him unable to leave, so he continued to drift away from her and towards his body. Ehcor's voice filled his head one last time as he separated from her, and he knew the sound would echo in his thoughts until he was with her again.

"Go with my blessing," she said, "and with the knowledge that I will always be awaiting your return."

The vast emptiness of space surrounded him, and the only lights he could see were distant stars winking at him from the other side of forever. In the next moment out of time, the universe collapsed in on him. Roche was yanked back into his body with shocking force, and he was on his feet before he was fully aware of his surroundings. Turning from the blank burnt wall of his cabin, Roche made for the door and threw it open.

Smoke invaded his nostrils, the hot dense smell of it returning his mind to the sweet acrid scents of Hell for a moment. Through the smoke he could see the fire, and feel its flames licking ever outward and upward to burn everything in its path. The deck had seen more years than any of the feet that walked it save his own, and it had taken on water only to dry in the thick hot air of a scorched world more times than any of them could count. No waves had washed over its scarred surface for some time, and the deck went up like tinder everywhere the fire touched it.

From some ways away the vessel surely looked like a small distant orange dot of light, with a tiny plume of black smoke rising from the flames to darken the night sky ever so slightly over the boat. Up close, there was nothing but smoke punctuated by brightly burning embers. Roche couldn't tell if the bright spots were showing him the lines of the deck or if they were fingers of flame grasping at the sky; even the frame he stood in was beginning to burn, and in moments he would be engulfed by the inferno.

Roche tilted his weight forward, and strode into the fire.

CHAPTER 39

The first few steps he took were blind. Roche waded through thick smoke and crackling flames, not bothering to adjust his eyes to try to penetrate the wall of fire. He knew the deck was clear for several strides, and expected to stop as soon as he stood on something that wasn't burning. No matter how far he went, he couldn't find a spot where he wasn't engulfed in the choking inferno.

His clothes had caught fire as soon as he stepped forward; by the time he stopped to get his bearings they had curled into ash and drifted away in smoldering pieces. Flames licked at his naked flesh. The feeling was more pleasant than painful, and Roche savored the sensation while adjusting his eyes to see through the inferno. Compared with the heat of Hell, the fire was more of a comforting warmth than a sweltering hot.

Looking past one wall of the blaze only showed him another. Roche turned in place to gaze in every direction, only to realize the deck was on fire from stem to stern. Flames leapt high in spots, but it was hard to tell if they originated on the flat walking surface or on one of the features affixed to it. He had no way to determine where the stairs that would take him belowdeck were, in the light and dark landscape of dancing red and orange punctuated by billowing black.

Roche took an uncertain step. The deck sagged under his footfall, giving way even more as he leaned his weight forward. Bringing his other foot down hard on the soft flooring, Roche felt the wood begin to splinter. He leapt up in the air, got a good look at the blaze that had once been a boat, and hit the deck hard with both feet. The boards shuddered when he struck them, and one of his feet punched through the flat flaming surface. He jumped up once more, and kicked downward in the moment before he landed again.

An explosion of flames engulfed him, sparks and burning wood rising to embrace him as he fell. The next moment Roche could see again, as he landed belowdeck in a shower of fiery debris. His eyes adjusted immediately to the darkness, and he was relieved to note the fire had not spread to the lower level.

He had time to hope Ehcor had been seeing into the future before he reached the oar room. If they had set the deck on fire first, the natives may not have had time to descend the stairs and play out the scene he had watched through her eyes. Maybe that moment was yet to come, and he could step in to save someone in what little time he hoped to have left.

Long before he reached the room, Roche knew it was too late. The lock had been sprung, and the door stood open; no one was nearby, and he knew what he would see in the cramped space before he saw it. First the smell hit him, even worse than before. Roche kept moving forward, although the stench of bile and blood had been drenched in the stink of death. The heat from the fire was not much to him, down here; but it was enough to increase the intensity of the odors spewing through the open door, and give him a moment's pause.

Roche pressed forward, holding his breath to escape the smell. A few more steps, and he was standing in the door frame scanning the room for life. Nothing moved in the space other than drops of blood, dripping quietly off dismembered bodies to puddle on the floor. Every one of their throats had been slit, and they all wore matching red smiles in death. Instead of looking like they had died in horror, the bodies appeared to be reclining peacefully where they had expired. Had they not been covered in their own blood from the neck down, Roche would have assumed they were all taking a well deserved break from their difficult duties.

He took one step into the room, then another. The smell climbed inside his nostrils, even as he tried not to breathe; and Roche let the gruesome sight burn itself into his brain. For some reason, he found himself hoping this stark memory would not slip away from him like so many others. He thought of the people who had done this, and let his rage build as he wondered if they had escaped.

The fire had been raging too long for them to have started it after coming here. Surely some of the smell of burning flesh drifting in the smoke was theirs, and that angered him even more. They were sure the world would keep turning without them, and that each soul would find the way to where it was going; yet they were willing to throw themselves into the fire and sacrifice their own future to speed the process along. The action belied their conviction, from where he stood; and Roche let the fire burn within him as he stared at the dripping gore.

Hot cinders had fallen through the deck with him. On the other side of the door, the fire was now spreading on this level as well. Roche was aware of it, and unafraid. He could hear the crackling flames getting closer, but he didn't turn until another noise reached his ears. The creak of the floorboards was oddly out of place in the whooshing burning cacophony, and he spun about immediately at the sound.

She was likely the only one left alive, at this point. Earlier, Roche had thought maybe he had seen some hope in her eyes. As she stood in the doorway, looking up at him, he realized it was not hope he had seen. The woman had shared her secret with him, tried to kill him, and even attempted to do him a kindness; but the whole time she had been waiting for death, and part of her had been disappointed every moment it didn't come.

They locked eyes, neither of them moving. Roche knew she could see the piles of death behind him, and feel the fire he could see creeping up behind her. Without words, he tried to tell her everything; he hoped his eyes were letting her see his thoughts, how he had meant to save her and all the others from this life. She seemed to be communicating her own silent message to him, that she knew nothing he could have done would have made her life worth living.

Without anger or resentment, she kept her eyes locked on his as the flames began to lick at her body from behind. Roche expected her to tense up, to wince at the pain. Instead she relaxed, and spread her arms so the flames could wrap themselves around her. He watched her clothes begin to smolder, blacken and burn; then they caught fire, and she became a being of flames with a simple ashen face. She wasn't smiling, but she wasn't grimacing either; her relaxed posture was echoed in her face, and her features looked serene.

Roche had not seen past the pain she wore on her face before. The circumstances of her life had twisted her countenance into a grim mask that had been forever fixed in place, and he had a sudden moment of clarity as the mask fell away. She was beautiful, under her torment. In another life men would have lined up to court her, instead of behaving like such savages that she had to hide herself and her beauty. For that moment he felt he was seeing her for the first time, and it was another memory he hoped would never slip away. The next moment her eyes rolled up into her skull, and she fell back into the flames.

Rather than go through the doorway and step over her body, Roche stomped the floor beneath his feet. The boards here were not on fire, not yet; but they were old and drenched in bile. It didn't take long before a hole opened underneath him, and Roche felt himself falling through. He did not expect the level below to be tilted, and he lost his footing when he struck the floor unevenly.

Piles of artifacts were everywhere, and he landed in one of them as he fell. Countless fishing nets and spears had been dumped unceremoniously below, and they had shifted with the boat to settle in a line along the middle of the lowermost deck. No one could live down here, or even keep their feet; so they had tossed what they had taken into the space, and left it to rot. Roche wasn't sure if he was disgusted more by the nature of the tools, or what the piles represented. For every spear he could see, at least one innocent native had died to row their boat and fill their bellies; for every net, there was an empty vessel drifting on the ocean that had once been full of hope.

At every stage, he had hoped to save someone from the fire. When he had realized no one could be alive on deck, he had descended below to break the rowers from their chains. After that, he surely would have gone to the sleeping quarters of the others if he hadn't encountered the woman and watched her beauty manifest only to go up in flames. In that moment, something inside him had switched. He hadn't realized it until now, but Roche didn't care if anyone else was alive on the boat. There was no way to save them, in the middle of the ocean; and he wasn't sure he would, even if he could.

He extricated himself from the clinging nets he had fallen onto, and stood on the uneven floor between two of the towering piles. This time when he stomped his foot, all of his weight and power went into the motion. He punched through the floor immediately, and was rewarded with a sudden spray of cold salty seawater. Hooking his foot into the hole, he pulled himself downward with one leg while stomping with the other. This time the hole that opened up was huge, and he passed through going one way while the sea gushed in going the other.

After the heat of the flames, the cool wetness felt good on his scaled flesh. Roche let the ocean embrace him, and pull him into its depths. He could see the dark shadow of the boat through the water, and the lighted ring of fire around it. As he continued sinking, the sight grew more and more distant; after awhile, he was surrounded in nothing but darkness.

Roche knew the descent would end in Hell; he could tell from the way he was being pulled rapidly downward. He let himself completely relax, and thoroughly enjoy the fall.

CHAPTER 40

Roche woke in Hell, with no awareness of having lost consciousness. One moment he was drifting slowly to the bottom of the ocean, awaiting a shift; the next he was lying on his back in the sand, dripping dry in the scorching heat of Hell. He rested there awhile, soaking in the scents of sulfur and burnt dust.

By the time he stood up and scanned the area, the seawater had dried to leave only a thin clinging layer of salt on his scaled skin. Long low mounds stretched out in every direction, and he stood in a shallow valley with limited visibility. Despite his nakedness, Roche decided to crest a nearby rise and have a better look around.

At first he only saw a few distant forms, too far off for them to spot his head as he looked over the rise. Roche kept moving in their direction, and soon found himself standing on a small hilltop with another valley below him. Something about the area seemed familiar; but it took him a few minutes to acknowledge the feeling, and a few more to place it.

Meanwhile, he kept walking. The sight below had captivated his attention immediately; he kept his eyes locked on the valley, as the details came clearer with each step. That handful of figures he had spotted at first were devils, as were the dozens of workers in the field beyond them; but what held his gaze so tight was what they were doing.

Plants too big to be called bushes towered over the devils, bent with fruits that were each as large as one of their horned heads. Every browned shrub had the fruits sprinkled generously throughout its foliage, and the devils picked them two at a time with ease. They had organized into a series of lines, each trail of bodies disappearing into the thick leafy growth. Only a few of the harvesters were visible from this far off, through the leaves; but he could see the string of devils passing fruits two at a time through the line. A wheeled stone box waited at the end of each line, to be trundled away and replaced with an empty once it was filled.

He stopped more than once, to stare in wonder. Already one container had been filled, and moved away; he watched a devil roll it down a long path away from him, to disappear over another rise. The whole time he was walking, the devil would kick his feet out to the side every few steps. Roche wondered if something was wrong with the devil, until he got close enough to hear the singing.

Then the noise reached him, the eerie echoing cacophony of a hundred devils raising their voices in song. If anything, it sounded more like chanting than singing; and they seemed to be deliberately varying their timing, causing Roche no end of difficulty when he tried to make out any actual string of words. All he could get from the rolling tune was that they had food, and they were happy for it.

He listened to the hypnotizing group chant, not realizing he had stopped walking and now stood out in the open. Just short of the field, he planted his feet and relaxed into the rhythm of the song. When a devil stopped and stared, with a fruit in each hand, the others in the line behind him turned to look as well. The rest of the devils kept singing, and Roche continued swaying along. It wasn't until one broke loose from the field and began running that he was snapped from his dreamy reverie and launched completely back into the moment.

The devil followed the same path the rolling cart of food had taken, moving much faster for having no burden. Roche knew he could catch the scaled runner, if he wanted to; but he didn't want to, so he just watched the retreating figure shrink slowly and disappear over the horizon. The others had stopped working, and they were moving to the edge of the field to gather in a tight knot. Instead of singing, they were murmuring amongst themselves; yet the murmurs sounded even more joyous than the singing, somehow.

To his surprise, they all came at him at once. Milling about but purposeful, the gathering moved closer until he could make out individual words in their urgent whispering. Their voices got bolder as they neared, and one addressed him as the crowd spread out to surround him.

"You there," the devil said. "You are the one called Roche?"

The question was nearly a statement, and Roche leaned in closer to see if he recognized the one doing the asking. No bells rang in his memory, but there was no way to tell if the memory didn't exist or if it just wouldn't chime for him. After a moment of hesitation, and another moment of consideration, he shrugged.

"Yes," he said. "I am Roche."

None of them heard him past the first affirmative word. A cheer went up at the sound, and the rest of what he said was drowned out by the happy collective cry. The devils filled what little space they had kept from him, and Roche was suddenly awash in a sea of crimson skin. All of them made tentative attempts to get close, and even brush against him, while each tried to keep a respectful distance. Instead of feeling overwhelmed by the tight knot of devils, Roche felt embraced by the small crowd. A hundred slight touches found his naked flesh in those first few moments, and he felt as though they washed the salt from his skin and the gruesome memories of the sea from his mind.

The cheer abated, only to be replaced by jubilant voices calling out questions to him. Again, the collective cry was too much to make out any particular set of words; until he heard one female burst out ecstatically and shout above the din.

"He is real!" she cried. "He is real, and he has returned to us!"

All at once, the crowd grew quiet. Whatever she meant by that seemed to be sinking in, in a completely different way for the devils than it was for Roche. He shifted uncomfortably under their collective gaze, and wondered if this was what an idol felt like. Immobile and awestruck, they stared at him with wide eyes until he noticed a new sound echoing over the long stretches of sand.

"Get back!" he cried, suddenly.

Some of the moments he had lived through had their own special kind of horror, and Roche suspected those sights would haunt his darkest hours for as long as he might live; but only one sound meant terror to him, and he could hear it now. Giant leathery wings crackled thunder in the distance, getting closer by the second.

He hadn't cared when one of the devils had run off; for the brief moment he had considered the possibility of him fetching a dragon, Roche had thought it might be a good day to see if he could indeed take on one of the flying monsters. He was itching for a good clean fight, after all the muck he had waded through to get here. Now, he had more than one life to consider: the devils still had him surrounded, and one good burst of dragon fire would turn the whole crowd around him to cinders. It didn't matter if he could withstand the flames; the devils could not, and they were clustered about him as tightly as ever.

"Get back!" he called out, again. "Don't you hear that? A dragon is coming! It could kill you all!"

They were still watching him, as if he hadn't spoken. He tried to shift one way or the other, and the knot moved with him. The deafening sound grew closer, and soon Roche could see a winged silhouette appear on the horizon. It looked big, even from far away; it only got bigger as it got closer, and he was certain Hell was about to rain down on all of them with its hottest fire.

As soon as he could tell it was black, Roche was sure the beast was Rendibite. That was the biggest black dragon he knew, and this monster was definitely larger than the only other one he knew. He kept trying to move away from the gathering, and they kept moving with him. Roche considered dashing away as fast as he could; but he wasn't sure if he could control the speed within him, or even call it forth. The last thing he wanted to do was hurt the very devils he was trying to protect, moving too quickly through them.

He didn't have time to consider another option. The dragon was covering ground swiftly, and before he knew it the beast was upon them. It shot up and into the sky of the endless cavern, dwindling to a deadly black dot; then it dropped from the smoky heavens to land nearby in a cloud of dirt and a series of small earthquakes that shook the ground under Roche's feet. As he waved away the dust hanging in the air, a familiar voice found his ears.

"Is it true?" he heard. "Roche, is that you?"

Making his way toward the sound, Roche grabbed the devil as soon as his face came clear through the lingering cloud. Forgetting his own nakedness for a moment, he clutched the transformed dragon to him in a fierce embrace.

"Laurentis," he said. "My friend. I am home."

This time when the crowd around them cheered, Roche could feel the sound in his bones. The noise rivaled the sudden explosion of the dragon's landing, and he could hear Laurentis chuckling as he crushed the devil closer to him.

"I see you found your land," Laurentis murmured into his ear, "and your people. Now let me go, and let's find you some proper clothes."

Roche released him, abashed but too relieved to feel it. He watched the dragon call out to the workers, suggesting they go back to work for a while before calling it a day. None of them grumbled, or hesitated to return to their duties; but every single one of them glanced back over their shoulders as they went, to catch a last glimpse of him. When Laurentis was done herding them away, he turned to Roche with a slight smile on his face.

"It has been a very long time," he said. "Come, walk with me. I will tell you what has happened since you left, and you can tell me what Ximena thinks of your return."

CHAPTER 41

Being back in Hell was a strange and surreal experience. Roche kept looking around as they walked, taking mental note of what had changed and what had remained the same. The air still smelled scorched, but it was mixed with the faint scent of dried fruit. Even the smoke that had hung in the air before seemed to have abated somewhat, or taken to drifting higher in the sky. In some spots Roche could see the rock roof above them, smooth and discolored by the many fires it had watched over.

More than once, they passed a cluster of huts alongside the sandy pathway. Devils stood in doorsteps watching them pass, and whispering to each other while pointing their way. Roche listened to the dragon carry on about crop schedules and how easy it was to lead happy workers until he began to tune out the words. He interrupted Laurentis finally, as they passed another series of stone and mud structures.

"I am glad things are going well here," Roche said. "I don't understand why everyone is so happy to see me, though; or why you called your workers my people. My interest in this place never waned, and I thought of it more in the other realms than I think of them here; but I have been away so long, I can't see how any of what is happening now could be attributed to me. Even my lands are only still mine because you have cared for them in my absence, when you could have just taken them at any time."

When Laurentis laughed, the sound was as sharp and loud as if he were still in his dragon guise. Some of the devils watching from windows smiled along with the conversation, as if they were just happy it was happening. Roche felt uncomfortable under the weight of so many awestruck stares, and tried to put his focus on the dragon's reply.

"It has been a long time, hasn't it?" Laurentis mused. "Even I have begun to see you as a legend, one of the hands that shaped the Hell of today. We were friends once, but when I invoke your name now it is in memory of what you made. I had always hoped you would return, to help this new world battle the old regime; but I never thought of claiming your land as my own. Once the fields you worked began to burst with food, I made sure every devil that worked it knew whose land they were on.

Maybe I could have taken it a long time ago; now everyone knows the best seeds come from your plants, and the best fruit grows in your fields."

Laurentis glanced his way as they walked, noting the discomfort on Roche's face when distant devils gawked at them. He chuckled under his breath, and went on.

"For generations," he said, "devils have worked your lands and known your name. Only dragons and Ximena would be old enough to have personal recollections of you being here before, but everyone knows that what you did changed life for all of us. You are a hero here, so you ought to get used to it. That, or do something awful and change what people remember you by."

Roche winced, and Laurentis noticed.

"Sorry," the dragon said. "I was not referring to anything you did to earn a reputation in the higher realms."

Biting his lip, Roche shrugged off the apology.

"You have no need to be sorry," he said. "What I did was awful, and worth remembering often. It is part of who I am, forever; if I thought you did not know and were not judging me by those actions, I would feel obligated to tell you what I had done."

The path they were on was wide, and worn. Others branched off from time to time, and they stepped from the main trail to one of the offshoots after awhile walking. Roche noticed there were no huts or devil spectators this way, and felt glad for it.

"You know," Laurentis said, "what happened in the mortal world was not entirely your doing, and not everyone saw the shift it caused in a dark light. You forced souls into Heaven that were not prepared for it, and I can see why the angels would be less than pleased with a sudden influx of undesirables; but you also sent many here. In Hell, the soul that is in touch with its humanity lifts the other devils up. Since the souls that belonged in human bodies were limited by the number of births happening, we ended up with a big beautiful dump of light. Have you noticed, it's actually brighter here?"

Roche had assumed that had to do with the lack of smoke hanging in the air, or his own memory failing him yet again; he nodded toward Laurentis, both in agreement and in gratitude to the dragon for pointing it out.

"I'm surprised," Laurentis went on, "that Ximena did not herald your arrival before it happened. Surely you came back because she invited you. It's strange, that she would not let everyone know you were here to support her."

Shaking his head, Roche kept his eyes on the narrow path in front of them. He noticed that the dragon's voice had changed when he brought her up. Laurentis seemed to be fishing for information, without having the confidence to come right out and ask. The first time he had mentioned the devil, Roche had shrugged it off and moved onto another topic. This time he faced the implied query head-on, spreading his hands as they walked side by side.

"She doesn't know I'm here," Roche replied. "I just, sort of…showed up here, and your workers were the first people I saw. I walked through a fire to get here, and drowned in the ocean; I didn't fully realize this was where I was headed until I arrived."

Glancing over, Laurentis nodded.

"I thought it was a little strange," he said, "you wandering around Hell naked and alone. It's a good thing another dragon didn't find you; they would have surely thought you were an indication of Ximena's intentions."

They continued on without words for a minute or two, both of them unsure of what to say. Finally Roche broke the silence, staring straight ahead and speaking in a clear and full voice.

"You said we were friends, before," Roche said. "That has not changed, in my estimation. You may suspect I am hiding something, but the truth is I have no idea what is going on in this realm. I can see it is different, but the details are beyond me. My silence is not due to any amount of secrecy; it is only an indication of my ignorance."

The dragon's shoulders shifted, relaxing as he nodded.

"Clearly," he said, "you have been away too long. The possibility that Ximena does not know you are here is pretty slim, if it exists at all. That means she is letting you come and go as you please, with no regard for the order the angels passed down to her."

Roche raised an eyebrow, without looking over.

"Order?" he echoed. "What order?"

Shrugging, Laurentis also kept his eyes on the path.

"She is supposed to bar your entrance to Hell," he said. "If she lets you in, she has been commanded to capture you and keep you in custody until an angel escort arrives to return you to Heaven. That's why you are lucky you did not encounter another dragon; you being alive in Hell would seem to indicate that you are here to support her; and if she needs your support, it is because she is against the old dragons."

Too many thoughts were whirling in Roche's head to speak them all at once, so he said nothing at all. He noticed a small structure in the distance, and that the trail seemed to end at its doorway. Something about the way the stones were piled to shape the building reminded him of something, but Roche couldn't put his finger on what it was. While they closed the gap between it and them, Laurentis shouldered the burden of carrying the conversation once more.

"She knows you're here," he said again. "She must be letting you know she has no intention of following their dictum, even if the angels say it came from on high. Of course, no world but Heaven would exist if she had not stopped taking orders from on high a long time ago. I suppose she is waiting for you to come to her, and I suggest you do so. If she tells you more than she is telling the rest of us, come find me and let me know if she intends to support the old dragons in the coming war."

As they had approached the little building, it had been easy for them to both keep their attention on the conversation. Now they stood at the end of the trail, facing the entrance to the small structure. Roche gestured toward it, noting that no actual door barred their way. He could see inside, and what he saw tugged at the back of his brain with more insistent recollection than before.

"What is this place?" he said. "Why is there no door?"

Laurentis inclined his head toward the room beyond.

"That is your house," he said. "Some workers decided to make it, to honor your contribution to their lives. Usually it sits empty, but devils come here to think and pray or keep the place up."

Stepping inside, Roche looked around in wonder.

"I know this house," he said. "It looks just like a home I knew in the mortal realm, before everything burned. Can you take me to the one who designed it?"

Following him into the cramped common area, Laurentis scanned the cozy space casually. He knew the place, and had been here before; but nothing about it had ever struck him as special. Roche could see that much in his eyes, even as the dragon shook his head. He had no way to tell him that this may well have been Adeb's house, except for being cast in stone; the thought of meeting his friend again in Hell started a churning swirl of delight and remorse within him.

"That devil," Laurentis said, "is long since dead. He may have passed into another life in Hell, or he may have been one of the few souls to go to Earth in recent years. I'm sorry, every devil that worked on this house has long since moved on."

Roche made his way to the kitchen table, smiling slightly at the fire crackling across the room. The last thing anyone needed was more heat in Hell, but there it was; he was glad for it, and the ambiance it lent to the space. He motioned for the dragon to sit with him, and turned to gaze at the flames while Laurentis got settled.

CHAPTER 42

So many of the details were familiar, while the place was still completely new to him. As much as the stone structure resembled the house he had once known, too many differences were woven into the design and decor to make him forget where he was. Rock and stone took the place of the wood in every occasion it had occurred, and the scorched scent of sulfur rolled off it in waves.

Laurentis sat with his back to the hearth, where it appeared stones had been chipped away or melted to resemble small logs. The rounds burned somehow, perhaps eternally. As much as the dragon held his attention, Roche felt his eyes going back to the unlikely and unnecessary fire time and again.

"You look much the same," Roche said.

He watched the dragon across the stone slab that made for a tabletop. Laurentis may well have stepped directly from his memories, much like the building they were in. So many things were the same; only the way he held himself and seemed to take an extra moment to consider his words when he spoke had changed. His eyes were the familiar still storm they had been before, masking his thoughts and giving his speech further expression at the same time.

"It is strange, isn't it?" Laurentis said. "Those like you and I live through so much, we watch other lives start and stop like they watch the days pass. Only our soul forms continue to grow, and we can see the fear in others when we simply take that form."

Roche's eyes found the fire. For the first time, he considered that maybe the burning beast within him was his own natural shape. He had thought of it as separate from him, when he had thought about it; but the dragon was right. Roche could no more divide himself from the fire within him than Laurentis could stop being a dragon. No matter how long either of them spent masquerading as devils, the dangerous reality always lurked just under their crimson scales.

"When I first saw you," Roche said, "it was a little terrifying. I hadn't realized how long it had been, or watched a dragon grow over time before.

I hoped it was you approaching, at first; when you got close I thought you must be Rendibite. I was not sure what to expect, but I was fairly certain it would not be good."

The dragon nodded, turning in his seat to follow Roche's gaze. Together they stared at the fire, and Laurentis sighed.

"I can't say you would have been in danger," he said, "but only because I have never seen you square off against one of us. The devils around you would have fought for you, and they would have died for you; and you would have definitely had a battle on your hands. Perhaps it would have been for the best, if you could have defeated him; but perhaps not. Any other enemy would be wise to pull back, in the face of a new and powerful opponent; but the old dragons might see it as an act of war, if you killed one of theirs. Rather than pull back and regroup, they may have set out to light the realm on fire."

They both realized they had lost themselves in the nearby flames in the same moment. Laurentis shifted in his seat, so his back was to the hearth again; Roche tore his gaze from the fire, and met the dragon's eyes over the table once more.

"You think he would have attacked me?" Roche asked.

Laurentis nodded.

"Not just Rendibite," he said. "Any of the old dragons. Now may be the best time in anyone's memory to be a devil, or a dragon; but the lines that separate us have been drawn with increasingly generous strokes as life has changed, and there is no soul in Hell that does not firmly stand on one side or the other. Being here means taking a side; since you're not a dragon, you must be here to stand against them."

Furrowing his brow, Roche leaned forward across the table.

"But you're a dragon," he said. "You stand against them. From what you have said, Ximena has not firmly planted herself on either side. Surely there is someone who exists outside all this, and can mediate."

Laurentis chuckled, and it was a dark and humorless sound.

"When your fields began to produce," he said, "Rendibite ordered me to burn them. I couldn't disobey without relinquishing my position and my life, but I could be clever about the way I carried out my orders. So I had the workers harvest the fruit, eat what they could and distribute the rest. Everyone was instructed to hang onto the seeds they found inside, and I burned what remained of the fields while the first demon fruit made its way into their bellies and their memories."

The dragon paused, and seemed to be recalling the events with a quiet pleasure. A slight smiled pulled at his lips as he went on, and Roche realized the dragon had changed more than he had first supposed. The stillness that had always lurked below the surface was now a solid sturdy sheet of peace. Something had changed inside the dragon, and it showed in his expressions even as his features remained the same.

"After I burned them," Laurentis continued, "they came back almost immediately, more lush and full than the first time. I could not have been more relieved, but I knew Rendibite had to hear it from me. We argued about what to do with the fields: he wanted to burn them each time they came up, fence them in and place guards to prevent anyone from harvesting even a single fruit. I was able to convince him that he would garner more power by working the fields and harvesting the fruit, and he agreed under certain conditions."

Shaking his head, Roche was not as disbelieving as his expression might have suggested. While he couldn't see any reason for the old dragon to behave in such a manner, he could easily picture Rendibite doing just what Laurentis was describing.

"He told me to harvest some fruit," Laurentis said, "but only enough to give those that could pay dearly for a taste of it. Rendibite wanted to create a rare delicacy, and keep it rare by distributing only a small fraction of what was being produced. He wanted me to burn the rest, even if it meant torching the fields daily."

Laurentis sighed again, and Roche found himself wondering how he had not noticed the differences in his demeanor before. He had watched the dragon draw on a deep well of anger in moments like these in the past; now Laurentis seemed to have a calm acceptance of the way things were, and what he had to do to change them.

"So I did the same thing I had done before," Laurentis went on. "I followed orders, and disobeyed at the same time. I had the workers harvest a certain amount, and cart them off to be traded at high cost. The rest I told them to discard, and leave alongside the fields. Without directly telling them to do so, I implied that each worker could take whatever they could carry from the piles they had discarded at the end of each day. There were so many, workers showed up the next day with their own carts. When I told Rendibite the product just wasn't selling at the high prices he thought it would command, he ordered me to drop the price and harvest more fruit."

A touch of humor had crept into his voice while he talked, and now Laurentis paused to chuckle under his breath. Once more, Roche was struck by the change in him. The laughter had no bitterness or anxiety beneath it;

instead it rolled out of him easily, the sound of both deep amusement and total acceptance finding its grave and jovial voice.

"The fields responded," he said, still chuckling. "We picked more, they grew more. The demon fruit became the great leveler, with every shift he made. With time, the devils began to grow in wisdom and wealth themselves. The days of eating dirt and living in fear didn't just end; they disappeared from memory, as generations of devils thrived due to your fields."

Now it was Roche's turn to laugh. He motioned at the dragon while the sound poured out of him, and he couldn't help but notice the tension and anger that sparked his own amusement.

"My fields?" Roche countered. "They may have played their part, but only because you played yours. How many times have you shifted your plan to help others, while risking your life by defying Rendibite?"

The dragon shrugged.

"Too many to count," he said. "But your fields have been as dynamic a player in all this as anyone. They have seemed to work with me, almost consciously. For every effort Rendibite made to destroy them, I had no solution but to wait and hope they would return. I stopped fearing for their life a long time ago, but before that I stopped fearing for my own. I stand on the side of the growth I see in this realm, and justice; and I will keep my feet firmly planted where they are until they have been burned out from under me."

Each of them was engrossed in the talk in their own way. Roche was letting his eyes drift from the dragon's face to the fire at will, absorbing the conversation as his gaze drank in the flames. The entire setting still had a surreal fog hazing its edges; from seeing Laurentis again after so long, to the sweet burnt scents hanging in the air, to the familiar strangeness of the little building they occupied. At best, Roche was delightfully disoriented by sitting here naked and talking with his friend once more.

The dragon had his own brand of reverie going on. Laurentis looked down at the table from time to time, watching Roche closely when he wasn't. They had each paused at his proclamation, and drifted off in their fashion. A movement across the room seemed to snag the dragon's attention, and he turned abruptly enough to cause Roche to turn as well.

Nothing could have been as surreal as her. At first she was just a shadow in the doorway, a darkness that seemed to empty the room and fill it at the same time; then the darkness swirled, and she stepped out of it. Still cloaked in shadows, she brightened the room by being in it.

"I don't mean to intrude," Ximena said, "but we all have much to discuss, and I'd hate to miss out on anything important."

Whatever tension had remained in Laurentis seemed to evaporate in that moment. He rose from his seat, turned to her and dropped to one knee. Looking up at her, his face was the picture of peace.

"My queen," Laurentis murmured.

CHAPTER 43

One did not seem to be the kneeling type; the other appeared unaccustomed to such treatment. Roche knew the dragon had been forced to kneel at Rendibite's feet for longer than even he could grasp, and that Ximena could not go for a walk in any of the lower realms without devils dropping to their knees all around her. Somehow this moment was different for both of them, and Roche could feel the simple motion made sacred somehow as it happened before him.

Instead of feeling awkward about it, Roche felt honored. Laurentis was clearly relieved to have a direct audience with the queen, and she was touched to have a dragon of any age show such homage. He was not ancient, but Laurentis was not young either; only a fool would not see him as a worthy opponent, or a significant ally.

Taking a step forward, Ximena reached out to rest her hand on his shoulder. The dragon raised his head for a moment, to meet her dark gaze; Roche could swear he saw tears shining in the dragon's eyes before he hid his face in another deep nod.

"Please rise," Ximena murmured. "Although I deeply appreciate the gesture, I am afraid I have failed you as your queen. I should have granted you the audience you requested long ago, and heard your concerns before things got so out of control. We could have been allies all this time, if I had examined your true intentions instead of suspecting you of being another dragon hungry for power. We might have even been friends, if what I have learned about you is true."

As he stood, and held her gaze as tightly as he held in his shining tears, Laurentis nodded gravely as she spoke. The simple gesture said it all, to Ximena and Roche: he understood, she was forgiven, and he was glad she was here at last.

Ximena turned, looking past the dragon to lock eyes with Roche. Maintaining eye contact with her was irresistible and trying at the same time. He could feel her dark warmth flowing into him, and reminding him of everything she had meant to him in all those memories he had let slip away. The sight of her had been enough to overwhelm his senses, when she first stepped into the room; the scent of brimstone found its way inside his nostrils as her dark delightful energy slipped into his soul, and the experience became as otherworldly as any moment a being who walks between worlds can have.

All around him, it was her. The air shimmered with darkness, softening the stone walls until they looked like scorched wood. She brought in both coolness and warmth somehow, and the fire swirled heat and tiny tendrils of smoke into the room on her currents. Roche could not recall ever having felt more at home, or glad to be calling a place home. Like Laurentis, he had forgiven her all her transgressions before she raised her voice to ask for it.

"Perhaps friendship with me is unwise, however," she said.

Laurentis turned, to stand beside her and tower over her small dark form. He could see the softness in Roche's eyes, and he inclined his head respectfully to honor what she had to say.

"I called you friend," she said, her eyes still on Roche's. "And I enlisted your help, to right what I saw as a terrible wrong."

She sighed, shaking her head as her shoulders slumped momentarily; Roche sat quietly, and let her take whatever time she needed to say what she had to say.

"The part you played," she said, "in what happened…up there. It was just a part that had to be played, and you were there through a much grander design than my own."

Breaking the intense eye contact for a moment, Ximena glanced at the fire burning brightly across the room. Roche followed her gaze, and drank in the feeling of losing himself in the flames with her. One part of him wanted to rush to her, and gather her up in his arms; the other longed to cry out, and ask why she had left him when he needed her most. Torn between two desires, he held his tongue and kept his seat. Still staring into the fire with her, he waited for her to go on.

"I went back," she said, "to look for you. All I found was the fire, and the robes I gave you floating on a lake of liquid flames. I was afraid you had been destroyed somehow, although I knew in my heart you must have survived. No matter where I looked, for the longest time, I could not sense you above or below. I tried to search the Heavenly realms, but I was denied access. That made me even more certain you were alive, but I did not get confirmation until I was instructed to detain you if you returned to Hell."

They shifted, at the same time; and once again Roche met her gaze. Ximena's cool darkness crept pleasantly into him through her eyes, and he could sense the sadness she had endured while searching for him. For the first time he wondered if she had felt as betrayed by him as he had by her; he could have returned to her long ago, and instead he had exiled himself from her presence voluntarily. His own fear had defined her intentions in his mind, and had seemed as real as the fire within him; now the assumptions he had made seemed silly, and foolish.

Briefly, he wondered if being near her had the same effect on everyone. Perhaps doubt crept in when she was not around, but her presence somehow washed away everything except a feeling of absolute trust. Such an ability would certainly serve her well; she was the devil, after all.

"I could not be more happy," Ximena said, "than to see you two working together. I would understand if either of you have reservations about including me in your plans, but I would implore you to put them aside for the sake of the realm. Action must be taken, before it is too late; and I need allies like you if I am to have any hope of wrestling control of Hell from the old dragons."

Roche stood, suddenly. Without thinking about it, he had given in to the urge to go to her. Before he could take a step, or cross the scant space between them to kneel before her or embrace her, he became keenly aware of his continued nakedness. He found himself standing there, facing her, as bare as he had been the first time they met.

With a casual motion, Ximena waved her hand before her. A swirl of darkness trailed the gesture, taking shape as her hand stopped in the air between them. The shadow had become his robes, untouched by all the trials the fabric had survived. As he took it from her, and settled the familiar weight around his shoulders, he heard his contented sigh echoed by Ximena. She was smiling when he stepped forward; and she didn't seem to mind that he bowed his head instead of kneeling. It was enough that he was smiling as well, and looking down at her with love in his eyes.

"I am with you," he said, "as I have always been."

Nodding, Ximena indulged in another sigh.

"You continued what we started together," she said, "and finished it by yourself. The devils in the mortal realm were a danger to humankind, especially during a time like this. I never thought to scour the seas searching for them, until I became aware that you were doing just that. If you are so willing to take the blame for whatever damage you caused, you really should take the credit for the good you have done. You may have saved the human race, by eliminating its greatest threat at its moment of utter fragility."

Roche scoffed, knitting his brow together.

"They survived," he said, "through a much grander design than my own. Nothing will change the fact that they would not have been so imperiled if not for me. Nothing I can do today will make up for the lives lost because of what I did yesterday."

For a moment he thought she was dismayed by his decision to throw her own words back at her; then she shared a shrug with Laurentis, and voiced the reason for her expression.

"Do you at least acknowledge the role you have played here?" Ximena asked. "Can you not see how much this realm has improved due to your influence? We may have had it hard at first, when Hell was flooded with souls that no longer had a place to inhabit in the mortal realm. Devils were back to eating dirt, there were so many and so few resources; but your fields flourished soon after, and now those hard times are distant memories for a few of us. Everyone else has long since forgotten them. But no one has forgotten you."

Laurentis laughed, a low rolling chuckle that implied far more than simple amusement. They both turned to him, to see him frowning through the laughter.

"He does not," the dragon said. "Apparently he is well versed in taking the blame for anything, but this original demon has trouble taking credit for the good he has done. He reminds me of another original demon I know, and her own humble example."

Bowing her head, Ximena was trying not to flush or trying not to laugh; maybe both. When she straightened once more, no hint remained of anything but total seriousness.

"If I am destroyed in this war," she whispered, "none of the good I have done will survive me unless devils like you do. This may be the cause I was made to fight for, and it might even be the battle I am meant to die for. No price is too high to pay, so long as souls like yours call this realm home. You are both welcome to summon me at will, as we get closer to the time to strike. I must go walk through more fires, to see if I have as many allies in these warm worlds as I hope."

The darkness deepened in the room, warm and cool air whirling once more to stoke the fire and send sparks drifting in every direction. By the time the embers had died in flight, the darkness had given way to the light again; and Ximena was gone.

CHAPTER 44

Of all the things Roche feared, the fire generated by a dragon definitely frightened him the most. He may have been afraid of being his own worst enemy, or the engineer of his own eventual demise; but he could save himself from himself at the last moment, or at least hope to. Dragon fire was a force beyond his control.

Conversations from their distant shared past had floated to the surface of his consciousness again, after spending time with Laurentis. Roche remembered how he had noted the heat and the distinct smell of the flames Rendibite had spewed forth. The dragon had told him that was nothing: every dragon had to hold back, when they were in burn mode. Once they got to a certain age, these old dark souls carried great destructive power in their bellies. Laurentis had heard some devils say the dragons could destroy all the lower realms a dozen times over if they wanted to, and leave it steeped in toxic fumes to choke the most hardy devil to death for lifetimes to follow.

Laurentis had gone on to tell him the old dragons laughed at such claims. An ancient dragon would nearly always scoff, and say they could actually destroy everything a thousand times over if they all wanted to; when Rendibite himself had discussed it with Laurentis, the elder had said all the realms would burn if the old dragons came together to scorch them. Even the mortal world could not escape that kind of destruction, and anyone left behind could not tell Heaven from Hell for eons.

Perhaps only a dragon could understand just what one of them could do, but one had tried to describe it to Roche a long time ago. He sat in his new old robes at his new old home remembering, long after Laurentis had gone. Not all the memories were of conversations they'd had, any more than all the conversations had been about the flames of dragons; but once Roche had done enough thinking, it seemed like that was all it came down to in every scenario. Then he stepped out the door, and dragon fire became his entire reality in a whole different way.

At one point, back then, Roche had mused aloud that maybe those flames were one of the few things that could destroy beings like him and

Ximena. Instead of brushing the thought aside, like he had hoped Laurentis would, the dragon had nodded in that solemn manner he'd had even in those days. He had said he hoped it was not possible, for such important incarnations to be destroyed; but if anything could do it other than God, it was dragon fire.

Laurentis had treated him to more than one show, telling Roche after each what his actions were illustrating. Most notably, he remembered watching the dragon skimming over the fields with a warm out-breath of cool flames pouring from his maw in a carefully controlled orange sheet. Then he had flown up out of sight, and sent a tight white beam of searing fire to outline the same field. The middle was lightly scorched, when it all was over; while the perfectly straight lines describing the border were smooth glass, and the sand around it smoked for hours. Laurentis had told him the searing beam was about a three for him, if he were to rate his flame on a scale of one to ten. He usually kept it more under a one, no matter what needed to be melted or burnt.

The first demonstration had left a smoky scent hanging in the air. Mostly it was the smell of crisped vegetation, and burnt dirt. Another odor was hinted at in that initial burn, and almost overpowering with the second fire; he could only liken it to the clean crisp smell during a lightning storm. Every other scent seemed burnt away by the intense aroma, and for the first time Roche had realized that some unusual smells triggered an automatic sense of terror in him.

Just as any being with a body moves without thinking in reaction to such triggers, Roche immediately dove aside as he exited the little stone structure. Most of the flame went past him, through the open doorway and into the space he had occupied a moment ago; the rest hit the wall, and scorched the stone. The rock started to melt almost immediately, and the straight frame began to sag as the fire shifted to follow him.

As soon as he hit the ground, Roche rolled to the corner of the house furthest from the flame. When he stopped rolling, he crawled along the sand as quickly as he could to round the corner and put more house between him and the source of the flame. He thought he saw a glimpse of scaled scarlet skin, flexing amongst the layers of reds and oranges and whites trying to burn him; but he couldn't be sure. Not that it mattered; if a black dragon could kill him, surely a red one could as well.

Pulling himself upright against the wall, Roche dashed to the next corner and pressed himself along the back wall. He could see wide open space before him, with trails in the distance to mark where foot traffic passed in these parts. Everything was sand, flat and easy to traverse; the worn paths did not make it any easier to walk the terrain, so much as they showed the way. Roche knew he could cover quite some distance in very little time, if he could rely on his speed to carry him; but that brought up questions he wasn't sure he wanted answered.

First, he wasn't sure his speed would kick in when he needed it. So many of his abilities had waned or stopped working entirely as his inner world continued to darken each day; and he couldn't remember the last time the world had slowed around him in response to danger, or by his willing it. The last thing he wanted to do was turn his back on a dragon and run twenty or thirty feet before realizing he was on fire.

Also, dragons were fast in flight. Lilia and Laurentis had both demonstrated that, a number of times. The latter had told him older dragons were even faster, despite their lumbering size. Even if Roche got out in front of it, he knew dragons have no top speed in flight; it would only be a matter of time before the beast caught him, and fried him from behind.

In the same moment he decided to step out from against the wall and face the monster, a giant reptilian head snaked over the top of the smoking structure and looked down at him. The thing's skull was bigger than he was, and the giant orbs that were its eyes locked on his as Roche stepped forward. He had considered the possibility that it was Lilia, after the glimpse of red he had caught earlier; but this monster was far larger than Laurentis, who was clearly older than her. Roche hadn't seen the red dragon for some time, but there was no way she could have grown to the size of this one even if they were the same color.

He saw its chest puff up as it came more into view, and watched the corners of its giant maw curl upward in a malicious smile. As it shifted its weight forward, hovering over the house, Roche realized it wasn't even flying. No pounding of wings assaulted his ears, and no downdraft of wind was blowing sand in his face. The creature was simply that big, it could step over the small stone structure as easily as Roche might step over a fallen body.

With a rumble that shook the ground under Roche's feet, the dragon swung a front leg forward and planted it in the sand. A giant cloud of dust erupted in every direction, while the dragon whooshed out another sheet of flame to torch him where he stood. Roche disappeared into the cloud of dust, pulling a curved blade from his mind as he dashed forward. Behind him, the back wall of the house was awash with fire; every lump was smoothed by the flames, every crack closing before the entire stand of stones began to sag and melt.

Perhaps he was not as fast as he had been in the past, but Roche remained every bit as strong. He swung the blade in wide powerful arcs as he stepped forward blindly, dispensing with all the weapons training he'd had and relying on raw power to save him. On the third swing, and the seventh step, the blade bit into the dragon's leg. Roche felt the weapon drag, scraping aside scaled flesh and trying to grind to a halt as it hit bone; he stepped forward, pushing with all his might, and drove the weapon forward.

His first triumph was the dragon's scream. While it remained bent on burning the pile of stones until it was a smoldering stack of reddening rock, Roche had sunk his blade deep into its lower leg. Now the dust was clearing, and he was still pressing forward. The dragon's scream turned to a howl, and its leg began to bend at the wound like it had sprouted an extra elbow several feet below the actual joint.

The monster's other leg came forward, so it stood straddling the smoking remains of the little home. Roche thought of running to it, and attacking the second limb; until he looked up at the dragon's head. Although its face was clearly twisted in pain, it was no longer breathing fire. Clearly it was waiting for him to step clear of it, so it would not burn itself with its own fire.

Roche pulled on the blade, and watched the dragon shift to lift it clear of him and the path of its fire. It took considerable effort to drag the sword from the wound, and he never stopped moving. Turning the blade as he spun, Roche buried the blade deep in the dragon's leg almost exactly opposite where his first cut had landed. The leg wasn't sliced off, but there was nothing left there to hold the dragon. Its foot stayed planted, while the beast pitched forward. Blood sprayed from the wound as the lifeless foot drifted forward, dousing Roche in an instant.

Then that old familiar sound pounded his ears, and shook his chest. Driving its wings downward, the dragon kicked up enough sand to obscure the view completely once more, and Roche was left to dash this way and that swinging his sword at the sky. Finally it found something, and made a satisfying squishing sound. In the next moment a scaled set of talons wrapped about his torso, and Roche was lifted up and over the whirling cloud of dust and sand.

He hung there awkwardly for a moment, feeling the dragon trying to squeeze the life from him. The monster had grabbed him at just the right angle, putting most of its leg and its entire body out of his reach; but Roche could still hack at the talons holding him, and that's exactly what he did. After he had sawed through two of them, and gotten a glimpse of how rapidly the other leg was healing as they flew, Roche hesitated as he prepared to saw through another.

Far below them, the hard expanse of sand stretched mercilessly in every direction. The best thing he could hope for, if he fell, was a hard landing followed by an even more difficult battle. Mostly, he was concerned about what might happen as he fell; the dragon would have time to make several passes, and sear him with that white hot laser fire Laurentis had shown him.

The talons he had chopped off were coming back, and the leg that had been dangling lifelessly a minute ago showed no sign of the wounds he had inflicted. Roche only had a moment to choose. With one swift motion, he cut through the last giant digit clutching him and should have sliced through his own side; instead the blade gently bounced off the flowing fabric of his robes, shaking loose wet sand and dried blood but leaving the material whole.

Roche expected to find himself falling. The dragon had flung him upward just as he cut himself free; it waited under him, flying casually with its giant maw cranked open. His plan to wrap the robe about himself and see if it protected him from the flames would not save him from being swallowed whole; so he twisted in the air, and angled himself so he could enter the giant toothy orifice swinging his sword. He closed his eyes, to block out the horrific hole he was about to fall into, or to utter one first and final prayer before being eaten; and that's when he heard another set of wings coming toward them.

Just as he thought he would be torn in two by a pair of dragons, or lodged in the throat of one as another arrived on the scene, Roche felt a smaller set of talons wrap about his flailing wrist. The force of the impact knocked his sword loose, and he watched it bounce off one of the larger dragon's teeth as the monster chomped down on thin air. In the next moment he was watching the giant beast's flying form dwindling to nothing in the distance. His arm felt like it had been torn almost entirely free of his body, and he twisted on the unresponsive limb to look the dragon that had saved him in the eye.

He wondered how he had thought the other dragon was her, even for a moment. All it took was one look at her, the cruel mirth that danced in her eyes even in her serpentine form; immediately he knew it was her. His healing arm twisted him around again, so he faced away from her; and the robes trailing from his body flapped loudly in the wind as she pumped her wings in a rolling rhythm of thunder.

"Lucky you got there when you did, Lilia," he muttered.

The pain from healing was always more intense than the wound itself, in his experience; Roche gritted his teeth against it, and was glad his back was still to her.

"I was about to seriously mess up that dragon," he said.

Her laughter rolled off her in waves, shaking his body from where she held him tight about the wrist. Roche didn't feel like fighting the grip, or her; instead he relaxed, and let his body dangle limp while the ache of mending screamed in his every cell.

CHAPTER 45

At the speed they were going, it was hard to tell how much distance they had already covered. Lilia kept flying faster, the ground below appearing and disappearing rapidly as they plowed through banks of smoke. Roche judged their ever increasing speed more by sensation than by the dizzying blur below; his limbs felt like they were being pulled from their joints by the wind, and then his skin began to feel as though it was being peeled away from his hands and face. The robes Ximena had given him fluttered behind, untouched by the flame and unmarred by the flight.

He focused on not looking down, or letting his dizzied disorientation show. Roche knew the dragon was pretending to ignore him, while paying close attention to his body language and expressions; he knew because he was doing the same, monitoring her as well as he could while acting as if he was oblivious. Catching a good look at her entire form proved to be difficult, from his angle; but he could see her serpentine face, at least the one side of it. Lilia was definitely watching him, as he was her.

Even setting down was painful, when it came. Lilia wouldn't do anything gradually in the air, other than build up incredible speed; instead of slowing the pounding of her wings, she stopped them immediately and swiveled the leathery appendages to catch the wind like dual sails. One moment Roche was dragging along in her wake, his face slowly peeling from his skull; the next he was flung forward, and felt his arm pulled once more from its socket as his weight lurched past her. They fell from the sky together, dropping like a huge misshapen stone until they were only feet above the hard sand.

Lilia swept her wings downward, in a single powerful thrust. A split second after his arm was pulled painfully away from his body once more, he was dropped unceremoniously to the scorched desert. The dragon hovered over him, putting Roche in the center of a small sandstorm. Wiping his eyes with the arm that wasn't dangling uselessly at his side, he traced his fingers over his features to make sure everything was in place. Roche watched her drift to the ground slowly, and waited another minute for the sand to settle around them.

Before he could get a good look at how much she had grown, Lilia transformed before his eyes. Whatever changes her reptilian form may have undergone, her devil shape remained almost exactly the same; even so, the amount of time that had passed made the differences seem more pronounced. A touch of girlishness had softened her face, before; now she was all woman, with no hint of vulnerability in her features. The look suited her, more than the suggestion of innocence ever had.

If her body had been at all lanky before, it had softened and filled in until she was nothing but curved sensuality from head to toe. Another element had taken shape in her mannerisms, as well; Roche could not deny the allure she had developed in the time since he had seen her last. Her energy had gone from reaching out, and feeling almost invasive, to a strong silent magnet drawing him in.

Even her clothes were different, although she still covered herself in shades of red that called out the color of her scaled flesh and the fire that dwelt in her eyes. Her dress clung to every curve while covering her completely from her neckline to her ankles and wrists, a perfect mix of modesty and sensuality. The only places where her skin showed were her face and hands, and a hint of flesh between where the fabric ended and her black heels began. Crafted to look like they were part of her foot, Lilia's platforms were more delicate hooves than shoes.

Silent, they were both looking each other up and down. Roche realized she must see some changes in him as well, and that she was assessing his appearance and mannerisms as much as he was hers. All the days that had passed were surely etched on his face somehow, described by his body language as much as the past had touched her without really altering her appearance in any way he could put his finger on. Although the changes had happened gradually for him, as they must have for her, he thought of how he appeared through her eyes while he watched her through his. Roche wondered what she saw, and how it looked from where she stood.

Who she had been before seemed superimposed over who she was now. Roche was in the presence of two versions of her: one standing before him, and the other generated by his own memories. So much had happened to him, and affected him deeply; Roche considered that he was meeting a completely different person than he had known before, and had trouble addressing her with the familiarity he had felt while dangling from her clawed talon.

Looking back the way they had come, Roche gestured at the endless expanse of sand and rock. He willed the two images of Lilia to come together in his mind as he spoke, and tried to keep his voice both grave and casual at the same time.

"Thank you," he said. "I had no opportunity to speak with that dragon before it attacked me, and was ill prepared to defend myself. As far as I know, I have never encountered it before. I don't understand why it was trying to kill me."

Lilia's eyes narrowed, flames dancing in their depths. She did not believe him, and found it amusing that the only soul in Hell who claimed to not know why the old dragons sought to destroy him was the one they wanted dead.

"She," Lilia said, quietly.

Another wave of euphoric strangeness passed over him at the sound of her voice. With a single word, she had characterized all the differences he had seen in her. Her voice was the same, but she had inhabited it more completely. Time had given her the chance to explore the range of expression possible to her, in every aspect of her being. From the way she animated her face to the manner in which she held herself, Lilia had gone from deciding who she wanted to be to being comfortable with who she was in the time they had been apart.

More than anything, that brief utterance cemented Lilia of today in his mind. Roche hadn't thought of her as young, before; but when he looked back on who she had been, he realized she was a dragon youth at the time. Part of him wished she had retained her reptilian form a minute longer, so he could have seen how much she had grown. She had grabbed him from the sky for a reason, though; and he sensed they had ended their journey where they were for a reason as well.

Wherever she had brought him to, he had never been here before. Roche thought back to what she had said, trying to pick up the thread without dwelling on the sound of her voice again. Looking around, putting his thoughts in order, he saw a clear demarcation where the smooth scorched sand ended and the rocky terrain they had come to began. The entire landscape from here on was violent stony upthrusts punctuated by oases of burnt chunks of rock. It looked like the stone had grown tired of living underground, and had reached up through the sand with giant jagged stone fingers too numerous to count.

"She...?" Roche echoed, bringing his eyes back to hers.

Lilia nodded, her lips smiling slightly while her eyes remained humorless and harmlessly seductive. The dancing flames did not make him want to embrace her, or touch her; but they drew him in just the same, as if some elemental part of her was calling to some undeniable part of him.

"The dragon you encountered," Lilia said. "Not an 'it', but a she."

Looking back the way they had come once more, Roche lifted an eyebrow. He was fairly certain they had gotten away clean, and that the beast had not followed; that didn't mean he was not still listening for dragon wings.

"Do you know her?" he said.

Even something as simple as a shrug had become a gesture uniquely characterized by the changes that had taken place in her. Lilia's whole body went into the movement somehow, yet it was so subtle he would have missed it if he hadn't been looking right at her.

"I know all the dragons," she said, simply. "I act as liaison between the dragons and the devils, and between the old dragons and the young. It is my duty to know all the dragons in Hell, and to make sure they are heard as clearly as the endless din of devil voices crowding the realm."

Instead of calling out her apparent prejudice, Roche nodded to indicate he had heard it and to show he didn't care.

"Other than you," he said, "that was the only red dragon I've ever seen. Is that how you tell males from females? By color?"

Lilia shook her head, and let the smile that had been tugging at the corners of her lips reach the flickering flames in her eyes. The expression was so much like one he had seen on her face before; but then it had seemed calculated, and now it looked completely natural. He couldn't help but feel the old chill image of her begin to melt away.

"Red dragons are rare," she said. "Either very few of us are born, or most of us are killed at a very young age by black dragons. It's hard to say which, and perhaps it's a bit of both; but the result is the same either way. Red dragons can be male or female, as can the black. Our color is more indicative of our powers than our sex, although most of the red dragons that live to maturity are indeed female."

She paused, perhaps to let how open she was being with him sink in. Without having any idea how to acknowledge it, Roche did not fail to notice.

"Black dragons are pure power," she went on. "They seek power in every form, and personify it more as time goes on. For a black dragon, fear is everything: they feed off the fear of anyone that glimpses them in flight and cringes at the sight, and delight as much in hunting down terrified transgressors as they do in punishing them. They love fear, as long as it is a fear of them; but they hate their own fear more than anything."

The smile lifted her whole face, and Roche couldn't help but be dazzled for a moment. Rather than appearing practiced, the expression looked well worn; Lilia had her share of happy thoughts, and this was one of them.

"And what do black dragons fear most?" she smiled. "Why... red dragons, of course. If they are incarnations of power, then we are incarnations of magic. Females tend to tap into our powers at a younger age, and thus have more chance of surviving the secret hunts the black dragons are rumored to practice. A red dragon must live a long time to be accepted into the world of dragons in any significant way, as must a black dragon; but when a few of us get old enough, we are able to keep them at bay. It is the red dragons that have kept order between devils and dragons so long; if not for my predecessors, all the realms would have surely been destroyed by now."

His grave expression played counterpoint to her easy smile.

"A thousand times over," he muttered.

Nodding, Lilia let her face fall to match his.

"At least," she agreed. "That is why I have such great concern right now. Even the old red dragons are beginning to consider life in Hell unbearable, with every last corner of all the lower realms overrun with devils. I have been working tirelessly since the influx of souls, trying to find a comfortable solution for everyone. Now that my greatest effort to date is complete, I may have compromised my standing with the old dragons by intervening with your little scuffle today."

Roche felt as though he should apologize, or thank her again; instead he remained silent, and went back over what she had said slowly in his mind.

"Tell me," he said. "What have you been doing? What is this greatest effort you speak of?"

Rather than answer him, Lilia walked briskly away from him and the desert. Her path was headed directly into a cluster of tall burnt stone, one giant slab leaning heavily against another. At first glance, the dark space between the stones was nothing but shadow; as she got closer, and he focused on the spot, Roche saw it was actually an opening.

Following her, as her careful strides seemed to want him to do, Roche came up beside her just as she stepped between the rocks and into the shade. His eyes adjusted as they stopped together, and he followed her gaze downward.

A giant bowl had been carved or discovered under the ground, and they stood at the mouth of only one of many openings looking down into it. Roche could see other access points, at various heights along the distant walls. It was hard to tell how far away they really were; he could only discern that the space was vast, and the other entrances looked like dots of light from here. The only way he could tell they were large enough to admit anyone was by the stairs, long winding steps carved in stone that illustrated the path from every lofty passage to the sandy streets below.

Without a population, the cavern could not be called a city. Other than that, it had all the hallmarks of a city in any realm. Clear pathways cut through every part of the level floor, describing wide streets along areas of commerce and narrow alleys through residential areas. Roche could tell where the bazaars would go, and could see the wisdom in setting up a multitude of them; the tall structures meant for housing would hold hundreds of devils, perhaps thousands. Rather than walk across the entire city for what they needed, everyone could get whatever they were looking for close to home.

Tearing his eyes from the scene below, Roche turned to Lilia. She was surveying the view, and smiling again. Although he had no desire to interrupt the chain of thoughts leading to her expression, or break the spell of her smile, he couldn't let himself assume he knew what he was looking at.

"You did this?" he said. "Why?"

Her smile didn't falter, as her eyes remained on the streets and the structures below. A few slow and measured steps brought Lilia to the closest set of stairs, the thin clinging fabric of her dress shifting and rolling with her movement; and she began to descend without looking back. Roche wanted to hear her answer as much as he wanted to see the city up close; but something about the empty space that looked like it should be full and the dwindling memories of his distrust of Lilia rooted him in place for a long moment.

Then he heard her words drifting back and up to him, and watched her fiery hair bounce lightly out of view. With one last look at the light outside, and the vast expanse of sand, he followed her deeper into Hell

CHAPTER 46

Their descent into the city was swift enough, as was her explanation of how it came to be; Roche tried to put his full attention to both, failing more than not. Every time his breath was taken away by a new vantage point, he lost the trail of the conversation; and each revelation of her motivation caused him to lose awareness of the city below almost completely. He did not miss a step, however; the stairs were wide and well placed, easily navigated despite their winding downward path.

Lilia spoke facing forward and looking down. Most of her words came out crisp and confident, flinted and clear; but every once in a while, her voice fell quiet under the weight of what she had to say. Roche quickly learned to pay more attention when her volume dropped, and found himself wondering more than once if she had changed as completely as it seemed.

"By the time I got to know the queen," she told him, "she had won the hearts of the devils, and the respect of the old dragons. She likes to say she was very young when she found me, but enough time had passed that her place in Hell was well established. Since I was not around yet when she was earning that place, I never really understood how the queen had come to be seen the way the denizens of the lower realms see her. I thought it was just the way things always were, and always would be."

Her deliberate omission of Ximena's name was not lost on him. Roche was not sure if Lilia was being respectful, and not calling the queen's attention to conversations she did not need to be bothered with; or if she was being secretive, and trying to keep what she was saying between them. So far, he had no reason to suspect it was anything but the former. The more likely scenario was that all devils and dragons spoke of Ximena that way, to avoid capturing her attention unnecessarily.

"Only the stories remained," Lilia went on, "to teach me what Hell had been like before, and to tell me what the queen had done to change it. She can be vague, especially when she is being humble; so most of what I learned was from others. The only examples I had that would explain the purpose of life for me were dragons, and dragons live a different life than devils. Or original demons."

The steps widened into a landing of sorts, a platform that was a little over twice the width of the stairs they had been taking. Roche had already wondered more than once how many steps there were, and how long they had taken to carve. Most of them were wide enough for two descending devils to pass two others coming up, and the landing she stopped at was large enough to hold over a dozen. He stepped up beside her as the path leveled out briefly, and looked over the city.

From here, they could see the sides of many of the taller buildings that hadn't been a part of the view from above. The site was well chosen, both in function and form. Devils coming up could rest here, and enjoy the sights while catching their breath; and those going down would not be impeded at all by them. Roche could see other landings below, along the path of chiseled steps; they were spaced at regular intervals, giving anyone climbing them either way spots to rest and gaze out over the city.

"It was you that made me see," Lilia breathed, beside him.

She spoke so quietly, he would not have heard her if they had still been walking. Torn between the view below and the urge to gape at her in mild shock, Roche kept his eyes on the city as she did. He waited for her to speak again, and was not surprised when she turned on her lifted heel and continued to descend the steps. This time he trailed her more closely, to catch every word she threw back over her shoulder at him.

"You did not belong here," she said. "Your powers were too great for a new soul, and your purpose was not in Hell. The devils were not happy to hear that another original demon was here, and the dragons were even less pleased. Nearly everyone expected you to be nothing but trouble, and many began looking for ways to destroy you or exile you as soon as word of your arrival had spread."

None of this was news to him. Roche had long been aware that many felt he had no place in the one realm where he might fit in. All the time he had been away, Roche had labored under the delusion that those opinions had not changed; if anything, he had expected to return to Hell and find he had more enemies than when he'd left. The way devils saw him now still had not sunk in completely.

"Then you made your mark," Lilia murmured.

Her words only barely found his ears, she spoke them so low. Another landing was coming up ahead, and he wished she would stop for awhile and tell the rest of her story. When she crossed it without slowing, Roche realized he would likely hear it all this way. The only view available to him would be the back of her head, and the city below. His eyes went from her fiery tresses to the breathtaking architecture, and he leaned forward to hear her better as she went on.

"I thought you would be scorned," she said, "when you left before finishing anything you had started. Instead you sent a giant influx of souls that did not belong here, the thinkers and builders and planners Heaven usually gets when souls on the upward path die. And the fruits that grew to feed them all…they were named after you, and with good cause. You earned your name and your place in Hell, even as the queen did; only this time I got to see it happen."

Looking over the city from this angle, Roche could see in through the windows of the nearby high buildings. His vision being what it was, he was also able to bring the distant openings up close to see beyond them better. Although none of the spaces were occupied, many of them had been furnished. He had never seen chairs or tables in Hell, aside from the ornate specimens owned by dragons or the queen; yet here were simple stone and straw seats to sit on, and beds to lie on.

Lilia was still walking, and talking; Roche hurried to catch up, and not miss anything she had to say.

"When Hell changed," she said, "I realized it was not who we are that determines our place. It is the things we do, and the lives we affect. To serve both the devils and the dragons, I devised and built this city. The ideas that came from the world of mortals helped craft such tall structures, and make it possible to house so many in a single building; but finding and preparing a location was a difficult and necessary first step."

As they came to the last landing before the final set of stairs, Lilia finally stopped and waited for him. Roche came up beside her once more, sharing the view and the space while listening in bewilderment. From here they could see the first couple levels of windows, and the walkway that began and ended at the base of the steps. The path widened almost immediately, turning into a cobbled lane with a tall stone archway for visitors and residents to walk under as they entered the city.

"I hope you don't mind," Lilia said, without turning, "that I build it on your land. Or under your land. However you want to see it."

Roche hadn't bothered to wonder why he felt such an immediate attachment to this place. With Lilia so close, it was hard for him to relax completely; but he sensed it now that he thought about it, and realized this was indeed one of the places in Hell that felt as though it belonged to him. They must have flown in a long and wide circle, only to return to the same area she had snatched him up.

"Why?" Roche asked. "Why in my territory? Don't you have lands?"

He wasn't angry, or even upset; just curious. Lilia's slow measured nod registered out of the corner of his eye, even as Roche's attention wandered the streets of the city below.

"I have lands," she said, "but they do not completely become mine until my ward dies. Until then, she has at least some say over what I do with my territories; and since she is arguably more annoyed with all these devils than anyone, I did not want to present my plan to her. Instead I brought it to the queen, and obtained her blessing to use your land. Then you returned just as it was completed, and I sought you out. To get your blessing, as well. And perhaps, to ask you to help me populate it."

After one last look at the lowest rooftops and closest buildings, Roche moved past her and began to descend the final flight. Lilia followed, as he had hoped she would.

"Your ward," he called back to her. "Does she know of this?"

Roche winced at her response, and was glad he had turned his back on her. The pain in his body may have healed, but the melting image of the little stone structure he had meant to call home was still burning in his mind. As the path leveled out, and the city stretched out before him, Lilia's words found his ears.

"I suspect," she said, "that is why she attacked you."

CHAPTER 47

At last, Roche was able to make eye contact with Lilia and hold her gaze. He turned in his tracks, just short of entering the city, and locked eyes with her. At first he was startled, taken aback by the new layer of churning fire in her eyes. Something had changed about her, to be sure; yet he still felt the old nagging in the back of his mind, telling him all those changes might not be for the better.

She seemed to be caught off guard in the same manner, and they eyed each other openly for a long minute before either of them spoke. The swirling depths of flame in her gaze drew him in and pushed him away at the same time, inviting him to look while not showing him everything. Neither of them appeared comfortable with holding the eye contact, or breaking it.

"Your ward?" he said, at last. "She is the one who attacked me?"

Lilia nodded, her head hardly moving. The entirety of her expression was in those fiery eyes, telling him everything she wanted to without revealing anything she didn't.

"Her name is Spessia," she said. "She is the oldest red dragon, and her magic is great. I am her ward, in the strictest sense of the word. However, she did not wish me to call her 'master' or 'mistress'; and she pointed out back when we formed our partnership that I would be taking care of her one day in more ways than she took care of me. Now that time has come, and I finally see why I have been calling her my ward all these years. Red dragons become as mad as black dragons as they grow into ancient status, and they are as difficult to contain. Perhaps more."

Still holding her gaze, Roche frowned slightly. He found himself wondering how much his own eyes were revealing, and if she felt as though he was trying to hide his thoughts from her. The least he could expect, Roche suspected, was that the suspicion she regarded him with was equal to his own suspicion toward her.

"How is she going to take this?" he asked. "You intervening, the way you did. Surely she knows it was you."

Once more, Lilia signaled assent with nothing but a flash of sparks in the fire of her eyes. Maybe there was a hint of fear in there, as well; just as he saw the vulnerability begin to creep in, she laughed and her eyes went to burning glassiness again.

"Of course," she said. "If she didn't recognize me, she can always divine who it was through her magic. I will explain to her that your destruction would have had serious repercussions, and might even start the war everyone is trying to avoid. I am ready to dedicate this city, and begin work on another. All we have to do is get the devils contained. They are communal creatures, so they will benefit from living in these conditions. The dragons can go back to leading their more solitary lives, unmolested by devils who do not know their place."

Roche laughed, but only with his eyes. He found the way she said so much with only slight shifts in her gaze compelling, and was imitating it without deliberately willing himself to.

"Whose side are you on, Lilia?" he said. "Really."

A smile pulled at the corners of her mouth, while she answered.

"I think I would say the same thing you would," Lilia said. "I am on everyone's side. If there is any way we can prevent war, that is the way I wish to take. Without that possibility, I would have to choose. As would you. And I think our answers would be much the same in that case, as well. You must know my allegiance lies with the queen, and the last thing I want is nothing but old dragons in Hell. Even Spessia has told me she expects me to stand with the queen when that time comes, and that she'll kill me first if we find ourselves on opposite sides. If all the old dragons die, everyone knows what that means for the remaining young dragons."

Roche narrowed his eyes, by way of nodding.

"You become the old dragons," he said.

Finally, Lilia broke the eye contact. Twirling on her elevated heel, she gestured toward the city.

"I have a place for you here," she said. "A fine estate, really a small castle. I would say they are better accommodations than the ones built for you aboveground, but that is no longer an option from what I saw. Can I show you what I am planning, and how many devils I can put in one building? Just this single site will change so much, and might even be enough to take the pressure off this situation entirely."

Looking at the open street indicated, Roche shrugged.

"I don't want a castle," he said. "I want to live in one of the other buildings, the ones you mean to house all these devils in. If I am going to encourage them to populate the city, and live there, I should show them I am willing to live there as well. Under the same conditions."

All at once, Lilia's body language changed. Her back bent a little, and then straightened; as if she was shrugging off a great weight. After letting out an audible sigh, she gave him an open and honest smile. It may have done more than anything to impress the change she seemed to have gone through on him, that simple subtle admission of relief.

"You'll help me, then?" she said, still smiling.

"Maybe," Roche replied. " I feel in part responsible for all the tension going on, and grateful to you for trying to find a solution. I don't want war, and you say you don't either. Let's have a look at your city, and you can tell me how you think everything is going to work."

For a moment, reading her eyes, Roche thought Lilia was going leap his way and hug him. Instead she turned her back to him, and crossed under the great stone archway.

Roche noticed, and not for the first time, that at least one thing about Lilia remained the same: she always walked as if she expected anyone trailing behind her to watch.

CHAPTER 48

Something about the city made Roche feel at peace, in a way he had never known. A blanket of calm came over him as he stepped through the archway, followed by another placid layer of tranquility that settled slowly over him while they moved together along the street. By the time they reached the building she had in mind for him, Roche was swimming in a sea of serenity.

Lilia spoke, pointing out landmarks along the way and telling him of her plans; he took in her words like he did the sights of the city, absorbing them without really making note of anything in particular. The sensation overwhelming his internal world had garnered his whole attention, and he had to make a special effort to assimilate anything he saw or heard in the moment.

Maybe this was the tide coming back in, for him. Roche had endured enough moments of despair, and days of darkness that felt as though they would last forever; perhaps the coin had flipped within him, and he was seeing the other side. He certainly had reason to be at peace. Part of his past had literally borne fruit while he was away, and the city around him was another testament to the impact he'd had.

Without laying one stone, or plucking a single fruit, Roche had somehow had a hand in all the changes he saw around him. The possibility that all those results were coming back to roost in him only made sense, and became a probability the more he considered it. He should have some sense of calm, and satisfaction; he was ensconced in good reason for the feeling, surrounded by the effects of his causes.

The sensation was like the one he had when he reached out to Ehcor, or when he closed his eyes to clear his mind as Laurentis had taught him. In those inner journeys, everything looked different: he could understand why some people let the world be the way it would be, when he looked at it from behind closed eyelids. Now he was seeing the world through those same eyes, but they were open. This moment was not one to be pushed and pulled into place by his inner judgements; it was meant to be absorbed, and allowed. No matter how long the moment lasted.

In this delightful reverie, he stopped walking when Lilia did without quite realizing they were no longer moving. She said something, and Roche let the words float in the burnt air between them for some time before he let them fall fully on his ears.

"This is not what I had in mind for you," she said, "but it is one of the structures built to occupy many devils. There are a few sizes of rooms, but not a lot of difference between them. You have to realize this will put you in the middle of everything, and all the devils will have access to you. They'll all be able to knock on your door, at any time."

Roche nodded, after he had registered what she'd said.

"Exactly as I would have it," he replied. "Anyone that wants access to me should have it, especially in this realm. The best way to get them to see I am not the stories they tell is to live among them. Since I have many places I can be, I will take one of the smallest rooms. It isn't as though I…"

Letting his words drift off, Roche was glad he had caught himself. Even in his unguarded state, he saw no reason to tell Lilia he had no need for sleep. He'd noticed that those who slept could not understand a life without it; even when they knew he never slumbered, it came as a surprise each time they were reminded. He could no more imagine a routine constantly punctuated by unconsciousness than others could conceive of his perpetual wakefulness.

"It isn't as though," he repeated, "I spend a lot of time at home. Even when I have had a place to call my own, I have ventured out more than dwelling in the structure."

She turned, in answer, and swept up a short bank of steps leading to a wide open entrance. Once more, he followed her. The first thing he noticed was how grand the main room was, and how the ceiling was nearly too high to make out. Squares of stairs wound their way up the entire height of the structure, and he could see doors cut into each wall on the first few floors. Beyond that, the sight was endless rising steps that showed him nothing but stone steps and railings.

"The least you can do," Lilia said, still walking, "is take a room on the first floor. It will make getting in and out easier, unless you are hoping for one of the better views of the city. Then we should go all the way to the top, where you can see nearly everything."

In the ocean of peace he was swimming in, the decision seemed like a much harder one than it should have. Roche wondered if she was trying to get him to take one choice or the other, and if her reasoning was helpful or nefarious. Trying to figure it out was too much, and he was afraid he had chosen exactly what she wanted when he seized upon the first idea that came to mind.

"In the middle," he said. "I don't need a great view, or easy access. Put me where I won't be in anyone's way."

Lilia didn't change course, and Roche didn't realize they had already been headed for the stairs until they began to climb them. He concentrated on the steps immediately in front of him, instead of the swishing fabric of her dress or the hypnotic thunk of her heels.

"Of course," she said. "I already have a room in mind."

From the look of the floor they stopped on, it was very much like all the others they had passed. They moved to the landing, and around the corner, to stand together in front of a door that also looked much like all the others they had passed. Roche nodded, when she gestured to the entry; and Lilia motioned for him to open the door.

The room inside was simple, but spacious enough. Stone furnishings were arranged to make the sitting area and sleeping nook seem separate without putting any walls between them. He believed this was what the other rooms were like, and could find no real fault in the design.

"This is great," Roche said, turning to her. "If this is the kind of accommodations you are offering to devils, you have my gratitude and support. I'll start spreading the word immediately, if you would like."

Lilia brightened, and Roche found himself again fearing she was about to embrace him. Instead she clasped her hands behind her back, and thrust her chest forward slightly.

"Thank you," she smiled. "I am hoping with all I am that this will alleviate the pressure that has been building. The sooner you can fill it the better, although I imagine you could use a little rest."

His eyes drifted from her to the room once more, settling on the soft stone bed in the far corner. Roche didn't need sleep, but he did have his own way of refreshing and renewing himself. From this lonely room, in the middle of an empty city, he could reach out to his other half.

Suddenly he wanted nothing so much as he wanted to be alone. With no distractions from the outside world, he could go to Ehcor and feel like himself for a breath of time once more. Roche let his eyes stay on the horizontal slab for a long minute, hoping she would see the longing in him and take it for exhaustion.

"You're right," he said. "First, I'll get some rest. Then, I'll get on with filling up your city."

Lilia clapped her hands before her, nodded solemnly and turned to go. For his part, Roche did his best not to show that he couldn't wait to close the door behind her.

CHAPTER 49

Once again, Roche left his body behind to fling his consciousness out across space. The darkness behind his eyes was the same familiar nothingness, images darting across the landscape of his mind without taking shape or giving up their meaning. In this place, he was calm and at peace; he knew Lilia had departed the city, from the way it felt. He was alone with his thoughts at last, and he couldn't wait to share them with Ehcor.

Next he expected to see stars come into view, accompanied by that vast open feeling he had when the shift occurred. He knew that was just the path to the place he wanted to go, and that he couldn't push his progress on it along with his inner insistence; but he had come to savor crossing the barrier, and didn't expect it to bar his way for long in his current state of mind.

Rather than what he expected, a completely different kind of darkness took shape around him as Roche tried to slip silently into infinity. The view from behind his eyelids was gone, but it was not promptly replaced by a perpetual night sky in every direction. Instead of expanding, the space around him seemed to compress; the black void felt like it was bearing down on him, wrapping itself around him. Not only were there no stars; the suffocating feeling of a palpable darkness embracing him was exactly the opposite from the empty endlessness of space.

Just as he began to grow uncomfortable, Roche felt a tendril of the inky nothingness reach toward him. He couldn't see it, against the backdrop of immediate and distant blackness in every direction; he could only sense it, the strange and somehow familiar touch of the void taking shape to brush against him. Roche knew his body was back in his new home, lying on a soft stone; yet he could feel the darkness on his skin, pressing against him as if it expected to absorb him or be absorbed by him.

He went from quiet discomfort to a mild panic when the sensation penetrated him, and the feeling began to sink into his sinew. Like a natural defense mechanism, the fire that always burned within him met the darkness as it tried to edge more deeply into Roche. The two came together, a tiny silent explosion happened within him, and the void retreated. Once more, he was alone in his own imagined skin; but the nothingness hovered close, already reaching out another invisible tendril to grasp at him without hands.

The inferno at his core had been awakened, and for once Roche was glad for it. He stoked the fire with his fear, and sent it out in all directions to meet the darkness before it came for him again. In every other world, he had kept a tight leash on the fiery rage within him; here, he let it go with abandon. Roche could feel the power gathering in him, even as it poured out of him. The sensation was completely different than when he had stomped around as a burning beast; although the fire had its own consciousness, that awareness was tied in with his. Rather than watching the power course unbidden through him, Roche was guiding where it went and what it burned.

At first, the darkness took the heat and light he was pouring into it. The void began to glow, but remained featureless and continued to stretch on into forever. Then the glow intensified, sparks began to fly in random patterned beauty all around him, and the nothingness burst into flame at last. Roche watched it rolling away from him, gathering at the edges of his consciousness. Darkness wrestled with fire just beyond his reach, too far to touch and too close to stop fighting it. The burning void formed a bubble around him; even if he could move in this place, he knew the blazing orb would move with him.

When he had lost his inner grasp and caused great destruction, Roche had suspected there was no power to match the fiery rage of his inner burning beast. In this calm state, he realized he had been wrong. He did not feel as though he was in complete control of the inferno, so much as he knew it was there to cooperate with him. Like a hunter with a leashed wolf, Roche understood he could guide the mind of the flames so long as he fed the beast to satisfaction. By itself, the rage in him was a fiery monster; under his direction, it could be so much more.

This was the place to find those limits and test them, with no fear of burning an entire world to fine ash. Roche began to reach out with the most intense heat within him, and push against the walls of darkness in particular areas. Almost immediately, he was rewarded with a sudden opening in the void; beyond it was a nothingness he knew well. As small and distant as the sudden portal was, he could see a handful of stars shining in the infinity beyond the window he had forced open.

Roche reached deep inside himself, readying the next blast of power and at the same time marveling at the blazing mind silently communing with his own. The feeling was sublime, his terror at his own rage slipping away as they became one calm consciousness. He knew he could blast a hole large enough for him to go through it, and he directed the inferno to a tight burning beam and sent it at the small opening he had already created.

In the same moment as the fire shot out away from him, a distant indistinct noise began to reverberate throughout the space he occupied. All this had happened in silence, and it did not seem strange to him to battle the void without sound until one entered the mix. Surprised, Roche let the fire within him smolder as he listened more closely.

Light and rolling, the echo took form when he put his attention on it. Immediately he knew the sound, and where it came from. Only one being he knew could laugh like that, somehow portraying complete innocence and utter sadness simultaneously. Roche pulled back the fire, and let the blaze die down; and instead of watching the darkness rush in at him, he heard her voice.

"My friend," she said, "my brother. What are you doing?"

She was nowhere to be seen; but then, he wasn't either. Nonetheless, Roche could feel her presence; it was all around him, like the void had been. Even though that darkness still lurked at the edges of his mind, she was between it and him. Roche was able to relax, and even feel slightly abashed.

"Ximena," he said. "What are you doing here?"

Another wave of her laughter washed over him, stark amusement untainted by anger or fear.

"I would ask you the same question," Ximena responded. "Why would you come to the barrier between realms, or seek to damage it? Do you not understand that one world's ceiling acts as another's floor, so to speak; and blasting through that barrier would see us all tumbling together into one reality that would be unlivable for everyone?"

He let her words sink in, along with his own embarrassment. The one place he thought he could do no damage was apparently the worst spot for him to test his powers. Rushing in to explain, he was glad they were not face to face. Now was not the time to see if his crimson skin could redden even further.

"My counterpart," he said. "I was trying to reach her. She has become a big part of my life, and my perspective; I knew in her presence, I could think clearly and get her view on my current situation."

The last thing he wanted to do was offend her, and Roche realized he may have done just that after the words had tumbled out of him. Ximena had shown him kindness and camaraderie, when he had been cast out by his own other; now he was back in Hell, and had been longing to commune with Ehcor ever since he got here. Rather than finding comfort in his reunion with Ximena, he was taking everything that had passed between them to someone else for clarity.

Ximena laughed again, putting him immediately at ease.

"Of course," she said. "I am glad you have paired up with her at last, and come to see her as part of yourself. Surely you know I do the same thing with my counterpart, merging our minds across worlds to maintain a balanced and comprehensive perspective on all the realms and the events occurring within them."

Nodding dumbly, Roche didn't register at first that she could not see the motion any more than he could actually feel it. He had imagined the relationship between Ximena and her other to be strained, a constant struggle with little or no calm communication between them. The thought of utter darkness and pure light coming together in any peaceful way boggled one part of his mind, while immediately making sense to another.

Perhaps the worlds were not at war with each other, by nature; maybe the friction was caused by their being joined together in an awkward reality sandwich, and these two great powers were struggling constantly to hold the pieces together. The idea was comforting and terrifying at the same time. Where he had once imagined great peace coming to all the realms if the two lead players could put aside their differences, now he had to consider that everything would fall apart if they were to stop cooperating.

"I have blundered once more," Roche moaned, "and I am truly sorry. Just when I think I have penetrated what seems to be and beheld what is, another layer of illusion gets stripped away to reveal an even deeper reality."

Now she was nodding, and Roche was glad he could feel it in this place. They were not mingled into one, as he and Ehcor could so easily do now; but they shared a connection here that passed feelings between them as easily as words.

"If you blundered," she said, "I must admit to my own regular blunders. No matter how much time I spend in these worlds, the reality of their workings continue to reveal greater secrets to me. I would have you see yourself as I do, and as I try to see myself. We are here to learn these secrets, and use our knowledge to make all the worlds into what they long to be. As much as others might like to see God as holding all the answers, beings such as ourselves have to understand that the worlds continue as a result of constant questioning. If existence held no further mystery, there would be no reason for it to go on."

Once more, the truth seemed obvious when he turned the issue and looked at it another way. As much as it frightened him to consider that the worlds were held together by beings as prone to confusion as him, the concept made a vague sort of sweet sense. Even as he reeled at the thought, he felt the knowingness settle into him with a calm equanimity.

He wasn't making any attempt to share his feelings with Ximena, any more than he was trying to hide them. Another round of tinkling laughter filled the unbounded space, and it was the sound of compassion.

"There is somewhere you can go," Ximena said, "that is tied to all the realms. You can contact your counterpart there, with no disturbance or intervention. As a matter of fact, you know the place already."

Suddenly, the scene around him began to swirl and take shape. Somehow he was in his body once more; although he could sense that he was still lying down somewhere else, Roche could feel his own form wrap itself around his consciousness as familiar sights came together before his eyes. The walls of Ximena's library were unmistakable, lined with shelves crammed full of books; he could smell the brimstone, and knew he could reach out and touch the ancient volumes even if his hand was really somewhere else.

"Is this a dream?" he murmured. "Or am I really here?"

Ximena's laugh had lost its jocular lightness; although she was not visible in the room, clearly she was still with him. The sound was solemn now, tinged with sublime sadness.

"That is a question worth asking," she said, "many times over, throughout the years. But the answer is long and ever-changing, and cannot be given to you by anyone other than you. Now is not the time for such wondering, however. I will show you how to make this space your own, to turn it into a portal and go through it while blocking others from following or disturbing the part of you left behind in your journey. Then I will leave you to commune with your other, with an open invitation to return to this place any time you wish."

The first instruction she gave was to get comfortable, and close his eyes. Roche knew he had already done that, elsewhere; yet he did as she asked, finding a cushioned chair and sinking into it. Once he closed his eyes, hearing her voice became much less disorienting. He could pretend she was in the room with him, speaking in his ear, instead of trying to picture where she really was or dwell on where he had left his body.

CHAPTER 50

Communing with Ehcor was like diving into a cool flowing river, for Roche. His entire being felt refreshed by the sudden immersive contact, all the anxious tension in him floating away in the current as he remained with her. Between knowing his body was in a safe place of such peace and being treated to access to Ximena's library, Roche showed up already feeling uplifted; in the angel's presence, he felt as though his very essence was vibrating in time with the universe.

Ximena had shown him how to seal off the room, even if he wasn't really in it. The words she taught him were some sort of spell; she told him to repeat them exactly, although the real magic came from holding his desire up to the light while uttering the phrases. He could hear her voice chanting with him, just as he could feel his body sitting in the chair. Rather than wonder if both or neither of them were real, he fell into an easy echoed rhythm with her until Ximena's voice fell away. The void he had inhabited earlier let him pass easily this time, and his mind sailed through the strange empty field without disturbing it or him.

From there, Roche found it easy to launch his consciousness into a more familiar nothingness. For the first time, he arrived in the space he had shared with his other before she did. It had never occurred to him that she had been there waiting for him each time they came together like this, until he found himself there waiting for her.

In the same moment she showed up, he understood: Ehcor could not watch him in the lower realms like she could in the mortal world, and she was not able to anticipate their meetings as easily as before. An emptiness existed between the mortal realm and the one he inhabited, as he had discovered; and it was hard for the angel to see clearly through it, despite her vantage point. The angel explained this to him without speaking, expressing her regret at not being there immediately without uttering any sound of apology.

Roche could feel her memories flooding his mind. All the moments he had experienced since sharing with her last rushed out of him and into her at the same time. He saw snippets of her recent past, talking with Trethis and meeting with other angels; the scenes were images without sound or context, and he focused more on what he was sending her way. Part of him had come here to merge with her, and bask in her light; that would always be a reason to come here. This time, however, he was definitely here for advice and guidance. Roche wanted to make sure she saw it all clearly, and understood his situation entirely.

When he felt emptied of all the twisted knots inside him, Roche had a moment of wondering about the scenes the angel had shared. Never before had he seen her moving so much about Heaven, or interacting with such a variety of other heavenly bodies. He was curious, and wanted to ask; but his own questions pressed at him insistently, and he dismissed the desire to pursue a more urgent one.

"The lower realms are on the brink of war," Roche said. "Whether I am there or not, it seems I am in the middle of things. On one hand, I feel as though I know what I need to do. On the other, I am not so sure I am in a position to judge the actions of others or mete out punishment based on that judgement. My involvement seems important to everyone, which means others think I can tip the balance with my decision. If I act, and do the wrong thing, I could wreak havoc in Hell as I did in the mortal realm."

Roche sighed, aware he didn't have to voice his thoughts here. Putting words to his feelings helped him process them, though; and Ehcor seemed to understand his need without him stating it.

"Of course," he added, "if I don't act, I may miss the opportunity to prevent something terrible from happening."

The angel considered, and used words to convey her feelings just as he had. At the same time, the internal sensations she was experiencing flooded his consciousness. Somewhere in there Roche sensed a sadness, and a secret. Once again, he dismissed her thoughts, in all their subtlety; his own were too foremost in his mind.

"When you choose," she said, "you think of everyone affected by your choice. You side with others that think of others, even those that would destroy them. There is no way to create without destroying, and that is what you would do with any destruction you may cause. Ask yourself if you are being thought of by your enemy as you are thinking of them, and if your allies would be thinking of you if they were your enemies. Even if I couldn't see into your thoughts, I could guess who you have chosen to support based on who I know you to be."

Somewhere in Ximena's library his body had seemed to take shape, although he knew his actual flesh and bones were back in the empty city.

The dual manifestations did not make him feel spread thin, or divided; instead the two restful places had stacked together to relax him like never before. Roche's entire reality was steeped in knowing; he could sense the inner workings of the universe ticking like a clock in the very fabric of his being. What being, he didn't know; with two bodies in different places and his entire mind here, he should have felt utterly confused by all of it. He didn't, however. Every part of him was calm and relaxed, even as Roche pondered the decision he had to make.

"What do you think I should do?" Roche asked her. "What would you do, if you were in my situation?"

Now her thoughts flooded into him, and Roche could see the angel had very strong feelings on this matter. The words that followed were hardly necessary; but like him, she defined the emotions she had shared with him when she spoke.

"I see no choice," she said, "or I wouldn't, in your position. You and I are the same as the queen and her heavenly counterpart. We cannot afford to see things from an eternal perspective, or contemplate allowing one of them to be destroyed. If the very thoughts of God can be snuffed out, the rest of us have bigger problems on our hands than a little dragon fire. Especially those like us. The cycle we live in may be part of a larger cycle, and we may all be gone someday in favor of some other system; but so long as we live, we must back the ones who make us who we are."

Roche had never thought of it that way, and she saw that he hadn't as he turned the idea over in his open mind. For a moment, he caught himself wondering if guaranteeing his own continued existence was reason enough to act. In all that he had seen, Roche had learned that things only look well ordered from the proper perspective. Why not allow a reality that made sense on the surface, and produced more light without so much agonizing fire?

In the same moment he thought of it, Roche knew he had to consider the other infinite possibilities. Perhaps this was the best consciousness could do, and any other option meant a series of worlds full of pain for all. Some greater cycle may indeed exist; but if they were at the pinnacle, the last thing he wanted to do was start a downhill race.

Her thoughts were as evident to him as his were to her, and Roche watched her disappointment at his first idea; when he moved on to the next, Ehcor seemed relieved. The entire time, her secret flitted like quicksilver through the sacred place. Roche couldn't put his finger on what it was or what it was about, and she let his thoughts fill the space until he only felt her peripherally.

"Can I ask you something?" she said, suddenly.

Swirling in his internal landscape somehow given shape, Roche could only nod without nodding. Ehcor felt his assent, and spoke again.

"Do you trust Ximena?" the angel said.

If it had been anyone else, in any other place, he would have immediately rushed in with an answer in the affirmative. Here, with her, he paused. In the silence that followed, Roche let the angel see how many times he had asked himself the same question. Every time, he had either discovered Ximena's true intentions and felt ashamed of his mistrust; or he had searched for evidence that was not to be found. He let Ehcor see his doubts, his shame, and his growing certainty.

He felt her relief before she spoke, and wondered about it for the moment he had before her words swept him away once more.

"It is as I thought it would be," Ehcor said. "You trust her so much it frightens you. Yet her actions have never given you any reason to fear, or to doubt her."

The relief was there in her voice, as well. Rather than determine its source, Roche found himself fascinated with the angel's curiosity about the devil. He had supposed she was aware of Ximena, and the role she played; yet he would have thought the knowledge was vague, and impersonal. Hearing the angel speak the devil's name surprised him, and made him wonder how much her thoughts dwelt in the lower realms.

"That's a strange way to put it," he said.

Roche thought about it for a moment, and spoke again.

"But true enough, I suppose," he said.

He was all set to question her, to find out why she had asked; as soon as his intention formed within him, the angel rushed in to explain. Later, Roche would realize she had given him a dozen opportunities to search her mind for answers; in the moment, the only answers he wanted were his own.

"That is how I feel about God," she murmured. "Not able to trust, and not able to find a reason why I can't. We must be designed that way, those and the few others like us. Perhaps we help keep things balanced, by having a distinctly different point of view than the rulers of the realms. Still, it only makes sense for us to support them."

For the first time, Roche finally consciously sensed the tension she was holding. He reached out to her instinctively, both out of curiosity and concern; a sudden wall went up between them, as impenetrable as it was invisible. If their togetherness wouldn't serve him, he doubted words would; yet he had to try.

"Ehcor," he said. "What troubles you?"

The wall almost took shape, as he felt it firm up between them. Roche knew he could call it out; but if she had thrown it up to begin with, it seemed unlikely that she would be the one to tear it down.

"Many things trouble me, brother," she said, blithely. "We certainly don't have time to completely cover all of it, especially when you come here so rarely. I must return to my studies, and you must return to your life in Hell. We will resume our lessons when you see fit to return regularly, and eventually there will be time for deeper sharing."

She gave him no time to respond, or protest; one moment she was there, chastising him while pouring her own feelings of guilt all over him; the next she was gone, and Roche was once again left alone in the place he did not think could exist without her.

CHAPTER 51

He was trapped.

After reeling from Ehcor's sudden absence, Roche had remained in the place they came together alone. For several minutes, he felt the reality of his own insides projected outward without her light to dispel the darkness. The peaceful feeling had not left him, which he found more disturbing than comforting; with all the unanswered questions he had, Roche's anxiety should have been at its peak.

First Hell had changed for him, then the very act of walking between worlds had been altered as well. Now the place he had thought did not exist without Ehcor was showing him new secrets. The last thing he wanted to do was rush off before soaking in the situation completely, like he had too many times before. The angel's guarded demeanor had alarmed him, at the end of their meeting; even in retrospect, it continued to surprise him that she had been able to keep something hidden from him in that sacred space.

Soon enough, he got curious about the two bodies he had apparently left behind. Getting back into the library was easy, and he sat up almost immediately in the seat he had relaxed into. The chair felt real, the books looked as they had before, and his physical encasement felt as familiar as it ever had; yet Roche knew there was another layer to his journey, and another form to return to. He relaxed immediately into the seat once more, and tried to send his consciousness back where it had come from.

Nothing happened, other than the usual vague imagery behind his closed eyelids. The calm was still seated deeply within him, the invisible trail to where he had just been remained open to him. All other pathways were closed to him, however; and after a few minutes willing them to appear within the network of possibility in his mind, Roche opened his eyes and sat up straight in his seat.

He was trapped.

Definitely.

Immediately after he had reassured his other that Ximena's intentions had always turned out to be pure and true eventually, Roche found himself doubting the devil once more. The library had appealed to him from the moment he knew it existed, and his thoughts had drifted to this room more than once while his life played out in other realms. All the information in those hidden pages called to him while he was anywhere else. Now that he sat amongst them, and could fetch any volume to plumb the depths of its secrets, all Roche felt was a desire to leave this room and return to the body he had left behind.

The idea struck him while he sat there, that perhaps he should relax and let whatever was happening play out. He had just told Ehcor he trusted the devil, after all; and what was trust, if not a knowing one carried through times of doubt? Like a spider on a hot stove, the thoughts skittered across his mind and leapt away almost immediately. Roche was sure, without even cracking the cover on one of the books, that he could not concentrate on its words or absorb its lessons. Knowing he could not leave this place would scatter the words before his eyes, and drive their meaning every direction but home.

Standing suddenly, Roche strode purposefully toward the shelves before him. He reached out, and ran his fingers over the various spines lightly. The books were all different sizes, from small skinned volumes to giant tomes bound in bone or stone. Each volume had its own texture, and its own emotional resonance; although few of them had titles on the outer binding, Roche could sense the nature of their contents through the light drifting touch of his fingertips. He went through a startling range of inner experience in moments, dark doom pouring over him only to be washed away by great hope. As his skin alighted briefly on each volume, Roche felt as though an entire lifetime of experiences had leapt from those books and into him.

Reaching up to the next shelf, Roche dragged his fingers lightly along the spines as he had with the line of volumes below. Immediately, he knew these were books about Ximena. Touching each of them briefly, he felt as though he was going back in time in her mind as his fingertips traveled slowly from right to left across them. At any other time, he would have been curious beyond his own control: Roche would have found the beginning, and started reading from there. If scenes began to fill his mind from simply touching the binding, he could only imagine the depth and detail he might absorb by opening their pages.

But he was trapped, and could not direct his curiosity to wonder about anything other than how he might escape. Even the way the books felt disturbed him; like that calm feeling that had pervaded his inner landscape since he had entered the underground city, he felt comforted by the feel of the books against his skin. He wanted to be free of this place, and this body he knew wasn't real; yet his own thoughts spoke to him in soothing tones while he remained in contact with the ancient tomes.

Snatching his hand back, Roche dropped his arms to his side. He felt his fingers curling into fists, unbidden; he sensed the fire within him starting to roil, and threaten to blaze. That taste of power he knew too well filled his throat, a throat that wasn't even really there; and Roche could find no desire within him other than to let it burn. His anger began to build, boiling into rage; he cried out, and his own voice surprised him.

"Ximena!" he yelled. "Let me out of this place!"

The exclamation echoed back at him, his own words forming another barrier that hemmed him in to this strange other reality. Roche let the seething fire within him leap from his belly and into his fingertips. Flames shot from his hands, first hitting the floor beside him and then changing direction as he raised his arms once more. The fire washed over the books before him, setting them alight and leaving them to burn as he turned a slow circle in the center of the room.

In the back of his mind, Roche knew he could always return to the place he had shared with his other. That single avenue was open to him, even if he couldn't go anywhere but here from there. He was bothered by the errant thoughts in his mind, and wanted to burn them away as he was the books. They persisted, however; and so did he. Roche watched the sheet of flames leaping from his hands as he covered the last of the volumes in fire, finally coming back to where he had started the slow destructive rotation.

The books had been burning, when he turned his back to them. Leather bindings had blackened, stone had begun to melt, and paper pages had given birth to countless flames before he had shifted his attention away from the shelf. As he turned to it again, Roche saw that the volumes he had sent the first fire to were whole again. They sat on the shelves, positioned exactly as they had been before and looking as though they had never been burnt.

Again, he set them alight. Flames poured from his fingertips, the fire going from a mixture of orange and red to a bright white as his anger intensified. Roche turned another slow fiery circle, only to watch the flames gutter out by the time he had completed the turn once more. There was no way he would burn through the shelves, or the walls beyond; even concentrating his contained explosion on one section of the library showed him what he could have guessed by now. Roche watched the books reform into unscathed perfection while fresh flames washed over them.

Letting his arms fall to his sides, and the fire to go out completely, Roche felt himself wanting to laugh at the absurdity of the situation. As far as he knew, he wasn't even here; although his body felt like the same familiar set of skin he was accustomed to, Roche also knew his actual flesh and bones were resting on a stone slab in a deserted city. He still wished he could wash away all these thoughts, and allow the rage to consume him; but they stayed with him, along with the desire to let loose a humorless cackle. Giving up the battle at last, Roche found his way back to the cushioned seat. He fell into it, and allowed the feeling of defeat to wash over him in stifling waves.

Closing his eyes, Roche relaxed into his inner darkness. The fury in him died down as the fire around him had, and soon enough he felt himself both frustrated and calmed by that pervading feeling of peace he had been carrying around with him since entering the subterranean city. His voice slipped from him once more, surprising him both with its words and its calm whispered tone.

"Ximena," he murmured. "Let me out of this place."

Although it issued forth from him, the sound was so soft he barely heard it. He certainly couldn't expect her to, wherever she was. As much as he expected to find himself still trapped in the room with only those whispered words to keep him company, Roche was not at all surprised to hear her respond almost immediately. Her voice came to him as it had before, drifting in from far away while sounding inside his head somehow.

"Of course," she said. "Did you recite the words I taught you?"

No matter how many times it happened, Roche never could escape the blanket of shame that came over him every time this shift happened. He chided himself for doubting her once more, and how foolish he was for not questioning himself first. As the words leapt to mind, she started to say them; and with his eyes closed, Roche chanted them with her. When they were finished, her voice came once more in his head.

"You are free to come and go as you please," Ximena whispered.

She said it as if it had always been true. Roche knew better, just as he knew she would not be in the room with him when he opened his eyes to look around for her. Nonetheless, he did look to see that nothing was there; and when he let his lids settle closed again, his inner landscape had completely changed. Just as she had said, he was free to slip from this strange temporary body to the one he had left behind; the way was as clear in his mind as the rage had been minutes ago.

CHAPTER 52

Once the way was clear, everything seemed to begin happening at once. Roche thought it would take days to spread the word about the city, maybe even weeks; but he soon found out how quickly good news could find its way to even the furthest reaches of Hell. When he walked out along quiet lonely streets, he could not have imagined how much they would change before he returned.

He knew where devils were clustered, working the fields that still belonged to him. Roche went there first, and began telling any devil that would listen about the underground accommodations. They all seemed to want to hear what he had to say; not long after he had arrived, the work had ceased completely. A steady stream of crimson bodies filled the trail between the field and the city within minutes, while a handful of stragglers drifted off purposefully in every other direction.

By the time he reached the next nearest row of fruiting vegetation, it was already almost deserted. A few devils had stayed behind, to finish what they had started or clean up for the day; they waved wildly at him, and gestured in the direction of the city. They were headed there as well, as soon as they finished up here. Roche turned away long before he got close enough for conversation, to move on in another direction.

A distant sound made him pause. He turned back to the field, just in time to identify the source of it. The black dot in the sky drew closer, the sound of dragon wings flapping got louder; and Roche had a wide smile on his face long before the monster descended loudly between him and the workers. Laurentis dismounted one form in the sky, to land deftly on his feet in the other; his smile was slight, but Roche could still see it tugging at the corner of the dragon's mouth.

"Not afraid of dragons anymore?" he said.

Roche shrugged, and kept grinning.

"Oh, no," he replied. "I'm more scared of dragons than ever. I seem to be getting better at telling you apart, that's all. You flap your wings in a unique rhythm, and move through the air differently. You may share a lot of common features, but each of you are physically arranged in your own way. Also, you're not exactly painful to look at in your present form; but you make for one profoundly ugly dragon."

Laurentis flinched, as if he had been struck. The smile fell from his face, and his eyes suddenly went wide. Roche could watch the gears turning behind the dragon's eyes, and was glad to hear him start laughing when the reality of the situation clicked into place in his mind. Surely he had seen his own serpentine form, and realized it was a thing of sheer beauty; his dragon shape was so uniquely striking that Roche knew he could rely on others having told him so many times, at the very least. When he had first seen someone toy with someone else in a friendly fashion, Roche had been similarly shocked; now he knew it added a layer to that kind of bond, instead of testing it.

Nodding, smiling once more, the dragon got it. He was so accustomed to being treating as a class above or below everyone he interacted with, such a gesture had a deeper meaning to it for him than it might for most others. Just as Roche had supposed, and experienced, the gentle jab created more lasting pleasure than it had momentary pain.

"You should see me when I first wake up," Laurentis chuckled. "My wings are all akimbo, and the series of horns on my head get bent every which way. I have to spend hours in front of a giant mirror fixing myself up to look so bad."

They laughed together, until Roche gestured toward the field. It was empty now, the last of the devils trailing off into the distance in the direction of the city.

"I suppose you're wondering," he said, "what's going on."

Laurentis shook his head, his face a gentle stone carving. He scanned the field without turning, watched the devils drift further away for a moment, then moved his eyes to meet Roche's.

"No," he said. "I know what is happening. The only thing I was wondering is when I might get my invitation, to come visit this amazing new city."

Sweeping his hand once more, Roche gestured to the path the devils were walking.

"How about now?" he said. "Although in all seriousness, I am going to have to ask you—"

"I know." Laurentis cut him off, kindly. "The city is not for dragons. I will keep my present form, even as we approach. If you would prefer I not visit at all…"

Roche shook his head, and waved away the dragon's concern.

"If you were any other dragon," he said, "I might agree. They'll all be happy to see you there, though; and it is a way to give your blessing to their having dropped everything to establish a new home there immediately. It's not too far, on foot; and it won't hurt to have devils see us walking together, on the path to the city."

Nodding his agreement, Laurentis turned and started walking. Roche was glad to fall into step beside him, and hoped they would get a chance to discuss what was coming as they walked. A full minute hadn't passed before a devil seemed to appear from nowhere, and started following them closely; then another joined, and two more after. He realized then that they would not just be walking into the city together; they would be approaching with a peaceful army behind them. Side by side they strode the wide path, and conversation was made impossible by the proximity of their followers and the growing rumbling sound of their feet as they fell.

CHAPTER 53

Laurentis was the first to notice, even if he did so only in passing. When they reached the entrance to the city, the dragon had insisted the crowd of devils following them go in first. He and Roche stood aside while they filtered in, and proceeded through the unassuming stone passage after the last of them had gone. As soon as they stepped inside, the dragon stopped and took in the view.

"It looks like it was made for dragons," he said.

While Laurentis had been gazing at a sight completely new to him, Roche had been reeling at the change in the familiar landscape. From up here, it looked like thousands of tiny insects were skittering along the city streets. He had never seen it occupied anywhere other than his mind, and Roche felt a tension that had been building inside him relax. Maybe it was the sight, or the city itself; somehow he felt most at peace here, and all the more so with so many devils walking the streets.

The stairways and paved footpaths had always drawn his attention as soon as he saw them. Roche had never considered how much of the city was actually in the empty space above the tallest structures. A dragon could leap from any of the solid platforms leading to a set of stairs, flap about at their leisure over the buildings and land easily in one of the wide even lanes. He glanced at Laurentis, and imagined he was seeing himself doing just that in his mind's eye.

Turning, Laurentis let one corner of his mouth curl upward almost imperceptibly. He saw Roche holding his breath, and shook his head.

"Don't worry," he said. "I won't. I will take the stairs, like everyone else. Did you say you only began to spread the word today? Look, they already have a bazaar set up."

Roche followed his pointing finger, and felt himself delighting in how easily and naturally so many devils were settling into the city. As Laurentis began to descend the nearest set of carved steps, all thoughts of dragons flying over the city were swept from his mind. They moved swiftly, the dragon calling back over his shoulder as he drifted down the stairs.

"Has Ximena seen it yet?" Laurentis asked.

Shaking his head, Roche realized the dragon couldn't see the motion. He noticed Laurentis had used her name, in a way that seemed deliberate; and that he spoke low enough so the devils descending more slowly below them would not hear.

"No," Roche said. "I wanted to fill it first."

His eyes kept going from the back of the dragon's head to the steps, then out to the city. Watching the activity below was making him a little giddy, and Roche was sure there were more than thousands of devils below. At least tens of thousands of red bodies streamed through the streets, their faces close enough now for him to see how most of them were smiling or laughing. As far as he knew, it may have been even more than that; he guessed at how many were making themselves at home in one of the many buildings made for it, and hoped he was right.

"It looks like you did it," Laurentis called back.

Roche nodded again, a little dumbfounded. The city didn't just look occupied; it appeared as though devils had been living there for some time. When he finally thought to look, he could see faces poking out high windows; and tapestries or tunics decorating many outer stone sills.

The first few times the steps had plateaued, Laurentis had raced across the level stone as quickly as he had been taking the stairs. Now they were nearing another, and coming up behind some slower moving devils. He paused this time, and turned so he might see Roche and the city at the same time. When Roche got close to him, the dragon repeated himself.

"I said," he murmured, "it looks like you did it."

Instead of nodding once more, Roche knitted his eyebrows together.

"Did what?" he said.

Laurentis gestured, sweeping his arm slowly to take in the city.

"You filled this place with devils," he said. "So…when are you going to invite Ximena?"

He was definitely stressing her name. Roche shrugged, and drifted closer to the stairs.

"Soon enough," he said.

Moving alongside him, Laurentis seemed to be fighting the urge to take him by the shoulders. He blocked the stairs, and searched Roche's eyes.

"This is her realm," he said.

Roche nodded, and shrugged.

"Of course," he said. "I know that."

Something hung in the air between them, other than the intense gaze of a clearly perturbed dragon. Roche sensed it, and that Laurentis needed something more from him. Without thinking, he spoke.

"Ximena is welcome here any time," he said.

A wave of relief passed over the dragon's face, spreading to become an invisible current that washed over the entire city. Smiles got wider, laughter grew louder, and the air was instantly clearer. Laurentis gestured to the steps, indicating that Roche should lead the rest of the way. They descended the final flight in silence, and were too crushed by devils wanting to be close to them both when they strode the streets. Without a word they crossed the threshold to the city and made their way to his quarters. Even in the hallways, devils came close without getting in their way. Roche had to usher the dragon through his door, and into his space, before either of them could speak without another hearing.

Roche closed the door behind him, turned, and nearly bumped into Ximena. She stood just inside the room, in what might have passed as his foyer had it been separated a little more from the rest of the open chambers. Her garb was simple elegant darkness, a silky shadow of robes that swirled shades of black without ever repeating a pattern. First she inclined her head at Laurentis, then did the same to Roche.

"Thank you," she said, "for the invitation. I hope you are pleased that I waited in here for you. The last thing I wanted to do was take away from the attention the two of you so richly deserve."

For a moment, he was confused. Roche had not burned her a scroll, or reached out to her in his thoughts; then he remembered how Laurentis had deliberately spoken her name, twice. He had waited for Roche to say it a third time, and the whole city had seemed to react. Apparently that was an invitation in Hell; at least, it was for the devil.

Roche began to move deeper into the apartment, toward the collection of chairs carved from stone. He was about to suggest they sit, when he noticed Ximena seemed to be particularly on guard. Still standing just inside the doorway, she glanced back and forth between them.

"I came because…" Ximena started, then drifted off.

Without moving, she seemed to sniff the air; after a long pause, she shifted her attention to Laurentis and frowned.

"The old dragons are planning something," she said. "I don't know what it is, but they are taking advantage of us holding back. While we consider the consequences of crossing them, they are plotting our demise. Laurentis, have you heard anything of this?"

The dragon nodded, solemnly.

"Not directly," he said, "but the older dragons that used to speak freely around me are falling quiet when I am near, and they make a special effort to behave as though all is well. They are not used to hiding their intentions, and are honestly quite bad at it. I don't know what is coming, but it is not more of them waiting to see what we will do."

Ximena shifted her attention to Roche, arched an eyebrow.

"And you?" she said. "Have you heard or seen anything unusual?"

Looking between them, Roche thought of saying that everything he had seen since returning to Hell seemed unusual. Instead he stared at the smooth stone floor, trying to order his thoughts. When nothing came to mind, he shrugged and shook his head no.

"Of course," Ximena said. "You have been busy. This city filled up quickly, and the devils seem to be settling in like…"

Again, she drifted off. This time Ximena appeared to be watching an invisible insect flying through the air, lazily crossing the space between her and him. She narrowed her eyes suddenly, and let a frown turn her lips into an unhappy line.

"Do you feel that?" she whispered.

Roche exchanged a glance with Laurentis, glad the dragon looked as confused as he felt. They shook their heads together, and watched her.

"This place…" she went on, quietly. "There is a feeling here, one that is both unnatural and yet somehow completely welcome. Where I should feel tension, I am relaxed. The fear I should have of what is to come is not there, in the place inside me that it should be."

As Roche began to feel the fool, again, he could see Laurentis nodding his agreement out of the corner of his eye.

"I feel it," the dragon said. "A general but also overwhelming sense of calm, like constant waves of…"

He trailed off, searching for the word.

"Serenity," Roche said. "I've felt it ever since I first entered the city. I thought it was…well, I honestly thought it was a feeling coming from within me. After all the problems I have caused, being part of a solution for once seemed to have an uplifting impact. I thought…I thought maybe that feeling was a reward of sorts. For helping others, or something."

The words sounded lame, even to him. Roche knew he should have sensed that the feeling was coming from outside himself, and taken better notice of how it had left him when he'd left the city for a while. Meanwhile, Ximena and Laurentis exchanged a look that appeared to speak volumes. Neither of them seemed to find Roche's naiveté amusing, or annoying; they looked as though they both continued to hope for such a payoff, even after all the time they had spent waiting.

"It's dragon magic," Laurentis breathed, his voice trembling slightly.

Ximena nodded, and pulled the darkness closer about her body.

"They are trying to lull us into a false sense of security," she said, "and perhaps trying to get us all in the same place."

She turned abruptly, and pulled open the door. Lilia stood on the other side, dressed in leather armor that protected her vital organs and showed nearly everything else. Her hair was loose, dancing flame that played about her shoulders while she motioned to them. When she spoke, she sounded like she was out of breath from running.

"Come on," Lilia gasped, "you've got to get out of here."

CHAPTER 54

The three of them stood there looking at Lilia, all manner of thoughts passing through their minds. Before any of them could react, she opened her mouth to speak again. In that instant a single strained voice reached through walls and windows to fill the air, and it looked as though the scream was coming from between Lilia's parted lips. She turned, as if she could see through the buildings themselves, and swiveled to face them once more.

"It has begun," she sighed.

Her eyes skidded off Laurentis, and moved to dart back and forth between Roche and Ximena. When she did speak again, all the subtle seduction was gone; her voice was a hoarse whisper, a desperate plea.

"You must leave," Lilia said. "Do whatever it is you do, walk between worlds, and get away from this place."

They shook their heads together, even as the single scream became a chorus of cries. Laurentis winced at the sound, and began to move his head sadly back and forth with them.

"Lilia," he moaned. "What have you done?"

The fire flashed in her eyes, and Lilia crossed her arms under her breasts. Rather than make her look defenseless, or innocent, the posture pushed her bosom forward and made her sheathed sword stick out at her side. Lilia appeared defiant, and capable of any deceit.

"I have done nothing," she retorted, "except discover the plans of the old dragons, and come here to save you from them."

Just as the screams began to die down outside, a fresh round of pained wails penetrated the walls again. Roche and Laurentis turned to Ximena, and were both surprised to see nothing more than a grim resolve in her eyes. She nodded to Roche, once.

"Take him," she said, inclining her head toward Laurentis. "Take him, and get out. Get as far away from here as you can."

Before he could form any kind of reply, Laurentis was already making for the door. Ximena moved to bar his way, and looked up at him with an almost pleading expression on her face.

"Please," she said, quietly. "Go with him."

Laurentis glanced to Roche, cocked an eyebrow at him.

"Where is he going?" he said, his eyes holding Roche's.

With a shrug, Roche indicated Ximena.

"Wherever she does," he murmured.

This was no time to be smiling, even if the dragon had been prone to such open displays of emotion; with the sounds of agony reaching them in waves now, Laurentis grimaced while his eyes twinkled his dark amusement.

"Then I will indeed go with him," he said, with finality.

Ximena made as if to throw up her hands, and whirled on Lilia.

"What are we facing?" she demanded.

Shaking her head, Lilia could not seem to choose a single response.

"All of them," she said. "Certain death. The old dragons are all here, to kill the devils that have flooded Hell. They mean to make a point, and show you all how nice it is here with less souls crowding the realm. You can't go out there. They'll kill you too."

Roche felt his rage boiling, and covered the space between himself and Lilia with more speed than he had known in some time. Glowering down at the armored dragon, he hissed at her between clenched teeth.

"Is this why you built the city?" he said. "Was this your plan the entire time? Did you use me to fill this place, only to attach my name to a massacre?"

When she didn't feign a shocked reaction, Roche felt his certainty begin to wane. Lilia looked more sad than anything, as she responded quietly to his accusation.

"I actually built this city to prevent this," Lilia sighed. "The old dragons had to change shape to come inside, since all the entrances are so small. Our only hope is to force them back through those same narrow passageways, and deal with them once and for all when they turn to devils and come out the other side."

All of them looked like they wanted to say more, Roche glowering down at Lilia while Laurentis watched the two of them with a pained expression on his face. Lilia did not seem fazed by either of their judging gazes; it was not until Ximena turned to rest her eyes on the dragon that Lilia's shoulders dropped, and her eyes fell. The queen spoke, and they all turned to listen.

"I will face the old dragons," she said. "They surely know most of the devils that flooded this place immediately were not the kind of souls that belong in Hell. They won't find their way back here until they have searched for life opportunities in the higher realms, and we can't wait for the reinforcements they may provide upon their return. I won't stop anyone from fighting beside me, but I will caution you all: defeating this enemy is not enough. We cannot let them have time to see the end coming. They can self-destruct, if they want to; and if they do it doesn't matter who is winning or losing. We must meet them at their best, and strike with certainty."

The queen brushed past all of them, striding into the hallway and leaping over the bannister. As she fell, she called back to them.

"The end must be swift," she cried. "Otherwise it could very well be the end of everything."

Together, the three of them rushed to the railing. They caught a glimpse of her transforming, changing from a slight lovely shape within dark shifting shadows to a drifting cloud of inky black. As soon as the smoky fog formed, it stretched immediately to the doorway below. In the next moment, it was gone.

Without a word, or a glance at each other, all three of them backed up a single step. They leapt over the railing as one, but two forms hung there in the air while Roche fell. He could feel the downdraft of their wings before he heard the sound of them lifting their bodies aloft, and all he saw when he finally looked up was the giant opening yawning wide over the series of rising steps. Funny, he hadn't noticed that before.

His body made a slight indentation in the floor where he struck, and his swift gait left a trail of flaming footprints all the way to the exit.

CHAPTER 55

Fires guttered along the street, small clusters of flame clinging to buildings and bodies where anything was left to burn. Blackened mounds huddled in burnt shapelessness, and Roche could only assume the charred piles were more bodies that had been cooked beyond recognition. Smoke filled the air, drifting upward in dark rolling clouds to obscure the monsters circling overhead.

The giant dragons were too numerous to count, gliding in long descending spirals or pounding their wings to climb high once more. Somehow none of them collided, as close as they came to each other in flight; the effect was mesmerizing as he looked up, and Roche felt he was gazing into a twirling tornado of serpentine flesh and leathery wings.

One ancient dragon was otherwise occupied. Even if Roche had not been able to tell Rendibite from the others, he would have known which black dragon he was by the way he was fighting for his life. True to his word, Laurentis had attacked the older dragon as soon as he had his chance; and from the looks of things, he was getting the upper hand. As quick as the older dragon might have been, Laurentis was faster. He darted around Rendibite's body while they were both in flight, biting and burning him while still on the move.

Roche could see the frustration in Rendibite's movements, the way his muscles jerked and twitched while he struggled to catch even a glimpse of his attacker. Meanwhile Laurentis slipped around him like a shadow, avoiding his desperate taloned swipes and short hot bursts of flame. Watching them, Roche suddenly pictured the smaller dragon sitting in stillness; he wondered how many of those inward peaceful moments had been spent imagining this violent outward one.

Overhead, the swirl of descending dragons was beginning to near the city. Roche thought to look for Ximena just as the first dragon cranked open its mouth to shower the streets with flame, and was not surprised to see her falling from the sky in a path to intercept it. He traced her descent backwards, to see where her streaking shadow had been: directly behind and above her, his eyes found the rocky outcropping she had just vacated.

Curled in a giant leathery ball, a red dragon was taking up every square inch of the stone plateau. Roche zoomed in on the strange sight with a thought, and noticed its eyes were closed; then he realized the thing was smoking, and pulled back his vision once more to get a better look. The dragon looked like an oven that had not been sealed properly: smoke seeped out of its skin in black puffs, gathering around it in a small dark cloud faster than it could dissipate.

A loud scream split the air, and Roche's attention was dragged back to the dragons descending on the city. At first he had thought their movements were random, as they relied on their own speed and skill in the air to prevent collisions; now he saw the pattern, and realized Ximena had seen it too.

She may not have looked dangerous, a small streaking shadow among a sky full of giant dragons; but whatever she did when she hit the first dragon made it scream like its very cells were on fire, and caused the dragons set to strike in its wake to hesitate as one. Their shared pause revealed the configuration he had missed before. Roche could see how they were set to strike, with one dragon swooping in to flame the streets while the next flew in its wake. As soon as the first pulled up, the next would turn on its blaze; and before the long line of descending dragons had reached its end, they would have covered the entire city in fire.

The strategy had clearly worked at least once before. Flames still sputtered everywhere he looked, even where only stone remained to burn. Every devil that had crowded the streets minutes ago had found cover, or been reduced to ashes. Roche could see them starting to poke their heads out of hiding places, only to glance at the sky and withdraw once more.

From where he stood, Roche was clearly in the path of the impending flames. Instead of watching a long line of fiery destruction rain down on the city, he saw Ximena engulf the first dragon in darkness for a brief moment and then move on. Whatever she had done to it stuck with the beast, and it wobbled in the air awkwardly while its thin screeching cry reached a piercing zenith. In the next moment it was silent, and fell from the sky with startling swiftness.

The ground rumbled when it struck, and the sound had barely died down before another scream split the air. Ximena had moved on to the next dragon in the formation, and was rapidly enveloping it in cloying shadows. Roche saw the others in line behind it begin to slip out of the pattern, and drift one way or another before starting another climb. He nearly leapt skyward, to catch one of them as it retreated; then Roche remembered the dragon on the ledge, and shifted his attention back to it.

Still occupying the same space, the smoking dragon was now almost completely obscured by its own toxic cloud. Before, Roche could have easily mistaken the source of the smoke; there was no question where it was coming from now. Waves of it rolled off the crouched monster, drifting through the small opening behind it and over the edge of the plateau. Whatever it was doing, the process was clearly building to some destructive culmination; Roche knew he had to act, even if he didn't know exactly what he should do.

Running seemed like a good idea, until he began to pick up speed. Dashing through the last dying embers of fire on the street did nothing to extinguish the small blazes, but somehow the flames leapt to his feet as they passed. He sensed a wet heat on his ankles, and felt it climbing up his calves; the sensation was like water spreading, making the places it touched feel both inflamed and drenched at the same time.

Ignoring the strange pain, Roche doffed his cloak and let it fall behind him as he spread his wings. The movement felt awkward, and foreign to him; but he ascended slowly over the streets until even the tallest reaching flames could not touch him. His legs were still burning, with pain and with fire; still he pressed on, pushing the ache from his mind. He flapped harder, rose more quickly, and soon came face to snout with the smoking dragon.

Its eyes remained closed, even as he tilted forward and hovered over it. The acrid stench of the smoke it was putting off filled his nostrils, and the invasive odor was almost overwhelming. Nothing about it was natural, or pleasant. Unlike every other kind of smoke he had smelled, this had the reek of concentrated chemicals about it. Roche shuddered, held his breath, and fell bodily on the dragon.

He expected it to unravel, and strike at him; but the monster remained immobile. The heat coming off it was as distinctive as the smoke, and it singed his hands as he tried to grip the slippery serpentine skin of the dragon's back. His feet were still on fire, but even they became hotter as he dug his heels into the beast's flesh. All he could do at first was try to hang on, despite the searing pain at every point of contact.

The swords he carried around in his thoughts came to mind. Roche was pretty sure the angel's blade would pierce the monster's smoking hide, and enough concentrated strikes would separate its head from its body if he could count on it to stay still. He stood up, almost crying out from the pain of putting all his weight on his flaming feet; before he could manifest a weapon in his grip, he looked down and out across the scene below.

Laurentis was still battling Rendibite, and they flew between Roche and Ximena just as he glanced their way. In one startling moment, it seemed everything they were doing separately took a turn for the worse together. Ximena had surrounded another dragon in her suffocating cloud, and hung there in the air with it while the monster screamed in agony. Instead of fleeing, several nearby dragons shifted into another formation. They came at the engulfed dragon from all sides, spewing flame at their lost comrade and burning the beast along with the dark shadow that had consumed it.

At the same time, Laurentis slowed in his flight directly in front of Rendibite for some reason. The larger dragon wasted no time reaching out, and sinking long sharp talons into his ward's exposed chest. His other foreleg reached out, wrapping around Laurentis and cradling his body carefully while Rendibite pressed the length of his claws deeper. Laurentis sagged in the powerful grip, his body going limp.

Roche wanted to go to his friend, and help him fight off the ancient dragon; he wanted to rush to Ximena's side, and take the flames for her. The last thing he considered was that perhaps his was the most precarious situation, until he felt the dragon begin to tremble beneath his feet. Tilting to one side and then the other, Roche looked down to see the red scales between his feet twitching wildly. The flesh began to bubble, and the monster started to smoke so violently that he could not see his own hand in front of his face.

Even as he realized what was about to happen, Roche also knew he had no time to leap clear of the danger. He dropped to his hands and knees on the dragon's back again, dug in his grip and held on with all his might. The aching was intolerable, and interminable; Roche wasn't sure if his fingers were clutching the dragon or if they had melted into it. He couldn't feel anything but pain, everywhere he could feel; and somehow all it did was grow increasingly unbearable the longer he held on.

Just before he cried out in agony, the dragon did what he knew it was going to do. All the smoke around it was sucked in toward it in a blinding wave, as if it was breathing it in through its scales; the trembling flesh under his feet was still for a moment, and all the sounds around him ceased in a sudden pregnant pause. He had one last clear look at Ximena and Laurentis, to see that their situations seemed worse than a moment ago; then the dragon exploded, and he was tossed into the air on a wave of liquid flame.

CHAPTER 56

In the moments before the explosion, Roche had imagined it. His mind had tried to calculate the damage it would do, without ever having seen what he was trying to picture. The best he could hope was that Ximena would survive, and maybe Laurentis as well; while he was hoping, he let himself picture the entangled black dragons being separated by the blast while the monsters attacking her were scattered. If the queen and his friend were not vaporized, the sudden explosion may give them a fighting chance.

As far as he was concerned, Roche was pretty sure the moments he spent imagining what was to come would be his final moments in any world. He let the thought settle in with surprisingly swift acceptance, and spread himself as wide as he could to mitigate the damage.

His body did expand, far beyond the reaches of what it should have been able to; but it didn't stop there. Roche felt the fire within him flare up in the same moment the dragon became countless flaming pieces, and somehow he wrapped himself around the explosion as it happened. The ground shook beneath him, and the stone ceiling trembled overhead. If it weren't for the plateau beneath him turning to so much sand underfoot, he would have been able to hold his ground while absorbing the blast.

As it was, Roche grew as he changed shape. The explosion pushed him outward in every direction, until he was filling the space the dragon had occupied and then some. He was already spilling over the side of the cliff before the outcropping began to give way, and there was nothing he could do to stop from falling once his descent began.

The burning beast was coming to life through him, and Roche was honestly glad for it. He embraced the change like he had the explosion, and let himself be grateful to have another string of moments in which he could imagine living to the next. Even if the monster within him had come without him calling, Roche still felt in control. Rage burned within him, but it was a healthy rage. The realm he loved was being threatened, and he could think of no better reason to be consumed by his anger.

And yet, he wasn't. A part of him wanted to see all the old dragons die, and he let the feeling fuel the fire he had become; but there were other thoughts in his mind at the same time. He still wished this could all stop, and the denizens of Hell could learn to live in peace. He still felt glad to be alive, and grateful to be consuming the explosion instead of being ripped to shreds by it. In his mind, the war went on; and it was more comforting to hear those sounds of inner battle than he had ever known it could be. That meant he was still himself, even as he fell flaming to the city below.

He had no wings in this form; he also really didn't have a body. The blazing beast was shaped like him, set on fire and blown out of proportion; but his very cells had transformed to burning cinders. His arms and legs were made of flames, and those flames were under his direction as much as the limbs they had replaced.

Roche stretched out as he fell, and willed his fiery fingertips to reach out to help his comrades. He saw his own burning arms shoot forward, the fingers splaying wildly as they exploded into the fray. His rapid descent slowed as he expanded, and his arms came down on several dragons at once. One flaming limb settled on Rendibite's back, while the other fell on the dragons between him and Ximena. He couldn't reach all of them, and gravity was still pulling him past the ones he touched; but the momentary contact had the desired effect.

The sensation in his fingertips was like nothing he had ever known. Roche could feel the scaled skin and the fire he was using to touch it at the same time. He let the heat of the explosion he had absorbed follow the sensation, and every dragon he was in contact with burst into flames. The monsters attacking Ximena all hesitated, even the ones that didn't find themselves on fire; and Rendibite was burning all over his serpentine body. The old dragon let the younger go, in the same moment that the team of dragons attacking the queen pulled back to reconfigure.

Still drifting downward, Roche took sad satisfaction in the chorus of reptilian screams that played soundtrack to his descent. At this point all he could do was look for a place to land where his flames would do the least unintentional damage, and hope his efforts had given his allies the respite they had needed.

From his vantage point, Roche saw the city in a way he hadn't before. The streets looked more like landing strips from up here, and it was clear most of the actual area that had been set aside was up here in the sky. As enormous as they were, the old dragons had plenty of room to navigate around each other in the air. The city had been nothing but a trap from the very beginning, and he had walked right into it.

One building stood out among the others, for several reasons. He hadn't noticed it before, and he could see why immediately; it was behind taller structures filling the space between it and the stairs he had always taken. The shape of it was different than the others, and it stood short and squat where they reached thin squared tendrils to the sky. Other buildings had stoops on the streets, while this one was surrounded by flat expanses of land on every side.

Tilting in that direction, Roche had time to wonder why he had not seen Lilia since they had each dashed off in separate directions. He supposed she could be flying overhead, lost in all the larger dragons and smoke that had gathered; perhaps she was even fighting them up there somewhere. Somehow he didn't think so, however. Roche could easily picture her slipping away, waiting until the fires had died down before proclaiming her allegiance to the victor.

The ground rushed up to meet him, and Roche fell square into the center of a field of dirt and sand. He felt as though he had been consuming the explosion as he fell, and that very little remained of that initial sudden blast; when he struck the city floor, he realized he had been wrong. Everything he touched was immediately consumed in flame, and he could feel the fine granules and soft soil under him turning to liquid fire. Within moments of landing, he was swimming in a small lake of churning lava.

Suddenly, his awareness expanded as it had done when he had taken this form before. Roche's vision was no longer confined to which way his flaming eyes were pointed, and he could see the entire city as if he was simultaneously looking down at it from above and gazing up at it from below. He saw that all the streets were burning, and the sky was choked with smoke; he could also see clearly that Lilia was neither above or below, and had escaped the scene as he had suspected.

For every moment he spent in that spot, the bubbling sea of liquid flame reached deeper into the ground below him. Roche kept trying to find purchase, succeeding only in setting everything he touched aflame. No matter which way he moved, he continued to sink further into the fire. The explosion was still shooting sparks and heat from his blazing body in every direction, and as much of him was submerged as was above ground.

He was glad to see the dragons had left Ximena alone for now, even if she had immediately started chasing them through the dense dark clouds of smoke hanging over the city. Laurentis had gotten past the reach of Rendibite's claws for a moment, only to recover quickly and dart around to the older dragon's back. Rendibite was trying to stay aloft, while also attempting to dislodge his opponent and put out the fires scorching his skin; his efforts were nearly futile, and the two of them were visibly losing altitude as one.

Dozens of dragons were circling, and began to descend in formation on the city once more. At first Roche was uncertain of their target, or their intention; as the spiral tightened, their purpose became clear in short order. Ximena was trying to break up the pattern, but she could only dissuade a couple of them from their paths before they began to strike.

Roche knew he couldn't climb out of the hole he had burned in the ground before the attack reached him, and he wasn't sure if their flames would have any effect at all on the inferno he had become. Letting his rage build as he waited for them to descend on him and layer him in sheets of fire, he reached out long blazing arms to embrace the heat and find out once and for all if dragon fire could truly destroy him.

CHAPTER 57

The dragons descended, forming an almost unbroken stream of scaled flesh falling from the sky. From snout to tail, they lined up to rain unending fire down on him. Roche could see it all, from every angle; yet there was very little he could do about any of it. He remained trapped by the lake of fire, sinking deeper for every effort he made to climb out. If the dragons' plan didn't work, and extinguish the blaze Roche had become, they would shift again and explore another approach; but if it did, he would be gone as the worlds moved on without him.

Once more, he found himself contemplating his own impending demise. Every moment Roche had lived had felt like a swift downward slide, and he didn't imagine anyone would begrudge him for embracing the veil of death when it fell over him. The promise of an eventual rise did nothing to comfort him. Instead the concept was alien, an unknown he could no more define than he could look forward to.

Thoughts whirled madly in his head while the world moved on at normal speed. Roche wondered if maybe this was the moment he was made for, that perhaps he was never meant to rise. All the darkness he had gathered within may have been sent to him, designed to put him at the very edge of his tolerance just as the web of worlds needed him to let go.

The first dragon in a long line of them opened its maw as the thought formed fully, and Roche stopped struggling in an attempt to climb out of the burning hole. Opening his giant blazing arms wide, he braced himself as best he could against the flowing fire underfoot and fixed his eyes on the dragon's. The beast was inhaling, puffing up its chest as it leveled out in flight not far from him; it blinked, and wavered for a brief second.

In the next moment, the fire came. Roche could see the blaze approaching, and felt the heat of it pour into him. Even as he closed his eyes, he saw everything; the dragon from above and below, the line of them coming in behind it to deliver one blazing blast after another. He also saw something he hadn't seen before, in all his looking: Roche shifted his attention, and focused in on Laurentis.

Ximena had been moving toward Roche, but he hadn't thought she would reach him in time to interrupt the river of flame the dragons had planned for him. He was right, and he had watched as she struggled with the monsters skimming the upper atmosphere. Eventually she might make it through all of them; but by that time the whole world would know if dragon fire was the secret to destroying Roche. Her efforts would eventually prove to be unnecessary or futile, even as hard as she was fighting; and Roche would either be long since dead or clearly no longer in need of aid by then.

Laurentis was closer, but Roche hadn't noticed the dragon any more than he had noticed all the other turmoil around him. The fight between the younger dragon and the older went on, and Roche had presumed nothing else existed for his friend as he battled for his life and his freedom. Suddenly the tussle shifted in the air, and Roche realized Laurentis had meant for it to.

For a moment he looked like he was faltering in flight once more, flapping his wings awkwardly in Rendibite's face. Roche could see he was actually getting between Rendibite and the line of dragons descending on Roche's position, putting his wings in his opponent's eyes to obscure his view. When the older dragon attacked, he swept gracefully aside; and Rendibite realized a moment too late that he was on a collision course with the dragon breathing fire down on Roche.

The two giant dragons came together with a loud meaty thud directly over Roche's head. All of their forward momentum ceased in that moment, and they began to fall as one. Roche wasn't sure if he was relieved or angry that the dragon fire had stopped. In the moment before they reached him, he poured everything he had into sweeping his arms into the sky to reach them first.

One fiery hand caught the dragon that had been trying to toast him, and Roche felt the monster's flesh begin to cook under his flaming fingers as he clamped down on its neck. The dragon began to shriek, and flail about; Roche watched as Rendibite was thrown clear, even as he pulled the other dragon into the pit of fire with him.

As soon as it realized what was happening, the dragon tried to close its eyes and curl into a ball. Roche was sure it would take some time for it to work up enough internal flame to explode, but he wasn't taking any chances. He did the opposite of what he had been doing this whole time, and dove deep into the lava below with the screaming dragon in tow. The creature struggled for a moment, then went loose in his grip; the next moment it was gone, dissolved in the liquid fire.

Rocketing toward the surface, Roche cried out as he broke through to open air once more. Laurentis had seized on Rendibite as he was thrown free, and was keeping the older dragon from taking off from where he had landed. Their battle on the ground was much as it had been in the air, the giant beast flummoxed by the swift actions of the smaller. Laurentis bit at him, rushed around his body, and bit at him again; by the time Rendibite reacted each time, he was being bitten once more. Roche watched the missing chunks of flesh try to heal as more appeared, and saw the deep purple blood of the older dragon staining the streets.

His leap took him nearly face to face with the next dragon set to flame him, and Roche reached out with both flaming hands to seize the monster midair. Ximena was watching from above, and he saw her disengage from the monster she was fighting to drift silently away in a completely different direction. He might have been confused, and wondered about it; but there was a struggling dragon in his grip. Putting her out of his mind, Roche plunged himself once more into the lake of fire under him.

Just before the dragon dissolved in his grip, Roche felt it trying to do the same thing the other had done. No explosion came, but he could feel a wave of dark emotion pass over him as the dragon turned inward. Roche found himself wondering why he didn't simply allow the dragons to end the world, much as he had wondered if he truly belonged in it anymore a few moments past.

The monster turned to fire, the flames changed to liquid, and the lava flowed between Roche's fiery fingers. When he lunged to the surface this time, it was more deliberate; he had time to see everything clearly, and the vision made his smoldering breath catch in his fiery lungs.

All the dragons had broken off, giving up their collective attack on him. Several had already found their way to ledges, or to cleared streets in the city below; the others were drifting toward some open spot, presumably to do what the few that had already found perches were doing. Together they were closing their eyes, turning inward and building up the flame inside them.

Ximena had anticipated the move. She had already descended on one dragon as it settled into an explosive ball, and was tearing it free of its moorings. Roche could see that she planned to drag it to him, and set it free in the flames; but even as she covered it in darkness and pulled it from the ledge, smoke began to puff out from the falling shadow.

A few of the dragons turned into devils when they hit a rock outcropping, and slipped through openings too narrow for a giant dragon. At first Roche thought they may be fleeing; but the thought was pushed aside for another, more likely possibility. If they could get far enough away before starting their explosive process, it would make reaching all of them in time impossible. Even if Ximena went after every dragon perched overhead before they began to smoke, and tossed them into his lake of fire, she could not chase down every one that had escaped in time.

CHAPTER 58

Ximena brought him the dragons, one after another; and Roche burned each of them. He knew others were slipping away, and might be exploding soon. The knowledge only made him more angry, and stoked the fire of his rage. As much destruction as he had wrought, the thought of others being able to cause even more frightened and disturbed him.

Even more disturbing was the thought that all of them were coming together on this. If it was true that the old dragons could destroy all the realms somehow, he still couldn't understand why they would come to the conclusion to act on it at the same time. His own damage had been done in fury, a passionate act in the moment which he came to regret later. The dragons were calm about their desire to end it all, cool and calculating as they planned their victory. If it came, it would be the last battle any of the worlds would ever see.

The fire he had become was not all flames and fury. As Roche burned one ancient dragon after another, he could hear their thoughts and sense their feelings as they expired. Not one of them was sad to be burning up, or angry at their own demise; to a dragon, each was certain their death was a contribution to the greater cause. They may have lived fiercely independent lives, for longer than any mortal or most immortals could imagine; but they were orchestrating this final act as one mind.

As much as he hated to think it, Roche couldn't help but agree with the idea as it flooded his mind over and over. Each dragon saw it their own way, but they all imagined the same result: those in the city would keep their enemies occupied while a few moved beyond their reach. By the time they had dealt with the monsters at hand, the others would be reaching the heights of their destructive power. Ximena could no more chase down both groups than Roche could climb from the lake of fire; all she could do was keep bringing him dragons, and all he could do was keep burning them to nothing.

Those thoughts were the only thing he couldn't seem to burn away, and they accumulated in Roche's mind like his rage had so many times before. This time he could step away from the thoughts, so to speak, and see them for what they were; yet observing them only made him increasingly angry, and soon his own fire began to burn with even more intensity.

It didn't make sense; yet in that way only emotions have, it began to. Roche started to think the best way to beat the dragons was to destroy the worlds before they could. Whatever he was doing to contain their destruction was an instinctive act, but that didn't mean he couldn't control it. All he had to do was let those explosions happen, and not pull in the blast like he had done with the others. Even better, he could gather up the energy of the dying ancients and create his own all-consuming fire. It would be his action that ended everything, not theirs; and somehow he thought taking that victory from them would count for something, even if it ended everything.

He was sure an eternity of rage would be harder to bear than a sudden and complete nothingness, and equally certain there would be no afterlife for those whose afterlife had been destroyed along with everything else. All the souls in the realms would evaporate into the flames, and the turbulent nature of the universe would know true and lasting peace.

And the dragons would not have caused it.

By the time the thought formed, Roche had lost count of how any dragons had perished in his lake of fire. He knew their feelings were influencing him; yet knowing was not enough to alter that effect. Whatever they were leaving him with was indistinguishable from the aspects of his inner landscape that came only from him, and he began to see the desire to end it all as his own.

Once the idea took hold, it seemed ridiculous that he would have ever seen things any other way. Roche found himself wondering why he had stopped his fiery destruction in the mortal realm at all, and why he hadn't taken it above and below when he was done there. A part of him was curious why he hadn't seen the way the worlds were and immediately set out to destroy them; that part grew the more he dwelled on it. Nothing made sense from start to finish anywhere he had been; and the only appropriate response to being plopped into the middle of all that, for a being like him, was to burn it all.

Someone was calling to him, from very far away; at first Roche thought it might be his own voice, and wondered why it sounded so tinny and far off. When the sound reached him again, he realized it was coming from above him. For the first time in several minutes, he put his attention somewhere other than inward. Lifting his fiery eyes to the sky, he saw Ximena and Laurentis circling overhead.

The dragon was streaked in purple blood, some of it his own; but also looked fully healed, if he had been wounded again. The queen was still in her shadowy form, drifting in the same flight pattern opposite Laurentis without any visible means of propulsion. Her voice came to him once more, and it sounded concerned this time.

"Roche!" she called out. "Do you hear me?!"

With his eyes still skyward, Roche opened his arms in a giant fiery embrace. He felt the energy of all those explosions within him, and the desire to let them loose as one. The rage boiled in him, to his molten core; and his outstretched arms began to pour thick acrid smoke into the city. Ximena's voice found his ears again, only barely reaching his mind.

"Roche!" she cried. "You must stop!"

Her words meant nothing to him. They were layered over with every other word he had ever heard spoken, by every voice he had known in his life; together the sound was noisy static, another annoying aspect of existence that needed to end along with everything else. Roche felt the energy building in him; he could see molten raindrops falling upward into the sky, cutting through the dark haze and trailing black smoke.

As one, Laurentis and Ximena changed the way they were flying. Both of them shot high into the air above him, only to hang suspended in midair for a long pregnant moment; then, moving in tandem, they began to fall together. In seconds they would dive into the lake of fire Roche was standing in, and they would burn to nothing moments before the rest of the world did.

CHAPTER 59

Everything could burn, as far as Roche was concerned. He had visited all the realms, and his memories of each were nothing but fuel for the fire he had become. The soft airy clouds above could be choked out by so much smoke, and the antiseptic scent of Heaven could be overwhelmed by the acrid stench of those new dark clouds.

Below was doomed from the beginning, giving slow rise to one ticking time bomb after another. The dragons were made to live forever, or until they brought eternity to a fiery halt; of course that day was going to come, if all anyone could do was wait for it. Sending a single solitary being to rule the realm was like damning Ximena to her own brand of Hell, and putting her in a sublimely uncomfortable situation she could never hope to get out of.

The mortal realm was caught between the two, and was none the better for it. All the worst of both bracketing worlds found their way into flesh form there, burying the best before it could rise. For every happiness the original demon had known among mortals, Roche had found a corresponding darkness that seemed to overwhelm that initial spark entirely. Nothing remained there for him, and his memories would die along with everything else.

If only those two were not spiraling downward, aimed to splash together into his lake of fire. They put faces to the destruction he was setting to unleash, and attached names to the deaths he was about to cause. Somehow countless was an easier number to annihilate than two, especially when it was those two. Ximena was falling, a streaking shadow given over to gravity with complete abandon; Laurentis had angled his body forward, and was set to meet Roche head on.

Shapeless in her descending darkness, Ximena had maintained only one feature from her usual form. Her eyes stared out at him from her shadowy fall, piercing the smoke between them and his soul beyond. The queen spoke to him silently in that stillness, admitting that his way seemed the only way. She had considered this outcome, even predicted it; if it was the last thing she did, Ximena was going to play her part.

Laurentis somehow also shared his thoughts in the slow stretching moments they had until they both drowned in his lake of fire. He had known it all would end one day, and had long since made peace with the knowing. The efforts they had made said enough about who he was for the dragon to allow this day to be his last, and he hoped maybe forever nothingness would mean some kind of eternal peace.

Their acceptance should have aligned with his own. Roche should have been delighted to have these two behind him, and so dedicated to the end he was prepared to bring to all this. His rebellious nature was not to be put to rest by their agreement, however. Immediately his mind went to what Hell might be when the young dragons became the old dragons, and what the queen might do with a chance to rule her own way.

He only had a moment, before they plunged together into his fire. Roche knew the dragon would burn, as the others had; and he was not so sure Ximena could withstand the flames any better. The explosion building in him had reached a blistering pitch, and he was set to unleash all the explosions he had contained in one endless blast.

Somehow, in that moment he had, Roche saw every aspect of reality coming together to create this event. The falling forms froze while his mind stretched out to encompass everything; he saw all that darkness he had remembered earlier, and at the same time he saw the light behind it. In the places where the darkness reigned, he looked beyond the cloying shadows to behold brightness like he had never seen. All the light that had ever struck his eyes could not add up to the luminous glow behind one dark spot, and somehow now he could see them all.

Since the beginning, he had seen demons riding angels and devils and humans; from the highest realm to the lowest, nearly everyone bore some yoke of guilt about their shoulders. Roche had seen the weight pulling them down, until this moment had stopped for him. Now he saw it lifting them up, buoying the fast falling souls while anchoring those on the rise. He realized what good could come from everything, not just demons; and beyond that, in this instant, he saw that the greatest darkness may be hiding the most brilliant light.

All of creation stared back at him, glowing with the hidden luminescence until he felt the darkness in him began to shine forth as well. His consciousness went from seeing everything to being confined in a small point of reference once more, the shock of his own mind coming back to him slamming into him almost painfully. Time moved forward once more, and Roche realized he was still gazing up at Ximena.

Looking into her eyes one final time, Roche watched them go wide as he shrunk further into himself. The explosion was going somewhere, and he hoped whatever he was made of would be enough to absorb the brunt of the blast. Roche turned everything headed outward suddenly inward, and let loose the hold he had on the accumulation of destruction.

The last thing he saw was the ground opening up beneath him, and a thick fall of lava gushing downward. Whatever part of the explosion he had not contained burst after it, filling the gaping orifice until the rocks forming it turned red and melted into smooth smoky walls. Roche was swallowed up in the rocks and sand that piled in after the implosive blast, and the only thought he had time for was one last wish.

Imagining it even as his own fire burned him, Roche saw Ximena and Laurentis being thrown clear of the explosion in his mind's eye. He couldn't be sure if he was seeing something that was happening, or if he was just picturing what he wanted to see; but seeing it made it possible to believe, and believing it meant he could let the flames consume him completely.

If they lived, there was hope for the realm; Roche had seen it is his last eternal moment. Drawing his mind in from everywhere had shown him what was happening beyond the city, and he wished with all his being that his sacrifice would not be for nothing.

In the next moment, the thought disappeared into flames.

CHAPTER 60

After long uncounted moments of darkness, the first shapes he saw were shadows cut from fire. Flames leapt high behind the figures as they surrounded him, casting all three of their faces into deeper pools of inky blackness. Roche sat up, and they stepped back as one. His vision swam, and then cleared; and he saw them for who they were.

Gazing down at him, Ximena's face was etched deeply with concern. She nearly clapped her hands when he sat up, and exchanged a glance with Laurentis as he allowed Roche's movement his own brief smile. The third figure was not a mystery to him, but her presence there was. Lilia stood over him as well, arms crossed under her breasts and a smug look of satisfaction smeared across her countenance. If anything, she looked disappointed that he had opened his eyes and sat up; more likely, she could not have much cared either way.

"I didn't die," Roche muttered.

His own voice was foreign to him, a guttural rasp that spoke more of fire than it conveyed actual words. Clearing his throat, he tried again. This time the only sound was a choked wheeze. He held his own hand in front of his face, to see if it was made of flames or flesh.

That was his arm, but it had been charred into a deep crusted black. As he watched the flesh grow back slowly, it resembled human skin for a fleeting moment; then it reformed perfect crimson scales over his sinew, finely wrought and carefully carved by the mind of creation itself. Energy filled his body, as it knitted itself back into existence; and Roche stood on new legs, reaching out to Laurentis for support. The dragon leaned in, to give Roche his shoulder; in the next moment, the assistance was no longer needed.

The original demon stood tall, and met each of their eyes in turn. His gaze went between Laurentis and Ximena, ignoring Lilia entirely.

"You saved me," he said. "You saved everything."

Ximena laughed, as Laurentis shook his head.

"We may have changed your mind," Laurentis said, "or whatever passes for a mind in that fiery creature you became. It was Lilia that saved everything, however."

Now Ximena was nodding, agreeing with one dragon while smiling at the other. She was clearly pleased with what Lilia had done, and was obviously even proud of her in some way. Roche found himself wondering about the relationship between the two of them, and not for the first time.

For a long moment, Roche had seen everything; but it was all together at once, and most of what he had seen was the energy behind the forms it took. As he had come back into himself, however, he had witnessed something else. Lilia had somehow foreseen what was to come in the battle with the dragons, and had slipped away to execute both her plan and her enemies when the fighting had started.

"Lilia," Roche breathed, "you waited for them. You and the other young dragons, you waited for them to change shape and try to leave the city. You met them as they tried to slip away."

His voice had come back to him, along with his flesh; but Roche still spoke in a hushed tone. He stared her down while he spoke, and the images he had seen in a fleeting moment came back to play out slowly in his head. Each retreating dragon had changed into their devil form, to fit through the opening; and Lilia or one of her cohorts had met them as they passed through. The young dragons didn't stand a chance, squaring off against the ancients while they were both in reptilian form; but they made short work of the devils they became in order to pass through the narrow exits.

Even the smallest dragon quickly overcame the ancients in their devil forms. Each of them clearly held a grudge against one or several of their elders, and they took those frustrations out on whichever devil came through their doorway. Roche couldn't get the memories out of his head, once they flooded in; he saw gruesome beheadings and flaming bodies behind his eyes, whether they were open or closed.

"And then you killed them," Roche said. "All of them."

Still holding Lilia's gaze, Roche shuddered a little when he saw a guiltless smile pull at the corners of her mouth. She was not just glad for what she had done; it seemed those same images were filling her mind, and she was savoring them as much as he was resisting them.

"We did," Lilia said, flatly. "And we would do it again."

She glanced at Ximena, and Laurentis; each of them inclined their head at the look, and met her eyes with gratitude in theirs. Roche had to remind himself that they had not seen the way she carried out her plan; all they knew was that their world still existed. They hadn't seen the cruelty Lilia displayed rushing from one egress to another, or the way she had made it a point to kill as many of the ancients herself as she could. They hadn't heard her orders, or the way she gave them; and they would never know what they had been.

Roche was as glad for the outcome as they were, and was just as grateful to be alive. The collective hate of the dragons he had burned was gone, only to be replaced by the kind of exhaustion even his healing abilities could not mend. After one last look at his friends, and the person he was most afraid of in all the realms, Roche sighed and turned to Ximena once more.

"My queen," he murmured. "I would like to visit your library, if that would be all right with you."

She exchanged a look with Lilia, which Roche thought nothing of until some time later; then Ximena smiled softly, and nodded.

"Of course," she said. "Take all the time you need, and tell your counterpart you made us all glad to know you today."

Laurentis and Lilia nodded at that, and Roche was reminded that he had his own dark desires to account for in all this. Still, he could not compare his moments of being carried away by stirred passions to the calculated horror Lilia had caused. When familiar faces had come into his fire, he had balked; when she had seen dragons she had known for longer than he could imagine, Lilia had made it a point to kill as many of them with her own fangs and fire as possible.

"She speaks truth," Laurentis commented, "and you look more like an angel than any devil I've seen other than her."

The dragon smirked, ever so slightly.

"But that flaming beast you became," he added. "That thing was a whole new kind of ugly on me, and I've seen some real ugly."

Lilia and Ximena turned to the dragon, their eyes going wide together. Laurentis cocked an eyebrow while he let the comment sink in, and Roche remembered how he had insulted the way the dragon looked when he transformed. He was no more in the mood to laugh than Laurentis had been back then, but he extended his friend the same courtesy he had received at the time.

Roche chuckled, a hollow meaningless sound; and after a moment, the others relaxed and joined in.

CHAPTER 61

Once again, a secret threw up an invisible wall between them from the moment Roche connected with the angel. He ignored it, just as he had before; at the same time Roche made note of it without really noticing, just as he had done before.

Being with Ehcor, even in this strange disembodied manner, was a healing balm spread over the pain of his soul. He was happy to find her there waiting for him, when he got there. Even more pleasing, she seemed content to not speak of what he had recently been through. Roche let the images play out in his mind, knowing she could see both what he had seen and what he had felt.

When he showed her the dragons' plan, and what he had done to address it, the angel watched the burning horror play out in his mind with calm equanimity. She did not waver until he had, and Ehcor somehow quietly expressed her disappointment in his desire to end it all without saying a word or displaying any expression. Roche knew she had hoped he would stay strong, and battle to the end; at the same time he felt her compassion for his weakness, and knew she would have forgiven him even if the worlds had ended.

He wondered if she would have stayed a different path, had the fate of the realms been in her hands as they had been in his; Ehcor sensed the thought, and pondered the possibilities herself. They both concluded that she would have done otherwise, for their own reasons: Roche could not imagine anything but the best out of her, and Ehcor could not foresee what the suffocating weight of centuries of darkness could do to a soul.

Their time in this place that was not a place was not always about interacting deliberately, or expressing their views succinctly. Roche needed to feel her intertwining with him, and sharing his soul as only she could. It had taken awhile for him to accept that she needed the same from him, for her own reasons; now he knew to open himself up as completely as he wanted her to, and let his view of all the worlds assemble itself into order for him through her eyes.

Together, they dwelt in that peaceful union for some time. It was not until Roche sensed a disturbance in her that he thought to wonder what the angel had been going through. She had been holding it back, expending more of herself on keeping something from him than she wanted to. Ehcor wanted to relax, and merge with him; yet that hidden thought in her mind was taxing her heart, and causing her pain.

Roche looked at it, effortlessly, and did the closest thing he could to laughing in this place. Part of him had known it all along, and simply not added the pieces together to make a whole; while another part of him had needed to stay in the dark, not knowing what was happening in this moment until the moment was upon him.

"Do not worry, my angel," he breathed, without breath. "I know why I was coaxed into this place, and what I will now have to endure. The judgement of all the realms must be weighed in my case, and the balance is likely to tilt in an unfavorable direction."

Her surprise was immediate, only to be instantly replaced by a wave of relief. To better define what he had seen, Ehcor spoke words that did not need to be uttered. Roche knew his fate, at least for now.

"They want to have a trial," she said. "I've heard talk of it, although no one will discuss the specifics in detail with me. It looks bad, for you; that's all they say, at least to me."

If he'd had shoulders, in this place, he would have responded with a light shrug. Whatever passed for a dismissive gesture here floated between them, and he saw that she needed his words right now.

"I know," he said. "The specifics of my actions are right here in my thoughts, in those memories I just shared with you. I can't see any reason for someone who did what I did to not be judged for it, and perhaps punished severely. If it was anyone else, I would say they must be held accountable. When you look at what I have done, can you deny that I should answer for those actions?"

Her denial was palpable, between them; but it was only a feeling. Ehcor could not come up with words to explain why he should not be judged, beyond expressing her fear of the outcome. In the swirl of thoughts and feelings dancing around them and through them, Roche felt what she wanted to tell him next. He spoke before she could, answering her question before she could ask it.

"I cannot run," he said. "You know that, better than anyone. Many places in Hell exist that could be a stepping stone to this world only we share; yet the only room that could contain me against my will is Ximena's library. You conspired with her to draw me there. You let her tell me it was the only path from Hell to you, and you kept the secret plans of my imprisonment from me even here."

To another, his words may have sounded accusatory. Ehcor knew his thoughts in this place, however; and she could see into his soul. The only feeling he conveyed along with his words was relief, and gratitude that everything had worked out the way it had. He even sensed how little she liked the word he used, and made sure not to refer to what was happening to him as imprisonment.

"You did the right thing," he said. "Ximena needed to know I could be…contained, and you helped her in the best way you could. To your credit, you did not keep the secret closely guarded; but as further evidence of my own obsessive nature, I did not question it or notice it consciously enough to wonder about it. Perhaps I knew what the two of you were doing, on some level; maybe I even helped in my own way, like you did in yours."

Ehcor seemed relieved at the thought, and at her decision to believe it as if it were true. Roche sensed her concern for him, and for what she was supposed to do next; he spoke kindly once more, since his words were clearly making his other feel more comfortable about the situation she had found herself in.

"Go, my angel," he said. "Report to whatever angel or devil has asked for it, and tell them whatever you remember about what we shared here today. Do not lie for me, or hide what you have seen. I will wait here, or in Ximena's library; and we will see each other in this place whenever you can come to meet me."

Roche could sense her wanting to speak; at the same time, the angel was very happy to know he was not angry with her. She did not want to taint the experience by speaking her doubts, and perhaps weakening his cheery resolve. Without a word, the part of her that was here embraced the part of him that was here. In the next moment, she was gone; and Roche found himself alone once more in that spacious endless nowhere.

CHAPTER 62

Not much time passed between his time with Ehcor and the first visit from Ximena. Roche knew he was trapped in the library, yet he didn't feel like a prisoner. The moments he had to himself were peaceful, and for the first time he was able to look back on his life without feeling an inevitable future pulling him forward. He never would have disengaged from the worlds on his own; with the decision made for him, the original demon was able to relax and allow a serenity like he had never known settle over his soul.

Ximena seemed surprised to find him seated comfortably, one leg thrown carelessly over the other as he leaned back into the giant cushioned seat. His left hand was behind his head, while his right held a book he had chosen from the surrounding shelves. The tome was ancient, one in a series that had caught his eye during an earlier visit. He was still on the first volume, nearing the final pages.

She swept into the room more than she appeared out of thin air, even if that's precisely what she had done. The shadows grew, before his eyes; and Ximena stepped from the darkness. Black shapelessness trailed behind her in long lazy tendrils, and encircled her in a slowly spinning vortex. In the middle of it all, the queen was simplicity swimming in complexity. A long dark gown hung from her neck to cover her arms to the wrists, and conceal her feet completely. The dress could have been another shadow, darker than all the others while similarly shifting and flowing with her every movement.

Glancing around the room, Ximena did nothing to hide her reaction. Her eyes were wide, brows arched over their dark roundness; a slight frown pulled at the corners of her mouth, clearly damming laughter more than it was expressing unhappiness.

"Hello," she said, cautiously.

Closing the volume carefully in his giant crimson hand, Roche set it aside and gazed up at her. He smiled, and shrugged lightly.

"Are you angry with me?" she ventured. "Or with your other? You should direct any such feelings you may have my way. Ehcor knew you would be imprisoned, and she wanted the environment to be one you would prefer. She chose this place, and she was the only one involved in the choosing that felt your confinement should be as much a reward as it is meant to be a punishment."

Roche held her gaze, allowed himself to be enveloped in her energy.

"Was she the only one?" he smiled. "Truly? This is your library, after all. Your own story is contained in these books, as is mine. You would reveal all your secrets to me, and call it imprisonment?"

Heaving a sigh that relaxed her whole body while slowing the spin of the shadows around her, Ximena peered at him with visible relief. Roche laughed, gestured around them.

"Did you expect me to be destroying the place over and over?" he chuckled. "I tried that, before; and I'm glad it had no lasting effect. This is the one place I would have chosen for myself, to be held. A part of me has longed to lock myself away in this space since I first saw it, and knew it for what it was. I want to read it all, even if I will forget it; even if the words change before my very eyes as I go back and read them again. So much of what I have longed to know is contained in these pages, and I am honored to be locked away with them."

Her smile was without guile, a relaxed and happy upturn of her mouth acknowledging that the situation might have been better while knowing it could have ended much worse. Seeing the expression, Roche pressed on.

"I know what I did," he said, "and why you are grateful to me. I also know what I almost did, and that your loyalty to the realm must be upheld above all else. Your cloak of darkness sets a certain expectation, but I have seen the light behind it. You shine brilliantly like a star to me, even now; and I'm pleased to say everything else seems to be brightening up around me as well."

Nodding, the queen allowed her smile to widen. The moment his soul had turned in its tracks, and began heading upward, Roche had known. A doorway had clicked open silently inside him, and a slow but certain coming together had started in his soul. This was the key to defeating him, knowing the cycles of his power; yet the books he had leafed through had already given him so many of her secrets. The one he felt most needed to be guarded seemed it would be safe with her, when he thought about it.

"I have hit bottom," he breathed, "and now I rise."

Her smile faded slowly. Roche thought nothing of it, until the queen spoke again. The words were as quiet as his had been, and he had to lean forward to hear her better.

"The demon rises," she murmured, "and the angel falls."

Before he could ask what she meant, or consider the meaning behind her words, Ximena shook off her grave mask to smile once more at him. This time there was kindness in her countenance, and no hidden sadness or concern.

"You might want to change your appearance before the trial," she said. "You look too much like an angel, with devil's skin. The council judging you are angels, but not like any you have met before. Their souls have never been human, or devil; and they never will be. They are powerful fixtures in Heaven, and they do not take kindly to demonstrations of greatness in others. Your features are too finely sculpted, your stature too tall and muscled. Think about how else you might appear to others, and try to choose a form that is not too spectacular in any way."

Raising an eyebrow, Roche searched her eyes.

"What kind of angels are these?" he said. "They sound like the dragons of Heaven, from the way you describe them."

She began to shake her head, to tell him more; Roche cut her off, by holding up one hand between them.

"No matter," he said. "I will learn of them soon enough, and I will accept whatever judgement they level against me."

Her countenance was clouded with concern once more, and Roche waved it off before dropping his scaled hand to his side again.

"I will change my appearance," he said. "You have advised me to do so, and I respect your counsel enough to heed it."

The last thing he saw, before she disappeared to be replaced by normal stretching shadows, was Ximena's satisfied smile.

EPILOGUE

One set of shelves was mirrored, and Roche cleared them to catch a better look at himself as he worked on shifting his appearance. He definitely needed to be shorter; though he knew that from towering over nearly everyone he had met, the original demon still wanted to keep a bit of his height. Looking over the tops of most heads would be easier than gazing up at everyone, and it was nothing compared with his former stature.

The muscles had to go, as well. Roche didn't really need them to be strong, and Ximena had said something about outward appearances of power; so he slimmed down, then decided to be a little defiant and built himself a beefy round body. He shrunk his horns down, until they fit neatly under the strange hat Ximena had given him; and when he looked at himself in the mirror the next time Roche was struck by how much he looked like a human. All he needed was a little age, and that weight was already burdening his soul. He simply let it come out, in his face.

His scales became skin, rough and old and touched with crimson. Human looked good on him, and Roche wore the hat and his new old body until the trial was held. Ximena never said anything about it, in the days leading up to the event; but he sensed she was pleased by his choice every time he saw her.

In the moment, he had sworn he would remember every detail of the trial; afterwards, Roche could only recall vague snippets of speech and fleeting forms. The place he was taken to reminded him of where he met with Ehcor, but everything he had made note of about the surroundings slipped his mind the moment it was over. He remembered looking straight at the angels, and burning the images of them into his mind; he had even made a point to count them, more than once.

Back in the library, Roche could not recall a single detail about the angels, or how many there were. He knew Ximena was there, and Ehcor; but the beings who sat in judgement of him were quicksilver in his memories, darting away every time he tried to put his mind on them.

The only things that stayed with him were when Ximena and Ehcor spoke on his behalf, and the final verdict that was delivered. Nothing about the voice delivering the words was there, or the face that spoke them; but the message itself got through to him, and was with him when he returned to his happy isolation.

He would stay here until it was deemed safe for him to be free; and thereafter, Roche would be exiled from both Heaven and Hell. The human realm would be his home once he was released, and any damage he might do would be restricted to that world. Part of him looked forward to the exile, just as part of him wanted to drink up the knowledge locked away with him in the devil's library.

Ximena came to see him often, in the countless time that he was imprisoned. They would sit and talk about what he was learning, and what he would do when he went to live among mortals. He learned to know when Ehcor wanted to meet with him, and they came together often to talk of demons and the role they played in the lives of their hosts. Roche felt as though the upward swing of his soul was giving him more energy every day, and a burning desire to begin the next stage of his journey.

Finally, one day, the decision was made. Roche didn't know how he knew it, but somehow he knew the order had been given to set him free of his confinement. The inner access to doorways between worlds opened up again, and he could see endless selections of earthly scenes to choose from. The sun was shining in the sky in some of them, and the people he saw looked robust and healthy like never before.

Roche put the thought out of his mind, and picked up again where he had left off reading. He would decide where to go, soon enough; but first, he had to finish Lilia's story. The book had been shelved right next to Ximena's, and Roche really felt as though reading it had given him a better view into the heart of the dragon.

Dear Reader,

As soon as I began writing the original 'Walking Between Worlds' trilogy, it was clear there was a lot more to this story than we could see through the eyes of a handful of demon hunters. Scenes played themselves over and over in my head until I wrote it all down, but I couldn't help wondering what had happened to bring the world of demons and angels to the place it was in modern day San Francisco.

The characters in those books revealed way more information than I could include in the trilogy, and it was both exciting and a little weird to know I was the only person in our world who knew all that stuff. From the very beginning, I wanted to tell this whole story. It was clear even back then that the only way to share this was alongside the characters that lived it, and I always knew the first book would need to be about Roche.

In the meantime, I didn't want to be known as the 'Walking Between Worlds' guy. Many other ideas were asking me to write about them, in their own way; and I wanted to write in as many genres as I like to read in. Before I could come back to this universe, I had to build others with zombies and space travel and body snatching in them. I had to explore other writing styles, and keep concentrating on getting better at telling all these stories I so strongly feel need to be told.

Honestly, I got a little scared about writing this book after awhile. I was afraid my voice may not sound quite the same as it did back when I wrote those first three books, or that the scenes wouldn't play out in my head the way they did back then, or that the characters I had wanted to write about for so long wouldn't be willing to speak to me for all the time I had let pass. I knew there were readers out there who loved the trilogy, and I didn't want to disappoint them. I was putting myself under a lot more pressure than I had felt back then, and I hadn't even started on the outline for the first of these prequels.

Then I did get started on it, and everything clicked into place. Roche became a constant thought in my head, a strange and scary companion of sorts; and the scenes played out just like they had in the past, while my tone seemed to naturally fall into the familiar cadence of telling this story I love to tell so much. The time I had spent writing other things made me better at coming back to this universe, while helping me appreciate how natural it would be for me to return.

I hope you loved this book, and that you are as excited to see this series take shape as I am. The next one will be about Lilia, if the ending didn't make that clear enough; and you might be surprised to find you have some sympathy for the scheming dragon once you know her story. I certainly did, and definitely was.

To help keep my attention on this series, please make it a point to post a review wherever you buy your books letting other readers know what you thought of this one. If I know people enjoyed this book and want to see the others come at you in a timely manner, I can adjust my writing schedule to make sure this series is my priority. Otherwise, I'll get to it…but I won't make any immediate promises as to when.

The best way to keep up with whatever I am writing, and promising, is to join the Secret Society of Deeper Meaning. You can also visit JayNorry. com to stay updated, reach out to me, or sign up for that innocent newsletter with the ominous name. I'll encourage you once more to leave a review for this book, to check out the other titles I have to offer on my website, and then I'll leave you with one last thought.

Thank you for sharing this journey with me. This book means a great deal to me, and writing it marked a completion for me that came with a certain measure of satisfaction. You are the one who makes the final connection, however. You add a whole new dimension to my writing just by reading, and I want to express my gratitude to you for that. You have a lot of books out there to choose from, and you picked mine. Thanks.

I hope you loved it.

All the best,
J.K. Norry

www.ingramcontent.com/pod-product-compliance
Lightning Source LLC
Chambersburg PA
CBHW032210180726
48284CB00001B/271